GALAXY

The Tranchillion
Encounter

S P LAKIN

ISBN: 149220966X
ISBN-13: 978-1492209669

This book is a work of fiction. Names, characters,
places and incidents are the product of the author's
imagination or are used fictitiously. Any resemblance to
actual events, locales or persons, living or dead, is
coincidental.

First published in 2016 by LakinsBooks.

This edition published in 2019 by LakinsBooks.

DEDICATION

I dedicate this book to my wife whose love and support meant everything to me.

Unfortunately, Samantha passed away, aged 45, before this book was released.

She was my rock, my world, my everything and had always believed in this project.

Thank you. Love you always.

A NOTE TO MY READERS:

This book has not been professionally edited. Any misspelled words or incorrect grammar or punctuation is purely down to me. I have improved in these areas and have reworked this entire novel using this knowledge. That is the reason for this second edition. Therefore, this book should not be used as an example of correct spelling and grammar. It is possible that the content is correct, but it is so easy to miss mistakes. If there are any – I apologize.

Please enjoy the story.

Thank you.

List of Characters

Space Federation

Neil Bolgon – *Warrant Officer, pilot of Star Cruiser One*
Andrew Bolgon – *Private, brother of Neil and copilot of Star Cruiser One*
Jim Bolgon – *General, father of Neil and Andrew. Commander of Sentry One*
Jennifer Bolgon – *Stewardess, mother of Neil and Andrew and Jim Bolgon's wife*
Michael Toddwell – *Assistant to General Bolgon*
John Stillson – *Assistant to General Bolgon*
Gwen Smith – *Secretary to General Bolgon*
Rebecca Chambers – *Research assistant with psychic abilities*
John Lyderattle – *Sergeant, Neil's friend*
Lisa Fowler – *Private, John's girlfriend*
Chloe Lewis – *Stewardess, Neil's girlfriend*
Daniel Meade – *Captain, captain of the 'Resolve'*
Alex Chamberlain – *Major, instructor at Sentry One*
David Turner – *Captain, captain of the 'Spirit'*
Keith Turnball – *Staff Sergeant, member of the original crew sent to Anthera*
Laura Henderson – *Lance Corporal, pilot and leader of Green Squadron*

Earth

Suzanne Cox – *Journalist for 'World News'*
Roxanne Taylor – *Journalist for 'World News' and a rival of Suzanne*

David Tressel – *Pirate, leader of the pirates*
Madeline Tressel – *David's mother*
Guy Travis – *Pirate, pilot*
Steve Cox – *Pirate, ex-husband of Suzanne*
Julie Statham – *Mother of Suzanne Cox and friend of Madeline Tressel*

Tranchillions

Zermiten Zemorphoride – *General, the highest-ranking officer on the 'Dragen'*
Tchzor Twochelope – *Colonel, is a psychic who is Neil's contact on Anthera*
Xornin Xenorphide – *Captain, captain of the 'Contention'*
Dwdoorian Dowdneer – *Colonel, covertly trying to take command of the 'Dragen'*
Marsup Maverphoride – *Lieutenant Colonel, Dowdneer's second-in-command*
Capustri Carphide – *Lieutenant, pilot*
Skliip Skillorpe – *Sergeant, General Zemorphoride's interrogator*
Murtle Mourneer – *Lieutenant, reluctantly working for Colonel Dowdneer*
Bernis Bowerphille – *Private, one of Colonel Twochelope's trusted soldiers*
Marsup Mayorpe – *Corporal, flight crew of the 'Contention'. Also, an engineer*
Putil Ptierwelope – *befriends Neil Bolgon*

CONTENTS

ACKNOWLEDGMENTS

Thank you to Michael Hall who helped adapt my new cover for this book.

I would also like to thank Smart Cartridge for the printer I bought from them and all the ink I use. Copies of this book are available to buy from here for as long as they stock it. Address printed at the end of the book.

I would also like to thank Shutterstock for the image they provided, for a modest fee of course, which became the front cover of this novel.

Thanks also go to everyone else who helped, in any way, with this project.

PROLOGUE

March 2169

Transporter 13 / Sentry One

Panic was spreading within the transporter. As it lurched sideways chief stewardess, Jennifer Bolgon, stumbled, causing her to fall hard on her left knee. She managed to pull herself upright and activate the passenger address system. Her face appeared on screens throughout the transporter.

"Everyone, try to remain calm." She wasn't feeling calm herself, but she needed to keep some semblance of control of the people in her care. "We are under attack and heading back to *Moonstation*. The star cruisers are out there defending us. I need everyone to put on your helmets which are in the backrest of the seat in front of you." Jennifer knew that, due to panic, some of the passengers would need reminding of the safety instructions she had recited before take-off. "They're self-moulding. Place them on your head and the helmet does the rest. I repeat, please remain calm so we can get everyone off quickly and safely – thank you." She switched off the PAS then made her way carefully towards the passengers.

The transporter took a direct hit on its engines and another on the communication array which shook it violently causing Jennifer to fall again. The lights dimmed and flickered, then went out completely. The sudden darkness caused adult screams to join the already crying children, then the lights blinked back on and Jennifer saw a small girl, around seven years old, stumbling over the various people sliding about on the floor. She must have already taken at least one tumble as she had tears running down her cheeks and a large bump on her right temple.

Jennifer reached out for the girl who clung to her. "Where's your mummy?"

The girl shook her head, saying nothing and tightened her grip. Jennifer pulled two helmets out of the nearest emergency cupboard and slid the first one over the girl's head then secured her own. By now it was almost impossible to stand as the pilot was fighting the controls just to keep the transporter moving in the right direction.

Jennifer, still holding the frightened girl, managed to look out of a porthole and saw they were closing in on *Moonstation*. The moon glowed in the background beyond the space station. As the transporter levelled out Jennifer carried the girl over to the exit. She noticed her colleagues directing passengers towards her and she prayed that the docking light would soon turn green.

"We're going to be all right. Try not to worry about your mummy. We'll get everyone off safely."

The girl nodded with tears still streaming down her face inside the helmet. The next five minutes seemed like five hours to Jennifer until she heard, and felt, the familiar clank of the magnetic clamps hold the transporter in position. The docking light turned green and she pressed the door release button. The door slid open and Jennifer, carrying the girl, hurried down the exit corridor using the see-through wall to support her injured knee. She looked around trying to spot their attackers but all she could see was *Moonstation* and the star-filled blackness of space. The rest of the passengers followed close behind.

She was half-way down the corridor when she heard an explosion behind her. She turned to look and saw two alien fighters flash past. Then the fire from the exploding transporter rushed down the corridor to engulf everyone in a fiery death. The corridor collapsed under the strain and heat of the explosion. What was left of the transporter and corridor drifted away from the space-station. The flames were extinguished as the air was sucked into the vacuum of space.

~

General Bolgon had took control of the situation himself. He was in the control room of *Sentry One* staring at the various screens in front of him. His mouth formed a thin line.

"They're starting to fall back. Keep the pressure on them."

[3]

"Sir!" One of the soldiers monitoring the screens interrupted from behind the general.

"What is it soldier?"

"They are attacking the transporters, sir."

"I thought they were out of range."

"All but one, sir. It turned back when the battle started."

"Get them some cover."

"I have already given the order, sir," the soldier was having trouble meeting the general's gaze.

"What's wrong?"

"Sir. It's the transporter. It's the one Mrs Bolgon's on, sir."

General Bolgon's eyes widened. "What! Are they in trouble?"

"They've taken a few hits. The star cruisers have engaged the enemy now which is helping but they are still attacking the transporter."

Send extra fighters there right now!" It was the first time in a long while that he had lost his cool during an operation. But his wife was on that transporter.

He watched the screens, focusing more on the battle swarming in the vicinity of *Moonstation*. It didn't look good for the transporter. His experience told him that it didn't have much chance.

"Where are those fighters!"

"They're seconds away, sir."

One of the comms channels died. Static was all they were receiving now.

No. What am I going to tell the children, thought the general. It was transporter 13's comm channel that had gone down. He strode over to the observation window to look at *Moonstation*. He could see the battle raging and

[4]

raised his binoculars to his eyes. The battle was still too far away to see properly but he could make out the space station.

General Bolgon drew in a short, sharp breath as he saw an explosion next to *Moonstation*. He lowered the binoculars and hurried back to the monitors. "Anything?"

"Transporter 13 is gone, sir. The bastards blew it up."

General Bolgon paled. He fought to remain in control of himself, but he was losing the struggle. He strode out of the control room. "Captain, you have the room," he managed before leaving. He could feel the tears welling. He could feel a tightness in his throat. It wouldn't do to show weakness in front of his troops. He had to get away before he collapsed in a useless heap. His life had just changed forever.

CHAPTER ONE

November 2171

In Space Orbiting Ganymede

(2 years later)

The star cruiser twisted and turned trying to evade laser fire from the pursuing fighter.

"Help, he's all over my ass!" screamed the pilot over the radio.

"On my way," replied squadron leader Neil Bolgon. "Bank right and dive."

The star cruiser turned and dived with the pursuing fighter matching the manoeuvre. The alien fighter was just starting to fire again when he was vaporised by Star Cruiser One.

"Thanks, sir. That was close," said the relieved pilot.

"Any time," replied WO1 Bolgon. "Now let's finish this."

The immediate airspace was swarming with fighters all trying to evade and kill each other. WO1 Bolgon took a few seconds to assess the situation and decided that his squadron could break off and go after the alien battleport. He'd had an idea and capturing the battleport was essential.

"*Resolve*. This is Red Leader requesting help with an attack on the battleport."

The reply was quick. "This is Captain Meade. Proceed. Blue Squadron will be with you shortly."

"Thank you, sir."

WO1 Bolgon turned Star Cruiser One to his new heading and opened to full throttle, followed closely by the rest of Red Squadron.

Two launch doors on the *Resolve* opened and out sprang all ten fighters of Blue Squadron and a boarding shuttle.

As Red Squadron neared the battleport a barrage of laser fire opened on them.

"This is Red Leader. Break off in twos and target each laser turret. We must have their defences down before the boarding shuttle arrives."

Six of Blue Squadron's fighters went full throttle leaving just four behind to protect the shuttle.

~

The combination of the ten squadrons of fighters, and *Resolve's* relentless battering of laser fire, was slowly depleting the number of alien fighters. They'd fought valiantly but were outnumbered. The presence of *Resolve* when they had dropped out of hyperspace had caught them off-guard. Their surprise attack on Ganymede had been forgotten as they fought off the human fighters.

Their mission had been to take over the colony set up on Ganymede, which they were going to use as an outpost to prepare future attacks on earth. The hostages they would undoubtedly have taken should have proved an effective shield against a counterattack. But they had failed miserably and lost many of their resources doing it.

Captain Xenorphide paced the bridge of the tranchillion battleport *Contention*. He watched the battle unfolding and realised it was not going his way. The star cruisers were evading their laser turrets and causing some damage.

"Send out the remaining fighters, we must not get boarded," he turned to the radio operator. "Order squadron seven to intercept that boarding shuttle."

The radio operator gave the order and waited for further instructions.

We may have to retreat, thought the captain as he carried on observing the unfolding conflict.

~

The leader of Green Squadron saw several alien fighters break off from the main battle and head towards the boarding shuttle. She immediately gave the order for Green Squadron to intercept them. Lance Corporal Henderson unleashed a torpedo towards the nearest alien fighter and scored a direct hit. It didn't deter the rest of them as they continued towards their target.

[8]

Two of Blue Squadron's escorting fighters' broke formation and engaged the oncoming aliens. As the dogfight continued, a growing number of fighters were destroyed on both sides. The remaining alien fighters were strictly defensive now, all thoughts of attacking the shuttle, gone.

The main battle surrounding the *Resolve* was continuing fiercely. *Resolve* had taken some damage but nothing of any importance had been hit.

~

"Recall the fighters," Captain Xenorphide instructed as he looked on despairingly at his depleted forces. "We have to retreat before it's too late."

"Sir," said Lieutenant Trulliphille. "Our defences will not hold up much longer. We have to leave."

"We will not leave our fighters stranded. Set up squads to repel boarders."

~

The alien fighters were beginning to disengage and head back to their battleport to escape.

After five minutes and only two casualties, the fighters of red and blue squadrons had disabled the defences of the battleport. While Blue Squadron remained in a defensive role outside, Red Squadron were about to enter the battleport and secure a landing platform for the imminent arrival of the boarding shuttle.

As Star Cruiser One entered the hanger WO1 Neil Bolgon spotted a welcoming party well protected behind transportable energy shields. He opened fire and managed to take out a few of the soldiers awaiting them.

[9]

They returned fire but their lasers were ineffectual against the shielded star cruisers. WO1 Bolgon set his fighter down and both he and his co-pilot, Lance Corporal Andrew Bolgon, leapt out taking cover behind the nearest object they could find. The other star cruiser pilots did the same, but they were all pinned down.

"When I signal give me covering fire," said Neil to his brother. Andrew fired off a couple of shots and nodded.

Neil turned around and pressed his back up against the vehicle they were hiding behind. He unfastened two grenades, primed them, then nodded at Andrew. Once Andrew started firing, Neil leapt out from behind their cover and threw both grenades before quickly ducking back down as laser fire narrowly missed his head and shoulder.

Moments later the grenades exploded, and inhuman screams were heard from the resulting carnage. Neil stood up again, weapon drawn, and shouted for them to advance. The other pilots moved forward while firing at the tranchillions. Neil and Andrew gave them covering fire. The grenades had destroyed the laser turret and killed a few of the aliens along with it. The battle was over within minutes and Neil posted sentries in strategic positions, around the hanger, to warn of any hostile forces that would inevitably come their way.

Neil climbed back into the star cruiser and activated his radio. "This is Red Leader. The docking bay is secure."

The shuttle appeared at the entrance to the hanger and slowly settled down. The rear ramp dropped down to reveal ten, four-man, squads marching onto the hanger floor, ready for combat. They were all wearing their armour-plated spacesuits.

Neil conferred with 2nd Lieutenant Ross who was the officer in command of the Space Federation Special Forces (SFSF) for this mission. They agreed on a plan and Neil went to join 'Bravo' team. Andrew followed Neil and each leader gave instructions to their respective units.

'Zulu' team and the remaining pilots set up a defensive perimeter. They needed to hold the hanger.

~

"To all pilots. This is Captain Xenorphide. Head for the moon. Do not attempt to come back. We are under attack and cannot defend your approach. I repeat, find sanctuary on the moon and wait for help."

Lieutenant Zielelope looked over towards his battleport and saw the concentration of alien fighters swarming around it. Several tranchillion fighters were attempting to board the *Contention* but were quickly destroyed. Lt Zielelope looked towards the moon and made his decision. "To all pilots. This is Lt Zielelope. Head to the moon. It is your only hope," he headed for Ganymede, hoping that some of his fellow pilots would do the same.

He landed the fighter in a relatively deep crater in the hope that it would be concealed from any surface scans. He powered down the fighter to avoid the possibility of being tracked. These aliens didn't have the same level of technology as his race, but tracking was a basic technology.

It was extremely dark, but his eyes were already adjusting, and he could see the terrain perfectly. He looked round as movement to one side caught his attention.

[11]

It was an escape pod from the *Contention*. It hadn't landed too far away. He reached inside the cockpit and pulled out his hand laser. He also slid five, fully charged, clips in the slots provided on his belt. He pressed a button inside the cockpit and the canopy slowly closed. Then he bent over until all six limbs were in contact with the surface and ran in the direction of the escape pod.

He saw two more pods impact in the five minutes it took him to reach the first one. They were within a reachable distance. He spotted four tranchillions standing around the pod and, after a quick scan of the area, continued towards them.

As he drew closer, one of them saw him and raised his weapon. Lt Zielelope raised all four of his hands in a *don't shoot* gesture.

The Tranchillion walked towards him after realising he was no threat. "I'm Putil Ptierwelope. Are there any more survivors, sir?" he had noticed the insignia on Lt Zielelope's spacesuit.

"Lt Zielelope," he acknowledged. "I've seen two more pods land over there," he half-turned and pointed in the direction of the pods. "After we've secured everything we can carry, I suggest we go and find them."

"Is there anywhere to hide?" asked Putil.

"Not that I've seen, but we *will* need to find somewhere. It won't be long before the aliens start searching for us."

"Do you know what went wrong?"

"No. But this mission was wrong before we left the *Dragen*. If I didn't know better, I'd say Colonel Dowdneer wanted us out of the way."

"That's just your imagination. The colonel would never..." he was interrupted by the others who had finished gathering essentials.

Lt Zielelope pointed in front of him. "That way. We should find another pod over there."

They began running in the direction that he indicated and soon came upon the pod. Lt Zielelope looked around. He couldn't see any sign of the tranchillions that had been in it. Then he spotted them walking along a rise. "Over there – let's go."

They ran in the direction the tranchillions were going. They rapidly closed the distance and five became nine.

"Do you have any weapons?" asked Lt Zielelope after introductions had been made.

"We each have a hand laser. Couldn't fit anything bigger in there, sir."

"That's all any of us has. It'll have to do. Now, as the senior ranking officer I'm taking command. I saw another pod back over that way. While we're searching for them keep a lookout for any possible hiding places. Move out."

~

Teams Alpha and Bravo had battled hard to get to the bridge. The alien captain had set up a decent defence. They were ready to begin their entry to take control of the vessel. Neil glanced over to his best friend, John Lyderattle, and nodded.

"Ready, Sergeant."

John nodded back. "Ready, sir."

With that brief exchange, a simultaneous attack on both entrances to the bridge commenced. They used flash-bangs and tear-gas first then burst into the room.

The bridge was in chaos from the sudden attack. The few aliens that could put up a fight were quickly taken down by accurate laser fire. The others surrendered and were bound to prevent any mishaps. The alien captain had been temporarily blinded by the flash-bangs and the tear-gas had him coughing and crawling blindly across the floor. One of the soldiers shot him with a stun bolt and he fell unconscious.

Neil found the radio but had never seen an instrument like it before. "I need someone to translate these symbols," he called out.

"Private Melanie McCoughlae reporting, sir."

"Do you know what these symbols mean, Private?" asked Neil.

"No, but I can soon work it out, sir."

"Okay. You go ahead and start deciphering them."

Neil touched the transmit button on the side of his helmet and spoke to the rest of the ten-man squads.

"This is Warrant Officer Bolgon. We have captured the bridge. Continue your current assignments. We need to secure this vessel."

WO1 Bolgon turned towards his brother and said, "Would you like to take the controls when we're ready to go."

"Yes, sir."

WO1 Bolgon looked at the info-pad attached to his forearm. He tapped a few buttons and the screen read 'BREATHABLE'. He tapped some more, and the front of his helmet opened. He pushed the helmet backwards off his head and it fell on its hinge to rest on his shoulder blades. He walked over to the unconscious alien captain and knelt beside him.

[14]

The alien had green skin and no apparent hair. He could see six limbs – two of which they stood on much the same as humans.

"Look like overgrown lizards, don't they," said Sergeant John Lyderattle as he stopped next to Neil.

"We'd better make sure their restraints are tight. We don't know how strong they are," replied WO1 Neil Bolgon without looking up.

He lifted back one of the alien's lips and revealed sharp-looking pointed teeth. He stood up. "Get them all secured. I want to get back home ASAP."

Once the battleport was clear and all the aliens were either killed or captured, three squads stayed aboard to maintain patrols around the ship. The rest boarded the shuttle and made their way back to the *Resolve*. A flight crew had been flown over in the meantime to fly the battleport back to *Sentry One*.

Private McCoughlae had finished deciphering the symbols. "I may not be one hundred percent accurate, but you should be able to fly it now, sir."

Andrew returned the salute and sat at the control panel, preparing to fly the huge battleport. "Thank you Private."

Private McCoughlae had labelled everything to make it as easy as possible for the flight crew to fly the ship.

"Is everyone ready?" called out LCpl Bolgon.

Numerous voices answered positively. He took hold of the controls. "This is Corporal Bolgon. We're ready for departure."

"Right, let's go," came the reply from Captain Meade of the *Resolve*. "Fall in behind. Next stop – the moon."

Andrew manoeuvred into formation with *Resolve* and they started the journey back home.

~

The small group of tranchillions had found the last pod in their area but they couldn't see any survivors. Lt Zielelope bent over and used two of his hands as extra feet as he searched the ground for signs of them. After a minute he stood up. "That way."

They set off, running on two legs, keeping some caution as the aliens would be looking for them by now. Ten minutes passed before Putil, bringing up the rear, spotted laser fire over to their left and let out a quiet squeal as a warning. He didn't need to say anything as they could all see the flashes of light.

"Do we see if we can help?" asked Putil.

"Of course, but we must remain cautious. Stay unseen in case the aliens outnumber us," said Lt Zielelope.

They all agreed then ran over as fast as they could, only slowing when they had closed in on the battle. There were three tranchillions left, all of which had taken cover behind a crashed tranchillion fighter.

"There must be at least twenty aliens," said Putil.

"And they're just the ones we can see," said Lt Zielelope. "Unfortunately, I don't think we can help them."

"If we could get closer, we could take them by surprise," said one of the pilots. "They won't last much longer."

"Okay. We'll try," said Lt Zielelope. "But if we get split up head over there," he pointed in the direction of his fighter. "If we're forced to run, we must try to keep the person in front in sight. Is everyone clear?"

They all got up.

"Single file. Let's go."

Just then Lt Zielelope noticed movement to his right and spun round to see two alien soldiers moving in their direction. The light on the alien's rifle swept over him then came back quickly and picked him out properly. Two flashes of laser light later and Putil had taken down the surprised aliens. They heard shouting coming from the direction of the battle.

"Follow me!" said Zelor as he bent over and used both sets of hands as extra legs. They all did the same and set off at an extreme pace.

They were half-way back to Lt Zielelope's fighter when Putil vanished. The following pilot stopped as fast as he could and used their warning squeal. The rest of them stopped and came back.

"Where's Putil?" asked Lt Zielelope.

"I'm looking now, sir," said the pilot. "He just vanished. Ah – here, there's a hole."

"Is it steep?" asked Lt Zielelope. He had just seen one of the alien fighters slow down where they had been spotted.

"No, sir. At least, not as far as I can see."

"Then we all go in," said Lt Zielelope. "We don't have much time," he was looking at the fighter advancing in their direction.

Lt Zielelope went in first, calling out for Putil, but there was no reply. The others silently followed him into the hole. They found Putil unconscious at the bottom of the tunnel in a small cave.

One of the pilots turned him over and checked his body. "There's no sign of any injuries, sir. He's lucky."

"We all are. If we'd stayed out there, we'd all have been killed or captured," said Lt Zielelope. "That alien fighter would've found us."

"What do we do now?"

"We stay here and make the cave larger. There are supplies in my ship which is not far from here. Let's hope the aliens don't find it."

They had a long wait ahead of them. Lt Zielelope was sure of it.

CHAPTER TWO

November 2171

The Moon

The journey back to the moon was uneventful and the work to repair the minor damage to *Resolve* had already begun.

Captain Meade and 2nd Lt Ross had been diverted to the debriefing room. Captain Meade had ordered WO1 Neil Bolgon to attend as well.

"You're back earlier than expected. I'd like an explanation as to why," said General Bolgon, the C.O. at

Sentry One. The general looked at WO1 Bolgon. "I didn't ask for you, son."

Captain Meade, being the highest-ranking officer on duty during the battle for Ganymede, cleared his throat and spoke first. "I asked him to attend, sir. He was heavily involved in the conflict and has seen the aliens up close."

"Go on."

"We were on our routine flight out to Jupiter when we picked up a blip on our radar. After further investigation, we found that an alien battleport had flown into our vicinity. I would hazard a guess that they had come to attack Ganymede or Europa. We intercepted and defeated the enemy and managed to bring home their battleport."

"You did check for a distress signal or homing beacon aboard the battleport," said General Bolgon.

"Yes, sir. A distress signal had been triggered but we shut that off. It's possible they could send out another vessel to look for the battleport."

"They must not know that we have captured their ship. If we move quickly, we might be able to use this battleport in an attack on Anthera," General Bolgon rose and placed his hands flat on the table around which sat his most trusted aides. "Is there anything else to mention?"

"Just that some of the aliens escaped to Ganymede, sir."

"I take it the colonists have been informed."

"Yes, sir."

"Ok, if there's nothing to add, that will be all, gentlemen. All of you," he said while looking separately at each of them, "will be interviewed individually over the course of the next twenty-four hours. Keep yourselves available." He stood up straight. "Dismissed."

They all saluted the general then left the debriefing room.

"Sorry for pulling you in Officer Bolgon. I thought you should be there in case I needed your account of the battle," said Captain Meade.

"Yes, sir. Will there be anything else?"

"Hang on a second," the captain had spotted Suzanne Cox, a well-known reporter for *World News*, approaching them.

"Any chance of an interview about your recent mission?" she asked Captain Meade.

He looked at her. The clothes she wore emphasised her athletic build and ample breasts. She had curly, brown hair and sharp, green eyes which seemed to be penetrating his normal self-control.

"No. The press conference will be held in a couple of days. You'll be able to get your story then."

Suzanne pressed him for more information, but he would not budge.

"How did you get this far inside the complex, Miss Cox?" he asked.

When he realised that she was not going to answer his question, Captain Meade waved his hand towards Suzanne as he said, "Officer Bolgon, escort Miss Cox away."

Neil took a step towards her.

She held her hands up and shrugged. "Okay – Okay, I'm leaving," she turned around with Neil following closely behind until she was past the security door.

Neil made his way back to the quarters he shared with his girlfriend. He was hoping that Chloe would be there.

He opened the door and crept inside, slowly searching the room for any sign of movement. Then he moved onto the next room. Still nothing. He finally decided that she wasn't there and brought up her work schedule on the television. He scanned the text for a few seconds then turned around.

"TV off," he said. "Music – Jenny Roman – section three."

The TV switched off and the sound system came to life. The sounds of Jenny Roman caressed his ears. He breathed in deeply and sighed. There was nothing quite like listening to your favourite singer after getting home from work. *Except*, he thought, *having your girlfriend there instead.*

He walked into the bathroom and switched on the shower then undressed and stood naked in front of the sink. His muscular frame, with all his battle scars, was reflected in the large five square foot mirror. He cleaned his teeth before stepping into the shower.

~

Chloe Lewis swiped her pass card through the door scanner and entered the quarters she shared with her boyfriend. She put her bag on the table near the door and walked straight to the kitchen. After making herself some coffee she sat at the dining table and rubbed her long, slender legs trying to erase the ache in her calves.

After she had drunk her coffee she walked into the bedroom and kicked off her shoes. She undid her dress and let it drop to the floor then removed her underwear.

"Hello honey," said Neil, standing naked in the bathroom doorway. "I've been waiting for you."

[22]

Chloe looked round and smiled as he advanced towards her. They embraced and kissed passionately. Neil lifted her effortlessly and carried her to their bed.

~

The starship *Spirit* was undergoing the final preparations for flight. Most of the crew and equipment was aboard and they were due to leave in an hour. Captain Turner had just received his orders in the observation room high above the starship. He was to go to Mars to collect Etherall from the mines and bring it back to *Sentry One*. It would then be manufactured into Etherum by combining it with Sodrum.

He looked down upon the *Spirit* and watched the crew preparing her for flight. He turned away from the glass and looked at General Bolgon. "Do you think we'll have any trouble on this mission?"

General Bolgon looked up from the reports on his desk. "It's always a possibility but I'm sure you can handle it, Captain. Is there anything else?" He returned to his work as the captain shook his head and left the observation room.

The final checks were being crossed off the list as Captain Turner arrived on the bridge. "Are we on schedule?" he asked.

"Very nearly, sir," replied Lieutenant Warner.

The one-thousand-meter-long starship sounded its one-minute warning siren and everyone near the huge carrier moved back to predetermined positions and waited for the *Spirit* to lift off.

The rear exhaust ports started glowing and then thousands of small jets underneath the vessel blasted towards the hanger floor. The *Spirit* lifted off, hovering four meters above the ground. The hanger doors opened, and the starship's exhaust ports glowed brighter as it moved forwards into the exit corridor and headed for space.

~

Suzanne Cox was standing at the front of the crowd of waiting reporters going over her questions and hoping that she could get them all answered. There was plenty of noise in the conference room, because of the media representation from most of the Earth's continents, but she concentrated on her notebook.

General Bolgon, followed by Captain Meade and Michael Toddwell, strode up to the lectern and placed his speech on it. A hush came over the crowd as everyone anticipated his words.

"First," boomed the general's voice over the loudspeaker. "I will inform you of recent events at Ganymede then, after I have finished, I will take your questions. Now be seated. When you are selected, you may ask your questions."

Everyone sat promptly as the general's commanding voice took effect. He gave a five-minute account of the recent battle at Ganymede and, as he fell silent, the onrush of voices started. General Bolgon ignored them and looked for the patient reporters who were showing their hands.

"Yes," he said as he pointed towards one reporter.

"Tom Singleton of the Sun in the United Kingdom," he announced. "Was this action taken with the Confederations approval?"

"No, it was a surprise attack on our Ganymede colonists and Captain Meade here," he gestured towards the captain with a nod of his head, "had a decision to make. In my opinion, he made the right choice. We have to protect our people from any threat whether they be alien or human."

"Next," he said as he pointed towards Suzanne Cox.

"Suzanne Cox of World News British Division," she paused then continued. "Could there have been a more peaceful solution to this situation?"

General Bolgon looked directly at her. "I'll let Captain Meade answer this one," he moved aside, and the captain stepped up.

"Thank you, sir. Now, Miss Cox. In answer to your question; we first attempted to contact the aliens, but they didn't respond. We tried again and then they launched their fighters. We had no choice but to respond in kind. The battle commenced until they retreated and left some of their fighters behind to fend for themselves."

Suzanne got straight in with another question before she could be passed over. "What truth is there about reports that the battleport was actually captured?"

"The rumours are just that – rumours. The battleport escaped and for all we know has returned to Anthera."

Again, Suzanne got in first. "Were there any alien survivors?"

"Yes, and they are being held at Ganymede."

The press conference continued with lots of questions being answered; some to the journalists' satisfaction, some not. After it had finished, Suzanne was walking away, talking into her recorder to remind her of things she must do later, when the general's aide, Michael Toddwell, approached her.

[25]

"Miss Cox, would you please accompany me to the interview room. General Bolgon and Captain Meade await you."

She nodded and followed Toddwell to the interview room while wondering what button she had pressed. They entered the room. General Bolgon and Captain Meade stood up and gestured for her to sit.

"Miss Cox," said the general. "Where did you get your information about the battleport from?"

Suzanne smiled, projecting a confidence which she didn't feel under the intense gaze of General Bolgon. "It's Ms Cox and my sources have to be protected general. You know that."

"I could hold you under the international secrets act, Ms Cox."

"You could, but you won't. Holding me would bring more focus upon your mission and you don't want that."

"I have an idea, Ms Cox. Well, more of a proposition really."

Suzanne was intrigued. "Yes, General."

"I would like to invite you to be our official reporter. You would still work for *World News*, but I would give you exclusive access to sensitive information about certain missions, on the understanding that you will only publish once I give the go-ahead."

Suzanne pursed her lips and gave herself a moment to consider the general's proposal. "Yes."

"Excellent, Ms Cox! You won't regret it."

~

Neil and Chloe glanced at the sign above the artificial park's door. It read 'Regents Park, London, England'. Each week there was a different park from around the world. They entered the room and into a perfect reproduction of Regents Park. The artificial park was created, for the residents of the moon, to relax in and remind them of earth.

They walked along path after path, taking in the scenery.

"You wouldn't know it was computer graphics, would you," remarked Chloe as they walked past numerous fields marked out with football pitches. "Is this really like Regents Park?" she asked, flicking her long blonde hair to one side in the way she knew Neil liked.

"Yes, but it's been down-sized. They have taken out some of the grassland in between the paths to fit it in the room. And possibly a couple of buildings have been removed as well."

They sat on a bench and watched some children at play in a nearby field. All around them were trees and open playing fields. Neil pointed in front of them and slightly to their left. "It's not been programmed in, but London Zoo is just beyond that wall over there. If we get to go back, I'll have to take you there."

"I would love to go someday," she said with a smile on her face. She rolled her piercing blue eyes upwards in thought then drew in a breath to speak when a young woman caught her eye.

She had blonde hair and looked as though she was in her early twenties. She approached them cautiously and looked nervously at Neil. He looked up and smiled. That seemed to give her some encouragement and she spoke.

"Are you Neil Bolgon?" she asked.

"Yes," he replied.

She let out a relived sigh. "Can we talk somewhere a little more private?"

[27]

"What's this about?"

"I was told to approach you, at this time and place, to pass on information in private. They were very specific about that."

"I'm sorry, you've lost me. What did you say?" Neil looked at her suspiciously.

"I need to tell you something when we're somewhere where no-one can hear."

"Who are you?"

"Rebecca. Rebecca Chambers."

Neil looked at Chloe and saw the look she was giving him. "I've never seen her before," he said defensively. "Honest," he added.

"He's telling the truth. We've never met before," said Rebecca.

Chloe shrugged. "Okay, Neil. I don't mind. Let's go back to our quarters."

"No," said Neil. He didn't want this woman to know where they resided. "We aren't changing our plans. We'll go to our favourite picnic spot and you can join us for lunch. It's in the middle of a field. There's open space all around, so no-one will be able to approach without us seeing them."

"That sounds good to me," said Rebecca.

Chloe held out her hand, "Chloe Lewis. Nice to meet you."

They shook hands with Rebecca still looking awkward and then set off in the direction of their favourite picnic spot.

Once they arrived, Neil spread out the towels while Chloe started unpacking the picnic hamper with Rebecca's help. When everything was laid out, and all three were seated around the picnic, Rebecca carried on with her story.

"An alien race called the *Watchers* contacted me. They are from the same part of our galaxy as the aliens currently attacking us. They view us from far away using their abilities to read minds and see through our eyes. They have been watching us for ten thousand years."

Neil rolled his eyes but said nothing.

"Why, and how, have they told you this?" asked Chloe.

"Because I'm psychic, they can talk to me. And I'm on *Sentry One* near to Neil."

Neil was twisting around; looking in every direction. "Okay, which one of them sent you?"

Rebecca looked blankly at him. "No one sent me. The *Watchers* talk to me in my head."

"No. Not them. The lads. Which one of them sent you? Was it John?"

"Sorry. I don't know a John."

"This is a wind up isn't it."

"No," replied Rebecca. "An alien race sent me a message psychically."

"Okay, if you can prove that you are psychic, I'll believe you. Then you can give us your message," Neil turned his attention to Chloe. "Do you remember what we were talking about a couple of days ago?"

Chloe looked thoughtful then she smiled and nodded.

"Okay then, Rebecca. Both of us will think about our discussion while you read our minds and if you get the right answer then you must be psychic. Are you able to do that?"

Rebecca nodded.

Neil turned to Chloe. "You didn't say anything to anyone about it, right?"

Chloe shook her head.

They fell silent and Rebecca started concentrating on their thoughts. After a short period of time had passed Rebecca opened her eyes and smiled. She looked at them and then started speaking.

"You were talking to each other about children's names. Neil likes the names James and John for a boy and Gemma and Samantha for a girl," she turned her attention to Chloe. "Chloe, you didn't mind James or John but would like a Thomas, and for a girl you would be adamant about Tanya," she paused and then said, "There is something else that you have to tell Neil, isn't there?"

With raised eyebrows Chloe said, "You've convinced me about your psychic abilities. But, just to make sure, why don't you tell Neil what you think I have to tell him."

"Are you sure?"

Chloe nodded.

Rebecca turned to Neil. "You're going to be a father."

Neil looked at Chloe. "Is this true?"

Chloe smiled and nodded. "I was about to tell you when she showed up."

Neil's eyes sparkled and he hugged her. When they parted he kissed her. "Love you."

"Love you too," said Chloe.

Neil looked at Rebecca. "Okay you're genuine. What's the message?"

"The tranchillions that attacked our first crew to land on Anthera, were led by a rather unpleasant colonel called Dowdneer."

Neil interrupted. "What are tranchillions?"

"Oh, sorry. That's what they're called. The aliens that are attacking us, I mean."

Neil nodded and signalled for Rebecca to carry on.

"Anyway, Dowdneer doesn't hold with the ideals of most their population and has designs on taking over their government when he gets back home. He just needs to add a few more believers to his cause. The Tranchillions are a peaceful race who think that we've attacked them. They're just defending themselves. You need to find a Colonel Twochelope. He will believe you when you talk to him, and together, hopefully, you will be able to find a peaceful solution to this war."

"Why will he believe me?"

"Because the *Watchers* have talked to him as well. They know that, by bringing you two together, this destructive conflict will end."

"Why do these *Watchers* care about what happens to us?" asked Neil.

"They didn't say."

Neil's hand subconsciously stroked his chin while his mind took in all this information. Then, after a few minutes, he looked directly at Rebecca. "Let's see what we can do about this situation."

CHAPTER THREE

November 2171

Anthera

Colonel Twochelope awoke with a bad headache. They had become more intense and much more frequent over the last two weeks. He swung his legs over the side of the bed and held his oval shaped head in his top pair of hands, while steadying himself with his second pair pressed down on the edge of the bed. He moaned slightly.

I'll have to see a medic, he thought.

The pain intensified and he slipped onto the floor still holding his head. Then the pain stopped as suddenly as it had begun. He heard a strange voice and looked around but there was no one there.

Then he heard it again. *Colonel Twochelope. Do not be alarmed*, the voice said. He looked around again but still saw no one. *Colonel Twochelope. I am inside your head. I am a Watcher. I have mind-reading and telepathic abilities and I need to talk to you urgently.*

Realization suddenly dawned on him, "Get out of my head whoever you are!" he yelled out.

There is no need to use your voice. That will attract attention to yourself. If you just think what you want to say, I will hear it.

I'm going crazy.

No Colonel. You are perfectly sane.

Where are you?

A long way away. Nearer to Tranchilite than your current location.

There's no way you are talking to me from that kind of distance

Our atmosphere amplifies our abilities.

Colonel Twochelope decided to go with the voice. *Why did it hurt so much when you spoke to me?*

It is an unfortunate side effect of making first contact. We can read your mind without any effect at all. But the initial time we contact you we must find the weak spot in your mind's natural barrier and break through it.

Have you read my mind before?

Yes, we have been watching your race for over twenty thousand years and the humans for ten thousand.

But if you can read anyone's mind when you want, you would have a tremendous advantage should you decide to attack us.

We are a peaceful race and would never attack anyone.

There's always a minority of people in any race that would use violence. If you can't attack others, you could be wiped out.

[33]

I did not say that we could not defend ourselves. If anyone decided to attack, we would know. All the people from that race who were a direct threat to us would be eliminated.

How?

We overload their minds which causes them to explode.

Have you done this to anyone before?

We have only had to do it once in ten thousand years. It was not a pretty sight for the survivors. They backed off immediately.

How close did they get before you killed them?

They had not left their planet.

Then how did you see what happened to them?

We can also see through other lifeforms' eyes. Some of us were watching while others were overloading the conspirators' minds.

You can see through our eyes. So, you see what I see?

Enough of these questions. I have a message for you that will mean the survival or destruction of the few of you that remain.

Col Twochelope considered asking some more questions. He had so many. But before he could ask, the *Watcher* continued.

The humans are not your enemy. Colonel Dowdneer is. Just over a century ago, when the humans were exploring their own solar system, they landed on Anthera, as they call it, which is the planet that you crashed onto. They were taking samples from the soil to see if there was anything useful to them when Colonel Dowdneer attacked. They barely escaped and headed back to their home planet. The colonel then reported back to General Zemorphoride that he had been attacked instead. All the loss of life in this conflict is a direct result of his actions. He plans to take control of your government when he gets back home. Starting this war with the humans was intentional. He knew it would weaken your defences enough so that he could take over at some point. He has secretly been gathering support for his cause and currently has forty-three percent of your remaining population on his side. The colonel sent

Captain Xenorphide to his death because he knew that he could not convert him. However, the colonel has not anticipated what the humans are capable of. They have a large military force and a history of using it. They are currently planning an attack against you. You would be outnumbered by about seventy to one. There would be no survivors.

The colonel took all of this in and realised how much trouble they were in.

What can we do about it? thought Colonel Twochelope.

That is why we intervened. We will not kill unless we must, so the best we can do is give you knowledge. We will shortly be contacting a human and we will tell him the same as we told you. One of them will seek you out. Between you an answer must be found or everyone on Anthera will die and the entire human race would be destroyed.

I thought you said they outnumbered us. Surely, they would wipe us out.

Yes, but they would only survive for another few years. Your Emperor has already sent out millions of probes searching for you. It would only be a matter of time before they find either you or your remains. They would send an army so large that Earth would be a smoking ruin with little to no survivors.

Why are you so interested in saving us; and the humans for that matter?

Colonel Dowdneer would eventually gain control of your entire planet and look to conquer every inhabitable planet he could find. He would find us and then we would be forced to kill again. We do not want that.

Okay, I'll think this over and await this human's arrival. Do you have a name?

His name is Neil Bolgon. He is the best soldier and pilot that they have.

[35]

How's he going to get here? Surly our defences would kill him the minute he turned up.

We do not know how he will arrive because they have not yet made their plans. All we do know is that he will be there and the two of you must meet and come to some arrangement.

How do I contact you again?

It is impossible for you to contact us. If we need to talk to you again you will hear from me.

Will it hurt again if you do contact me?

No, that is a one-time side effect. Your barrier has been broken so I can talk to you whenever I want.

Is there anything else I need to know? The colonel was greeted by silence and he repeated his thought. Still there was no answer.

"I guess that's my answer," he said out loud. He realised that at some point during the conversation he had lain back down on his bed. Twochelope got up again to pour himself a strong drink and then settled down to think about all that he had learnt.

~

Colonel Dowdneer turned slowly to look at his potential recruit. Sergeant Thrillorpe had accompanied two of Colonel Dowdneer's guards.

"Sir," he said as he stood to attention.

"Sergeant, would you be so kind as to allow me some of your time?"

"Of course, sir."

"Good. I've been watching you for some time and I think you would be perfect for my restructuring plan."

"What plan, sir?"

Colonel Dowdneer ignored the question. "You have been outspoken on several topics. One of which gained my attention. Your view on these humans was what helped me decide to call you here."

"I don't like them. They are dangerous and should be eradicated before they wipe us out."

"Exactly. I have seen enough of this present governments squandering of our military resources. They would not do what is necessary, so I intend to take over. I want you to be part of my army."

"How are you planning on taking over, sir?"

"By force of course. These fools that are running it now would never bend to my will, so they would have to be taken out. We could be the most powerful race in the galaxy if only they would use their might," the colonel, who had been pacing the room, turned back to face Sergeant Thrillorpe. "You would increase in rank as soon as I take over and get all the privileges that brings with it. So, what do you say?" the colonel had closed the gap between them and was just a few feet away.

"You've made a mistake, Colonel. I may not agree with a lot of the general's decisions, but I would never turn against him, which is what you are asking me to do. My answer is no."

"Foolish – foolish boy," said the colonel. He walked over to the door control on the far side of the room. "There's a reason why only my most trusted soldiers are here. You are about to find this out."

The two guards that had escorted him to the colonel suddenly grabbed him. They dragged him, struggling and shouting, over to the airlock. His eyes widened when he realised what the colonel was about to do.

"But you can't. I'll be killed."

"That's the idea," the colonel waved him goodbye showing his sharp, pointed teeth with a large smile.

"You'll have as much chance as the others who defied me. Which is, admittedly, slim."

One of the guards hit him over the head with their rifle and then they threw him into the airlock.

"You have about thirty seconds to put on the suit I provided before the outer door opens. Good luck, Sergeant."

Colonel Dowdneer pressed the door release button and watched as the inner doors closed, sealing Sergeant Thrillorpe in. The automated voice cut in on the speakers, *Warning, safety protocols have been removed. Warning, safety protocols have been removed.* After a few seconds had passed, the automated voice restarted. *Warning, twenty seconds until outer doors open. Warning, fifteen seconds until outer doors open.*

Sergeant Thrillorpe was desperately trying to get the protective suit on while still feeling groggy from the blow to his head. "I've changed my mind. I'll join you. Please!"

"Too late," replied Dowdneer. "I could never trust you."

The automated voice continued now on its ten-second countdown. *10, 9, 8, 7, 6, 5, 4*, he had just got hold of the helmet and was lifting it towards his head when, *2, 1, outer doors opening.*

Sergeant Thrillorpe looked up with surprise on his face as he was sucked out of the airlock.

Colonel Dowdneer moved away with a satisfied look on his face. "Turn the safety protocols back on and adjust the ship's log before you leave. Cameras as well. No traces." He left the room to go to a scheduled meeting with the general. The rest of his men left after they had reset the system. The outer door closed again, leaving no trace of what had just happened. The colonel was always careful about his recruitments. Only his most trusted men got to see what happened to all those who opposed him.

~

Colonel Twochelope had decided to keep all he had learned to himself. He did not know who had already been recruited into the employ of Colonel Dowdneer. He knew that the general would be unprocurable for Dowdneer. But if he told him what he knew the general would almost certainly try to do something about it. Then, after the general had been disposed of, he would be the next target. This might bring about an early takeover and he could not risk that.

Colonel Twochelope arrived at the conference room, paused as the guards signed him in, and entered to take his place at the table. The general, as always, would be the last to enter. He looked down at the scheduled topics and saw one subject that interested him above all others. It was about the battleport that had gone missing with Captain Xenorphide in command. He looked up from the list as the door opened.

In strolled Colonel Dowdneer leaving his two personal security guards at the door. He sat down in his usual place, two seats to the left of the general, and crossed his legs.

Moments later, the general entered and took his place at the head of the table. The room was in total silence waiting for General Zemorphoride to start proceedings.

"Right, officers we'll start this meeting with suggestions from all of you about how best to ration our food. We need to make it last until our people find and rescue us."

The meeting had been going on for an hour when the final topic came about. Colonel Twochelope could not help looking in Colonel Dowdneer's direction when the general brought up the mission that Dowdneer had sent Captain Xenorphide on.

"I take it that we were expecting Captain Xenorphide back already," the general directed his statement towards Colonel Dowdneer.

"Yes, we were expecting him back two days ago," replied Dowdneer.

"Then why haven't you sent out a search party already?" asked the general.

"They may have had problems; he is only two days overdue. I was just giving them a little longer in case they turned up. I didn't want to send out another battleport only for Captain Xenorphide to come back after it left."

"If they're in trouble they'll need our help. Those two days could mean the difference between their life and their death."

"I'm sorry, General Zemorphoride I was trying to save resources."

"Then why send them at all?"

"The plan was to take over a colony the aliens had set up on one of the moons around that ringed gas giant. From there we could attack them while finding new materials to help us."

"I think it was an unnecessary risk. If we have lost that battleport then I will hold you personally responsible."

Colonel Twochelope spoke out. "I think that Colonel Dowdneer sent him on that mission to get rid of him. It's a little-known fact they dislike each other," he paused in thought then added, "Perhaps hate is a better word."

"On what basis do you accuse Colonel Dowdneer of these actions, they seem unfounded to me."

"Just observations, sir," Colonel Twochelope inwardly cringed as he realised his mistake.

"You should not accuse anyone of something like that unless you have proof. Do you have proof?" asked the general, looking directly at Colonel Twochelope.

"No, sir. I have no proof."

"Then be quiet. Colonel Dowdneer, do you have you anything to say to Colonel Twochelope?"

Dowdneer removed his gaze from Twochelope's direction and declined to comment.

"Well, if this is not going to be taken any further, then let's think about getting our battleport back."

When the meeting ended, Colonel Twochelope left the room and was heading back to his quarters when two of Colonel Dowdneer's guards blocked his path. Twochelope looked behind him and saw Dowdneer approaching.

"What was that all about?" asked the colonel.

"Nothing, I have just observed you two in the past, added two and two together and come up with fourteen. I'm sorry if I caused you any embarrassment in there."

"No no. No embarrassment. But I don't appreciate the implication that I might have sent Captain Xenorphide on a suicide mission." *Even though it's true*, he thought.

"Like I said, I was wrong and I'm sorry. What more can I say?"

"You just watch yourself, Colonel. People can have little *accidents* from time to time," he leaned forward and whispered in Colonel Twochelope's ear. "You know what I mean."

[41]

"Are you threatening me?"

"No, it's a promise. If these cameras weren't here, I would have already warned you properly. Just watch yourself."

Colonel Dowdneer took Twochelope's hand and shook it, for the benefit of the cameras, before he could react. Then Dowdneer walked off with his entourage following him.

Colonel Twochelope felt warned. *I'd better watch out now. Why did I provoke him?*

~

Colonel Dowdneer paced his room angrily muttering words under his breath. He stopped and looked at one of his guards. "How did he know about my relationship with Captain Xenorphide? I always keep my affairs low key. One of you must have been talking to someone about it," he carried on walking briskly around the room.

"Was it you?" he asked a guard.

"No, sir. Definitely not, sir."

Dowdneer looked round towards the next guard. "Was it you?"

The guard shook his head. "No, sir."

Everyone denied having said anything about what the colonel did behind closed doors.

"We would all die for you and would never betray you, sir," said the colonel's second in command.

"Then he must have found out some other way. We must be even more careful than usual," said Dowdneer.

He took his place at the head of the table and the rest of his most trusted soldiers took their seats.

"All of you are to find out how he knew of our dislike for each other but do it discreetly. I want to know how much of a threat, our friend, the colonel is. And, if we must, we will neutralise him."

CHAPTER FOUR

November 2171

Mars – Etherall Mining Facility

Captain Turner looked down from his vantage point, in the control room set high in the canyon wall, watching trucks carefully picking their way across the dusty surface of Mars, bringing Etherall back to his starship.

The mining of Etherall is an ongoing operation which continues through the night. It is brought up from the mines and stored in warehouses ready for when a starship comes to take it away.

"I'm going to get some sleep now. If something important needs to be brought to my attention let Lieutenant Warner know," he returned the salute offered him and left. The mining officer watched Captain Turner disappear then resumed his duties.

~

A large silver truck loaded with Etherall slowly trundled towards the *Spirit*. It moved into position under the cargo hold, ready to offload the 500 crates it carried. A dozen men climbed up to the top of the neatly stacked crates and took hold of the hooks that had been lowered towards them. Each one attached their hook, to the base on which the crates sat, and then moved away. The team leader held up his hand, in a thumbs-up sign, signalling to the winch operator. The slack was slowly taken up and the straps tightened then the crates started rising. They spun slightly, and swung a little, as they were lifted upwards into the waiting starship.

Inside the mine, three more trucks were being loaded. One truck was nearly full and would be ready to move within the next ten minutes.

A shadow moved on the far wall then another followed. The two men had stealthily worked their way this far without being seen. They also had two more accomplices on their opposite flank and another two towards the rear of the mine.

The two at the rear entered the security room and fired off two sleeping darts. Both security guards slumped to the floor and one of the men disabled the alarm system. They changed into the security uniforms of the unconscious guards and locked the door behind them. They walked to the truck and one of them looked

[45]

at the export documents thrust into his hand by the mining officer. After signing them he gave the clipboard back and the mining officer checked the documents himself then moved on to the next truck.

The other four trespassers had also taken down their targets and were now dressed in mining uniforms. All six of them got into the truck. No one had noticed the two dressed as security get in. They seemed to be getting away with it so far. The truck pulled out of the loading bay and started on its way towards their starship.

~

Lieutenant Warner was overseeing the loading of the last few trucks himself and was busy talking to a pair of miners. He stretched his arms upwards and moved his head from side to side. His neck felt stiff and he didn't like wearing his spacesuit. He was used to dress-uniform as he spent most of his time inside the *Spirit*, on various missions, or in *Sentry One*.

He looked around taking in the magnificent scenery of the red rock faces that surrounded him and sighed at the sight. He never failed to be impressed by this planet's landscape and the sun was also an amazing sight to behold when reflected with the red tinge of the Martian lands that surrounded him.

He noticed a flash of light in the distance and diverted his attention towards it. He gestured to the nearest soldier. "Hand me your binoculars."

The soldier removed them from his belt and placed them in the outstretched hand of Lt Warner. The binoculars were specially designed to fit up to the visor of his helmet. He adjusted the focus and frowned. He lowered them slightly and squinted into the distance.

Then he spotted the light again and raised the binoculars once more. He saw a vehicle but couldn't quite make it out, so he adjusted the focus a little more and increased the magnification again then he saw it. One of their trucks was heading in the wrong direction.

He lowered the binoculars again and shouted some instructions to the nearest security officer. Two security buggies raced off in the direction of the truck.

"I want a star cruiser launched immediately," he ordered.

We need to catch that quickly, we can't afford to lose any more Etherall, he thought. He raised the binoculars to his eyes again and found the truck just as it disappeared out of the canyon. He lowered his gaze a little and saw that the buggies were only halfway across. They would catch the truck, but he was relying on the star cruiser to stop it.

Lt Warner looked up as the star cruiser emerged from the *Spirit* and sped after the fleeing truck.

~

"There it is," said David Tressel, the leader of the thieves, as he raised his arm towards their awaiting starship. The driver didn't respond. He was too busy concentrating on the uneven surface to acknowledge anything.

They were approximately one hundred meters away when a star cruiser flashed overhead and then banked away sharply.

"We must get back to the ship as fast as possible or we're finished!" shouted David.

"There are two buggies closing in from behind, sir," reported one of the thieves from the rear of the truck.

The pilot of the star cruiser looked out the side of his cockpit towards the truck as he banked round for another pass. "Sir, they're only one hundred meters away from their ship. Please advise."

'Fire some warning shots. See if that stops them. But don't destroy the truck.'

The pilot banked again and came in low, firing off his lasers a few meters in front of the truck. It swerved slightly but the driver regained control and carried on towards the starship.

"They're going to kill us," panicked one of the men in the back.

"No, they're not," said the person next to him. "They won't risk the cargo we're hauling."

~

Captain Turner strode on to the bridge to take over from Lt Warner.

"Captain on the bridge!" announced one of the soldiers guarding the entrance.

"Report, Lt Warner," ordered the captain.

"One of our trucks has been stolen and we're in the process of retrieving it," replied the lieutenant.

"Cripple their ship before they can get to it," said the captain. "Send three squadrons. This could turn nasty."

~

The pilot of the star cruiser received his instructions and turned back towards the thieves' starship. He locked onto one of the landing supports and released two torpedoes as the starships laser cannons fired on him. He narrowly avoided the lasers and climbed out of danger.

The landing support collapsed after the impact of the torpedoes and the starship tilted over to one side sending out a large cloud of red dust as the hull bit into the dusty, rocky surface.

"That should hold them up, sir. Only a skilled or desperate pilot could take off in that now, let alone land it again," reported the pilot.

The truck skidded to a stop underneath the starship and they all got out and assessed the damage to their hull.

"We'll never get out of here now!" screamed one of the men.

David gave him a warning glare. Then he started pointing as he gave his orders. "We're going to have to load this manually now! The loading door is too high up damn them!" he shouted. "Set up a defensive perimeter underneath the ship to protect us while we load as much of this as we can. That way the star cruiser won't be able to pick us off."

From high above the star cruiser turned towards the starship once again. It dived towards the ground and, at top speed, sped past at a low level to observe them then he pulled up again.

"Sir, they're still trying to load the Etherall but from what I can tell it'll take them some time to load any significant amount. Their loading ramp is at least three meters off the ground which is slowing them up."

~

Captain Turner paced the deck of the bridge and then stopped, looking towards Lt Warner. "Have another transporter ready to go but keep them on hold. And tell the troops already on their way to launch their assault. Try to take prisoners if they can." And with saying that he started pacing the bridge again.

~

[49]

The two security buggies had pulled up and the soldiers were now using them for cover while returning fire. It was a stand-off.

A large shadow loomed above them and they looked up. The transporter had arrived. It settled down and out poured one squadron who set up their mobile shields and slowly started their advance towards the stricken starship. The transporter had taken off again and was landing on the opposite side to offload another squadron of soldiers, then once more for the final squadron on the one remaining side. After it had offloaded the third squadron the transporter took off again and moved to a safe position to observe. The shields had absorbed what little laser fire had come their way from the damaged starships lasers.

All three squadrons closed the distance with minimal losses due to the mobile shields in front of them. As they got within range, they switched their lasers to stun and were now beginning to attempt to take prisoners.

David could see that it was all over as far as defence was concerned and ordered the retreat. They had about a quarter of the load of Etherall on board which was enough to cover their expenditures and with a good number of them dead or captured they would still have a decent amount each to live off for another six months.

The loading bay door started to close, and the last two men got stunned as they ran up the closing ramp. One fell to the floor of the ramp and the other ended up unconscious with his head and shoulders tilting over the edge. As the ramp closed there was a sickening crunch, combined with some tearing and squelching, as his head and shoulders were cut clean from the rest of his body.

One of the Space Federation soldiers looked at what remained of the dead man and smiled. "What a way to go," he joked as he looked up at the starship.

"Move it people. Get away from the ship," ordered one of the team leaders. They all backed away as the engines started firing up.

The star cruiser circling above saw the exhaust ports begin to glow. "They're attempting to take off, sir. What are your orders?" reported the pilot.

~

Captain Turner approached the microphone. "How much Etherall have they got?"

One of the team leaders spoke up. "I'd say about a quarter to half the load, sir."

Captain Turner thought for a moment then turned back to the microphone. "Fire a homing beacon. We'll follow and retrieve the Etherall later." He turned to Lt Warner. "Order everyone back to the ship. We'll leave as soon as possible," he paused and then added, "Have all the crates been loaded yet?"

"Yes, sir," replied the Lieutenant.

"Then I'll inform General Bolgon what's happened," and with that parting comment he left the bridge to report privately to the general.

~

The starship, still with one corner resting on the ground, fired two of its downward thrusters nearest to the damaged landing strut. The ship started shaking and moved slightly upwards. The thrust increased and it started rising more rapidly. At just the right moment the pilot applied all downward thrusters and it lifted off the ground. He fed in the main engines and the ship moved off, starting to climb. The soldiers on the ground scrambled back aboard the transporter. The truck and both buggies started the long drive back to the *Spirit*.

CHAPTER FIVE

November 2171

The Moon

"How can you even suggest making a full-scale assault? We don't know if they're indigenous or if they crashed there," argued Michael Toddwell with one of the other strategists mulling over proposed battle plans against Anthera.

"They can't be indigenous. Anthera's too far away from the sun. It can't support life."

"As far as we know. What if an alien race has developed the technology to sustain life wherever they see fit?"

The strategist shook his head and decided to move past that point. "So, you're suggesting we send a small survey team to Anthera to find out what we're up against; is that right?"

"I'm not suggesting anything yet. But that would make more sense than risking our entire military force against an unknown enemy. If they are indigenous, then they control Anthera. If they have crashed there, then they'll be localised to one area."

"The informant said it was just one crashed mothership we're dealing with."

"That's if we can trust her. I'm still sceptical. I think we need to be sure of the forces we're up against before we go in," said Toddwell.

"What if we send in this small force and they get killed before they can send a message back."

"That would obviously have been wasteful. And, like I've already said, I'm not suggesting anything like that yet. We must exhaust all avenues of attack before we commit to any one suggestion."

"If only we could talk to the captured aliens and get one of them to tell us what we need to know."

"That would be nice but…" Michael paused. Another idea had struck him. "That psychic. Perhaps she could read the minds of the tranchillions for us. Plus, I'd be more inclined to believe her story if she managed it."

"If she can that would definitely help, but they don't speak our language so how would she translate what she heard?"

"I thought you didn't trust her," said another strategist. "If so, why do you keep using the name she gave them?"

"One name's as good as any other. It's better than saying 'alien' all the time," replied Toddwell. "We'll have to think some more about this. Carry on with your plans and I'll get to work on finding a way for the psychic to understand tranchillion." Michael left the room and headed for General Bolgon's office.

~

Michael arrived at the outer office and entered. He walked up to the secretary's desk and smiled.

"Hello Mr Toddwell. The general is in. I'll see if he's available," she picked up her phone. "Michael Toddwell to see you, sir," she paused as she listened to the response. "Okay, sir," she replaced the receiver. "You may go in, Mr Toddwell."

"Thank you," he replied as he walked towards the office door. The secretary pressed the release button on her desk. The door slid open as he approached and closed automatically behind him. He walked up to the desk and saluted.

"Sir," he said as he stood to attention in front of General Bolgon.

The general returned the salute and gestured for his friend to sit down. They had an agreement that, after the formalities were out of the way, they would do away with formal talk. No more saluting, no more 'sir'.

"So, have you come up with anything interesting yet?" he asked.

"There are a few conflicting ideas, and all of them need additional information gathering before they can become viable. That's why I'm here, Jim."

"Oh yes."

"About that psychic Neil has hooked up with."

"Yes, although 'hooked up' isn't exactly how I would've put it."

"I was thinking that perhaps we could get her to read the minds of the tranchillions to see what we're up against."

"Interesting. I take it that you're trying to come up with a way for Rebecca to understand the tranchillion language."

"Yes, she'll need to be able to translate their language, which is a bit of a stumbling block."

"I'll get Neil to bring her here and we'll come up with something," General Bolgon rose and strode over to his drink's cabinet.

"Will you join me in a whiskey, Michael?" he asked with his back still turned.

"No thank you, I'll pass. I'd better be going," Michael got up and made his way to the door. He looked back as his hand hovered over the door release pressure pad. "I know it still hurts, Jim. We'll get the one responsible for her death. Take it easy with the drink, okay."

Jim held up his glass. "I appreciate your concern Michael." He drank some more and walked back over to his desk as Michael left the room. He sat back down and placed the glass on his desk then opened a drawer. He carefully lifted out the picture of his wife and stared at it. He broke down and sobbed as he lifted the picture to his forehead. "I'll see you later, Jen." He let out a couple more sobs. "Much later."

~

Neil and Rebecca were walking briskly to General Bolgon's office. "Did your dad say why he wanted us?" asked Rebecca breathlessly.

"No, he just said that he wanted me there and I was to bring you along."

"Can you slow down a little please?"

"Sorry, I sometimes forget that I walk fast," he slowed the pace. "Is that better?"

"Yes, much better thanks," she was watching the way he moved and was beginning to wish she had met him earlier – like, before he had met his girlfriend. Her eyes wandered down to his bottom and she inhaled sharply.

Neil looked around at the sound. "Are you all right?" he asked.

She blushed at the thought that he'd caught her looking at his behind. "Yes, of course."

They arrived at General Bolgon's office.

"He's waiting for you. Step right in," called out the secretary. She buzzed them in, and the door slid open, allowing them to enter.

"Ah, Neil, Rebecca, sit down. I have a proposition for you."

They sat and waited for Jim to carry on.

"Mr Toddwell has come up with an idea. It needs a bit of work but we're going to press on anyway."

Neil shifted in his seat.

"We want Rebecca to read the minds of the tranchillion prisoners to gather information about Anthera. We want to know how many of them there are, where about on the planet they are, and how strong a military force they have."

[57]

"How's she going to do that?" asked Neil.

"We'll interview them one by one. Someone will ask them carefully selected questions, and hopefully get some answers, while Rebecca will be reading their minds in the next room."

"I don't understand tranchillion. How am I supposed to read their minds if I don't know what they're thinking?" Rebecca seemed flustered at the idea.

"Someone will come up with a solution soon enough," replied Jim.

"When do we get started?" asked Neil.

"As soon as the questions have been selected and we find a way for Rebecca to learn their language."

"Back on the battleport there was a language expert amongst the soldiers. She managed to translate the tranchillion symbols into English so that our flight crew could fly the ship back here. It might be worth bringing her in on this."

"What's her name?" asked Jim.

Neil thought about it for a few seconds then he clicked his fingers. "Private Melanie McCoughlae."

"Right. I'll get Private McCoughlae and Michael to work together on this and maybe you'll understand tranchillion within a couple of months," Jim said to Rebecca. "Go get some rest. You'll be notified when we want you."

Neil stood and saluted the general. Rebecca awkwardly did the same. Then they left the office. Outside, Rebecca looked drained from her encounter with General Bolgon.

"I forget how he can affect some people," said Neil while taking her hand to help steady her.

"He's so intense. You must obey him," she paused while looking for the right words but settled for, "You know what I mean."

"Yes, I do. But you haven't been military trained. That's just years of authority in his voice."

"Well, it looks like I'll be interviewing them then. It doesn't look like I have any choice."

"If it helps, the tranchillions won't be able to see or hear you. Someone else will be interviewing them. You'll just be reading their minds."

"Okay, but I'll need a favour."

"What's that?" Neil let go of her hand.

"Will you come? All this is new to me and I only trust you."

"Okay, I'll see to it that I'm available when you have to do this."

"Are you all right now?"

"Yes, thank you."

They set off in different directions to their quarters.

~

Neil awoke the next morning and turned over to cuddle up to Chloe, but she wasn't there. He drew his elbow up beneath himself and half sat up in bed.

He focused on the *en suite* doorway. "Darling, are you there?" Silence. "Honey, you all right," he called out louder in case she was in the next room. Still no answer. Neil got up and, without dressing, left the bedroom, heading for the kitchen. Chloe was nowhere to be seen.

After he'd made a coffee, he decided to check the answering machine. Chloe sometimes left messages on there for him if she had to go out. There was only one

[59]

message and that was from a panic-stricken Rebecca. Chloe must have gone to meet her.

A few minutes later, as he was finishing his coffee, Chloe walked in. Neil got out of his chair to greet her and realised, too late, that Rebecca was with her. He cleared his throat and said, "I'll just get dressed then."

He hurried off into the bedroom. Rebecca was completely red-faced with embarrassment.

"Please take a seat. I'll get you some coffee," said Chloe. "Don't be embarrassed. We often stay naked when we've not got to go out."

Chloe came back with the drinks and sat down opposite her. "He'll be out in a moment then you can tell him what's troubling you."

Neil walked back into the room and sat next to Chloe after checking her face for any signs of anger.

"Sorry about that, Rebecca. If I'd known you were coming, I would've been dressed."

"It's okay," she replied, still feeling rather awkward.

"What's wrong?" Neil asked her while taking the cup of coffee offered him by Chloe.

"I had another conversation with the *Watchers* last night. They have instilled the entire language of the tranchillions into my head. They said that it might take a couple of days for my brain to sort it all out but after that I could help program the language translator that the military have been developing."

Neil was chuckling. "That'll annoy military intelligence."

"What will?" asked Chloe. "And what's so funny?"

"Oh, that a young, non-military, woman knows about their secret project," Neil got up and plucked his jacket off its peg. "I'll go and report this to dad. I suggest you

[60]

get as much rest as possible. These developments will obviously bring things forward."

He left the room and Chloe resumed her conversation with Rebecca. They were rapidly becoming best friends.

~

Two days later, Rebecca felt confident that she was fluent in tranchillion. It was as if she'd been speaking it her entire life. She had just confirmed all that Private McCoughlae had already given them. They had their questions and the language translator was ready to receive the information from her head.

"Now, Miss Chambers. This will hurt for a few seconds, but we'll only have to do it once," said the technician who was about to attach the translator to her head.

"Go ahead," was all she said in reply.

He attached it to her then switched it on. She stiffened and closed her eyes tight. After six seconds had passed, she relaxed. The technician switched off the device and removed it from her head.

"I'm sorry that you've had to go through this, Miss Chambers but it will hopefully save lives."

"It wasn't too bad actually. More like a sudden headache than painful."

They set off for the interview room. Part-way there Rebecca asked, "Won't I have to ask them the questions?"

"No," replied Neil.

She walked on a few more steps looking puzzled.

"What are you frowning for?" he asked her.

"Frowning. Oh, you mean," She pointed to her forehead and relaxed. "I'm not frowning. I was just thinking, you know, kind of puzzled."

They turned a corner and were almost at their destination.

"About what?"

"If I'm the only one who knows tranchillion, how's the person who interviews them going to ask the questions and how's the tranchillion going to know what they're saying?"

"There will be two translators. One will be attached to the interviewer and one to the interviewee."

"Won't the Tranchillion remain silent?"

"More than likely, but that's why you're involved. The interviewer will ask the questions and it won't matter whether he answers because you'll be reading his thoughts. And in turn you'll be connected to a computer that will be recording everything you receive."

Rebecca stayed silent for the rest of the walk and seemed a little happier than before. Besides, nothing bad could happen. She had the legendary 'Neil Bolgon' at her side.

They entered the secure side of the interview room to be behind the one-way glass where Rebecca would be hooked up to the machine. Michael Toddwell and Suzanne Cox were already sitting at the only table in the room. Suzanne had agreed to the general's conditions on the understanding that she could be present at every major event. This was one such event that she had been invited to attend.

After they'd finished for the day, Neil took an exhausted Rebecca back to her quarters.

"Will you come in for a minute. I have a couple of questions to ask you," she said as she opened her door.

"Of course, but I can't stay for long. Chloe will be wondering where I am."

They both entered her room and the door slid shut behind them. Rebecca collapsed into her armchair and Neil sat opposite her.

"What was your question?" he asked while leaning forwards, hands clasped together and elbows on knees. She smiled and looked back at Neil with her stunning brown eyes.

"How long will these interviews go on for?"

"Well, we did three today and, with an earlier start tomorrow, we should get the remaining eight finished. So hopefully, we'll have all the information we need by tomorrow night."

"What happens then? Will you be finished with me?"

"I'm not sure. But I imagine that we could possibly need your further assistance."

"Could you get me a glass of water please. I'm thirsty."

"Of course, but then I'll have to get going."

Neil left Rebecca to sit in her chair while he fetched her some water. When he got back, she was fast asleep. He looked at her a little more closely than he had before. She had similar hair to Chloe's, just shorter, and a slightly narrower face. Her breasts were smaller. That was one place that he'd forced himself not to look at before. Her body was slim and her stomach flat. The shirt she had on was almost skin-tight, so he had little trouble noticing, now he was looking. He put the glass down, after drinking some, and watched her sleeping for a moment.

[63]

He decided he'd better carry her to bed if she was to get a good night's sleep, so he opened her bedroom door and looked for her bed. The sheets had been folded back halfway to air the bed he presumed. He pulled the sheets up to her pillows. Then, he walked over to her and gently fed his arms behind her neck and shoulders, and the backs of her knees, before lifting her up. She murmured some ineligible words and brought her free arm around his neck. He felt some familiar stirrings with this contact, but he suppressed them and carried her to the bedroom.

He lay her on top of her sheets, and she murmured again as he removed his arms from underneath her. She turned over and, after removing her shoes, he backed out of the bedroom. Neil reached into his trousers and adjusted himself. That was the first time since Chloe that he'd reacted that way to any female. He picked up the glass of water and finished it off then put it in the sink and left.

~

Neil entered his quarters and headed straight for the bathroom. He switched on the shower and then undressed. He stepped into the water and felt the warm droplets running all over his body. He always found a shower soothing after a long day.

Chloe entered the bathroom. "May I join you?" She didn't wait for a reply. Her dressing gown fell to the floor and she opened the shower door. Neil pulled her towards him. They kissed as the water started to soak Chloe as well. Their hands were exploring each other's bodies and Chloe brought her leg upwards, bent at the knee. He held her under the knee with one hand and gently caressed her face with the other while kissing her passionately.

[64]

Suddenly, he grabbed her bottom with both hands and lifted her up while stepping towards the tiled wall. She wrapped her legs around him as her back pressed against the tiles. She reached down for him and gasped as she guided him into her. They made love and moaned with pleasure until they both climaxed together. They opened their eyes, smiling at each other as the water started to clear away the signs of their love making.

After their shower they went to bed, laying on their usual sides.

"Neil, what do you think of Rebecca?" asked Chloe while watching his face.

"She's a nice girl who's braver than she makes out, why?"

"You seem to be spending a lot of time with her recently, that's all."

"Oh, Chloe. It's just work. Nothing more."

"You don't need to be there while she's reading minds."

"I'm just there for moral support. She trusts me and, right now, we need her to do this for us. If I didn't go along, I think she'd refuse to do it."

"Do you fancy her?" Chloe's face was set straight. Not a hint of a smile.

"Of course not. I'm with you and would never sleep with another woman."

"That's not what I asked," she said, now looking more suspicious than ever.

"No Chloe. I don't fancy her."

"She fancies you. I've seen the way she looks at you."

"No, she doesn't. Don't be silly."

"You might not have noticed, but I did. I'm telling you – she wants you."

"Don't you trust me?"

"Of course, I trust you. It's her I don't trust; or any other woman for that matter."

"It takes two people to have an affair and I don't intend to stray no matter how beautiful or persuasive she may be."

Her anger grew. "Has she asked you to fuck her?"

"Chloe! Of course she hasn't. I've never heard you use language like that before. What's got into you?"

"You said she was beautiful and persuasive."

"I was talking metaphorically."

"Just make sure you don't mess with her, okay."

"Okay... okay." Neil turned away, now feeling slightly worried about this sudden outburst from Chloe.

She lay on her back and looked up at the ceiling, wondering if she'd gone too far. She decided that she hadn't and was glad that Neil now knew how she felt. Chloe closed her eyes and turned towards him. She cuddled into him and, satisfied that they had as much contact as possible, laid her arm over his body. He lifted his arm to allow her to place her hand on his chest. Happy that all was still well with him, she drifted off to sleep.

Neil was thinking about Rebecca, trying to recollect if she had ever flirted with him. He couldn't think of a single time. He also thought about the last time he'd been with her, and how her touch had affected him.

I can control myself so there's no problem, he thought. It took him another half an hour to go to sleep. He drifted off, dreaming about them both.

The next day, during the interview sessions, Neil was watching Rebecca to see if she was showing any signs of liking him. He couldn't see anything but, then again, she was concentrating on her work.

They stopped for an hour's lunch, mainly to give Rebecca a rest, and then they carried on until late afternoon. After they had finished, the officers from military intelligence looked very pleased.

"We will analyse the findings and then get back to you, Neil," said Michael Toddwell before turning his attention to Rebecca. "And thank you, Rebecca, for all that you've done."

"I have a question," said Rebecca to Michael.

"Go on," he replied.

"All of the tranchillions were clear about at least one thing. They thought we attacked them. How can they all think the same thing?"

"Probably because that's what they were told. In your own report, you mentioned that this colonel, what was his name?" he paused trying to remember the tranchillions name.

"Dowdneer," suggested Neil.

"Yes of course; Dowdneer – that's it. He attacked us then reported back to his CO that it was the other way around."

"But what if the *Watchers* have their own agenda and want us to believe that it was one rogue colonel to lure us into sending out someone on their own?"

"I can vouch for the first contact with those fucking aliens," said a voice from behind them. It was one of the officers from military intelligence.

[67]

"Over sixty years ago I was one of the crew members of the shuttle *Reconnaissance*. I know first-hand what happened."

"Really," Rebecca thought he only looked around thirty but was intrigued to hear his story. "Can you tell us about it?"

"Well, we were approaching Anthera and all seemed appropriately quiet. There were no signs of life on the radar, which was admittedly short range, so we decided to land. We'd only been out of cryosleep for an hour and were a bit groggy to say the least. We landed with no problems and set about taking soil samples. We were generally enjoying ourselves and thought we were alone. We'd been there for five days and were close to finishing our survey when Collins, he was one of our team, spotted something in the distance. We sent out two men to investigate and started packing our gear. After about five minutes we noticed Collins and Fredrico were running towards us. We then saw the aliens closing in on them. Collins went down from a shot to the back and Fredrico managed to get back to us. We couldn't return fire as none of us had weapons, so we hurriedly threw the equipment back in the *Reconnaissance*. They were using lasers just like out of a science fiction movie. We didn't have them back then. We lost two more men before we retreated into the shuttle. As we blasted off, they tried to take us out. The shuttle was badly damaged but still operable and we narrowly escaped. We felt ourselves lucky at the time that they couldn't follow to finish us off. We sent a message on to space command and set the autopilot for home then we all got into our sleep chambers and settled into cryosleep for the journey back.

Unfortunately, we'd led them to earth. But we were happy just to be alive."

"How old are you?" asked Rebecca. "You don't look old enough."

"I was twenty-eight when I left for Anthera in twenty-fifty-two so that makes me about one-hundred-and-forty-seven years old. But because of the cryosleep I have only aged three years."

"I don't know whether I could have done that. I couldn't handle losing everyone close to me."

"Yes, everyone I knew was dead by the time I got back, but we knew that was going to be the case before we left."

Neil broke them up and advised her it was time to get back to her quarters.

"Will you walk me back again, Neil?"

He paused, but only for a couple of seconds.

"Of course, but I can't stop this time. I've got to get back. Chloe is expecting me."

Rebecca turned back to the military intelligence officer. "What's your name?"

"Keith. Keith Turnball."

Neil escorted Rebecca back to her quarters and then made his excuses and left. He didn't want to annoy Chloe by staying with Rebecca any longer than he had to.

~

It was late evening, the next day, and the latest meeting had been going on for four and a half hours. They'd discounted three plans already and were undecided about the remaining two options. Neil had joined them half an hour previously and was listening in without making any comments.

He listened to the arguments for and against both plans. Each had their merits but, without really knowing what they were up against, he didn't fancy either. He got up from his seat and joined Michael Toddwell at the round table around which they were arguing about the different plans.

"I have an idea. It's dangerous but I think it'll work," butted in Neil.

One of the strategists said in a slightly mocking tone, "What is this great idea, Mr Bolgon?"

"Before we go wading in, causing unnecessary loss of life, I could go in using a *Chameleon suit* to disguise me as a tranchillion. I could walk among them and gather information that way."

"It would never work," said the same strategist that had mocked him only seconds earlier. "The technology is new and unproven. What good is one man against an entire army of tranchillions. There could be fifty thousand or more of them."

"Or there could be fifty to a couple of hundred," replied Neil.

"That would still be too much for a solitary soldier to handle."

"Yes, but with the chameleon suit on, and an extreme amount of luck, they would never know I was there."

"If the suit failed, you'd be dead or wishing you were."

"I don't mind taking that risk. I joined the armed forces to make a difference. If this could end the war, I've got to try."

"How would you get there? If you arrived in a star cruiser, and was spotted, you'd be destroyed before you could land."

"We could use the captured battleport."

"But it's a huge ship. It takes a crew of at least eight to fly it properly. And anyway, how would you explain the length of time you were gone."

"That's for you lot to work out. I've just given you the idea," said Neil. He walked towards the exit then said, "Let me know if you come up with a plan that works."

Neil left the room, heading for the docking bay that Chloe would be arriving in soon. He missed her even though she'd only been gone for twenty-four hours. He sat and read the latest edition of World News on his e-reader while he waited.

The shuttle arrived and the doors slid open. All the passengers came pouring out, walking in different directions. Once all the passengers were clear, the flight crew started to leave the shuttle and Neil stood up.

He saw her appear from the corridor in her red and blue stewardess's uniform. He hurried over and gave her a warm hug, then they kissed.

"I've missed you," he said.

Smiling, she replied, "I've missed you too."

They parted and Neil carried her bag. They walked back to their quarters talking about everything that had been going on since they'd parted.

~

The next day Neil, Chloe, John Lyderattle and Lisa Fowler were all sitting down to lunch when Michael Toddwell appeared and asked Neil for a quiet word. He got up and excused himself then followed Michael over to a quiet corner of the restaurant.

"We have the plan sorted. It's dangerous and there's a good chance you won't survive but we require your input to finalise the plan. As soon as you're finished join us in your dad's office."

"Of course, Michael. I'll see you soon."

Toddwell left and Neil re-joined his friends.

"What was that all about?" asked Chloe.

"He wants to see me later. He has a plan he wants me to go over," Neil smiled and then the conversation returned to more happy thoughts. They didn't have much time for these get-togethers, but they sure enjoyed them when they did.

When the meal was over, Chloe went with John and Lisa back to their quarters and Neil set off for his rendezvous with Michael and his father.

Neil arrived there in a happy state of mind. Chloe and his friends always had that effect on him. But his mood was about to change when he heard the plans.

"So, you want me and Rebecca to escape here disguised as tranchillions while avoiding any human casualties; break out the other tranchillions being held here; go to Ganymede and raid their prisons and then set off for Anthera; is that right?" Neil was amazed at this latest plan.

Michael kept eye contact. "Yes, but no one can know that you have gone, or the mission could be a failure before it's even begun. Not even Chloe or John must know."

"But she's bound to know I'm missing."

"Officer Turnball is going to be wearing a third chameleon suit, disguised as you, and will be sent out on a mission with the *Resolve*. He is perfect for the role as no one will miss him."

"I'll call in sick to cover the few who know me," said Keith.

"You know, Michael. This could work. How long would I have to complete my mission?"

"One month. That's the longest time the *Resolve* can be away without raising at least some suspicion."

"I don't think I can spring the tranchillions and get away from *Sentry One* without casualties. Even if I managed to take them down without using weapons, I couldn't guarantee the real tranchillions would do the same."

"We already have plans for that. At the time of the breakout, most of security will be policing a concert across the other side of the complex. It'll still be hard, but I feel confident that you'll find a way."

"Will Rebecca be able to handle this mission?"

"It doesn't matter that Rebecca has no military training. The replicater that carries her tranchillion's character traits, will take control of her actions as long as it's attached to her suit. She will become a tranchillion."

"Why do I have to do this?" Rebecca blurted out.

General Bolgon looked at her. "Because your psychic abilities may come in useful there. You need to be near Neil if the *Watchers* talk to you."

Rebecca lowered her eyes and nodded.

"When do we do this?"

"In two weeks," said General Bolgon. "Everyone in this room has two weeks to get ready and make these plans fool proof. No one else is to know about this mission. The only people who do know are here in this room and that's the way it's going to stay. I want my son to return from Anthera, so if anyone leaks anything, I'll personally court martial them. Is that clear?"

"Yes, sir," replied everyone in the room.

[73]

Rebecca felt sick at the thought of going to Anthera, even if Neil would be with her. She knew how dangerous this could be and wasn't relishing the thought of it one little bit.

CHAPTER SIX

November 2171

Earth

The sleek silver and black spacecraft entered earth's atmosphere and headed for England. As their altitude dropped, Denmark and Holland gradually gave way to the horizon as did Ireland. They were headed for the east-midlands and home. They levelled off above a town called Hinckley heading north towards Earl Shilton. They flew over Burbage woods then swooped down skimming the trees until they came to what looked like an old farmhouse. The craft slowed and hovered near a large barn. Three of the four landing struts opened as the barn doors slid open to reveal a high-tech hanger for the spacecraft. The pilot skilfully guided the damaged vessel into the hanger and settled it down, compensating for the area where there was no landing strut.

Being careful to avoid the landing thrusters, a maintenance crew wheeled over a makeshift brace to hold the spacecraft upright until another landing strut could be welded into place. The pilot cut the last of the remaining downward thrusters and the spacecraft settled onto the temporary brace.

"Woo. Not bad, not bad at all," said the co-pilot while wiping his brow with his forearm.

"I'm the best pilot you'll ever see," said Guy.

"Don't get too cocky or you'll come unstuck."

"Me – never," he laughed.

Guy Travis – a twenty-five-year-old pilot, who no one could mistake for being modest, got up from his seat and made for the exit. As he walked down the exit ramp, he saw Madeline and held out his arms to her.

Madeline, in contrast, was just as lovable and jovial as Guy, but she would never acknowledge it when complemented. She didn't look her fifty-five years as she bustled her way towards him, smiling fondly. She was like a mother to him and the rest of the crew.

"Mads, how the heck are you?"

"Better now you lot are back," she took a few more steps. "Were there any casualties?"

They embraced and Madeline ruffled Guy's black hair in a friendly gesture.

"You'll have to ask the captain that. I don't have all the information, but I do know some died," he replied as they parted.

"Mother. You know what I told you about talking to him," said David with a sly smile on his face. Guy stepped to the side so Madeline could see her son advancing towards them.

"I'll talk to whoever I like, and don't you forget that," she mocked while waving her finger at him. "So, who was killed then?"

"Can we take this inside, mother? I don't want to talk about this in front of the crew."

"Oh yes, of course, you're right."

They walked towards the house with their arms behind each other's backs while Guy made his way to the wash house. He needed a shower after being cooped up in the spacecraft for so long.

David and his mother entered the house through the back door and turned left into the kitchen.

"Sit down, David. Have a cup of tea," she said and picked up the kettle. She took it over to the sink and began filling it with water. David sat at the old wooden table and looked around the familiar room. He did enjoy being home.

"What happened then? I thought this was supposed to go through without a hitch."

He sighed and leaned back on his chair while running his fingers through his short black hair with his eyes closed.

"It was all arranged, and we never made a single mistake. All the guards were taken down quietly and without harm. We thought we'd got away but then a star cruiser intercepted us. We must have been spotted."

"Could your contact have had second thoughts and tried to take you all out."

"No, I don't think so. He's making too much money out of this to double cross us. Anyway, I'm sure he'll contact us soon, then we'll find out what went on."

Madeline sat opposite David after putting the tray on the table.

"Mother, why don't you get yourself a proper drinks dispenser? It takes a lot less effort than this old-fashioned method you use."

"Look, I like my old wooden table and I like making tea with tea bags and a teapot. If I had machines to do all the work for me," she shrugged and continued, "then I wouldn't have anything to do."

"Okay, forget I said anything," he accepted a biscuit. "Thank you, mother," he said, smiling.

"Right, back to business. Three were captured – Jones, Murphy and Weston. Another three were killed – Trent, Samson and Thorpe. Jefferies was stunned on the way up the ramp, but he fell safely in the middle. Trent was also stunned, but he was hanging half over the edge and lost his head and shoulders as the ramp closed. His remains have been taken to the usual place."

"Oh, that's terrible. I'd better inform their families and arrange the appropriate ceremonies."

"I'd recommend a closed casket as his head and left arm are still on Mars or in *Sentry One*."

They finished their tea and biscuits and Madeline started making some calls. David went to get washed and changed. It had been a long trip.

~

Captain Turner watched the numbers roll by as the turbo lift carried him to the bridge. He heard the familiar sound of excess air being pumped away as the lift slowed to a halt and the doors slid open. He walked into the noise of hundreds of crew members talking to each other and generally going about their business.

"Status report," he ordered as he stood near the observation screens. Lt Warner stood to attention then recited what he knew.

"The ship has entered Earth's atmosphere and is somewhere in the Leicestershire – Warwickshire area of England. Once we've descended ourselves, we'll be able to pinpoint exactly where they are, sir."

"Good, good. I want a squad readied for when we get the go-ahead to go after them. You sort the details while I report to the general. Just make sure you're ready."

They saluted and Captain Turner left the bridge to send his report.

He entered his private quarters and connected to the general. "Sir, we have arrived back home and are orbiting Earth. The ship has entered the atmosphere and headed for England. I request permission to go after them, sir."

"That's a negative, captain. I'll inform the local government and get back to you. If there are any developments let me know."

Captain Turner gave the co-ordinates of the starships approximate location to the General, then altered frequencies and dialled a new number. He figured he had time to talk to an old friend while he was waiting.

~

Guy, David and a couple of friends were just getting in their car when Madeline called for David to come back. She was standing outside the front door waving madly. David got back out. "Sorry guys, hopefully this won't take long," he hurried over to his mother.

"What's wrong, mother?"

"There's a phone call for you. The one you've been expecting."

He disappeared inside the house and picked up the handset. "Yes."

"Why hasn't your mother got a video phone yet?" said the voice on the other end of the line.

"She's old fashioned that way. Now, what the hell happened on Mars? You said that this one would be a piece of cake. Your words not mine. I lost three men and had three captured."

"First, you don't speak to me like that. May I remind you who you're talking to."

David tried to interrupt but the caller was having none of it.

"Stop interrupting or you'll have to find another accomplice and I'll see to your downfall, personally."

Again, David interrupted. "Don't threaten me. I could just as easily bring about your downfall as you could mine. Let's not forget that."

"Point taken. Let's not try out either scenario then. Now, to answer your question. Lieutenant Warner spotted our truck driving in the wrong direction. It was purely a miracle that he saw you. I could do nothing about the resulting battle without revealing myself to them. I'm sorry for your casualties and will do my best to get your men either released or sprung from prison."

David sighed. "I suppose that'll have to do. Do you want to meet sooner or are we leaving it as planned?"

"There's a big change of plan. You have a homing beacon attached to your hull. You'll have to destroy it immediately. We're orbiting Earth as we speak. Once we've obtained permission, we're coming to take back the

Etherall. We're not close enough to pinpoint you, but as soon as we enter the atmosphere, you're as good as found. If you cut the signal, I'll try to divert the search away from your base or at least delay it somehow. I'll contact you again when it's safe."

David could not believe what he was hearing and signalled for his mother. He then turned his attention back to the phone. "Hold on a sec," he said, then lowered the handset again.

"Mother, get everyone back in the house and set up a meeting in the lounge."

Madeline nodded and left.

"Okay, I'll take care of my end and will be waiting for your call. Oh, and if this all goes wrong, it's been lovely doing business with you."

They ended their call and David hurried to the lounge to break the news. He entered and waited for everyone to file in then held up his hands to signal for quiet.

"There's a homing device attached to the hull of the *Intrepid*. The SF will be down here soon. So, unless you all want to spend the next twenty years in prison, we need to find, and destroy, that device quickly. They are orbiting Earth right now and as soon as they get the word, they'll descend on us. They know the general area of our location but if they enter the atmosphere before we destroy the homing device then we're finished, any questions?"

They all got up. "Let's find it then," said one.

It took two minutes to find the device. David took it over to the acid-filled barrel which they had for occasions such as this. Amongst other uses it was a brilliant way of getting rid of metals.

[81]

"Couldn't we distract them with it instead," suggested Guy.

"How?" replied David.

"I could take the sky kite up and look for a suitable moving object to drop it in. What do you think?"

"Do you know, Guy. That's a brilliant idea. Get her started right away. I think you should have about ten minutes before they arrive. Make sure you've offloaded it by then or the ploy won't be nearly as effective," he handed over the homing beacon.

Guy got in the sky kite, started her up, and pulled the canopy over him. He signalled he was ready and opened the throttle. The sky kite soared into the air.

Guy decided to head south and, just as the ten minutes were up, he swooped down and spotted an open-backed lorry just outside Rugby. It seemed to be heading towards Hinckley which would hopefully send them in the wrong direction when they found out they had the wrong target.

After dropping the beacon into the lorry, he turned the sky kite back towards Hinckley and headed for home. A minute later he noticed a large military troop transporter with SFSF written on the side descending about two miles to his west. His heart quickened as he anticipated them turning towards him then he relaxed and smiled as he realised they hadn't noticed him. It seemed to be working, for now.

~

"The signal's coming from that truck," said the navigator.

"We've been had," said Captain Turner. "We must stop that truck and see where it came from. Then we can start our search from there. Lt Warner, organise the troops. Equip them with Etherall detectors and hopefully we'll find them before the day is out."

The transporter flew over the truck and set down on the road a little further up, completely blocking the way forward. As the truck, and several other vehicles, came to a stop, four Special Forces soldiers advanced towards them. Two of the soldiers stopped at the cab and the other two climbed into the back to find the homing device.

"Have you seen a black and silver spacecraft today?" asked one of the soldiers.

"No. What's this all about? You're blocking the road."

"The people we're looking for placed our homing beacon in your truck. Where did you originate from?"

"You could've caused an accident," continued the man, oblivious to their questions.

"We need to know where this truck came from."

"Get it moved. I've got deliveries to make."

One soldier pushed him against the truck. "Look you idiot. We haven't got time for your bullshit. Now where did this truck come from?"

The man looked the soldier in the eyes then folded. "Willoughby's. It's a building firm in Rugby, but I haven't seen anyone messing with the truck."

"Okay, what's the postcode for Willoughby's?"

"What do you need that for?"

"We can locate the business quicker, now what's the postcode?"

The two soldiers returned from the back of the truck with the homing device. "Got it, sir," they said as they carried on past towards the waiting transporter.

"I don't know. I just work there."

The second soldier looked at the side of the truck. "Never mind. We've got the address. Let's go." They left him bewildered by the side of his truck as he watched them march back to their transporter.

A few more motorists had got out of their cars and were staring in disbelief at the soldiers. It was not an everyday occurrence and a couple of them went to see if the truck driver was okay.

The transporter lifted off and headed towards Rugby just as two police cars arrived on the scene. The police officers got out and were just as amazed as the civilians.

Two minutes later, the transporter landed in a field next to Willoughby's and the entire squad filed out in formation waiting for orders from their CO. Captain Turner exited the transporter and climbed onto a Jeep to address the soldiers.

"I want you all split into groups of four. We'll spread out in a circle and continue outwards for a radius of thirty miles. Each squad leader will have an Etherall detector. I want you all to knock on doors and ask about sightings of the spacecraft. If your detectors find any traces of Etherall you have the authority to enter and search. Set your weapons to stun and don't fire upon anyone unless you absolutely must. Is that clear."

"Sir, yes sir," replied his troops.

"One more thing. We have two days to find the thieves and the Etherall then we *will* be asked to leave. Your squad leaders already have all the available Intel so any questions you have should be directed to them. Dismissed."

Every soldier saluted the captain then they all filed away to their starting positions and the search for the Etherall began.

~

The sky kite turned to line up its landing and gradually descended towards the ground. Guy skilfully guided it into a soft landing and steered straight into the hanger. He cut the engine and the propellers slowed to a stop. He undid his straps and jumped down onto the dusty floor, then took off his helmet and passed it to a waiting maintenance man.

"How did it go Guy?" asked David. "We saw the SF transporter landing to the south."

"Very well indeed. I dropped the homing beacon in a moving truck and then got out of there. After a minute or two the transporter appeared and went after the truck. I was a couple of miles away by that time, but I was still crapping myself in case they changed direction and came after me."

"It's a good job you dropped it when you did. Another thirty seconds later and they would've had you. Well done, Guy. Now, let's decide on the next stage. We need to clear this whole area of any tell-tale signs of our operation and we also need to get the Etherall out of here as fast as possible. They'll use Etherall detectors and *will* find it."

David turned to his mother. "Let's get going. I think we'll have about twenty-four to thirty-six hours to get everything cleared."

"Do we close the road or not?" asked Madeline.

"No, I don't think so. This road is hardly used and what does come down drives straight past us. It would raise suspicion if we closed it and word would be bound to get back to the SF."

[85]

"Okay, David. I'll start arrangements for some extra trucks; how many do you think we'll need?"

"About five."

David left his mother and walked towards the hanger with Guy. "I think we'll divide the Etherall into eighths and load a quarter of each truck with it. To cover ourselves, the other three quarters will be loaded with cattle or hay in case we get stopped for any reason. You get the idea?"

"Yes, David. I'll get right on it."

Guy left David's side and gathered a group of men together to start dividing the Etherall. David took his mobile from his pocket and pressed his thumb on the screen. The phone beeped as it unlocked. "Steve," he said to the phone. He waited a few rings then smiled as he heard his friend's voice.

"It's me. Do you still need some work?"

'Yes mate. I can't find anything.'

"Good, I've got some for you if you're interested. It's manual work but I might be able to find something more permanent for you later. What do you think?"

'Brilliant when do you want me to start?'

"Right now."

'I'll finish up here and come straight over.'

"Great. You'll be lifting and carrying in the farmyard for a start."

'Sounds fine to me. See you soon. Oh and, David,' he paused.

"Yes."

'Thank you.'

"It's all right and thanks for your help. We really need it, bye."

'Bye.'

David pressed his thumb on the screen again and the connection was terminated. He'd walked back to the house during the conversation. He entered the hallway through the front door and waited for his mother to finish on the phone.

"I've enlisted Steve. Can you think of anyone else we can trust to help?" he asked as soon as Madeline replaced the receiver.

"Not off-hand but we should already have enough help to get the Etherall loaded onto the trucks in time. I've only managed to hire four trucks. Do you want me to try another company?"

"No, four should be fine. We'll just have to load the trucks with more Etherall to compensate. If we get ours off soon there will be less chance of them being intercepted. I'll get back to Guy to amend the instructions. Can you warn the warehouses to expect the trucks please?"

"Of course, darling. I'll get right on it."

David left the house and went in search of Guy.

~

One day had passed when Captain Turner's unit arrived in Hinckley to continue their search for the Etherall. So far there had been no sign of it. All they'd achieved was to annoy the residents of the areas they'd searched, and they had also been slowed down by the police until it was made clear they'd been given the clearance to search any buildings they wanted to. So far, no force had been used on the protesting citizens. The Space Federation soldiers were facing mounting resistance almost everywhere they went as word spread about their activities.

[87]

"Someone's going to get hurt before long, sir," said Lt Warner.

"If we use minimal force during our search, we should be okay, but it is getting harder to inspect everywhere now that the civ's are locking their doors and refusing us entry," replied Captain Turner.

"May I suggest that we only search commercial buildings unless the detectors pick up anything inside a private residence, sir?"

"I think we're going to have to, Lieutenant. If they were going to spread the Etherall over a wide area, we should have come up with at least one positive response from the detectors by now."

The Captain rubbed his brow, head bowed with eyes closed, and thought for a moment. He lifted his head and opened his eyes.

"We have to change our approach. Apart from the trouble we're causing, we have twenty-three hours left to find the Etherall before we're called back. Take one soldier from each search group and make up as many four-man squads as you can. They will be assigned new, smaller, search areas within the current ones, and are to focus entirely on none residential buildings. That should speed up the search considerably. Now off you go. I'll meet you in area six," he paused as he found it on the map and tapped it. Lt Warner saluted and left to arrange the new orders.

"Driver – area six," said the captain as he got back in his vehicle. He leaned forward and pressed the privacy button then settled back into his seat. He reached into his pocket and pulled out his private phone. Instead of saying the name he searched the menu and manually dialled it from there. He waited for a few rings and smiled as his old friend answered.

'Hello, how are you?' asked his old friend.

"Fine – fine, listen. I've got a few minutes spare and I'm in Hinckley. Could you meet me for a coffee?"

'Of course, where are you?'

"Is *Jeffreys* still open?"

'Yes, I'll meet you there. I wasn't expecting you to call again so soon. Is everything okay?'

"Yes, fine. I just happened to be here and thought I'd give you an update."

"Right, okay then. I'll be right over."

"Bye."

He cancelled the call and put the phone back in his pocket then closed his eyes and contemplated recent events. He just had to get some of the Etherall back. It was the second time in the last eight visits that he'd been hit. *I shouldn't have agreed to another job this soon*, he thought.

The vehicle pulled up and Captain Turner pressed the privacy button again.

"We are here, captain."

"Good, you stay with the car and I'll have a look around. Call me when the others arrive."

"Yes, sir."

He got out and closed the door behind him. He didn't recognise any of the shops anymore. Turner crossed the road and headed in the direction of *Jeffreys*. He hoped it hadn't moved since his last visit. God knows, almost everything else had. As far as he could make out it was just the banks and building societies that had survived the passing years.

~

[89]

"Nonsense dear, it's been absolutely ages since your last visit. I won't hear of you paying for anything while you're with us."

"But mother, that's the reason I want to pay. It's the least I can do after all that you've done for me."

"Suzanne, will you please stop arguing with me. I will not budge on this matter. Now put your purse away."

Suzanne shrugged and put her purse back in her handbag. "Okay, mother if that's the way you want it."

Julie smiled. "You always were a stubborn girl, Suzie. That's what makes you so good at your job," she looked at her watch. "We've still got a few minutes to kill before coffee. What about a spot of clothes shopping?"

"Okay, mother but are we just trying them on or are you actually going to buy something this time?"

"You never know dear, you never know."

Suzanne felt happier now than she had for a long time. There was no pressure on her to meet a deadline. There was no one around that she had to keep an eye on for a story. No one to meet for an interview. It was nice just to relax for a while. Now that the latest story that she'd been working on had gone cold, she had decided to take a week, maybe two, off to take stock of her life.

"Are you listening to me, Suzie?" repeated her mother.

"Oh, sorry, mother I was miles away. What did you say?"

"What do you think of this colour?"

"I think it suits you, mother. You have got to try it on."

Julie put the dress in her basket, along with two others, and a nice hat that she'd had her eye on for months. Together, they walked to the changing room, stopping off twice to handle a couple more garments, and waited in a small queue for a changing room to become vacant.

Suzanne waited outside while her mother tried on the clothes periodically calling for her to have a look. Ten minutes later, Julie put all the garments back on the rail outside the changing rooms.

"You're not going to buy any of them. Not even the hat. Why?"

"I'd feel guilty about buying them. I'll probably get them next week."

"But they might be sold out next week."

"Well if they are then it obviously wasn't meant to be."

"You don't change. Well, don't start moaning to me about them being gone when you look for them next week."

Julie smiled. "Let's get some coffee."

~

Captain Turner entered Jeffreys café and selected a small cubicle at the back. He sat down to wait for his old friend to arrive.

After a few seconds had passed a waitress came over to him. "I love a man in uniform."

Turner looked up and caught the wink she'd given him. "Coffee please."

"Oh, okay then. Black or white, sir?" she replied, quite taken aback that he hadn't taken the bait. She was used to getting complements and the odd date from her seductive wink.

"White thanks."

[91]

She turned away and walked back to the kitchen. When she returned with his coffee, she set it down. "There you go."

He raised his hand in a dismissive 'thank you' gesture without removing his eyes from his tactical map.

He was still studying it when a shadow fell across his table. He looked up and invited his old friend to sit.

"Look," said Turner as he half turned the map towards his friend. "This is where we are now. I'd say, within the next six hours we'll be at your place. Do you think that's enough time to clear out?"

"It'll have to be, David."

"There's something else I need to ask of you. I think it'll make all this seem a little more authentic to the SF."

"What do you need?"

"Some Etherall left behind for us to find. I think it'll satisfy them if we got some of it back. What do you say?"

"You've already got most of it back. We only managed to load a quarter of it in the first place."

Captain Turner shrugged. "Well?"

Tressel sighed. "I don't think that'll be a problem given the time frame. We'll more than likely have to leave some behind. I don't think we can get it all loaded in the next six hours."

"Just make sure you're not there when we arrive."

"I'm not happy about leaving any of it behind. Not only will we lose a lot of money, but we won't be able to go back there ever again. Mother loves that house. It's been in our family for generations."

"I suggest you don't let on to her in advance then."

"That's our home…" David cut short what he was about to say as he caught sight of a young woman, with curly brown hair, enter the café with another, older lady.

[92]

"Be very careful what you say now."

"Why?" replied Captain Turner.

"Look in the mirror behind me. Do you see that woman behind you who just entered?"

"Yes."

"Her name is Suzanne Cox. She's an old friend of mine; childhood friend to be precise. And she's also a reporter for World News. When she spots me she'll come over to say hello."

"What the hell do we do now? If she recognises me, how are we going to explain what we're doing here together?"

"Let's try to avoid that if we can. You go to the toilet. When you come back out head straight for the exit. Hopefully she won't have seen us together."

Turner got up and made his way to the toilet ready to do his disappearing act.

"Who was that?" asked Suzanne.

David raised his head then stood up with open arms. "Suzanne! How, the devil, are you?"

"I'm fine. Just taking some time off to visit my parents. Now, who was that?"

"A friend of mine. He's a captain in the SF." *Shit, how do I get out of this one?* "Would you like to meet him?"

"Yes, I would."

Captain Turner emerged from the toilet and walked towards the exit.

"David," said David as he signalled the captain.

Turner changed direction and addressed his friend. "Yes, David."

"Suzanne would like to say hello."

She held out her hand and Captain Turner took it.

"Nice to meet you, captain."

"Hello. How does someone of your beauty know this ugly son of a bitch?"

Suzanne smiled. "We have been friends since our school days."

Captain Turner let go of her hand. "Look, I'm sorry but I've got to go. My men will be arriving shortly, and I need to get on with my mission. Goodbye. It was lovely meeting you."

Turner left the café, hoping that this chance meeting wasn't going to come back and bite him on the ass.

"Childhood friends then, David?"

"Yes, I've known him for a long time. Anyway, enough about him. Let's talk about you. You're looking lovely, Suzie."

"Thank you, David. May we join you for coffee?"

"Of course, although," he paused to look at his watch. "I've got to get going soon. I have a lot to do today."

Julie Statham sat down. "How are you dear?" she asked David.

"I'm fine, Mrs Statham."

"And how is Madeline?"

"Mother is fine as well."

"Let me get you a coffee and we can catch up on old times. It's been so long since we've all been together in the same room."

"Okay. Just one though. I really have to be going."

CHAPTER SEVEN

November 2171

The Moon

Rebecca struggled with the *chameleon suit* trying to get it over her shoulders. The suit was like a pair of overalls. She had one arm in, but the suit seemed to be resisting her attempts to put it on.

"Here, let me help you with that," said Neil as he moved behind her to hold the suit on her shoulders. "You'll have to take your bra off, Rebecca or it's going to be uncomfortable when the suit tightens."

"Really! I've only just got it on," she sighed. "Turn around then, both of you." She checked that both men were looking away then let the suit drop. She removed her bra and then pulled the suit back up again. "Okay."

Neil turned back and helped her with the suit. "Now, just press that button on your wrist," he paused while she found the button. "That's good, now type in your access code and the suit will mould to your body."

Rebecca typed in her code and gasped as the suit finished tightening. She looked at herself in the mirror. "This doesn't leave much to the imagination, does it."

"Wow, Rebecca. You look lovely," said Neil.

Rebecca blushed slightly then said, "A little too revealing don't you think."

"Not at all," said Keith as he circled her. He playfully smacked her bottom. "Not at all."

Rebecca let out a little squeal at the sudden, unexpected contact.

"Once you apply the replicater anyone who sees you will think you're a tranchillion," said Neil.

Keith and Neil activated their suits then Neil picked up all three replicaters. Each one was sealed in a clear plastic bag and labelled with their names. He gave Keith and Rebecca theirs then removed his from its bag.

"You two don't look bad either," said Rebecca, her eyes hovering over Neil slightly longer than Keith.

They pulled on their chameleon masks which moulded to their suits upon contact.

"Time to see if they work," said Keith. He slotted his replicater into a slot on his chest then twisted it until it clicked. As Neil and Rebecca watched, he slowly changed into an exact replica of Neil.

"That's incredible," remarked Rebecca. "He looks just like you, Neil, only naked."

"I just want to try something," said Neil as he placed his replicater back on the table. He walked over to Keith and, without warning, threw a punch straight at his head. Keith moved on pure reaction and countered the attack. This sparring went on for two minutes at an unrelenting pace until Neil created a gap between them and said, "That's enough."

Keith stopped at the command with neither of them having connected. They were both breathing heavily.

"I'd say the replicater works," said Neil.

"I have no idea how I did that. Your combat skills are amazing," replied Keith.

"I've never seen anything like that before. Remind me never to piss you off," said Rebecca.

"The replicater not only tells the suit what to look like, but also how to react to certain situations. It gives the wearer all the knowledge of the subject it's replicating." Neil pointed at her replicater. "Try yours, Rebecca." He moved back over to the table and picked his up.

"Am I going to appear naked as well? Looking at Keith is rather off-putting," said Rebecca.

Neil threw Keith a towel which he wrapped around his waist.

"Is that better?" asked Keith.

"Very much so," Rebecca slotted her replicater in and slowly transformed into a tranchillion. Two extra arms seemed to grow from her ribs. Her own arms thinned and extended by a foot. Her neck lengthened and her head changed to a more oval shape. Her skin tone changed to a light green and her teeth and ears became slightly longer and pointed.

"Did that hurt at all?" asked Keith.

[97]

"No, it didn't. I don't know how, but it didn't."

"The suit grows the extra bits it needs around your body. It's all just an illusion," said Neil. "You can be touched on your extra arms and nobody would know they weren't real. The tech really is amazing."

"Where are your reproductive bits?" asked Keith.

Rebecca looked down. She still had breasts but couldn't see anything normal between her thighs.

"They must open up somewhere when they need to go," she said.

Neil threw her a towel then slotted his replicater in and transformed into a tranchillion. The difference between them was slight. Neil's tranchillion was taller than Rebecca's and hers was a darker shade of green. He also didn't have any reproductive organs.

"Do you think we'll pass, Keith?" asked Neil.

"Oh yes, definitely. Both of you are kinda creepy. If I didn't know it was you, I'd already be reaching for my laser. By the way you're still speaking English. Why's that?"

"Take out your replicater and all you should hear is the tranchillion language," said Neil.

Keith removed his replicater and slowly changed back into himself.

Neil moved over to him and said, "Is that better? Can you still understand me?"

Keith stepped back and shrugged his shoulders.

Neil removed his replicater and waited for the transformation to be complete. "I asked if that was better."

"I couldn't understand a word of it. You'd better be careful when we put the plan in operation. You were rather scary when you walked over to me."

"If Rebecca and these *Watchers* are right, the tranchillions are actually a peaceful race. We've just got off on the wrong foot. In the future, if everything goes well, we'll be walking among each other and not even thinking twice about it."

"I hope you're right, Neil. I think it'll take a while as there's bound to be a lot of prejudice against them for a start," said Keith.

"It'll be the same for them. They won't trust us either. It *will* take some time, but we'll get there," said Neil.

"We're getting a little ahead of ourselves here," said Rebecca. "I mean – at the minute both our species hate each other. I don't know how you're going to pull it off, Neil but we'll be counting on you to find a way."

"Let's get out of these suits and prepare for tomorrow," said Neil.

Once they had changed, they left the secure room and went their separate ways. Neil headed for General Bolgon's office and both Keith and Rebecca returned to their rooms.

~

Chloe and Lisa strolled past shop after shop, both happy with the way their lives were going. They'd just bought new outfits for the concert. It was going to be brilliant and tonight couldn't come soon enough.

Lisa had become Chloe's friend through their boyfriends. Lisa was just as tough as John and she had to be. She had been a soldier in John's unit for over three years. She was extremely fit at thirty-four and kept her black hair short to fit in with the boys. She was slightly shorter than Chloe but refused to wear heels.

[99]

"How did General Bolgon get 'Independent Women' to play here on such short notice?" asked Lisa.

"I have no idea, and what's more, I don't care," replied Chloe. "Tonight's going to be amazing. I can't wait to hold Neil in my arms while listening to them."

They made their way back to Chloe's quarters to try on their outfits once again. Both felt like teenagers going to their first concert. It had been a long time since either of them had done anything like this.

They entered Chloe's quarters and changed into their outfits in the lounge. Chloe went into the kitchen to make some tea and Lisa lay back on the sofa.

"You know something Chloe!" she shouted.

"What's that!"

"While I'm looking forward to the concert, I'm actually anticipating what me and John will get up to afterwards!"

Chloe appeared in the kitchen doorway. "Why's that?"

"John's going to be horny as hell after watching those four girls singing and dancing wearing practically nothing."

"Oh yeah, I hadn't thought of that. Do you think Neil will be as well?"

"Girl, if he wasn't then he wouldn't be a man. They are gorgeous. Hell, given half a chance, I'd do them myself."

Chloe started laughing. "Lisa, you're terrible. Probably right, but terrible," she re-entered the kitchen.

A few minutes later she carried the tea into the lounge and found Lisa on the phone. She put the tray down on the coffee table and waited for her to finish.

[100]

"Okay, sir. I'll be right over," Lisa cancelled the call and turned to Chloe. All the joy on her face had disappeared.

"What's wrong?" asked Chloe.

"The *Resolve* is leaving in one hour on some mission that's just come up. I'm sorry but I have to go," Lisa gave Chloe a hug. "I was so looking forward to tonight as well."

"Neil will be going, won't he," said Chloe.

"Yes. All of *Resolve's* crew will be going."

"Look, stay and have your tea. Five minutes won't matter."

They both sat on the sofa feeling disappointed with the turn of events. The phone started ringing and Chloe used the TV to answer it.

"TV on; answer phone," she said, guessing who'd be calling.

Neil's face appeared. He looked sad even as he smiled.

"Hello, babe. How are you?"

"Not good. You're going again aren't you."

"Yes. I've just been bleeped. Hi, Lisa. You all right."

"Yes. I'm just finishing my tea then I'm off."

"Do you know how long you're going to be gone?" asked Chloe.

"Not yet. Unfortunately, I've got to go straight to the *Resolve*. I just called to say I love you and I'll see you soon."

"Can't you come and see me before you go?"

He ran a hand through his brown hair. "I'm afraid not. I'm the other side of the complex, not far from the ship. I won't have time to get there and back, sorry."

"I'll see you soon then, Neil. One more thing before you go, please be safe."

"Try not to worry too much, Chloe. I'll be back soon. Love you babe. Look after junior for me. Bye."

Chloe looked down at her stomach and a tear ran down her face.

Lisa gave her another hug. "You'll see him soon. Before you know it we'll all be back here laughing and giggling."

They parted and Lisa held Chloe by the shoulders looking directly into her eyes. "I must go now. You look after yourself and the baby," she nodded towards Chloe's belly.

She got up and walked over to the front door. She pressed the pressure pad then looked at Chloe again. "I'll have to find something else to wear that dress to now, won't I."

Chloe nodded. "You be careful as well, okay."

"Of course. See you."

Lisa left the room and the door closed behind her. Chloe dragged herself off the sofa and walked into the bedroom. She started crying as she sat on the bed. She didn't know why but something was different about this mission. Sighing, she lay back with her feet still dangling over the side.

Perhaps it's my hormones making me emotional, she thought.

~

The guards stationed outside interview room one saluted Neil as he faced the door they were guarding. Neil returned the salute then a guard opened the door and he stepped inside. Neil set the case he was carrying on a table at the side of the room. The tranchillion, who was sat at a table in the centre, said something that Neil

[102]

couldn't understand so he ignored him and opened the case.

He pulled out the *chameleon suit* and set it down on the table then he undressed and put it on. As the suit finished tightening around Neil's body a back door opened and in walked Keith Turnball carrying a similar case.

"Hello, sir," said Keith.

"Hello, Corporal. Are you ready?"

"Yes, sir."

Neil handed his clothes to Keith and removed a tranchillion uniform from his case. He waited for Keith to put on the *chameleon suit* and plug in his replicater. Keith began slowly turning into Neil.

The tranchillion moved backwards in his chair as far as his chains would allow and started making noises, which Keith started understanding towards the end of his transformation. Then Neil stretched his mask over his head and inserted his replicater. He began to turn into Captain Xenorphide.

They both got dressed in their appropriate uniforms and Neil walked over to the tranchillion. "What do you think, Captain?"

"What the hell's going on here?" the captain sounded badly shaken.

"We're putting our plan into action tonight, Captain. That's all you need to know."

Neil turned to Keith. "Right, we'll get started. Is there anything you need to know?"

"I just want to say good luck sir. You're going to need it."

"Good luck to you too, Corporal. I do have one thing to mention before we part. If I don't make it back before you, don't fuck my wife."

"Yes, sir. But I would never do that, sir."

"Just making sure."

The back door opened and in walked John Stillson and two security guards.

"You both ready?" asked John.

"Yes, sir," said Keith.

Neil nodded.

The guards unchained Captain Xenorphide and took him out the back door. Neil sat down and allowed himself to be chained up. Then John left through the back door, taking Neil's case. Next, he entered the back of interview room two where Rebecca had changed into her suit. He helped her with it and waited for her to change into Staff Sergeant Carphide. He exited the second interview room after Rebecca had been chained up. Along with four guards he escorted the two tranchillions to isolation where they were to stay for the rest of their visit.

Keith, now looking like Neil, knocked on the front door to interview room one and the guards stationed outside opened it. Keith walked out.

"Secure the prisoner. It's going back to its cell."

Keith walked into interview room two and stood in front of Rebecca. He gave the thumbs up sign and she acknowledged it. They talked for a few minutes to pass the time.

"That should be long enough don't you think," said Keith.

"Yeah, I think so. Good luck, Keith," said Rebecca.

"You too."

He left the room and gave the order for her to be taken back to her cell as well. With everything going to plan so far, Keith set off for the *Resolve* and the hardest part of his side of the plan. He now had to be Neil Bolgon for however long it took.

~

Chloe had decided to go to the concert, but her heart wasn't in it anymore. She hoped that when the music started, she would forget about everything; at least for a couple of hours. She'd arranged to meet some of her friends to go with instead of Neil and was now waiting for them.

There was a lot of security on duty which she supposed was only to be expected. People were all heading in one direction past her. There were no tickets needed as the Space Federation was paying for it all.

Chloe saw her friends approaching and smiled as they all greeted each other. She wasn't sure who three of them were, but they were friends of Kelly and Rachel, so she was looking forward to getting to know them.

"Thanks for letting me join you. Everyone I was going with is off on the *Resolve*."

"It's fine, Chloe. Really, we're glad you're with us," said Kelly.

Kelly was one of the few girls who was taller than her. Her black dreadlocked hair suited her dark skin and overall look.

All six of them walked over to the entrance and stepped inside. The sound of instruments being tuned was coming from the stage. A steward pointed in the direction he wanted them to go. Chloe could smell the electricity in the air. A sense of excitement coursed through her. Maybe it was going to be a good night after all.

~

Keith was sitting in a toilet cubicle, fully clothed, trying to compose himself. He was going to be working on a starship for the first time since his last mission to Anthera.

Right, you can do this, he thought. He looked down towards the replicater, which he couldn't see, and twisted a dial. Now he was fully Neil Bolgon he would act like him; walk and talk like him and, most importantly, he would know his way around the starship. He could always twist the dial back again to be more himself, but that was only to be done in private. He didn't want to let Neil or the general down especially as Neil's life could depend on it.

Keith got up and stepped out of the cubicle. He left the restroom and walked towards the *Resolve*.

"Hey, Neil. I've been looking for you everywhere," said Andrew as he ran over to him. "The captain wants to see you right away."

"Okay, Andrew. I'll see you later."

Resolve was due to depart within the next half-hour and the final checks were being performed. Keith walked up the boarding ramp acknowledging every salute on his way to the bridge.

~

It was time for the escape and Neil was as prepared as he was going to get. He had the replicater turned down so he could use his own skills. He still looked like Captain Xenorphide, but he didn't trust the captain's abilities.

Neil called out to Rebecca. "Are you ready?"

Rebecca appeared at the bars of her cell and nodded. The other eight tranchillions in their cells all started asking what was going on.

"We're getting out of here. Follow my lead and try not to kill anyone," said Neil.

"Why's that, sir?" asked one of the tranchillions.

"I don't think we need to be at war with these aliens. If we can get back to the *Dragen* I'm going to try to convince the others to stop attacking. Besides, if we get caught during this escape, they may go easier on us if we haven't killed any of them."

"But they started it. If we back off what's to stop them from killing us, sir?"

"I've been observing them while we've been here. They haven't mistreated or harmed us in any way. If they were truly hostile, we'd have been killed or experimented upon by now."

"Do you think we can escape?"

"We'll have a good try. I think it's possible. If you follow my lead and we do this quietly we may have a chance."

"Okay, sir."

A guard opened the outer cell door and locked it behind him again. "You lot quiet down will you. I'm trying to listen to the concert."

Oh, what's the use, they can't understand me, he thought.

"Okay everyone. Stay quiet. I need to draw him towards me," said Neil. He started calling the guard, hoping he would come close enough. The guard approached Neil's cell.

"You're the one making this racket, are you?" He stopped just short of where Neil needed him.

"Hey, ugly. Come over here!" shouted Rebecca. The guard turned around to look at her and she sprang towards her bars, reaching for him with a snarl. Her aggressive movement startled him causing him to take a

[107]

couple of steps backwards. That was all Neil needed. He grabbed the guard and pulled him back towards the bars. While holding him with two arms he put one more over the guard's mouth and with his last arm found the pressure point in the guard's neck.

The guard slumped and Neil took the strain with three of his arms. He unhooked the keys from the guard's belt and then let him slide to the floor. Neil unlocked his cell and dragged the body into it. Then he unlocked Rebecca's cell and in turn let all the others out.

"Everyone wait here and stay quiet while I see what we're up against."

Neil crept towards the cell block door and unlocked it. He left it open and crept towards the guardroom. He stood up slightly and peered in through the window. The other guard was too busy watching the concert on the TV to notice the monitors. Neil threw the keys at the open gate and readied himself.

The guard looked round at the sudden, unexpected noise and then at the monitors. He saw the wide-open cell block door and scrambled out of his chair. He drew his stun laser from his belt then opened the guard-room door which Neil was hiding behind.

Neil silently cursed as Rebecca appeared at the cell door. The guard aimed his laser. He wasn't far enough out of the doorway to grab so Neil improvised. He kicked the door hard – knocking the guard over. His laser skidded across the floor and Neil sprang towards him. The guard raised his hands defensively with a look of terror on his face as Neil landed on top of him. Neil found the pressure point in the guard's neck and put him to sleep then picked up the laser and went back to the others.

"Grab the other laser from him," he pointed towards the unconscious guard in his cell, "then close all the cell doors and follow me."

They followed Neil to the guards' room. He'd already picked up the unconscious guard and was placing him in his chair. To anyone passing by he would appear to be watching the concert. Neither of the guards would be waking up before they got to the battleport. Neil unlocked the gun cupboard and handed out the remaining lasers.

"Set them to stun then follow me," said Neil.

They all obeyed and stealthily set off down the corridor. Neil slowed at a corner and peered around it. There was no one coming so he signalled the others and set off again. They were not far from the hangers now. Neil hoped that everything was going to continue this smoothly.

There were two guards stationed outside the hanger. They could not approach without being seen so Neil moved back slightly and addressed the other tranchillions.

"There are two guards outside the hanger doors. When they go down there's a good chance that all the remaining guards will be alerted to our presence. Who's the best shot?"

"I am, sir."

"I'm going to work my way around the other side and when I signal, you take this one and I'll take the other one. Then we all head straight for the hanger doors and hope there's not too much resistance."

Neil headed off up a corridor and disappeared out of sight. The other tranchillion moved into position and waited.

[109]

When he saw his captain position himself the other side of the hanger doors, he levelled his laser and fired at the guard. Neil fired his laser as well and both guards dropped to the floor. They regrouped at the doors and, after a brief pause, burst into the hanger and rushed towards the battleport.

The sudden onrush of tranchillions took the few technicians and soldiers by surprise and most of them were stunned within seconds. There were just two left, but they had the tranchillions pinned behind cover. Neil knew they didn't have much time. The soldiers would have radioed for back-up which meant they had two to five minutes.

"Switch to live fire and hit their cover. I'm going to flank them," ordered Neil. The pinned tranchillions returned fire and the new threat forced the soldiers to duck behind their cover. Neil moved with lightning speed and got alongside the two soldiers.

He broke cover and levelled his laser while running straight for them. He had almost reached them when the nearest soldier caught sight of him and screamed with fright. He tried to bring his laser towards Neil, but the stun beam hit him in the chest, and he fell against the other soldier. By the time soldier two could react Neil was upon him. He knocked the laser out of the soldier's hand while simultaneously grabbing and lifting him with two arms.

The look of terror on the soldier's face, as Neil held him a foot away from his own, did not surprise him in the least. Neil, once again, found the pressure point in the soldier's neck and the body he was holding went limp.

Neil dropped the soldier and headed for the battleport. The rest of the tranchillions broke cover and ran over to Neil.

"I want everyone on the flight deck. We have minimal crew and will need everybody to make this work."

Neil stepped onto the ramp. "Last one in closes the hatch. Let's go." Neil headed inside.

Moments later, he arrived on the flight deck and looked around. He saw two crucial positions were empty.

"I need someone to fill in for the 'co-pilot' and 'engine management' positions. Quickly now. The aliens' backup has arrived."

They lifted off and headed out into space just as the Space Federation soldiers were setting up their big gun.

"That was close," said Neil.

"Where to, captain?"

"Our original target. We have to rescue as many of our soldiers as we can, then we'll head back to the *Dragen*."

Once they were clear of the moon the short-range hyperspace arms folded out and rotated towards the front of the battleport. Then they were gone. They'd started their short journey towards Ganymede and Neil allowed himself to relax slightly. They had managed the first part of the plan superbly well, but the next part was the most difficult and dangerous.

~

General Bolgon shifted in his chair. All around him there were people singing, or trying to sing, the songs that were coming from the stage and several loudspeakers around the hall. Everybody was having a good time and the general was glad that he'd decided to set up the event. To

[111]

his left sat John Stillson who looked like he wasn't enjoying it.

"John," he said, but the noise in the hall was too loud. He raised his voice. "John!"

Mr Stillson looked around, "Sir!"

"Something wrong?"

"Not really, sir!"

"Come on John, what's wrong?"

"I'm just thinking about recent events and hoping everything goes well, sir!"

"I'm worried as well, but we are here to enjoy this!" the general moved his arm in a half circle. "This may be your last chance in a while to do something like this!"

"Okay, sir!"

The curtain behind them parted and a messenger entered the VIP box. He stood next to the general and bent to his ear to give him a message. He had to repeat it a little louder because of the music. The general faced the messenger and said in a raised voice, "What sort of disturbance?"

"A breakout, sir!"

"Who's broken out?"

"The tranchillions, sir!"

"How many?"

"All of them, I think. I haven't been given any details, sir!"

"Okay, go back and tell Mr Toddwell I'm on my way!"

The messenger left and Jim got up from his seat, "It's started John. Let's Go!"

"Yes, sir!"

They left the VIP box and headed for the holding cells. When they arrived, two very disoriented guards were giving statements to the MPs on duty.

"What's going on?" asked General Bolgon.

"The tranchillions have escaped and neither guard knows which way they went, sir," replied one of the MPs.

"We'll find out soon enough. They won't exactly blend in anywhere," said the general.

The MP who'd answered the general received a message on his communicator. He held it to his ear.

"Sir, they have just entered the hanger where their ship is being studied. There are just two of our soldiers holding them off. They're requesting backup, sir."

"I'll bet they are. Get every available MP and soldier over there right now."

"Sir."

The general turned to John. "Let's go." Two MPs, John and the general hurried in the direction of the hanger bays, leaving behind two MPs and the medical team.

"Are there any casualties?" asked the general.

"None so far, sir. Those two back there were knocked unconscious. One of them was tricked into getting too close to the bars and the next thing he knew he was being revived by us. The other guard saw a tranchillion at the main cell door and went to intercept when he was knocked over by the guard-room door. The last thing he remembered was a tranchillion leaping on him then he blacked out."

"Let's hope it stays that way."

They arrived at the hanger doors and entered with lasers drawn. There were already ten soldiers firing towards the battleport with two more setting up an LC300 laser on a tripod. The last two tranchillions ran up the entry ramp and disappeared into the darkness.

"Advance! If they close the ramp, they're as good as gone!" shouted the general.

But before anyone could get close, the ramp closed. Seconds later, the engines started up and the battleport lifted off and flew up the tunnel making its escape into space.

Good luck son, thought the general.

CHAPTER EIGHT

December 2171

Ganymede

Ganymede was on the dark side of Jupiter. Everywhere, except the human colony buildings, was in total darkness. The guards patrolling the fences couldn't see too far beyond them unless they requested a spotlight to be aimed their way. They didn't expect much, if any, trouble as most of the tranchillions that had landed on Ganymede, and evaded capture initially, had now been rounded up or killed.

On the other side of the fence, about fifty meters out, lay three tranchillions. They were on a scouting mission, trying to find any weakness in the aliens' defences. They were hidden by the rise and fall of the land. When combined with the pitch blackness of the night, they were virtually invisible.

"It's time to get back," said the squad leader.

They moved away from their observation point and headed back in the direction of their camp, covering their tracks as they went.

Suddenly, three dark shapes rose, as if from out of the ground, and took them completely by surprise.

"Do not raise your weapons. I'm Captain Xenorphide and I demand to know your names," said one of the dark shapes.

All three tranchillions were frozen with fear. They couldn't believe how easily they'd been captured.

"Captain. We thought you were dead, sir."

"We were captured but we managed to escape. Now, what are your names?"

They gave their names and Rebecca checked them off her list.

"How many are left?"

"There are another five of us at our camp, sir."

"Good. Take us there."

They set off for the camp.

"We'd better hurry, sir. The light will be returning in another half an hour and we're still twenty minutes away."

They arrived at the camp as the sun started to appear from Jupiter's shadow. The camp was a natural hollow in the moons crust that was only a few meters deep.

"How did you find this cave?" asked Neil.

"One of us fell down it when we were running from the aliens. If he hadn't, I'm pretty sure we'd have been captured or killed by now."

"We need to get the rest of our men out of that base as soon as possible. Has anyone come up with a plan yet?" asked Neil.

"To be honest, sir. We were just trying to survive. Our food supplies are running short though and a few of us were thinking of giving ourselves up just so we can eat."

"That won't be necessary now. My shuttle's only five minutes from here. I'll call it in when we're ready to go and we'll get off this moon."

Neil opened his rucksack and produced some of his rations. "These will help for now." A few seconds passed. "I have recently promoted Staff Sergeant Carphide to lieutenant," he pointed at Rebecca. "She's now my second-in-command."

"With respect, sir. I don't think we'll be able to get anyone out of there. We are outnumbered and any assault on that base will be suicide or, at the very least, a sure-fire way of getting captured."

They followed the three tranchillions to their hideout. Once inside, Neil found out the others' names.

"Who was in charge here?"

Lt Zielorpe spoke up. "I was."

"Okay. You can stay behind to keep order while I take two of you with me when the darkness returns. We'll recon the area then go in the night after."

"Sir, yes sir," they replied.

"How much air have you got left?" asked Neil.

"Plenty sir. One of our ships is an hour north of here. Two of us go to fill up our tanks when supplies run low."

"Everyone, get some sleep. Lt Carphide and I will take the first watch," said Neil.

They crawled up to the entrance of the cave and peered out into the weak sunlight. There was no-one around, so they crawled out onto the surface and Neil used his binoculars in a full three-hundred-and-sixty-degree circle.

Due to the rise and fall of the rocky surface there was nothing to be seen in any direction, but Neil knew the human base wasn't far away.

"Let's go back inside, Rebecca. Are you okay?"

"Yes. These chameleon suits are amazing. I feel nothing but confidence."

They lay on their stomachs and crawled backwards into the cave, just far enough for the entrance to be visible, and kept watch.

~

After dark the next day Neil, Rebecca and a third tranchillion were laying down observing the activity around the colony's buildings. Neil swept his binoculars across the complex. He could see the dome-shaped forcefield, which covered the entire complex, shimmering with light when the searchlights passed over it.

"Over there is a building which, if I'm not mistaken, is the prison. The writing on the sign outside is the same as where we were being held. It's only a guess but it's our best bet. It also has two guards posted outside and, as far as I can see, it's the only one being guarded," said Neil as he passed the binoculars to the other two tranchillions. "It's got to be the one."

Neil waited for them to finish with the binoculars. "Now all we need to do is find a way to extract them."

Rebecca handed back the binoculars. "How are we getting in there?"

"*We're* not. I'm going in on my own through the fence. But tomorrow night we'll get the *Contention* to land in front of the building."

"You're going in on your own, sir," said Rebecca.

"Yes. I'll see if I can pinpoint where our men are. Then I'll withdraw and we'll finalise the plan, ready for our assault tomorrow night."

"But you'll be captured, sir," said the third tranchillion.

"Not if I'm lucky," Neil rolled on to his back, removing two short-wave radios from his belt and handed them over.

"Set them to channel one. When I'm ready to come back out I'll click the transmit button twice. You two will then distract the guards and I'll try to slip back out unnoticed."

"Aren't you forgetting something," said the third tranchillion.

"What's that?" replied Neil.

"The forcefield. You won't be able to get past it."

"I'll be able to walk right through it. It's more like an atmosphere shield. All it does is keep breathable air in. If it was designed to stop solid matter from passing through, you'd be able to see it all the time."

"Oh."

"What if they see you?" asked Rebecca.

"Then it'll be a lot harder to extract our men tomorrow. Let's try not to let that happen."

Neil rolled back onto his stomach and, with one final sweep of his binoculars, he said, "Meet me at the rendezvous." He set off towards the perimeter fence.

The nearest guard had just passed Neil's position. He used his laser cutter on the wire fence, keeping his body

[119]

between his work and the watching tranchillion, then pulled the flap open and crawled through. He was using a *human* tool and didn't want to try to explain it to him. He then folded the fence back and secured it in position with very small clamps. Unless the guards looked closely, they would never know it had been cut.

Neil placed the last clamp on the wire fence and, still crouching, turned to see if he'd been spotted. There were no lights directed towards him, no shouts, no laser fire.

When Neil was happy that all was well, he set off for what he thought was the prison building. There were no windows, so everything had to be artificially lit. If he could find the power generator that would greatly improve their chances during the planned rescue.

Neil completed a circuit of the building. The only way in was the front door which was guarded. That wouldn't normally be a problem for him, but he had to stay undetected. He slipped the radio from his belt and spoke softly into it. "I need a distraction to get in."

"Okay, hang on, sir," replied Rebecca.

"Stay safe both of you," said Neil.

He waited for a while. Then a searchlight was switched on and aimed at the fence. Neil couldn't see what was going on, then he heard laser fire and one of the perimeter guards dropped to the floor. There was some more laser fire then the other guard, who had just closed in on the search-lit area, screamed out and fell clutching his leg.

"You stay and watch the door. I'm going to see what's going on," said one of the guards blocking Neil's entry into the building. The other guard stayed where he was and raised his binoculars. While looking through them the guard wandered far enough away from the door and Neil saw his chance.

He left the cover of the shadows and silently moved towards the door. He would normally have taken care of the guard to eliminate any surprises later, but he knew he couldn't. He placed a code breaker on the door which he'd smuggled from *Sentry One*.

The light on the code breaker changed from red to green. Neil removed it and opened the door. He slipped inside and quietly clicked it shut then observed the room.

There were two levels. The upper level was accessed by metal stairs and balconies. The cells were situated around the exterior walls with the guard room positioned in the centre. All four walls of the guard room had large observation windows.

Neil waited for the camera, pointing in his direction, to turn away then he ran over to it and stayed as close to the wall as possible. When the camera had turned back past him Neil hurried to the nearest door. He peeked inside and, satisfied that no-one was there, stepped in, closing the door behind him.

He removed his backpack and uniform then the replicater and transformed back into himself. Then he took one of the guard's uniforms off its hook and put it on. He put the replicater inside a small plastic bag then placed it in his backpack. He stowed it in the corner nearest the door before leaving the room.

He methodically walked past every cell and took a head count. There were eighty-seven tranchillions and three drunken human soldiers overall. During his survey, he found the circuit breaker which would knock out the lights. Luckily, it was in the same room as the door release controls.

Neil made his way back towards the room where he'd left his backpack and removed the borrowed uniform. He slotted the replicater into its slot and twisted it into its locking position. The transformation into Captain Xenorphide began.

He put his tranchillion uniform on again, picked up his backpack, and opened the door slightly to check on the camera. Neil pressed the transmit button on his radio twice then darted over to the camera and repeated his earlier manoeuvre. He arrived at the exit and attached the code breaker once again. With the door unlocked Neil opened it slightly and saw one guard standing about a metre away. He couldn't see if the other guard had returned and just had to take a chance.

Neil stepped outside and knocked out the surprised guard before he could turn around. He fell to the floor and Neil squatted next to him. The other guard hadn't returned yet, so Neil made his way to the fence. He'd just finished re-sealing the wire when the unconscious guard was found.

Neil returned to the rendezvous and found no one there. He checked his surroundings, but it was almost impossible to see anything in the darkness, even with his improved eyesight. He held up his radio and spoke into it.

"I'm at the rendezvous. Where are you?" he asked.

After a few seconds a voice answered, speaking softly. "We're not sure. He's been hit and I've helped him away, but the aliens are close. Need help."

"Is that you, Lt Carphide?"

"Yes. Please hurry. They're close. I can't carry him anymore."

"Okay. Leave your radio on transmit and I'll follow your signal. I'm going silent now so as not to give away your position. Just hold on."

Neil paused to check his equipment. He didn't have nearly enough weapons to take on a large force. He hoped that he'd find them before the SF guards did. He spent a few minutes adapting his radio then triangulated their position and set off to find them.

After five minutes of travelling in the darkness, Neil had closed in on the signal from Rebecca's radio. He could see several flashlights swaying from side to side searching for the tranchillions. Neil closed the gap as silently as he could and saw two tranchillion forms curled up on the floor as the guards were taking it in turns to kick them. They were laughing with every blow.

The officer in charge ordered them to stop the beating. He walked over to the tranchillion that was moaning with pain on the ground and grabbed her head, pulling it back sharply. "You killed two of my friends so I'm going to repay the favour and put you out of your misery," he let her head drop and viciously kicked her in the stomach. He pulled his pistol from its holster as he pushed her onto her back, holding her down with his boot. He aimed at her head.

Neil had no choice. First, he targeted the officer and pulled the trigger then shifted his laser to the next two targets that were facing his direction and fired twice more. The officer spun round and fell to the ground then the other two soldiers, who saw where the shots came from, went down in quick succession.

One of the remaining soldiers aimed at the tranchillions on the ground and the other two raised their lasers to where they thought Neil was. He had already moved position and their laser fire just gave them away. He fired three more times and they all fell to the ground.

Neil ran to Rebecca and saw her holding her stomach and her head with both sets of hands. Then he looked at the motionless form of the third tranchillion before examining his body. As far as he could tell there were no broken bones. He had a laser wound in his left leg and was unconscious.

Neil heard noises behind him. He looked and saw at least twenty flashlights heading in their direction. The only plus point was that, in this darkness, they could easily miss them. But there was always the chance that the soldiers could get lucky.

"Rebecca," Neil whispered into her ear. "Stay still and quiet. I'm going to lead the re-enforcements away and then we're out of here."

Rebecca grunted. Neil sprinted off to attempt his diversion. Enough people had died already so Neil decided to place a few shots at the advancing soldiers' feet. Then he sprinted off again, leading them further away from Rebecca. He paused and faced the soldiers again. Their shots were hitting the ground about ten metres away from him. Neil let off two more rounds then started sprinting again.

One shot almost hit him as their reactions to his fire quickened. They began to spread their fire in a wide arc and Neil was forced to dive to the ground. He stayed still for a few seconds then, when the shots were no longer coming in his direction, he started crawling back to Rebecca.

Neil paused again and looked behind him. The soldiers were twenty meters away and searching where his last shots had come from. Neil rose from his prone position and quietly ran in a combat crouch. As soon as he'd put some distance between them, he began to sprint.

Neil closed on Rebecca's position and slowed to a crouch. He checked for her radio signal again then followed it. He hadn't been far away. Neil knelt beside her and helped her into a sitting position.

"Where ... are ... they?" she asked between breaths.

"A good distance away unless we make a lot of noise. Can you stand?"

"I'll try," she grunted with a pain that flowed through her ribs as she moved.

Neil helped her to her feet. "Do you think you can make it back to the others?"

"I'll have to. Just don't go walking too fast."

"Hold on. I've got an idea."

Neil opened his backpack and produced some rope. He tied one end to himself and the other end to Rebecca.

"Now if you stop or fall, I'll know, and won't lose you."

"When did you pack rope?"

"When I'm going on stealth missions, I have a mental list of things I always pack."

"But I didn't see you pick it up."

"I had already stashed it inside the *Contention* before the breakout."

Neil shouldered the pack then crouched at the tranchillion's side before lifting him onto his shoulder. "Let's go."

They set off at a slow pace back to camp having to stop several times for Rebecca who was managing quite well considering her injuries.

"You're doing well – keep going soldier," encouraged Neil as they drew nearer and nearer to camp. Rebecca stayed silent as she stumbled on. Neil looked up towards the sky and saw they didn't have much time left. He stopped walking and, as gently as he could, lay the tranchillion on the ground. He was still unconscious, although he had shown signs of waking up a couple of times.

"Sit down, lieutenant. We're not going to make it at this pace. Keep a watch in that direction," he said as he pointed back the way they'd come.

"Try not to sleep and I'll be back with help as soon as I can." Neil untied the rope then looked at Rebecca. "One more thing. Don't fire unless you have no choice as you'll give away your position."

Rebecca nodded and tried to smile. Neil set off for the camp at a much quicker pace.

~

Twenty minutes had passed. Rebecca was beginning to wonder if Neil would make it back in time. There was roughly half-an-hour of darkness left and the desire to get up and try to find the camp was almost overwhelming. But instead she kept her eyes on the horizon looking for any tell-tale signs of flashlights. So far there were none but that wouldn't last forever.

She turned her head quickly to her right. Rebecca thought she'd heard a noise, but there was no flash-light, so she concentrated on directly in front again. Then she saw a light in the distance.

Oh damn, she thought. *They're sure to find us now.* Rebecca lay still on her stomach and aimed her pistol at the flashlights.

She sensed something to her right and turned her head again. Standing there, with a rifle pointed directly at her head, was an SF soldier.

He switched on the side-mounted light at the same time as he switched off the night-vision mode on his visor. The soldier raised his hand to the side of his helmet and started speaking. "Found them, sir."

The soldier paused while receiving instructions then released the button on the side of his helmet and shifted his aim to the tranchillion on the floor. There was a flash of laser fire and the tranchillion's life ended. Rebecca looked up at the muzzle and waited for her turn.

Then a laser fired and the soldier standing over her fell to the ground with a loud thud. Several lasers fired all around her and Rebecca looked for a target but couldn't see any. The whole situation confused her. Her head felt heavy and she closed her eyes before resting her head on the floor. There was silence. She felt someone turn her over.

"Lieutenant Carphide, are you okay?"

"They shot him. They just shot him."

"Right you two, pick them up. We need to get back to camp, fast."

Rebecca felt herself being lifted and all she could think about was the soldier shooting an unarmed, defenceless, tranchillion then she passed out.

~

"Listen," said Neil. "In an hour, we'll begin our offensive to rescue our captured soldiers. There's a possibility that some of you won't be coming back but we must attempt to release the prisoners. There are eighty-seven of our people in that building and we *are* bringing them home."

[127]

There were cheers and fists raised in salute of Neil's speech.

"I'm going to take a small force with me to free them and the rest of you will be taken to the *Contention* with Lt Zielelope providing cover for the shuttle. Later, I'll radio for the *Contention* to pick us up outside the prison building. With any luck, we'll all be going back to the *Dragen* with a full crew. If the *Contention* is in danger of being boarded," Neil paused while assessing the soldiers in front of him. He pointed. "You will take command of the *Contention* and set course for the *Dragen*."

"Sir," said Lt Zielelope as he saluted.

"Let's get on with the final preparations. Everyone knows what they're doing so let's get to it."

Neil walked over to where Rebecca was lying. Her eyes were closed. He reached out and touched her shoulder and her eyes opened.

"How are you doing Lieutenant?"

"Much better, but my ribs still hurt."

"I don't have much choice but I'm afraid I'm going to have to ask you to come with me on the assault. I should be sending you to the battleport with the others but if I don't make it back," Neil lowered his voice to a whisper, "you'll be on your own on Anthera."

"I'll be all right. It was the shock more than anything."

"What was?"

"Seeing the SF soldier kill the unconscious tranchillion. It was uncalled for."

"Yes, it was, Lieutenant. But he was under orders. We can sort that out if we survive our mission, okay."

"Okay, sir."

Rebecca laid her head down again and closed her eyes. Even with this tranchillion's training running through her mind she was still finding it difficult to accept the losses of war.

Neil bent over her once more and whispered in her ear. "If I should die out there tomorrow get yourself out of sight and remove your replicater. With some luck, you'll survive. Then, when it's safe, ask to speak to my father. Everything will be fine then, and you'll go home."

~

Neil's five-man team were watching the patrols, out of view of the sweeping searchlights, trying to figure out how long they had between sweeps.

"They've stepped up security. There's now only a five-minute window before the searchlight passes the same position. That isn't enough time to get to the fence, cut it, get through and clamp it back together before the light catches us. So, this is what we're going to do," Neil settled his intense gaze on Lt Carphide.

"You're going to stay here and act as lookout. If you see anyone getting within two minutes of us double click the transmit button on your radio."

Rebecca nodded. "Yes, sir."

"The rest of you will come with me. There are some loose rocks down there. I want you to cover me with them then get back to the Lieutenant as fast as you can. Once the light has passed over me, I'll cut through the fence, clamp it, and hope like hell that I make it to the prison without being seen."

"I still think it would be best if one of us came with you," said Putil Ptierwelope.

"No. It's too risky. I've done it before. I can do it again. When I'm inside, every time the light passes over the entry point send one click. I'll be waiting for the signal to cut the power so be ready to make your assault when the light above the entrance goes out."

"Understood, sir."

They waited for another two minutes before the searchlight passed.

"Ready, ready, now go!" commanded Neil. He set off at a sprint towards the fence. The other tranchillions kept pace with him and Neil dropped to the ground near the fence. The others started piling rocks all over him until there was no sign left, then they all raced back to Rebecca. As they settled next to her the light approached Neil's position. Rebecca held her breath in anticipation.

"Where did the captain learn these things?" asked one of the tranchillions.

Without taking her eyes off Neil, Rebecca said, "He wasn't always a captain. He used to be a soldier like you. Everyone is used to him commanding the *Contention*, but in more extreme circumstances he takes a more 'hands-on' approach."

"After seeing him in action I'd die for him," commented Putil Ptierwelope.

Rebecca looked at him and said, "You just might yet, you just might."

The light passed over Neil and he started to shrug off the rocks. Then he scrambled over to the fence and pulled out his laser cutters. Three minutes later, he was through. Then, after he'd clamped the fence back together, he sprinted towards the prison building, melting into the darkness as he got further away.

Neil appeared in the pool of light at the entrance and, in one fluid movement, disarmed one guard before spinning him around as a shield. He locked one of his arms around the guard's throat and squeezed until he fell unconscious. Neil brought his laser to bear on the other guard and fired a stun shot. Both guards fell to the floor and Neil slipped silently into the building.

"That was amazing," said one of the tranchillions. "We normally use our power and aggression against our foes."

"That would attract too much attention," said Rebecca. "Even so, that was different to last time. I suppose he doesn't have to worry about leaving guards lying around this time."

The searchlight passed the entry point again and Rebecca sent one click on the radio then waited for the light to pass again.

Inside, Neil avoided the camera and slipped into the room to change appearance. He came out dressed as a human guard and walked towards the guard room. There were five soldiers inside with one monitoring the cameras. Neil walked up to one guard, returning his smile. Then he pressed the pressure point in his neck and drew his laser. He stunned the other four guards with accurate laser fire. With the room cleared, he left. He was about to walk away when another guard appeared.

"Hold the door!"

Neil re-opened the door and let him enter the room then, as the guard paused in mid-step, he fired his laser again and another one was out of the way.

Neil quickened his step now as they would surely be found soon. He heard a shout and looked around.

"What's wrong!" he called back.

"Unconscious guards here. Sound the alarm!"

"Okay."

Neil stepped into the control room. "Sound the alarm. There's an intruder," he said to the guard that had stood up holding his rifle. The soldier turned back to the console and Neil fired his laser once more then closed the door. He opened a locked cupboard by smashing the lock with the butt of his pistol and took down several rifles. He set each one to stun before placing them on the desk.

Then Neil stripped off his uniform and inserted his replicater. He had finished the transformation, and was adjusting his tranchillion uniform, when the door burst open. The guard's forward momentum stopped when he saw the tranchillion before him. He'd been expecting a human. Neil moved fast towards the surprised guard and punched him hard in the face. The guard stumbled backwards from the impact then fell in a heap on the floor, blood pouring from his broken nose.

"*Contention*, this is Captain Xenorphide. Need pick-up, now," said Neil into his radio before clipping it back onto his belt. The radio let off a click.

He opened every cell door then switched off the power. He used the butt of one of the rifles to bend the lever on the power terminal to prevent it from being switched back on. He waited for his tranchillion eyes to adjust to the dark then picked up the other two rifles which he slung over each shoulder. He drew his pistol and strode towards the exit. The guard on the floor grabbed Neil's leg with blood-soaked hands in a feeble attempt to stop him. Neil yanked his leg away and fired a stun shot at the guard before leaving the control room.

He reached the cell floor and saw several tranchillions slowly poking their heads out from their cells.

"Okay everyone!" shouted Neil. "I'm Captain Xenorphide! Make your way to the exit as best you can! When you reach it, the *contention* will be waiting for you directly ahead! Run to it as fast as you can as we won't have long before alien re-enforcements arrive!"

The few remaining guards were soon overpowered by the sheer number of tranchillions pouring towards them. Neil held back to let them go and slowly followed them towards the exit.

~

The rest of the team had barely arrived at the entrance before the tranchillions burst out of the prison building, shielding their eyes. The *Contention* was settling on the ground fifty metres away. Two of Neil's team ran for the battleport and settled in defensive positions on either side.

Rebecca and Putil stood near the entrance, watching for approaching hostiles. As more and more tranchillions poured out from the building, and headed for the waiting battleport, Neil's team had begun to open fire on SF soldiers that were closing in on their position. They were only perimeter guards and didn't have any heavy artillery, but it wouldn't be long before they were in serious trouble.

About half of the tranchillions were on board when Rebecca spotted headlights in the distance. They were sure to have heavy weaponry on board. *Come on Neil*, she thought. *Get out of there*. The Jeeps closed in on them and laser fire from their mounted LSR500 lasers started felling dozens of tranchillions at a time.

Neil exited the building. He'd already lost fifteen tranchillions inside the building. They'd been trampled on in the stampede for the door. Several had also been killed by the guards who were shooting wildly in every direction before they got trampled underneath the onrush of bodies trying to get out.

Now he saw them being killed outside as well. He un-slung two of his rifles and threw them to Rebecca and Putil then he holstered his pistol and brought his rifle into firing position as he set off towards the Jeep, which was still moving.

Neil crouched and took aim. He held his breath and fired. The tyres on the right side of the Jeep disintegrated and it flipped over as the driver lost control. He looked around. Five more Jeeps were closing in.

"Let's go!" he shouted while waving his free arm towards the battleport. Neil ran towards it and laser fire started hitting the tarmac around him. He stopped and turned, already crouching again. He fired at the Jeep as did Rebecca from a different angle. The Jeep veered off to the side as the driver panicked and Neil again took out the tyres.

The Jeep came to a standstill without flipping and Neil, Rebecca and Putil poured laser fire towards it, forcing the occupants to exit on the other side for cover. They continued firing whilst moving backwards towards the battleport, keeping the soldiers pinned behind their Jeep.

By the time the other four Jeeps arrived there were only a few tranchillions left to board. All five of Neil's team kept the vehicles suppressed until everyone was aboard then they ran up the boarding ramp.

"Go go go!" shouted Neil. The order was signalled towards the pilot and the ramp closed. Everyone not strapped in was thrown to the side as the *Contention* took off and headed for space.

[134]

CHAPTER NINE

November 2171

Earth

Two Jeeps rumbled along the dirt-track road kicking up dust as they went. They were on their way to the only farm down there. A truck going in the opposite direction skidded to a stop when the first Jeep pulled up at an angle to block its progress.

"What the ell ya doin," said the driver of the truck, in a slightly raised voice, as he stepped down from the cab, waving his arms in the air. "I got cattle in back and I gotta be careful wit em. Ya make me stop suddenly. I'll ave to check em." He moved to the back of the truck, mumbling under his breath.

"That's good, sir," said one of the SF soldiers. "We were going to ask you to do that anyway."

The angry farmer paused at the catches on his back door and looked at the soldier. "Why's that en?"

"We are looking for stolen Space Federation property and are searching every lorry, farm-house, business, shop, garage," the soldier leaned closer to the farmer. "No exceptions."

"Unless ya got a court order ya ain't lookin in ere sonny."

"We don't need a court order. We have these," the soldier extended his rifle towards the farmer.

"Ya don't frighten me sonny. I know me rights."

As the soldiers were about to physically restrain the farmer, Captain Turner strode up and signalled for the soldiers to stand down.

"Sir. I'm Captain Turner of the Space Federation. I can assure you that we do have permission to search anywhere we want. I suggest you let us search your truck and we'll be on our way."

The farmer looked at him and shrugged. "Go ead en but I'll be complainin to me councillor." He began opening the catches.

"As will many citizens – I'm sure," replied the captain.

"I'll do this myself, soldier," said Captain Turner, holding out his hand. The soldier handed over his Etherall detector and stood back from the truck.

Captain Turner climbed in the back and turned the sound down on the detector then switched it on. He tried to walk forwards but the cows were too tightly packed in. The Etherall detector's lights changed from red to green which meant that there was Etherall present, but he ignored the lights. He switched it off again and turned the sound back up. He jumped down from the truck and handed the detector back to the soldier.

"Nothing here," he turned his attention back to the farmer. "You may go about your business."

The farmer, who had seemed agitated, visibly relaxed. He climbed into the back and patted one of the cows.

"Let's go," ordered Captain Turner.

All the soldiers got back in their Jeeps and carried on towards the farm.

~

"Right, that's the last one. Close it up," said David.

"What about these?" asked Steve, pointing towards the last of the Etherall.

"We load as many as we can into the cars and leave the rest. I really don't think we have very long."

David's attention was diverted from Steve as one of his spotters came running towards them.

"David, I mean, Mr Tressel sir," he paused for breath. "They're here," he half-turned and pointed down the road. "They've stopped Trevor's truck and are searching it now."

"Right, Peter. Round up the others and get out of here," he looked at Steve. "Get as many workers as you can and load the Etherall into the cars."

"Okay, David. I'll get right on it," Steve set off for his car.

David ran towards the house. Once inside he shouted, "Mother, they're here! Where's Guy?"

Madeline appeared at the top of the stairs. "He's in the hanger, I think."

"Okay mother. Hurry up and get in the car. We're leaving."

[137]

David hurried back outside and found Guy talking to one of the engineers.

"We have to go, Guy. Get the ship out of here. Fly low initially and we'll meet you at the northern warehouse."

"Okay, David," Guy ran back into the office area. "Let's go, everyone aboard, right now!"

David noticed the last truck driving towards the road and ran after it. The truck was about to turn onto the road when David banged on the side. The truck stopped. David opened the passenger door and stepped up to see the driver.

"Turn right and go the long way around. The SF are on their way. They've already stopped Trevor."

"Right you are. Thanks, boss."

David closed the cab door and ran back to Steve. "Are we ready to go?"

"Yes," said Steve as he slammed the boot down. They both looked towards the remaining Etherall.

"It's a shame to leave it," said Steve.

"Yes. But at least it'll keep David happy. He gets to go back saying that he managed to retrieve some of the Etherall. Now get to the warehouse. I'll see you there."

David and Steve got in separate cars which were already occupied by the remaining staff. Steve set off in the same direction as the last truck and David drove over to the house. He pulled up outside the front door in a cloud of dust.

Madeline came out carrying her handbag. She locked the door behind her then got in the car. "They let Trevor go. I don't know how they didn't detect the Etherall."

"Was there a captain with the soldiers?" asked David.

"I couldn't make out the rank but one of them was definitely an officer."

"David. It must be David. Let's get out of here."

They drove off after the other two vehicles, leaving behind everything that was dear to them. David looked in his rear-view mirror and saw Guy lifting off in their ship. *That's good, at least everyone got out.*

~

Two Jeeps turned into the farmyard and pulled up outside the farmhouse. Soldiers poured out from both Jeeps and covered all angles for any possible attack. Captain Turner stepped out and looked around. "It looks deserted, Henry."

The soldiers were already conducting their search. Two of them were knocking on the farmhouse door. The captain and Lt Warner marched over to them.

"Keep trying," ordered the captain.

The soldier rapped on the door again; harder this time. "Open up! Space Federation! Open Up!"

"Sir, we've found it!" the shout came from the barn.

They hurried over to where the soldiers were beckoning them and looked at the open crate.

"Etherall," said Lt Warner.

"Check the house," ordered Captain Turner.

The two soldiers at the farmhouse door broke it down and entered with their rifles ready. After two minutes had passed, they came back out. "No one inside, sir."

"We must've barely missed them," said the captain. He walked back over to the Jeep and brought up the local road map on the computer display.

[139]

"That's our current location," said Turner, pointing at the screen. "They didn't go that way because we'd have seen them so that only leaves…" He scrolled the map slightly east. "There. Now, if they turned left that would take them into a built-up area with no access to the motorway. If they turned right…" He scrolled the screen to the east, then towards the north-east, following the marked road.

"There," he tapped the screen. "Junction 21 of the M1. That's the focal point. If they're not there yet they soon will be. Mobilize every unit. I want roadblocks at both exits of the M69 going southbound. If they get to the M6 they'll be gone. The other option that way is Coventry. They will lose us there. Now, going back to junction 21. If we trace it south to junction 20…" he paused again as he scrolled the screen southwards.

"There, that's Lutterworth. Get a roadblock on junction 20 before the southbound exit…" he scrolled the screen back northwards. "Damn it. Junction 21a isn't very far. They could've got off there. If they have then we've lost them, so we'll concentrate our roadblock at…" he scrolled the screen north-west, following the M1 then moved it back northwards again until he found the next exit.

"Junction 22. The A50 – A511. Set up roadblocks there. That's all we can do. Send the instructions Lieutenant."

~

"How long's it been since you last saw her, mum?" asked Suzanne.

"Oh, about two weeks, I think. We used to see each other most days but you know how it is as you get older," replied Julie. "Besides I phoned her yesterday."

"So, she knows we're coming then."

"No."

"Are you sure surprising them will be okay?"

"Of course. I never announce my visits to Madeline."

"Do you think David will be there?"

"I should think so, but there's someone else there that you know dear."

Suzanne knew what her mother was like and adding 'dear' to the end of a sentence usually meant she was displeased or up to something.

"You're not trying to match-make again are you. You know what happened last time."

"Your problem is that damn career of yours always gets in the way."

"I do important work, mother."

"You tell tales on, or about, other people dear," she corrected.

"I'm damn good at my job and I won't apologise."

"Well, I just hope you don't look back on your life when you're fifty and regret not having a social life. Remember dear," and Suzanne copied her mother word for word in the last sentence. "You're only young once." They looked at each other and started laughing.

Julie turned onto the Tressel's farm drive and pulled up outside the house. "What's this?" she said as she stopped the car.

There were two Jeeps parked in the yard which obviously didn't belong to the Tressels'. As Julie and Suzanne got out of the car, two Space Federation soldiers walked over to them with their rifles raised.

"Keep your hands where I can see them," ordered one of the soldiers. Both women raised their hands and stopped walking.

"What's going on?" asked Suzanne.

"Is this your farm?" asked the soldier.

"No. We're just visiting. What are you doing here with those guns?"

"Come with me," said the soldier as he pointed towards the house with his rifle.

"Are we being arrested or taken prisoner?" asked Julie.

"The captain will answer any questions you may have, madam."

They were led to Madeline Tressel's house and told to sit at the kitchen table. Suzanne was about to start protesting when she saw Captain Turner enter the room. She stared at him and nearly cried out in recognition but a subtly mimed 'no' was enough to stop her. There was something in his stare which told her to stay quiet.

"Carry on with your search. I'll handle this," said Captain Turner. He pulled out a chair from under the table and sat opposite the two women. "Lieutenant, could you find out how the mobilisation is going, and report back thank you."

After the Lieutenant left, Suzanne spoke up. "What's going on here?" she asked as she leaned over the table.

"Don't we know him from somewhere," said Julie while waggling her finger in the air.

"Yes mother, we saw him at the café, yesterday."

"Ah yes I remember," Julie looked at David with a frown on her face. "What are you doing in Madeline's house and what have you done with her?"

"Mrs Cox, we haven't done anything…" he paused as Julie interrupted.

"Statham; my name is Julie Statham – not Cox."

"Sorry, Mrs Statham. I'm going to explain, as best I can, what's happening. But I don't have much time, so you'll have to settle for the shortened version."

Turner looked at Suzanne and let out a sigh as he sat back in his chair and crossed his arms. "I really could've done without this, but here goes. I have an agreement with David Tressel. It needs to stay secret for both our sakes. David and his family are now in a lot of trouble because their last mission went wrong, and we've traced them back here. I've tried my best to hold up the search and they *have* got away."

"What's he done?" asked Suzanne.

"I think you should hear it from him. If you really are a good friend of his I suggest not printing any of this."

"But you haven't said anything. Why have they left?" asked Julie.

"It amounts to theft, Mrs Statham. I supply the time and date for David to steal, from the Space Federation, something that is very valuable. I really can't say any more. I've got to go and try *not* to capture any of David's people."

"Is Steve Cox involved?" asked Suzanne.

"I don't know any of David's employees by name. It's better that way."

Julie sat back in her chair and put her hand to her mouth then she removed it again as she said, "That's what I was going to tell you about. Steve, just yesterday, accepted a job working for David."

Suzanne sank back in her chair and closed her eyes. She still cared for Steve. Their break-up had been her

[143]

fault because she'd spent too much time working and not enough time attending him.

There was a knock on the door. David got up and walked over. He opened the door and saw Lt Warner. "Yes."

"Everyone is ready, sir. It's time to go."

"I'll meet you in the Jeep," David turned back to Julie and Suzanne. "I hope you make the right decision. All our fates are in your hands."

Captain Turner stepped through the door and closed it gently behind him. Then he set off at a brisk pace to catch up with his Lieutenant.

Suzanne got up and started pacing the kitchen. Julie sat still, thinking about Madeline and David. She couldn't understand why they'd do something illegal.

"I can't believe this. My best friend's a thief and I had no idea," said Suzanne.

"I've known Madeline nearly all my life and I didn't know about it either."

"What are we going to do?" asked Suzanne.

"I think we'd better get in touch with Madeline and David as soon as possible."

"Yes, let's get out of here and phone them as soon as we get home."

Julie got up from the table and Suzanne stopped pacing the room. They left the kitchen and drove home.

~

So far, all five of David's own trucks had made it to, or were near, their destinations. That just left the four hired ones and themselves. The only two trucks he was worried about were the last two to leave. Trevor should be okay as the SF had already let him go once. It was Peter's truck that was most vulnerable.

"Let's hope we catch up with Peter. We could provide support for him if the need arose," said David.

"He can't be much further ahead. He didn't have a very big head start," said Madeline.

They passed junction 21a, breaking the speed limit to catch up with Peter. They spotted him another two miles later and slowed down to settle in behind him. David used the radio.

"Hello, Peter."

'Hello. Is that you behind me?'

"Yes, fancy a little back-up."

'That would be lovely, thanks.'

They carried on down the road and everything seemed fine until a large shadow fell across all three lanes. Madeline pressed her head against the window, straining to see what it was.

"It's a Space Federation ship, David. What're we going to do?" asked Madeline.

"I'm thinking." A few scenarios crossed his mind, but he didn't think any of them were good enough. They were getting closer and closer to junction 22. He was running out of time.

"Peter, you listening?" asked David.

'Yes. How the hell are we getting past that?'

"I'm going to forge ahead. I doubt they'll be stopping cars, so I'll drive past them then pull onto the hard shoulder and prepare for a little ground work. Just hang on. I promise we'll try our best to get you out of this."

David indicated and pulled into the middle lane then accelerated away from Peter's truck. It wasn't long before the traffic started building up.

"The ship must've landed at junction 22," said David.

"Make sure you're in the left-hand lane before we get stuck in traffic," said Madeline. "Once we're past the blockade it'll be easier to pull over onto the hard shoulder."

David frowned at his mother's comment. *As if I didn't already know that*, he thought. He indicated and steered to the left, pulling up behind the first in a long line of vehicles waiting ahead of them. Two minutes passed before they started moving again and then it was slow going.

"Did you lock the boot, David?" asked Madeline.

"It locks automatically when the engine's running, mother."

"We don't want them looking in the boot."

"I don't think they will mother. They're just searching trucks and trailers – look."

They were closer to the giant ship and could now see how the traffic was being filtered. Many cars were getting through relatively quickly in the right-hand lane. David sighed at that. But all trucks, vans and cars with trailers were being guided to the hard shoulder and forced to open their loads for a search. They pulled up beside a soldier and David opened his window. Madeline seemed to shrink in the back.

"What's going on?"

"We're searching for stolen property. You can go through."

"What's been stolen? I mean, it must be valuable for you to hold everyone up like this."

"I'm not at liberty to say, sir. Move along," the soldier started waving them through and David decided he'd pushed his luck far enough. They moved off. After they'd put a little distance between them and the blockade, but before the junction 22 turn off, David switched off his engine and dipped the clutch. He steered the coasting car onto the hard shoulder and switched on the hazard lights.

"With any luck they won't investigate us. We seem to be close enough for the trucks to mask our advance when we spot Peter being stopped," said David. He got out and lifted the bonnet. After a couple of minutes, he closed the bonnet and phoned Peter again while leaning against the front wing of the car.

"Peter, how far away are you?"

'I'm being waved into the hard shoulder. I'd say there are about four or five trucks in front of me. I hope that whatever you're going to do, works.'

"So do I. Can you see if they are searching more than one truck at a time?"

'Not from here.'

"We'll just have to hope there's nothing in front of you when they begin their search. Remember to give us a call when you're next."

'You bet I will.'

A soldier was approaching as David rang off. He looked up with a smile.

"What seems to be the problem?"

"We've run out of fuel because you held us up for so long."

"Ah, sorry. We can't help you with that. We use different fuel. We might be able to spare a few men to help push it to the nearest petrol station. I'd have to ask the Sergeant though."

"There's no need. We'll be all right. I've phoned for help. My brothers on his way with a petrol can."

[147]

"Okay. Sorry for holding you up and your current trouble."

David nodded and gave a quick smile.

The soldier walked back towards the blockade.

David's phone started ringing and he lifted it to his ear. "Yes, Peter."

'They're closing up the truck in front. Any minute now, I'll be in trouble.'

"We're on our way."

David put the phone back in his pocket and knocked on the glass before moving to the boot. He glanced at the departing soldier then opened it. He ignored the Etherall in full view and felt along one of the inner panels. There was a click and the side panel dropped down to reveal several laser pistols. He passed one, through a gap in the back seats, to Madeline. She switched it to 'stun' then placed it in her lap and covered her legs with a blanket.

The three men, Xavier, Julian and George were now out of the car. They each took a pistol and set them to 'stun' before tucking them into the waistband at the small of their backs. David closed the boot.

"Let's go. Take as many as you can, *quietly*. If we get into a fire fight we'll lose so let's try to avoid that," said David.

They moved towards the blockade under the cover of the latest two trucks to be released. All the SF soldiers were concentrating on the traffic ahead, so it wasn't too hard to get close.

"Xavier and Julian. I want you to take out as many soldiers as possible without being seen. Then George and I will take out the ones searching the trucks. When we've taken them down fall back to the car to cover our retreat. Let's go."

Within seconds Xavier and Julian had surprised and stunned several soldiers and signalled for David and George to commence. David crept down one side and George stunned his first soldier then crept down the other side.

They both paused near the back of the truck. There were two soldiers stood behind it with Peter who had now seen them. David moved his lips asking silently, 'how many inside'.

Peter mouthed back 'two'. Just then the Etherall detector gave off a soft and continuous tone. George and David ducked back out of sight as the two soldiers with Peter turned around and peered inside the truck. David and George moved around their corners. Both soldiers on the ground sank to the floor as the stun pistols did their job. The two soldiers inside appeared from behind the hay.

"It's here…" was all they could say before David stunned one and George the other.

"Get back in the cab and when George joins you, get going. Turn off and find cover as quickly as possible. That ship will be searching for us soon. Now go," ordered David.

Peter ran back to his cab while David and George pulled both soldiers out of the back and then closed the doors. Some of the waiting commuters had stepped from their vehicles and were calling to the soldiers near the ship. It was time to go. They ran down the left side of the truck and George gave the thumbs up sign to David before climbing into the cab.

David sprinted back to his car, all thoughts of stealth abandoned. Xavier and Julian were watching for any movement from the SF soldiers. The truck moved through the gap and drove past them. David got in the driver's side and started it up. He moved off as soon as Xavier and Julian had got back in, following the truck off the motorway.

~

Julie turned onto her drive and pulled up outside her front door. She got out and marched towards her house. Suzanne hurried after her.

"Do you even know what you're going to say to her, mother?"

"Not yet," she said without looking back. "But I need to find out the truth," she paused when she got to the front door and looked at Suzanne. "Do you really think they did what that soldier said?"

Suzanne looked at the ground and that was all the answer that Julie needed.

"You *do* think she's done it, don't you?"

"Yes. I mean, why else would he have said that. It incriminates him doesn't it."

Julie leaned closer to the retinal scanner and it scanned her eye. '*Welcome home Mrs Statham*' said the automated voice as the front door clicked open. Julie pushed the door and entered with Suzanne following her in.

"Please remember how long you've been friends, mum. If this is true, she couldn't have risked telling you before. She'll need your help and support not your anger and rejection."

"I'll decide what I need to say, Suzanne. Right now, I'm pissed off and I don't mind if she knows it," Julie entered the lounge and sat in what she called her 'phone chair'. When you spent as long on the phone as she sometimes did it was nice to be comfortable.

She picked up the receiver and said, "Madeline Tressel – mobile."

The phone started ringing and Julie looked at Suzanne. "Could you make some tea please?"

"Of course, mum," said Suzanne. She left the lounge and headed for the kitchen. Suzanne switched on the kitchen TV and the drinks dispenser. She looked up as she heard the news and stared intently at the screen.

'There is chaos on the M1 at junction 22. A large Space Federation spaceship has landed on the motorway and caused fifteen-mile-long tailbacks. They seem to be searching lorries for something. We don't yet know what, as the soldiers are not saying anything. What little we do have has come from motorists. One said a few minutes ago that there was a disturbance and several soldiers were shot. A lorry sped from the scene and a man was seen running towards a car parked a little further up the motorway. A similar occurrence has...'

Suzanne switched it off, realising that she should've been there covering it for World News, but her mother needed her here whether she knew it or not. The machine finished dispensing the tea and Suzanne put both cups on a tray then carried them to her mother.

Julie was in the middle of an argument with Madeline and didn't see Suzanne straight away.

"But how could you not tell me about it," Julie stopped while listening to her friend. "Well no, of course not. Is Steve involved as well?" again she listened. "At least that's something then. So where are you going?"

Suzanne sat down opposite Julie and saw her frown. Suzanne settled back in the sofa and waited for her mother to finish on the phone.

"I know she's a reporter but that doesn't mean she can't keep a secret, or me for that matter," said Julie. She seemed to be calming down now. "All right. But promise me you'll ring as soon as you can." She listened to Madeline's response then said, "Okay, bye then – bye."

"Is everything sorted, mum?" asked Suzanne.

"Sort of," she paused while thinking. "You can ring Steve after they phone back. He is involved, but only since yesterday. It seems it'll only be the Tressels' that the SF can pin anything on. Everyone else will be able to return home eventually. At least he wasn't involved in stealing from the Space Federation. Although, he has been handling stolen goods."

"Did he know they were stolen?"

"I should think so, Suzanne. He was helping them load crates of Etherall onto the trucks."

"What was that you said about keeping secrets?"

"Oh, that's the reason she gave for not telling me about it years ago."

"She was probably right to keep it from me. At the start of my career I would've printed a story on them, and named names, because I wanted to get the truth out there and, I suppose, to prove myself to the editor. But nowadays I'm not so sure that everything I find out about should be made public."

"What did you say?"

"You heard. I've been sitting on a story since the middle of November which I can't even tell you about. There are lives at stake."

"But surely you can share something, dear."

"No. No I can't. If anything got out, they'd trace it back to me and I'd be on the run. These people don't mess around. I can only submit the story when the appropriate time comes."

"All right, Suzie. I won't ask you about it again."

They both finished their tea and Julie switched chairs to sit next to Suzanne. Mother and daughter cuddled together to watch some TV. They were both thinking about what they'd just learnt.

Later, Suzanne's mobile started ringing. She sat up and plucked it from the coffee table.

"Hello, Suzanne Cox speaking," she said.

'Hello, Ms Cox. Mr Stillson here. I'm afraid we need you to come back to *Sentry One* as soon as possible. It's time to release your story, but we need to go over it with you. How soon can you be here?'

"I'll get the next flight out, Mr Stillson."

'Thank you,' the line went dead.

"What was that about?" asked Julie.

"It looks like the story I couldn't tell you about is soon to be released. I've got to go, mum. Sorry."

"It's okay, Suzie. You *nearly* managed a week off."

They hugged each other.

"I promise I'll be back soon, mum," Suzanne got up and walked over to the lounge doors. She turned back to her mother. "If you should hear from Steve could you tell him I love him please."

Julie's eyebrows raised. "Of course, dear. Maybe you two could get back together one day. You did make a lovely couple you know."

"I know mum and if I…" she paused as she changed her train of thought. "When I see him again, I'll tell him.

Perhaps I could change my ways. We may still have a future," Suzanne smiled at her mother.

"I hope so. You two deserve each other. You're a good match. I've always thought so. Remember, Suzie; you're only young once."

Suzanne let the old saying of her mother's go this time. She let go of the doorframe and disappeared upstairs.

~

Captain Turner's Jeep sped along the hard shoulder, receiving angry car horns as he went. Several cars started following him down the hard-shoulder and, as he pulled up next to the SF ship, he signalled for the soldiers to stop them coming through.

The lead car screeched to a halt as three armed soldiers blocked the road. The driver got out of the car full of rage.

"Get back in your car, sir," said the first soldier.

The man pushed him hard and he fell backwards. Without hesitation, a second soldier fired a stun shot and the man fell to the ground, unable to move or make any more noise. Two other drivers were approaching, and the third soldier warned them to go back to their cars. He had his rifle pointed towards these two. They saw the other man on the floor and all the fight left them.

The first soldier got back up. "Return to your vehicles or you'll be detained."

They turned back and walked briskly to their cars.

"Pick him up and take him inside," said the first soldier.

Captain Turner had observed the altercation. He said, "Who's in charge here?"

[154]

The first soldier answered. "Sergeant Jenkins, sir."

"And where's he?"

"Over there, sir," the soldier pointed behind Captain Turner.

"Thank you, Private Harris. But remember your basic training lad. When a superior officer even so much as looks at you – you salute," his voice had risen throughout the rebuke so that everyone in the immediate vicinity could not help but hear.

Private Harris swallowed imaginary saliva and saluted the captain, "Sir, yes sir."

Captain Turner returned the salute and said, "That's better lad, now get to it."

"Sir," replied Private Harris who looked red-faced towards his fellow soldiers. The captain walked over to Sergeant Jenkins who saluted sharply.

"What's the situation, sergeant?"

"Err … we got sloppy, sir and they got away."

"How long ago was this?"

"A minute ago, sir. We were about to send some Jeeps after them."

Captain Turner looked at his watch. "We've only got one hour left before we must leave. Go ahead with your plans, sergeant. But we need to set up a rendezvous point. Every vehicle must be back by eighteen hundred hours. After you've set that in motion get this ship moved to the rendezvous position so these people can be on their way."

"Sir, what should we do about the idiot who assaulted Private Harris?"

"Let him go, I'm sure he won't try anything like that again in a hurry. Now I'm going to leave Lt Warner in charge while I go back to the *Spirit*," David faced his lieutenant.

[155]

"Make sure that we're off the planet by no later than eighteen hundred hours," they saluted each other. Captain Turner climbed aboard his shuttle. Moments later, he was gone. He was glad to finally leave. Everything that could go wrong – had, or mostly everything anyway. He just hoped that he'd still have a job next year.

~

"Of course, I couldn't tell you about it. The less people that knew the better. If you knew anything, and something had gone wrong, then you'd have been an accessory. You don't want to go to prison, do you?" Madeline was close to ending the call on her friend, but she supposed she owed her some of her time.

"He only got involved yesterday to help load the crates. That's all. The only way he could get implicated is if someone snitched on him," Madeline listened to her friend. Seconds later she said, "I can't tell you that yet. It's better that you don't know until all of this has died down. Anyway, Suzanne's with you isn't she. She would report it to that paper of hers in an instant." Again, she waited for Julie to finish speaking then said, "I've got to go now, Julie. Speak again soon."

Madeline paused while Julie spoke. "I promise, Julie. Bye," and with saying that she cancelled the call. She looked at her son. "That was awkward. They visited the farm while Captain Turner was still there. She knows about our work now and has promised to keep it a secret. I'm still not sure about Suzanne though. I wouldn't put anything past her when it comes to her job."

David looked at his mother. "I'm as sure as I can be that Suzanne won't say anything because we're friends and she still loves Steve."

"It didn't stop her before," replied Madeline.

"Do you think we've lost them?" asked Xavier.

"That depends on whether they got a description of this car or Peter's truck, but I should think that we're safe," said David. "They haven't got long left for another search. And there are multiple exits from the junction 22 roundabout, with lots of other routes off each road after that."

"When we get there, we'd better let Steve know that Suzanne knows about our activities," said Madeline.

"Right, back to the present," said David. "Who's hungry? I know a great pub near here and the food is excellent."

"Hadn't we better put some more distance between us and the soldiers?" asked Julian.

"No. They wouldn't be expecting us to be sitting in a restaurant, eating. Besides, if they spot the vehicle and move in on it, we'll see them and leave in someone else's."

"You mean steal someone else's, David," said Madeline.

"Of course. If they get that close, then adding car theft on top of our Etherall thefts won't matter too much I think."

They all laughed.

"Let's get some food," said Madeline.

[157]

CHAPTER TEN

December 2171

Anthera

The battleport emerged from hyperspace in orbit of Anthera and started its descent to the damaged mothership. As it entered the atmosphere a squadron of tranchillion fighters raced up to meet it.

"Identify yourselves," ordered the lead fighter.

"This is Captain Xenorphide. Clearance code TR1530XE1TE," replied Neil.

"Standby while we clear the code."

Neil stood still looking directly at the camera and waited.

"Standby, sir. The general wants a word."

The screen with the pilot's face on went blank and was replaced by the light-green skinned face of General Zemorphoride.

"Hello, Captain Xenorphide. Sorry for the unusual protocol here but we need to make sure you're who you say you are," said the general.

"That's fine, sir. We're rather late back. I'll tell you about it when we land, sir."

"Who's that next to you, captain?"

"Neil looked to his left then said, "That's Lieutenant Carphide, sir. My second-in-command. We had trouble and I promoted her beyond normal protocol because I needed to, sir."

"Okay captain, we'll talk about that later. You may land. I want a full report after you've cleaned yourself up."

"Thank you, sir."

The screen went blank again and then the lead fighter pilot's face reappeared. "You have clearance to land, but we'll escort you down, sir."

Neil turned from the screen. "Let's take her down. It's time to land this thing and get some well-deserved recreation time."

There were cheers from everyone present. They had a new-found respect for their captain. He'd saved them all.

The battleport slowed as it approached the mothership and a docking bay door opened to allow them in. The battleport flew inside and, as the doors closed behind it, settled on the floor. The battleport doors opened and out walked what was left of the crew, soldiers and pilots. Some of them were taken to medical while the rest were taken to two large waiting rooms for processing.

The last to leave the battleport were Neil and Rebecca who were cheered all the way down the ramp by their crew. They both waved back then saluted the crowd. All the cheers stopped abruptly as every one of them returned the salute. Neil had already gained a lot of tranchillion supporters, but he didn't know if they'd remain friendly if he revealed himself, so he still had to be careful.

They got on board the tranchillion equivalent of earth's 'astroport' and were taken to get cleaned up. After they'd washed and changed clothes, Neil and Rebecca were guided to General Zemorphoride's conference room.

Neil sat in Captain Xenorphide's chair and nodded to all the officers' present. He noticed a colonel watching him a little more closely than the rest. He searched Captain Xenorphide's memory for the colonel's identity and found him to be Colonel Twochelope.

The doors opened and in walked Colonel Dowdneer leaving his personal security guards at the doors. He looked at Neil and, for a fleeting moment, Neil detected animosity on his face.

Rebecca had been seated on her own at a side-table as her alter-ego, Capustri Carphide, wasn't a normal member of the council. Neil looked at her and nodded slightly. She didn't seem relaxed at all. Rebecca moved one of her hands down to her stomach and Neil knew she was adjusting her replicater. She visibly relaxed and Neil felt relief that she would now hold herself together.

In walked General Zemorphoride and took his seat at the head of the table. He looked at his notes briefly then he fixed his commanding gaze on Neil.

"We'll start with you, Captain Xenorphide. Before we get to hear your story, perhaps you'd like to enlighten me as to any more improper promotions you may have made."

Neil hoped that he hadn't messed it all up before he'd even begun but he couldn't have done it any differently.

"There were no others, sir."

"What rank was Lieutenant Carphide before you promoted her?" the general already knew the answer but wanted the entire council to hear it from Captain Xenorphide.

"She was a Staff Sergeant, sir."

"So, you have taken it upon yourself to promote a Staff Sergeant four ranks higher than normal. You're sailing very close to being stripped of your captaincy, so you'd better have a damn good reason for doing it."

Colonel Dowdneer loved this rebuke so much that he started laughing.

"What are you laughing about colonel?" asked the general.

"Sorry, sir. I don't know why. I just found it funny."

The general looked back towards Neil. "What happened to your previous lieutenant, captain?"

"Lieutenant Trulliphille must have been killed, sir. After I was knocked unconscious, I never saw him again."

"Didn't you have other lieutenants on board?"

"Not at that time, sir. Lieutenant Zielelope was one of the officers we rescued after I had made Officer Carphide a lieutenant."

"We'll decide her fate at the end of the meeting. Get on with your statement."

Neil recounted how they had been all set to attack the colonists when an alien starship intervened.

"We didn't know it was there until it got closer. We fought them but lost, sir. They captured the *Contention* and several soldiers including myself. A lot of our fighters made it to the moon but most of them were captured."

Neil also recounted how everyone left alive on the *Contention* were taken to the moon of the aliens' home planet and held prisoner. Then Neil told them about his escape and the resulting rescue of the tranchillion prisoners on the gas giant's moon.

"I had to promote beyond normal protocol because so many were lost or had died and, at that time, most of my crew were still imprisoned. All I ask of you, sir, is that you let Lt Carphide keep her rank. From judging her during the battle I know I can rely on her as my second-in-command, that is if I should be allowed to carry on my captaincy, sir."

General Zemorphoride sat back in his chair and pondered all that he'd heard. "It sounds to me that, apart from everything leading up to your capture, you performed exceptionally well and saved many tranchillion lives in the process." He paused and stood up, looking at every officer. "I hereby promote Captain Xenorphide to major in recognition of his courage and bravery in a highly stressful and dangerous situation."

There was applause from every officer in the room except Colonel Dowdneer who looked like he was going to protest. Instead, he sat back in his chair and eventually pretended to join in with the others.

The general raised and lowered his uppermost two arms and the room quietened once more. "I'll allow Lieutenant Carphide to keep her unprecedented promotion for the time being and will review it in due

[162]

course," he sat down again. "That'll be all. The rest of the agenda will be left for another day. Dismissed."

They all filed out and Rebecca joined Neil as they left the conference room.

"You'd better get some rest Lieutenant Carphide and I also suggest that you go to medical as well."

"I am tired Ne..." she stopped herself just in time.

Neil said, "Get some rest."

Rebecca nodded and then noticed a tranchillion approaching.

"Excuse me, Major. May I have a word."

Neil saluted Colonel Twochelope. "Yes, sir. How may I be of help?"

"We've known each other for more years than I care to mention, and you seem a little, different. Is everything all right?"

"I guess it was the imprisonment, sir."

"Could be, could be. You don't happen to know anything about any of the aliens do you. Any of their names perhaps?"

"No, sir. I don't understand their language."

"Okay. Just ignore me. I've got a lot on my mind. I'll say one thing though," he looked around to make sure no-one was listening. "Watch out for Colonel Dowdneer. I'm sure that he sent you away hoping that you wouldn't return. I believe that it was a suicide mission although, without any proof, I can't say anything more about it."

They saluted each other and Colonel Twochelope walked back in the direction of his quarters. Neil and Rebecca walked together for a short distance until their paths separated.

"That was our contact, Rebecca. Colonel Twochelope. I think he's suspicious already."

[163]

"I think so too," replied Rebecca.

"Right, see you soon. Remember, if you need me just come and visit."

"Okay, Major. Be careful yourself."

They parted ways and went for some much-needed sleep.

~

Colonel Dowdneer caught sight of Colonel Twochelope and newly promoted Major Xenorphide talking, about him no doubt, and felt like he might have to push his plans forward. He picked up his two security guards and headed for his secret meeting room.

He entered after his security guards had checked every possible hiding place within then sat and waited for his advisers and highest-ranking followers to arrive. Five minutes later they'd all arrived and Colonel Dowdneer started the meeting.

"I really thought that once the *Contention* failed to return, we'd seen the last of Captain Xenorphide but now we'll have to deal with him. He was a pain in the ass before he left and I'm damn sure he'll be watching us even closer now. His apparent ally in Colonel Twochelope also has me worried," Dowdneer shifted his weight then continued. "I want someone on them at all times. If they seem to be trouble, then we'll neutralise them both. Let me remind all of you; we're not yet ready to take over. Any action taken against either of them will be the start, or end, of our hopes to take charge. If anyone finds anything, come to see me straight away."

Staff Sergeant Onimechelope stepped forward. "Sir, I think I may have found two more suitable recruits for our cause."

"Good. Bring them before me at the usual place tomorrow. We should only need a dozen more before the balance will be suitably tipped in our favour."

He looked around at all the officers in front of him. "Lieutenant Mourneer, have you finalised the back-up plan yet?"

"It's not ready yet. I just need a few more days to make sure the plan's viable."

"Okay, due to recent events, I'll give you two days. If you haven't finalised the plan by then I'll have you killed and someone else can take over."

Lieutenant Mourneer's already pale green skin almost turned white. "I'd better carry on right away then, sir."

"Okay Lieutenant. Off you go. Make sure it's ready."

Mourneer left the room hurriedly, muttering to himself.

Colonel Dowdneer started laughing and said, "I just love messing with him. He's so easy to scare." He looked around and saw how they were all looking at him. "What!" He was still laughing.

They all filed out one by one, leaving Colonel Dowdneer alone to think about proceedings.

~

Colonel Twochelope, along with two privates, was bouncing along Anthera's surface in one of the *Dragen's* rovers. He had a feeling that the recent disappearances were not accidental. He believed that Colonel Dowdneer had something to do with it and was out on the planet's surface, looking for evidence. He looked at the message on his electronic notepad again and re-read it.

'Colonel Twochelope, sir. I'm sorry to bother you with this but I've heard that you don't see eye-to-eye with Colonel Dowdneer. I

[165]

don't have anyone else I can talk to. Recently my friend, Sergeant Thrillorpe, was called to a meeting with an anonymous person. He decided not to go but then disappeared. This happened almost a month ago. I've told my superiors about it and they've said they'll look into it. But nothing has come of it yet. You are my last hope of finding out what happened to him. I last saw him talking to some of Colonel Dowdneer's men. I'm sure that has something to do with it. I thank you in advance and hope that you'll look for him.'

Colonel Twochelope put the notepad away and looked back out the window. He didn't expect to find anything out here. It had been a month after all. And the body, if there was one, could have drifted in any direction for miles by now. He'd already exhausted his other options. There was no sign of him anywhere on the *Dragen,* so he had decided to give it two days outside. After that he'd have to find another way to take down Colonel Dowdneer.

"Is that something, sir?" asked one of the privates, pointing to their left.

"Could be private. Take us over there."

The rover changed direction and headed for what looked like a rock. But it was moving very slowly. As they drew nearer it became obvious it was a body and they stopped next to it.

"Go out there and bring it on board. We must get the body back as soon as possible and run some tests."

Once the lifeless body was secured aboard the rover, they set course for the *Dragen.* Colonel Twochelope hoped that this would finally be the evidence he needed to nail Colonel Dowdneer.

They were nearly half-a-mile away from the mothership when Twochelope spotted movement to their left.

"Stop a minute, private. Hand me those binoculars," Twochelope looked through them and saw another rover heading out towards the mountains.

"How much fuel do we have left, private?"

"Three quarters of a tank, sir."

"There's a rover over there, heading towards the mountains. Follow it but maintain your distance."

The rover turned towards the mountains.

"I don't want whoever is driving it to know we're following."

"Okay, sir."

"Once we've only enough fuel to get back to the *Dragen* we'll turn around and go back. I hope it stops before then. I'd like to know what they're up to."

They followed the other rover until it arrived at the base of the mountains where it slowed and seemed to be searching for something.

"Sir, we'll need to turn around in another two minutes if we're to make it back."

"Keep following until you absolutely have to stop."

"Yes, sir."

They followed it for a further two minutes until the driver stopped the rover. "We can't go any further, sir. We'll be running on fumes by the time we get back."

"Understood, private. Stay here and switch off the engine. I'll observe as best I can."

The other rover stopped, and the driver got out. There seemed to be no-one else with him. That, at least, broke the rule about never going out on your own. He

[167]

watched through the binoculars trying to get a glimpse of a face.

Twochelope turned the magnification up to maximum and looked through the binoculars again. The tranchillion turned his head in their direction and Twochelope clicked a button on the side to save the face on the binocular's files. *Got you*, thought Colonel Twochelope.

"There should be enough air in these suits to make it over there and back," said the colonel. "When he leaves, we'll take a walk over there and see what he was doing."

"Do you want us both to come, sir?"

"No. You can stay with the rover. If anything happens to us, I want you to go back and get help."

"Yes, sir."

The other rover moved off and drove further along the base of the mountain. It eventually disappeared out of sight. They checked each other's suits one final time.

"Everything okay?" asked the colonel.

"Yes, sir. Ready to go."

They opened the airlock and stepped onto the surface, closing it behind them. They made their way over to where the other rover had been parked. Colonel Twochelope knelt by the tyre tracks in the sand and then looked around.

"The footprints lead over there," said Colonel Twochelope while pointing towards the mountain. They followed the footprints and arrived at the foot of the mountain where there were signs of a lot more activity on the ground. There was a small gap in the side of the mountain and the colonel noticed a cross etched into the rock just above the entrance to the cave.

"What does that look like to you, private?"

[168]

"It looks like he's looking for a cave. Not just any cave though. It probably needs to be large. I'd say he's marking all the none-suitable caves with a cross, so he knows that he's been there before."

"Not suitable for what though?"

"I don't know, sir."

"Let's get back to the rover. We need to find out whose body we've found, and I would also like to know whose photo I've taken."

When they got back to the rover, and were on their way to the *Dragen*, the colonel placed his hands on the two privates' shoulders. "No-one must know about this. You *must not* tell anyone without my prior consent."

They both nodded and concentrated on the journey back to the *Dragen*.

~

Neil awoke and sat up in bed, listening intently. Someone was in his room, sneaking about. He left his bed and silently moved over to the door. He opened it slightly and looked through. The intruder was across the other side of the room. Neil slipped through the doorway and kept to the shadows until he was close enough to see what was going on.

The tranchillion left something stuck to the back of his desk and then moved on to the bathroom. Neil reached behind his desk and felt something small and round. He pulled at it and held, what could only be, a listening device in his hand.

He stood up and marched straight for the bathroom. He opened the door and walked in on the surprised tranchillion.

"What are you doing here?" demanded Neil.

The tranchillion bumped the back of his head on the sink as he tried to get up but Neil had sprung on him. He grabbed the tranchillion with all four arms and lifted him up against the wall with some force.

The intruder fought back and dropped to the floor as Neil was forced to defend himself. Neil hit the tranchillion with a vicious right-hook to the jaw and heard a crack. But he didn't stop there. He grabbed hold of the dazed tranchillion and forced him over to the sink. Neil turned on the tap and, after a few seconds, held the intruders head under the water.

He pulled the struggling tranchillion's head clear of the water and said, "Why are you bugging my room?"

There was no answer, so Neil forced the tranchillion's head under again for longer the second time. He was spluttering and thrashing his arms about as Neil pulled his head clear.

"I repeat, why are you bugging my room?"

"I'll not tell you anything," spluttered the tranchillion. Neil's response was to push his head back under the water again. This time he left it there until the tranchillions struggles grew weaker, then he pulled him back out and let him fall to the floor.

Neil dragged the tranchillion out of the bathroom by one of his feet. The semi-conscious tranchillion's head kept jerking about as Neil dragged the limp body across the room and left him lying on the floor. He walked over to his front door and leant out. "Runner!"

A runner appeared from around the corner. Runners were being used, as the communication system was damaged in the crash.

"Could you tell General Zemorphoride that Major Xenorphide needs an intruder picked up from his room."

[170]

The runner set off and Neil closed his door then sat in a chair near to the groaning tranchillion. He waited for ten minutes until four military police arrived and picked up the intruder.

"Follow us, sir."

Neil got up and followed them to the general's office. Once the tranchillion was secured in a seat the general sat in his usual chair and Neil sat next to the un-talkative prisoner.

"What were you doing in the Major's room, Private Treesomelope?" demanded the general. Private Treesomelope remained silent.

"You will answer me soldier or I'll make your life a misery. Normal rules don't apply while we're stranded here."

There was still no answer from Treesomelope. He just looked at the floor and refused to say anything. General Zemorphoride sighed and signalled for Sergeant Skillorpe to begin his interrogation. Neil watched as the Sergeant brutally beat the soldier into submission.

"What was he doing in your room?" asked the general.

"Placing listening devices, sir."

"Why would he want to do that I wonder?"

"I'd say that someone here isn't happy that I'm back and is trying to find out if I'm a threat to them," said Neil.

The general held his hand up and said, "I remember something from one of our meetings while you were away. It was about Colonel Dowdneer. Colonel Twochelope said something about you two not getting along and accused him of something. It was all dismissed as there was no evidence. Perhaps it's about that."

General Zemorphoride turned his attention back towards Sergeant Skillorpe. "Concentrate your questions around Colonel Dowdneer."

The sergeant nodded and continued with his interrogation. General Zemorphoride addressed one of his runners. "Bring me Colonel Twochelope."

The runner departed.

"This is stupid. We shouldn't be fighting amongst ourselves. We should be concentrating on our defence against the aliens. All this is just going to weaken us."

Neil crossed his arms. It was still too early to tell the general about himself. Like the *Watchers* had told Rebecca, the colonel was his best bet, but he still had to be careful.

A few minutes later a runner entered the office. "Sir, Colonel Twochelope is out in a rover."

"Send him here as soon as he gets back."

The runner nodded and left the office.

"Are you all right to stay while we wait for Colonel Twochelope?"

"Of course, sir. I'm intrigued to find out anything that might have to do with a conspiracy against me. I have been, and always will be, one-hundred percent loyal to you general," said Neil.

"Send security round to Major Xenorphide's room to sweep it for listening devices and have them bring back the evidence to me," said the general to one of his aides.

"Your room will be clear again soon. Let's hope that we find out why your room was being bugged."

Sergeant Skillorpe stopped his interrogation and walked over to the general. "I don't think he knows anything. He keeps saying that a sergeant gave him the order to place the listening devices, but he doesn't know a name."

"Great. Now how do we find out who's behind it?" commented the general.

"How certain are you he's telling the truth, sergeant?" said Neil.

"I'd say I'm about ninety-eight percent sure sir. No one's gone above interrogation level three before and this guy was up to level five."

"Take him away and get him cleaned up. Then to medical," said General Zemorphoride.

"If it was Colonel Dowdneer who ordered this then it seems he has a lot of support and is also very clever," said Neil. "He didn't send anyone traceable to him to plant those bugs. There's no connection between him and this soldier."

"I'm still not sure that Colonel Dowdneer had anything to do with this," said the general. "He's one of my most trusted officers. He's the one who reported the attack from the aliens all those years ago."

"With all due respect, sir. Couldn't he have been lying back then. He may have attacked them and caused this war."

"I won't hear anything bad said about him. He's also my friend. If anyone brings me proof, that'll be different. Until then, I advise everyone to keep their comments to themselves," said the general.

Another runner entered the office. "Colonel Twochelope has arrived back with a body and will be with you shortly, sir."

"Okay, thanks. That will be all," the general leaned back in his chair and stretched his uppermost arms above his head then sat forward again. "Not long to wait now."

~

Rebecca stepped out of the shower and the water automatically stopped. She'd played around with that feature when she first got in by stepping in and out of sensor range. She had found the stop/start of the water hilarious. *I'll have to tell Neil about that*, she thought.

Beads of water ran in uneven lines down her body following her various curves as she walked to the drier. Rebecca stepped into this machine and her skin wrinkled all over as powerful jets of hot air dried her body effortlessly. She covered her face with her arms as the hot air became uncomfortable.

Next, she walked back over to the bed she'd slept on for the last six hours and lay down, still naked. She reached down between her legs and gently started rubbing herself while thinking about Neil. Her back arched as two of her fingers found their way inside herself. She moved them around as they got wetter and wetter, then she let out a cry as she climaxed.

If only Neil wasn't with Chloe, she thought – not for the first time.

Rebecca got up and tried to make sense of the kitchen. Everything was different to what she was used to. She looked at various packets and containers and couldn't decide which was drink and which was food. It never occurred to her to put the *Chameleon Suit* on and use Lt Carphide's knowledge to help her.

She turned on the tap at the sink. At least water was still water. That would have to do. She gulped it down, quenching her thirst then, after putting the glass on the counter, she walked back into the main room and sat in a large chair.

What the hell am I doing here? she thought. *I'm well out of my depth. I want to go home.*

[174]

You are doing an important job Rebecca; one that needs to be done, said a voice in her head. Rebecca sat upright and looked around, subconsciously covering her breasts with her arms and crossing her legs, until she realised that it was a *Watcher* that had spoken to her.

Would you mind not frightening me when you make contact, she thought.

How would you like me to do it, as I cannot think of a way? came the reply.

I don't know, some sort of signal so that I know you're about to speak to me.

It does not work like that I am afraid. You will just have to get used to it.

Okay, what do you want?

First, you had better put some clothes on. Rebecca looked down at her body and blushed. *I do not mind seeing your nakedness, but if anyone other than Mr Bolgon should enter your room then you would be in serious trouble.*

Rebecca got up and rushed into her bedroom. *Can you see me?*

I see through your eyes, so only when you look at yourself.

Are you male or female?

Male, but do not worry about me seeing you like that. Our bodies are very different to yours so, let me say, there is no physical attraction on my part.

Rebecca struggled with the *Chameleon Suit* again, but she couldn't get the damn thing over her shoulders. She was beginning to wish she hadn't taken it off.

Are you having trouble there Rebecca? asked the *Watcher.*

Yes, I am. I can never get this damn suit on properly. I'll have to wait until Neil comes.

"Oh, damn it!"

I will make sure that Neil is the first person through the door, said the *Watcher.*

How are you going to do that? she thought back.

Colonel Twochelope has just got back. I will speak to him and get him to tell Neil that you need him. The rest will be up to you.

There must be another way, surely.

There was no answer this time.

"Great, alone again," Rebecca sat in the large chair with the suit around her waist waiting for Neil to turn up. As the minutes passed by, she drifted off to sleep. She was more tired than she'd thought.

~

Colonel Twochelope stepped out of the rover onto the hard metal surface of the *Dragen's* docking bay. The two privates, who were carrying the body between them, followed the colonel out of the rover. They were crossing the docking bay towards the control centre when a runner hurried towards them.

"Sir, I have an urgent message for you," said the soldier.

"Okay, what is it?"

"General Zemorphoride has requested your presence in his office, sir."

"Tell him I'll be right there," said Colonel Twochelope. He turned to the two privates. "Get that body to the medical bay. No-one, except me, is to go near it no matter what rank they are. I'll be along as soon as I can."

As Colonel Twochelope was walking towards his meeting with General Zemorphoride, the voice in his head started up again and he ducked into a nearby room so he could concentrate on what was being said.

[176]

Hello colonel. I have an urgent message for you.
Go ahead.
After your meeting with General Zemorphoride you must take Major Xenorphide to Lieutenant Carphide's room. That is all.
Why do you want me to do that?

Again, there was no answer. It was beginning to annoy him that he couldn't decide when a conversation was over with the *Watchers*.

He left the room and continued to the general's office.

When Colonel Twochelope approached General Zemorphoride's office both security guards stepped aside to allow him through. He opened the door and saw the general sat behind his desk. He walked over and saw Major Xenorphide sitting in a chair to one side.

Neil got up from his chair and saluted Colonel Twochelope then sat back down after the colonel had taken his seat.

"Colonel Twochelope. I've asked you here because I'm hoping that you can shed some light on a recent event involving Major Xenorphide."

"How may I be of assistance, sir?"

"Major Xenorphide has just foiled an attempted bugging of his room. Now I remembered you said something in a recent meeting about Colonel Dowdneer and the Major. We were just wondering what your opinion was."

"Sir, you told me that unless I had proof, I wasn't to make accusations against him."

"That's true but we're not in the conference room now. There's only us three here so I'll allow you to give us your opinion. There's only one thing I request of both of you. Anything said in this room stays in this room."

[177]

They both agreed to Zemorphoride's demands and Colonel Twochelope told them of his suspicions.

"I said in the meeting that I thought Colonel Dowdneer and, the then, Captain Xenorphide disliked or perhaps hated each other, giving only my observation as evidence, which obviously isn't a good enough reason to have brought it up in a conference meeting. I'm sorry for that general."

"Quite all right. Carry on."

"After the meeting was over, I was surrounded by Dowdneer's soldiers and the colonel himself warned me not to interfere. If the cameras hadn't been there, I'm sure he would've been warned me differently."

The general shifted uncomfortably in his chair but said nothing.

"Also, various soldiers have been going missing since we've been stranded here. I'm sure that Colonel Dowdneer is behind those as well. I recently received a communication on my notepad about a Sergeant Thrillorpe who is one of the missing soldiers. This communication resulted in me looking at the missing persons list. There have been seventeen missing persons listed in the last sixty years since first contact with the aliens. The reason this hasn't been picked up before now is because, I believe, Colonel Dowdneer is secretly recruiting his own army from within ours. Anyone who doesn't join him gets executed. I believe that in those sixty years only those seventeen soldiers have refused."

The general interrupted him at this point. "If that's true then he would have control of the entire army by now," he shook his head. "I'm sorry colonel but I don't believe it for a moment."

[178]

"Sir. I think he only recruits roughly eight to ten soldiers a year. Any more would raise suspicion. Especially if some of them refused. Taking that number into account he could have recruited somewhere in the region of five-hundred soldiers in the last sixty years."

"There are only one-thousand and sixteen of us left now. So, you're saying he has nearly half of my soldiers under his command. What would be the point of this, colonel?"

Neil now knew the size of the threat facing them if this went wrong but he couldn't allow the humans to finish off these tranchillions. The imminent arrival of a much larger force would literally kill every human on earth if that happened. Neil decided to speak up himself.

"If I may say something, sir."

General Zemorphoride looked at him and nodded.

Neil continued. "I believe, due to my recent encounters with the aliens, that they wouldn't attack anyone without provocation. In all the time we were imprisoned by them we were not mistreated. It wasn't until I orchestrated our escape that any lives were lost. Both sides lost soldiers the day I rescued the others, sir. It was unavoidable. I'm starting to think that when the original contact with the aliens happened, one of two things took place. One, the aliens involved either thought they were threatened, or they were a rogue group and attacked Colonel Dowdneer. Two, the colonel did initiate the attack and cause this conflict."

Both tranchillions looked at Neil, deep in thought, and there was silence for one, long minute. Neil didn't know if he'd gone too far but it had seemed like the right time to speak up.

"Colonel Dowdneer is one of my closest friends on this ship. But, if he's gone bad, I'll execute him myself," said General Zemorphoride. "But I still find it extremely difficult to accept this. If I'm to believe he's guilty of anything you'll need to find evidence of any crimes he's perpetrated. Only then will I confront him with this. Is that clear."

"Yes, sir," they both replied.

"Now, Colonel Twochelope. I believe you brought back a body from outside. What's happening with this?"

"I'm holding it in the medical bay for further analysis, sir," said Colonel Twochelope.

"Let me know what you find," there was a pause. "Dismissed," he ordered as he looked between them.

They left the general's office. After the door closed behind them Twochelope said to Neil, "We have to go to Lieutenant Carphide's quarters straight away."

"Why?" asked Neil.

"It's hard to explain. I just know we need to go there right away."

"Then let's go."

~

Rebecca was still asleep when Neil knocked on her door. Even though Neil knocked louder the second time she still didn't wake up.

Neil used a command override and the door opened. He stepped inside Rebecca's quarters and saw her asleep on a chair, looking very human. He could tell, even from this distance, that she was asleep, and not dead, because he saw her bare breasts rising and falling with her breathing.

[180]

Before Neil could stop him, Colonel Twochelope had entered the room. "Is everything okay? Where's the lieutenant?" The colonel stopped short as he saw Rebecca sitting, asleep, in the chair in front of him.

Neil moved behind the colonel and drew his pistol. The colonel's initial shock of seeing the alien had worn off and he drew his pistol. "Where's Lieutenant Carphide?"

"She's in front of you colonel," said Neil. "I advise you to put your pistol back in its holster. We have a great deal to discuss."

"Why are you pointing that at me?" the colonel had half-turned towards Neil.

"Put yours away and I'll gladly do the same."

Colonel Twochelope reluctantly holstered his pistol and looked back towards Rebecca.

Neil holstered his as well. "Now, you're about to see something that'll probably shock you. I hope you'll do the right thing colonel."

Neil removed his replicater from its socket and slowly changed back to his normal self in front of Colonel Twochelope's eyes. The colonel's mouth opened in amazement as he stared at them. "You're both aliens. How did you do that?"

Neil replaced his replicater and changed back. "I'm sorry. What did you say? This only translates your language when it's inserted into the suit."

"I said, how did you do that?"

"I'll tell you later, but I need to know that I can trust you, colonel."

"You… you're that Neil Bolgon that the *Watchers* told me about, aren't you?"

"Yes. And from what I've seen of you so far, I'm sure that I can trust you. I'm normally good at judging people, colonel. That's why I allowed you to keep your weapon."

Colonel Twochelope looked down at his hip but didn't even think about going for his pistol. He looked back towards Rebecca. "It's all true then. The whole Dowdneer thing. The *Watchers*. I'm not going crazy after all."

"I don't believe you ever thought that, sir," replied Neil. "Now if you'll excuse me, I must see to my rather uncouth friend here. Her state of dress is not at all appropriate."

"Of course. I'll just sit over here while you sort her out."

Neil removed the replicater again then he touched Rebecca on her shoulder, but she didn't wake up. He held her shoulder firmly the next time and shook her gently. "Rebecca, wake up."

Rebecca awoke and saw Neil standing in front of her and she smiled.

"I think you'd better put those away, Rebecca."

She looked down and her cheeks flushed red.

"I... I needed a shower and I couldn't get the suit back on properly..." she stopped speaking when she caught sight of Colonel Twochelope watching them.

"That's a tranchillion, Neil."

"I know, and I've already partially explained who we are. Now, let's get that suit back on and blend in again."

Neil held her suit on her shoulders and she pressed the button on her wrist then typed in her access code and the suit began tightening up around her body.

"Go and find your mask and replicater. We'll be waiting for you," said Neil.

[182]

He watched Rebecca hurry back to her bedroom then inserted his replicater and changed back into Major Xenorphide.

"What's happened to Xornin and Capustri?" asked Colonel Twochelope.

"They're being held in the most secure holding cells we have. Only four other… no, make that eight other humans know that the switch has been made."

"What you told General Zemorphoride back in his office. Was it true?"

"Yes, it's all true. They're safe and well, believe me. It was unfortunate to lose so many tranchillions during the escape, but I suppose it was inevitable."

"Why did you risk your life to save our people?"

"I needed more crew to fly the battleport. But once I found out this whole war between us was just a big misunderstanding, I had to release as many as I could."

"Neil, I commend your bravery and obvious skill in combat, and I thank you."

"You're welcome, colonel," said Neil, smiling as Rebecca re-entered the room.

"That's better," said Twochelope. "You can walk around freely again now. I suggest, what's your name?" he paused.

"Rebecca."

"Rebecca. I suggest if you want a shower in the future, while you're still here of course, you should make sure Neil is around to do you back up."

Rebecca forced a smile. "I will, thanks."

"How did you know I'd had a shower? I thought you couldn't understand us while we're in human form."

"Your hair was damp, and you weren't dressed."

"Oh."

[183]

"I've got some business to attend to so, if you'll excuse me, I'll be getting back to it."

"One thing before you go," said Neil quickly. "You'd better have your room swept for bugs as well."

"I've been doing that for a while now. Ever since the *Watcher* first spoke to me, I've been extra careful. I don't trust Colonel Dowdneer anymore. Your re-appearance may have brought his plans forward so we could both be targeted very soon. Be careful Mr Bolgon."

"We'll be careful and remember to think of us as the major and lieutenant when speaking to us."

"Don't worry. I'm not stupid. See you around," Colonel Twochelope left the room and headed in the direction of the medical bay.

"I'm sorry about my appearance when you turned up, Neil. I didn't mean to fall asleep."

"It's okay, Rebecca. It all turned out well, didn't it?"

"I suppose so. It's just that I don't want to be the one that gets you killed; or me for that matter."

Neil could see that she was getting upset so he held her in his arms. They parted and removed their replicaters so they could see each other's true forms. Neil looked into Rebecca's brown eyes and said, "I'm sorry that you've had to come here. But I'll protect you to the best of my ability. Let's relax for an hour then get down to business."

They sat next to each other on the sofa and Neil let her rest her head on his chest as he put his arm around her.

"What business is that, Neil?"

"You're going to read minds so that we can find out who's with Colonel Dowdneer, and who isn't."

"Okay, Neil. I'll do whatever you want me to do."

[184]

~

Colonel Dowdneer was sitting in his office going over his carefully laid plan. Some parts of it seemed to be going wrong and he was wondering how. He was still on course for his take-over, but the wrong people were becoming aware of him.

The latest developments were also alarming. No-one could connect him to Private Treesomelope but now General Zemorphoride was aware that something was going on. It was going to make things a lot more difficult. He slammed his fist down on the desk. He was so close now.

The office door opened and one of his security guards entered with his pistol drawn. "Is everything all right, sir?"

"Yes, yes. I'm just a little annoyed. Good response though. Well done."

The guard backed out and closed the door. A knock came from the secret door on his right. Dowdneer pressed a button underneath his desk and the door moved backwards slightly then slid to one side.

In walked Dowdneer's most trusted messenger. He handed the colonel a notepad which he read with some interest.

Subject: - *Colonel Twochelope / Major Xenorphide.*

Comments: - *Have tailed both the colonel and the major to Lieutenant Carphide's room. They went straight there from General Zemorphoride's office. No further details as the room isn't bugged. Will report any further findings.*

Colonel Dowdneer wiped the notepad memory then handed it back to the messenger. "That'll be all."

The messenger left the way he came in and Dowdneer pressed the button again. The secret door slid closed. He now had some new complications to consider.

He leaned forward and pressed the intercom button. "Get me Lt Col Maverphoride," he ordered.

~

Chief medical officer Lance Corporal Silmerwelope marched back over to the two privates guarding the body that Colonel Twochelope had brought in. "That's enough now. Let me see the body," he ordered.

"Sorry, sir but we've been given orders by Colonel Twochelope to guard this body against anyone. That includes officers."

The chief medical officer reached out to physically move the privates out of the way, but they reacted by drawing their weapons. "Please, sir. Do not make me use this weapon."

Lance Corporal Silmerwelope hesitated then backed away from them. "I'll have you court-marshalled for this you insolent little..." he was interrupted before he could continue the insult.

"Leave them alone, corporal," said Colonel Twochelope. "They have legitimate orders to keep anyone from looking at that body without me being here. Now, I want you to do an examination. I want identification and cause of death. Get to it, corporal." He turned his attention to the two privates, who had now holstered their pistols, and winked at them.

"You two will be promoted if you keep this exemplary performance up. I know that was hard but you both did very well."

They saluted Colonel Twochelope.

"Stand guard outside and let me know if anyone wants to get in."

They moved out of the room and stood guard at the doorway. The chief medical officer had now moved the body over to the examining table and removed the suit.

"Anything interesting yet?" asked Twochelope.

"There was no helmet and judging by the condition of his body, and what's left of his face, I'd say that he died of sudden oxygen starvation and de-pressurisation."

"I'll look through the files and try to match his face to a name while you work your magic, corporal."

The chief medical officer nodded then pulled a mask over his face and picked up his tools.

Colonel Twochelope sat at the chief's desk and brought up personnel files on screen. First he typed in 'missing persons' and then scrolled down the names until he found Sergeant Thrillorpe. He compared the picture on screen with what was left of this body's face. They were similar but he needed more before he could be sure that it was the same man.

He got up and took a fingerprint from the body then sat back at the desk. After he'd applied the fingerprint, the computer verified that it was Sergeant Thrillorpe. Now all he had to do was tie this body to Colonel Dowdneer somehow. That was the tricky part. He noted his findings then brought up the photo recognition programme. He scanned his notepad photo of the rover driver into the computer and waited.

After a few seconds had passed the screen stopped on the file of Lieutenant Mourneer. Now he had got the person who'd been out on his own in the rover. He saved the file to his notepad and left the desk after clicking out of the files he'd been accessing.

[187]

"His name's Sergeant Thrillorpe. If you find anything noteworthy – send for me."

"Yes, sir."

Colonel Twochelope left the medical bay and set off for General Zemorphoride's office.

~

In the time it took Lt Col Maverphoride to arrive, Dowdneer had received two more reports regarding Colonel Twochelope. The first was a standard report on his leaving Lt Carphide's quarters alone and the second was a report on him spending a while in the medical bay with two soldiers posted outside. He'd been seen leaving the medical bay but had left the two soldiers on guard at the door.

"What took you so long?" asked Dowdneer as Lt Col Maverphoride entered his office.

"Sorry, sir. I was on the other side of the ship. I came as soon as I got the message."

Colonel Dowdneer waved away his answer. "Never mind. I need you to pick up one of these three using allies that can't be traced back to us. We need to extract information from them." Dowdneer handed over his list to Maverphoride.

"Sir, are you sure? The disappearance of any of these could lead to trouble."

"That's a risk I'll have to take. They have all started seeing each other way too much. I think they suspect something's going on and I need to know what they know."

"What's to happen to which ever one of them I manage to interrogate?"

"I would think the answer to that is obvious, Marsup. Be ready for the take-over, as these actions we're about to take could lead to our hand being forced early."

Lt Col Maverphoride left the office quietly. He was not happy about this latest order. He was beginning to think that Colonel Dowdneer was losing his cool, and that could be dangerous for everybody connected to him.

~

Rebecca woke up and realised that she was sitting next to Neil with his arm around her. He was asleep. She gently removed his arm from her lap and was about to get up when she looked at his peaceful face. While she had the chance, she had a good look at his body. She'd already, fleetingly, seen him naked. But even with the chameleon suit on she could see every minute detail of his body.

She bent her head towards his face and kissed him on his lips. Neil stirred and responded. He kissed her back which took her by surprise. They started kissing passionately, their eyes closed. Rebecca leant backwards, getting ready to undo her suit again then he said a word which completely ruined her perception of what was going on.

"Chloe," said Neil. He reached for her again as he opened his eyes, smiling. It was then that he realised it wasn't Chloe in front of him. They parted quickly and Neil got up.

"What just happened?" asked Neil.

"We kissed."

"I thought you were Chloe. Why would you kiss me?"

"Because I love you Neil. Ever since I met you, I've known that I can't have you but that doesn't stop my feelings."

"There's no way, Rebecca. No way I'm going to cheat on Chloe."

Rebecca moved closer. "But she's not here – I am."

She was right. Chloe was right, he thought.

"No, Rebecca. I won't do it. You're beautiful and god knows I'd love to, but I won't cheat on her," Neil walked to the kitchen, his throat suddenly feeling very dry. Rebecca followed him.

"Are you sure, Neil? She doesn't have to know. I'd never tell her."

"How do I know that, Rebecca."

"Oh, come on, Neil. If I caused your relationship with her to break down, you'd kill me. I'm sure of it."

"The answer is still no, Rebecca. We have a baby on the way. It's not worth the risk of losing the two people closest to me."

After he'd finished his water, he turned to face her and couldn't help looking hungrily over her body.

"This isn't the time or place for this anyway," he said.

Rebecca could sense his resolve weakening. She knew he wasn't ready yet, but she could work on him later. The seeds were planted. She just had to wait for the right time to sprinkle on the water.

"Okay, Neil. I'll back off. But remember that the offer will still be there if you need someone while we're stuck here. After all, I'm the only other human here."

"Don't get me wrong, Rebecca. If I wasn't with Chloe, I'd love to be with you, but I can't."

Rebecca plugged in her replicater and started the transformation. Neil did the same.

"Let's get on with this mind-reading mission of yours," said Rebecca.

They left the room and went in search of Colonel Twochelope.

CHAPTER ELEVEN

December 2171

The Moon

Kelly woke up with her best friend's red hair in her face. She gently kissed the back of Rachel's head and ran her fingers through her hair then reached over Rachel's, still sleeping, form and squeezed her breast gently. Kelly moved her kisses to Rachel's ear and licked her earlobe. Rachel responded to Kelly's touch and turned onto her back.

Rachel reached out and pulled Kelly's face towards her own and they kissed. Kelly shifted her weight then brought her leg over and knelt astride Rachel's naked body. Rachel caressed both of Kelly's breasts and Kelly placed her own hands on top then she leant forwards and they started kissing again. They both found each other at the same time and gasped as their fingers entered.

Chloe, also in the bed, opened her eyes and looked at them. She watched them enjoying themselves and it made her long for Neil even more. He'd only been gone for two days yet it felt like a week already.

"Do you two mind. You're in my bed," said Chloe, not really meaning it. "If Neil knew what you were doing in his bed, he'd hit the roof."

Kelly looked at Chloe without stopping. "No, he wouldn't. He'd want to watch." She grinned.

Chloe smiled at the thought. "Yeah, you're probably right there."

"Join us," said Rachel. "You may like it."

"No. Sorry girls. Even though you're not male it would still be cheating."

"I'm with Eric and he doesn't mind," said Rachel.

"That's because you let him watch – you pair of tarts," said Chloe. She swung her legs out of bed and stood up.

"Hey. We're offended. Take that back," said Kelly, trying not to smile.

"No, you're not. Can I get you anything?" Chloe had started walking over to the bedroom door.

"Are you sure you won't join us," said Kelly, admiring Chloe's body. "It's such a shame to waste a body like that on a man."

Chloe left the room, without comment, and walked to the kitchen to make some coffee. She also made three lots of toast then brought them into the lounge and sat at the dining table.

"Your coffee and toast's ready!" she called.

Kelly and Rachel left the bedroom, still naked, and joined Chloe at the dining table.

"Are you both working today?" asked Chloe.

"I'm on afternoons," said Kelly.

"I'm on the morning shift," said Rachel.

"You'd better hurry up then," said Chloe. "You only have forty-five minutes before you're late."

Rachel looked at the clock. "Shit! I'm going to be late." Rachel finished her toast, took a mouthful of coffee, then ran back to the bedroom.

"I'm surprised she doesn't get fired how often she's late for work," said Chloe.

"Cameron's a big softy. All she has to do is look cute for him and he gives in," said Kelly.

"He's not a very good boss though. I swear he's just there to ogle the girls."

"At least it means we can get away with lots of things."

"I bet he's never had a girl, judging from the way he is around them."

"Well I could change that. He deserves to have some fun, I think."

"He'd expect you to become his girlfriend though, Kelly. I'm not sure he'd understand the term 'one-night-stand'."

"Hey, you make me sound like a whore," said Kelly indignantly.

"Come on, Kelly. You've slept with, how many men?"

Kelly looked thoughtful then said, "Yeah, I can see where you're coming from, but I don't charge them."

"That just makes you cheap," said Chloe as she leaned sideways to avoid a playful slap aimed at her shoulder.

They both started laughing and Chloe said, "I love you Kelly. You're the best friend a girl could ever have."

Rachel walked back in the room. "What you two laughing at?" she asked.

"Nothing. Just banter," replied Chloe.

Rachel stopped at the table and finished her coffee. "It's been lovely girls. Thanks for letting us stop the night, Chloe."

"It's okay, both of you."

"How do I look?" said Rachel giving them a twirl.

"Lovely, Rachel. Now go and try not to make poor Cameron come in his pants," said Kelly.

Rachel winked at her and walked over to the front door. She looked back at them. "Only if he leaves me alone," she said before leaving the quarters.

"Have you got to work today?" asked Kelly.

"Yes. I'm on afternoons as well. Transporter seven, I think."

"We're working together today. How lovely," said Kelly with a twinkle in her eye.

Chloe got up. "I'm getting dressed."

Kelly followed her to the bedroom. "I may as well get dressed then."

"Are you still hoping for us to have sex, Kelly?"

"I'll keep trying, Chloe. Look at you. You're gorgeous."

"Okay, I'll have a word with Neil and maybe we can get together."

"She's breaking. Finally, she's breaking."

They both got dressed talking about anything and everything.

~

Captain Turner had been back for just over twenty-four hours. He had already gone through all that had happened with General Bolgon. The general hadn't been happy that they'd lost so much Etherall, but he had conceded that Turner had, at least, got some of it back. He had handed over the details of both Madeline and David Tressel to leave their fate in the general's hands. That night he'd drunk too much alcohol. So, on top of his guilt about giving away his friends he'd also had the constant companion of the sick bucket.

Why did Henry have to spot the truck? he thought. He'd done a lot of thinking since his return but none of it helped. He felt terrible about the *Tressel's* predicament. It was an unusual feeling for him. The great captain of the *Spirit* making life changing decisions every time he was aboard.

Now look at me, he thought. *A lousy drunken mess. Not fit to command anything.*

David had decided that he couldn't allow them to fend for themselves and formulated a plan. He thought it was a good one. He'd been up half the night trying to make it work in his head before the alcohol had taken effect.

David picked up his phone and called the Tressel's. He left it ringing for a while and was about to ring off when Madeline answered.

"Hello."

"Hello, Mrs Tressel. Is David there?"

"Captain Turner. Is that you?"

"Yes, can I speak to David please?"

"Of course. I'll just get him."

A minute went by until David answered. "Hello, David. What's up?"

"Is there room in your plans for an extra pair of hands, David?"

"Are you asking me for a job?"

"And a place to stay until I find my feet."

"Have they found out about you?"

"No, not yet. But it won't be long before they do, and I'd like to be gone before then."

"But we need the Etherall. It's our main source of income and it could take us years to find another source we can trust."

"I've thought of another way you can get Etherall. You won't be making as much because you'll have to buy it."

"How's that going to work, David?"

"I can't go into details over the phone, but it'll work. Trust me."

"Okay, get yourself back here and we'll talk about it. Ring once you've landed and I'll pick you up."

Captain Turner cancelled the call and started writing his resignation note, detailing all he'd done. When finished he sealed it in an envelope addressed to General Bolgon. The end of one career was nigh and the start of a new one was on the horizon. He felt better after looking at it like that.

David picked up the letter and put it in his pocket. First, he had some last-minute arrangements to make then he'd deliver the letter to General Bolgon.

~

At mid-day, Suzanne Cox arrived at *Sentry One,* ready for a meeting with the general. But, with it being lunchtime, she was hungry, so she decided to stop off at the café.

Suzanne ordered her meal, downloaded a newspaper, and took a coke with her to find a table.

Presently, a waiter brought her food over and she began to eat. After finishing her meal, she got up feeling better for the food and left the café. It was a ten-minute walk to the general's office, so she had time to answer the call of nature nagging her.

When she arrived, she smoothed her skirt and straightened her blouse. She'd already checked her hair in the toilet. Suzanne entered the outer office and approached the secretary's desk.

"One moment please," said the secretary, Gwen Smith. She finished with the papers on her desk then put them in a tray and looked up. "Yes."

"Suzanne Cox of 'World News' to see General Bolgon."

"I'll see if he's ready for you, Ms Cox," Gwen picked up the phone and talked to the general. After a few seconds she put it down. "Would you please take a seat. The general will see you soon."

Suzanne nodded and sat in one of the indicated chairs. While she was waiting both Michael Toddwell and John Stillson, who were the general's main assistants, arrived and were sent straight into his office. Suzanne saw a magazine that took her fancy and started flicking through it.

After several minutes had passed the door to the general's office opened and Mr Stillson stepped out.

"Could you come in please, Ms Cox."

Suzanne put the magazine back and got up. She walked over to Mr Stillson who stepped aside to allow her access to the office.

He looked at Gwen. "Could you hold any calls until we're finished, Gwen. Thank you." He walked back into the office and the door slid shut behind him.

Suzanne sat in front of the general's desk and Michael and John sat either side of her. She studied the general's clean-shaven face and saw the intelligence behind his brown eyes.

"It's time for you to release your story about the battleport," said General Bolgon. "There's already talk of its existence going around, due to the escape of the tranchillions on November the thirtieth. I'm about to tell you about that escape and the reasons for it. You'll appreciate that I, again, cannot allow you to print all the details I'm about to give you. You'll find that lives are at stake here. I will not let any current mission fall into jeopardy because of anything you might print."

"Okay, general. I'm listening."

General Bolgon told her about the escape and that it was really Neil who had done it. He told her about the people who knew about the mission and he gave her the most recent news he'd just received only minutes earlier.

"Are you saying that humans were killed on Ganymede and Neil may have been the one who did it?" said Suzanne with surprise in her voice.

"Judging by the few details we have; I'd say that Neil is the only one capable of pulling off that escape. I'm sure he had no choice when he killed the few soldiers that he did."

"Tell that to their parents and loved ones," replied Suzanne.

"Neil knows only too well how much it hurts to lose someone you love, Ms Cox. That's why I'm sure he had no alternative on Ganymede."

"How many casualties were there in total?" she asked.

"The report says that fifteen soldiers were killed, ten were stunned and ten soldiers injured."

"That's quite a list, general," said Suzanne.

"Obviously, there were a lot more casualties than I'd hoped for, but I will not judge Neil until I have him back here face to face."

"Does it make any difference that he's your son?"

"No. I'd follow the same protocol for any of my soldiers."

"Just for balance. How many tranchillions were killed?" asked Michael.

"Thirty-eight," replied the general after looking at the report again.

"I wouldn't call that a very good rescue," said Suzanne.

John butted in. "There were eighty-seven tranchillions held prisoner at Ganymede, Ms Cox. I'd call the ratio of lives saved to lives lost a pretty successful mission."

"Spoken like a true politician," said Suzanne.

"That's enough!" ordered the general. "Ms Cox, you may write your original story about the capture of the battleport and add the information about the Ganymede incident. But, Ms Cox, no mention of Neil or Rebecca must make it into the story. When this whole sorry mess is cleared up, and my son's safely back home, you can go ahead with the rest of it. You'll be able to give Neil's side of events as well then."

"That's if he ever makes it back," said Suzanne.

"Of course, he will. I can't afford to think any other way," said the general. "Once you've completed your story, come back to me and we'll go over it," he stood and signalled towards the door. "Now if you'll excuse me, I have a lot of work awaiting me."

The general watched Suzanne and Michael leave then turned to John. "Fifteen sounds just right for the new project. We could have three, six-man squads. All we'd need is three squad leaders."

"I'll get onto Ganymede's BC and tell him to put them in cryo."

"Very good, John. I'll see to Captain Meade myself."

~

All the arrangements were made. His flight left in half-an-hour, and his rendezvous with David Tressel was a go. Now all he had to do was hand in his resignation and get off the moon before the general closed it down to stop his escape.

Captain Turner really didn't want to leave his post, but he couldn't live with the guilt of his criminal activities anymore. It was all in the letter. All he'd done. How sorry he was and all the regrets he had at leaving in the way he was planning. But at the same time, he didn't want to go to jail.

He knew that the general read his mail in the mornings. He was normally out of his office making sure that everything was running smoothly during the afternoon.

David entered the general's outer office and walked over to the secretary's desk. He waited until she'd finished on the phone then handed the letter to her.

"Can you make sure the general gets this, Gwen."

She smiled at David. "Of course, captain. Is there anything wrong?"

"No, Gwen. I just wanted to say goodbye to you before I go. I'll miss our little chats."

"Go, David. What do you mean?"

"It's all in the letter, Gwen. You may read it when the general wants it filed."

Gwen got up from her desk and walked round to him.

"What are you doing?" he asked.

"I've always wanted to do this," she said as she reached up to hold his face in her hands. Then she moved in closer and kissed him. He started to respond before gently pushing her away.

"Gwen. I didn't know you felt this way."

"I always have but I didn't dare do anything about it with you being an officer."

"That wouldn't have mattered," he stopped talking as he heard voices approaching the general's office door. "Is someone in there?" he asked.

"Yes. The general, Mr Toddwell, Mr Stillson and Suzanne Cox."

"Oh hell, I'd better get out of here," he started towards the exit just as the office door opened.

"Hello, captain. Nice to see you. He's free now," said Michael Toddwell.

David turned back to the office. He could see all his carefully laid plans falling apart. "Hello, Michael. It's nice to see you too."

Suzanne followed Michael out. She looked at David, her face blank. "Captain."

She's already told them, he thought. *Why else would she be here?* He spoke up. "Ms Cox."

They walked past and left the office. Gwen handed him his letter and he gave a quick smile before entering the office. All he could foresee in his future was bars. He could see no way out. David walked over to the general's desk and saluted.

"I'll get on with my calls, sir," said John.

"Okay, John," the general looked at David. "Sit down, captain. How may I help you?"

John left the room, unnoticed.

The question caught David by surprise. Perhaps he didn't know after all. Then he realised he was still holding the letter.

"Is that for me?"

"Err… yes, sir," David held it out and wished he was anywhere but here. After the general had took the letter David started rubbing his moustache with his fingertips.

"Are you all right, captain? You don't look your normal self."

David shifted his weight. "No, I'm not, sir. All your answers are in there." He indicated the letter.

General Bolgon leaned back in his chair and opened the letter. David saw his expression change multiple times whilst reading it.

The general put the letter down. "So, captain. You're the leak. What should I do about that?"

"You knew about it!"

"All I knew was that someone was feeding the thieves information. I just didn't expect it to be you. I was thinking more along the lines of Lieutenant Warner."

"No, sir. He didn't have anything to do with it."

"Who else knows about your involvement, captain?"

"No one, sir."

"Come on now. Be honest with me. I'm trying to feed you a life-line here."

"Apart from their leader, two civilians know, sir."

"Who are they, captain?"

[203]

"Suzanne Cox and her mother," said David, bowing his head.

"What!" exclaimed the general. "Suzanne knew. Why didn't she tell me I wonder?"

David knew he wasn't looking for an answer, so he kept quiet.

"Look, David," the general gestured with his hand. "You don't mind me taking this to a personal level, do you?"

David shook his head.

"I can't accept your resignation. We'll be sending god knows how many soldiers to Anthera soon. I need my best people there. The crew of the *Spirit* already know and respect you."

David couldn't believe his ears. Here he was thinking he was going to be court-marshalled and the general was instead asking him to stay.

"In that case, sir. I'd be proud to lead the *Spirit* into battle.

General Bolgon handed the letter back to David. "You'd better have this back captain. I only have one condition. I want nothing but the best from you on the mission. At the minute, you're not thinking straight, or you would not have owned up to your activities."

"What are you suggesting, sir?"

"I think you need some time off; a little R&R. You can start straight away but I want you back no later than the third of January, is that clear."

"Sir, yes sir."

"Dismissed."

David stood and saluted the general and he'd half-turned when an idea popped into his head. He turned back.

"Is there something else, captain?"

"Yes, sir. I haven't worked out the details yet, sir. But I'd like to turn my associate's activities into a legitimate business."

"We already have several buyers for our Etherall and Sodrum, captain."

"I know, but if these associates of mine can be persuaded to work legitimately then there will be less Etherall going missing, sir."

"Okay, Captain. Work out a business plan. Get me all the details and I'll consider it."

David left the office and stopped at Gwen's desk. He kissed her passionately. When they parted, she had a shocked look on her face.

"See if you can get some time off and call me on this number," he had produced a pen from one of his pockets. After he'd written it down on her notepad, he held her by the shoulders and said, "I've got a month off to recharge my batteries. I'd like you to come too if you can. What do you say?"

"Of course, David. I'd love to. I'll ask Mr Bolgon and let you know."

They kissed again.

"We should have done this years ago, Gwen. I didn't know you felt this way," he caught sight of the time and hurried to the door.

"I've got to go, or I'll miss my flight. Call me, okay."

"I will."

~

Suzanne was back in the café with her laptop on and a sandwich in her hand. She was trying to work out how to write the story without giving away any of the information that the general wanted kept quiet. The key elements needed to clarify the story were classified. She held her head in her free hand while she tried to think.

"Can we sit here please?" asked a tall, slim female with brown skin and black, dreadlocked hair. "There are no other tables, or we wouldn't have bothered you," she continued.

Suzanne moved her gaze from the lady in front of her and looked at her friend. The friend was three inches shorter, looked older, and had long blonde hair which reached down to the small of her back. She was also slim with fair skin and blue eyes. Suzanne moved her hand in the direction of the spare seats. "Of course, please sit."

Both women sat and set their drinks on the table. They were dressed the same in their stewardesses' outfits. Suzanne looked back at her screen. She could not think how to write it.

"Are you a writer?" asked dreadlocks.

"A journalist. Suzanne Cox," she held out her hand.

"Kelly Hanson," said dreadlocks as she shook her hand.

Suzanne offered her hand to the blonde.

"Chloe Lewis," she said as she shook Suzanne's hand.

"We are stewardesses," said Kelly.

"I guessed," replied Suzanne.

"Anything important you're writing there?" asked Chloe.

Suzanne closed the laptop and said, "Some of its classified so I can't tell you about it."

"Are you having trouble? You didn't seem to be writing very much," said Kelly.

"It's complex and certain classified elements have to be left out. I'll do it later in my room."

"Sorry we disturbed you, Suzanne," said Chloe.

"It's all right. I wasn't getting anywhere, and I needed a break."

"I know your name from somewhere," said Chloe.

"I work for World News. I'm up here quite often."

"That's where I heard your name from. Neil mentioned you once."

"Neil?" Suzanne paused trying to think of a Neil that she knew. "Neil who?"

"Bolgon, Neil Bolgon. He's my boyfriend."

Realization spread across Suzanne's face. "Oh my god Neil. Yes, I know Neil. He's the one who escorted me away from the security area a while ago."

I've got to be careful here, she thought.

"How is he?"

"He's away on a mission. We were supposed to go to a concert together."

"What concert?" asked Suzanne.

"It was two nights ago. I still went with Rachel and Kelly though."

"I wasn't here then. I was visiting my parents back on earth," said Suzanne.

"It was a good concert. Sorry you missed it," said Kelly.

"I hope Neil comes back to you soon," Suzanne stood up. "Excuse me. I must get going. It was nice to meet you both," Suzanne waved then left them to their drinks.

"What did Neil say about her?" asked Kelly.

"Something like she keeps popping up asking awkward questions and that they had her under control or something."

"It strikes me that it would be very difficult to control her. That is unless she wanted to be controlled."

"What do you mean?"

"I think they must have something on her. Either that or they've threatened her. She's the one who broke that big case about the diamond theft involving her father-in-law. I think he was involved in the theft and Suzanne found out about it. She wrote the story and dropped her father-in-law in the shit at the same time. Her divorce followed not long after."

"I'll bet," said Chloe.

Kelly looked at her watch. "Christ we're going to be late." They got up. "We're just as bad as Rachel," she added jokingly.

They hurried off to work. With a little bit of luck, they would just about make it.

CHAPTER TWELVE

December 2171

Anthera

"It's been two days Marsup. Two days since I gave the order. What's going on?" said Colonel Dowdneer.

"I've selected Lieutenant Carphide. She should be the easiest to break, sir. But she's always with Major Xenorphide," replied Lt Col Maverphoride.

"Pick them both up then. And don't call him major. He doesn't deserve the promotion."

"Sorry, sir. Slip of the tongue. I have thought of picking them both up, but I think that Colonel Twochelope would raise the alarm within a day of them going missing, sir."

"Then take him as well, Marsup. I need to find out what's going on with those three."

"Okay, sir. If you're sure."

"Of course I'm sure. We'll start the take-over as soon as questions are asked about any of them. It's still a little early but my hand's being forced. Despite all my carefully laid plans they've still managed to suspect me, and I can't figure out how."

"I'll get right on it, sir."

Colonel Dowdneer dismissed Lt Col Maverphoride with a wave of his hand and resumed reading the report from Lt Mourneer. Finally, something seemed to be going right. He'd found three caves large enough for his followers and with a few months of drilling, all three could be joined together via tunnels.

Colonel Dowdneer sat back in his chair. It was just a shame that the only thing that seemed to be going right was the back-up plan.

The two new recruits seemed to be fine as well. He was glad that he hadn't had to kill them. It was always such a waste when they defied him.

~

Colonel Twochelope sat at his desk and waited for the knock on his door. He'd seen the arrival of Lt Mourneer in his, newly installed, secret camera above the office door.

"Come in."

His door opened and in walked, a nervous looking, Lt Mourneer. "You wanted to see me, sir."

"Sit, lieutenant," said Colonel Twochelope as he indicated the chair in front of his desk. "It has come to my attention that you've been breaking rules, lieutenant."

[210]

"Really, sir. What rules?"

"Driving a rover without back-up. Why were you out there on your own, lieutenant?"

"I needed to get away for a while and I fancied a drive – you know – to be on my own."

"Bullshit, lieutenant. I saw you. What were you examining the mountains for?"

Lt Mourneer visibly cringed at the question and started looking around for an escape route.

"Answer me, lieutenant or I *will* hand this conversation over to the general and his favourite interrogator."

"I can't say, sir. I really can't."

"And why is that lieutenant?"

"Because he'll kill me, sir."

"Who lieutenant? Who will kill you?"

"I can't tell you that either, sir. He has too many followers. I'll be killed."

"You're an officer in the emperor's army, lieutenant. You swore an oath to protect Tranchilite's citizens from harm. Hell, we both did. If this person continues, where do you think he will stop. He's killed people, lieutenant. I can stop it from happening, but I need you to tell me who. I can't protect you if you don't give me a name."

"I'm sorry, sir. I can't tell."

Colonel Twochelope changed his approach. "I know it's Colonel Dowdneer. I also know he has roughly five-hundred soldiers in his pocket. I know that he's going to attempt a take-over soon. He won't stop there, lieutenant. He'll eventually get back to Tranchilite with all opposition here crushed. He can make up any story he likes to whoever rescues us. The government on Tranchilite will be overthrown and all remaining tranchillions will be forced to fight, and conquer, every race of aliens they come across."

"If you know all this then why haven't you stopped it already?"

"I have no proof. Without that the general won't listen to me."

Lieutenant Mourneer thought about what he'd just heard and lowered his chin to his chest. "Okay, sir. I'll tell you everything I know. You can protect me though, can't you?"

"Of course, lieutenant. Of course."

~

Over the last two days Neil and Rebecca had managed to catalogue almost every tranchillion on board the *Dragen*. Some had been easy to link to Colonel Dowdneer and others had to be asked questions to get them thinking about him first. They had used Colonel Twochelope for help with the questioning as his influence could get most of the soldiers into the interview room.

Colonel Dowdneer had five-hundred and four followers including the two new recruits he'd got his hooks into during their mind-reading mission.

On top of finding all that information, Rebecca had found out they were being constantly followed by a team of five. Rebecca had read their minds and what seemed constant was that they were all waiting for her to be alone. She told Neil and they had decided to stay together until the danger had passed.

They were in Neil's room trying to make sense of their findings. Neil got up from the chair. "We have to bring Twochelope into this now and give him the update. He knows how many tranchillions the colonel has in his grip but this new direction can mean only one thing," he paused.

"What's that, Neil?"

"They're going to try to take us by force if necessary."

"What about Colonel Twochelope?"

"They'll take him as well. I'd say we'll be fighting off Dowdneer in as soon as five to eight days."

"Let's take this to General Zemorphoride then. He must know about it before it's too late."

"Take what to him, Rebecca. All we have is your mind-reading evidence. He will require proof before he takes Colonel Dowdneer down."

"There's got to be something we can do."

"Let's hope that Colonel Twochelope has had some luck with his investigation."

Neil put his jacket on. "Let's go."

Rebecca got up from her chair and gathered all the notes. "Shall we take these with us, Neil?"

"No, put them in the usual place, Rebecca," he said as he picked up his weapons from the table in the lounge.

Rebecca put the notes in Neil's secure box then hid it in plain sight on the shelf. It looked just like any other ornament except that it was hollow and heavy.

She was walking back into the lounge as Neil reached out for the door control. The door opened just before Neil pressed the button and in burst four tranchillions – knocking him to the floor.

In a blur, Neil had removed his pistol from his holster and was bringing it up when the tranchillion stood over him fired a stun shot. He fell unconscious.

Rebecca tried to get back in the bedroom but was stunned in the doorway. Her momentum took her as far as the bed. The top half of her body bounced off the edge of the bed and she lay still on her side. Two of the tranchillions picked them up then carried them away for interrogation.

~

Colonel Twochelope was hiding behind a tall bookshelf in the darkest corner of his office. He'd seen four tranchillions enter his outer office, on his secret camera, with their weapons drawn. So, he'd prepared an ambush of his own.

The door opened and a stun shot hit his chair, knocking it over. He stayed hidden and waited. The first of the four tranchillions entered his office and started scanning the area. He didn't see Twochelope in the corner. A second tranchillion entered and walked in Twochelope's direction.

The colonel shot both tranchillions with stun bolts then he moved over to the doorway and peeked through. The other two had taken cover and were waiting for him to appear. It was a stand-off and he couldn't figure a way out. Their cover was too good. If he stepped out to fire, then he'd be stunned before he could get a shot off.

Twochelope bent his hand holding the pistol around the door frame and fired a couple of blind shots at them. There was no laser fire returned but moments later a stun-grenade hit the floor of his office and rolled towards his desk.

The bright light and ear-piercing buzz emitted from the grenade forced Colonel Twochelope to his knees. He looked up as the two tranchillions rushed into his office. He fired his laser, but his aim was affected by the ringing in his ears and the stubborn refusal of his eyes to focus.

[214]

He missed. The two soldiers didn't and Colonel Twochelope sank into unconsciousness.

~

When he woke up, Colonel Twochelope had been stripped naked and was strapped into one of Colonel Dowdneer's electric chairs. He looked around but his vision was still blurred and all he could make out were shapes and shadows.

"He's waking up, sir."

"Okay, get to work on him. I'll inform the colonel."

There was a sudden jolt of pain as electricity was passed through Colonel Twochelope's body. He resisted the urge to scream and his whole body relaxed as the power was cut. An unseen door opened and closed.

"Now colonel, I warned you about messing with me. I know you're up to something. What I want to know is, how you knew about my plans," said Colonel Dowdneer as he walked out of the shadows and into the only source of light in the room. The heat from the spotlight was causing Twochelope to perspire. Visible beads of sweat were slowly making their winding paths down his body. He said nothing.

"Turn it up a notch," said Dowdneer.

This time he couldn't help but scream from the pain and once the power was cut, he shouted at them, "Fuckers! I'm going to kill every one of you! You're de..." His rant cut short when the power was turned back on and his whole body stiffened as he screamed again.

His body sagged forward in the chair when the power was cut. Only his restraints held him in place. The colonel's interrogator lifted his head up and held it so he could see Dowdneer.

"Tell me what I want to know, Tchzor and it'll all be over," Dowdneer used Twochelope's first name on purpose. Trying to use a more personal approach. "No more pain. No more suffering. I can keep this up for days. What do you say?"

Twochelope was breathing heavily now and hadn't the strength to hold his head up by himself. He couldn't gather any saliva either so spitting at the colonel was out. He stayed silent.

Dowdneer turned away from him and spoke to his interrogator. "Keep up the good work and let me know if he breaks. Make sure he suffers but don't kill him yet." He walked into the shadows, leaving the room.

He entered the second interrogation room. All three rooms were separated by one wall so he could enjoy watching the torture of whichever victim he chose with little effort. In this room, strapped to a table in a pool of light at its centre, lay Lieutenant Carphide. She was also naked. This room was designed to pray on a person's fears. Four feet above Rebecca was another table, turned upside down, onto which a crude set of spikes of different sizes had been welded.

Colonel Dowdneer appeared out of the darkness. "Lieutenant Carphide. No doubt you can hear the colonel's screams from the next room. He's not being very co-operative, so I'm forced to electrocute him, until he dies if necessary. Is that what you want for yourself?"

"No … no."

"Good, then maybe you would tell me how you know about my plans."

"What are they for?" she asked as she moved her eyes from Dowdneer to the spikes above her.

"I suppose I should tell you what trouble you're in. It might help you to make up your mind a little faster," he paused as he bent over her and said, only inches from her ear. "You have an hour before that drops on you and ends your life," he stood up straight. "Now, how do you know about my plans?" he ran a finger down her arm and traced the outline of her body with his nail. He moved it along her ribs and then over to her stomach. She tensed as he started moving his finger towards her legs. He smiled then removed his hand.

Rebecca stayed silent, praying that Neil would find a way to rescue her before the hour was up.

"There is another way, lieutenant," said Dowdneer as he leaned over her and unsheathed his knife, "that I'm not beyond using if I have to." He ran the blade across her stomach, then between her breasts, and paused at her neck. He applied a little pressure. Just enough to frighten her then he put it away again.

"You now have fifty-five minutes to tell me what I want to know," he said then he stepped backwards out of the light and made his way to his last victim.

Neil woke up. His arms and legs were strapped to some sort of rack, but he couldn't make out what it was because he was in total darkness. The room felt cold and he could sense the presence of someone close by.

"Who's there?" said Neil.

There was no answer and Neil realised he'd better save his strength until an opportunity to escape presented itself. There was always a way. He just had to recognise it when it occurred. He heard a door open and shut then a single powerful spotlight, aimed directly at him, was switched on. He closed his eyes for a few seconds then opened them in a squint.

[217]

"Who's there?" he asked again.

"It's no secret, thanks to Twochelope, that I hate you, Captain Xenorphide," said Colonel Dowdneer. "I don't believe you should have been promoted so, while you scream and beg to die, I'll refer to you as captain."

"Shut up, Dowdneer. Cut me down from here and let's see if you can beat me fair and square."

"Do you think I'd give up my advantage," Dowdneer said as he pulled out his knife and turned it round in the glare of the spotlight. "Do it."

Suddenly, the rack that Neil was tied to fell forward, and Neil realised, a split second before he entered the water, what was going to happen and held his breath. While he was under, he tried to manipulate the ropes binding his wrists to the rack. Then he was brought up again.

Dowdneer punched him several times on his body and face then he backed out of the light and reappeared, moments later, with a long metal pole which he used to beat Neil with. He'd been expecting yelling, screams, swearing, anything like that, so he was surprised when Neil stayed silent.

Neil was concentrating on controlling his pain. He could survive weeks of this kind of torture unless they took it too far and killed him.

"Drop him again!" yelled Colonel Dowdneer.

In the next room, Rebecca had heard the colonel's yells of frustration and realised he wasn't getting his own way. She knew that Neil must be close by and that gave her the courage to wait it out.

Everything had gone silent in Colonel Twochelope's room. He'd passed out from the pain and his interrogators were waiting for him to wake up again. They were in no hurry.

~

General Zemorphoride was in Major Xenorphide's room. He hadn't heard from the major or Colonel Twochelope for over five hours. Under normal circumstances that wouldn't have bothered him, but they had an agreement to check in every four hours. He didn't believe that Colonel Dowdneer was trying to take over, but he couldn't dismiss it either. Now both officers that had said something against Dowdneer were missing and at Colonel Twochelope's office there had been signs of a struggle.

"Keep searching for them and get Colonel Dowdneer to report to my office right away," he said to his runner.

The general turned around and the door to Major Xenorphide's room closed behind him. He had now begun to worry what would happen if the colonel and the major were right about Dowdneer. He had to get back to his office and work out all possible scenarios. He didn't want to be caught unawares and just hand it over. He was in an emotional turmoil. Colonel Dowdneer, his most trusted friend and ally, plotting against him – it couldn't be true.

His secretary gave him a message, from one of his runners, when he got back to his office. '*Lieutenant Carphide has not been seen since this morning. Will report any further news*'.

He sat behind his desk and checked the charge on his pistol then he placed it in the quick release harness under his desk.

Ten minutes had passed before Colonel Dowdneer entered his office looking agitated. He indicated for Dowdneer to sit which he duly did.

"You look annoyed, Dwdoorian. What's wrong?"

"Nothing, sir. Just having a bad day."

"The reason I'm calling you here is that three officers have recently disappeared, and I was wondering if you had seen them."

"Really, who's missing?"

"Colonel Twochelope, Major Xenorphide and Lieutenant Carphide."

"Haven't seen them, sir. Why are you asking me?"

"I'm asking all of my officers, Dwdoorian. I trust you the most, so I asked you first. Just keep your ear to the ground and if you see or hear anything, let me know."

"Fine, sir," said Colonel Dowdneer as he stood up. He left the general's office eager to carry on with his interrogations.

General Zemorphoride watched Colonel Dowdneer depart his office. That had neither proved nor disproved the accusations made against Dwdoorian, but he was now leaning more towards the conspiracy theory.

He pressed the intercom button. "Get me a runner."

A runner entered the office and waited for instructions.

"Send word to maintenance to get the bunker ready," he said then dismissed the runner. He settled back in his chair and waited for the next officer to arrive for questioning.

~

While Colonel Dowdneer was away, Neil had been busy. He'd managed to loosen one of his wrists by wriggling his hand around. He'd damaged his wrist, making it bleed underneath his *chameleon suit*. He ignored the pain.

After another tug at the ropes they loosened enough for him to pull his hand free then he untied his other hands. The room was still pitch black and he listened for the presence of any other tranchillions. He thought he could hear breathing over to his right. One, maybe two guards. He set about untying his feet.

Neil swung round the back of the rack and landed lightly on the floor. In the silence of the room though, his landing was amplified.

"If you don't want dunking in the water before the colonel gets back, I suggest you stay still," said a voice to Neil's right. He pushed the rack from behind then crept towards the sound of the voice. There was a splash as the rack fell into the pool and a sudden commotion began in the room.

Neil homed in on the voice then something bumped into him from behind and he swung around and grabbed what must have been a tranchillion's arm. He swung all four fists upwards and one of them connected with the tranchillion's jaw who then skidded across the floor and thudded into the wall.

Neil turned back to where the original voice had come from just as the spotlight lit up the floor behind where the rack should have been.

"Hey, he's in the water. Pull him up. Pull him up quick."

Neil was still moving as the empty rack emerged from the water and back into the spotlight.

"Where is he?" said one voice.

"Turn on the lights," said another.

[221]

The room flooded with light and, as his eyes adjusted to the glare, Neil saw four tranchillions in the room. He grabbed the nearest one by the head and twisted his neck fast. There was an audible snap and the dead tranchillion dropped to the floor.

The naked form of Major Xenorphide picked up the dead tranchillion's laser. As his eyes adjusted to the light, he took out the other three before their surprise could develop into a response.

Neil made it to the door as it opened and shot the tranchillion who entered the room. He looked through the doorway into another darkened room and saw Rebecca in the centre beneath a pool of light. She was strapped to a table, looking terrified. He edged through the doorway looking for any signs of resistance and found none. After switching on the lights, he hurried over to Rebecca.

"Hurry!" she screamed. "My hour's nearly up!"

Neil had managed to undo two of the four straps holding her down when they heard a click. Neil dived to the floor as the trap was sprung. The spikes dropped towards Rebecca with a thud. Neil closed his eyes, took a deep breath, then got up, expecting to see Rebecca skewered. The spikes had stopped two inches from her body and Rebecca was wide-eyed, holding her breath, and laying very still. Her ability to scream seemed to have deserted her.

Neil found the controls and managed to reset the mechanism, then he unstrapped the rest of Rebecca's bindings and lifted her off the table. She remained still and silent. Neil looked into her wide open, non-blinking eyes. He slapped her hard on the side of her face and she snapped out of the trance she'd fallen into. Her eyes were moving quickly from side to side.

Rebecca started crying. Seeing those spikes rushing towards her had nearly broke her spirit completely. Neil held her face in his hands.

"Rebecca. It's me, Neil. Can you hear me?"

Her eyes stopped moving and she focused on him then nodded.

"Good. I need you to get yourself together and gather weapons and clothes. I'm going after Colonel Twochelope. If anyone comes through any door – shoot them," said Neil.

"I don't know if I can, Neil. I… I almost died."

"But you didn't, Rebecca and you live to fight another day," said Neil. He held her gaze. "You can do this. You must do this." He closed his eyes for a second. "Turn your replicater up to full. You won't be able to make your own decisions, but I've got a feeling that we'll be fighting our way off the planet soon. You'll need all of Capustri's training to stand a chance of escape."

Rebecca reached down and turned the replicater up to full. Now the only control that Rebecca had over her reactions was not to harm Neil. She started removing clothes and weapons from the bodies.

Neil moved over to the door of the last room and opened it. He saw Colonel Twochelope slumped in an electric chair in the middle of the room, again with a spotlight trained on him. Neil could sense a trap, but he had no choice. He had to rescue Colonel Twochelope. He walked through the door and waited.

There were no shots fired so they still wanted him alive and conscious. That gave him a chance. He took a few more steps into the room and the door slammed shut

[223]

behind him. He squinted as the room was suddenly filled with bright light.

"Drop your weapon captain," said one of the tranchillions. Neil stayed still, mentally calculating his best course of action.

"You won't kill me. I'll bet that Colonel Dowdneer wants me alive," said Neil.

"We only need one of you alive, but the colonel wants to make that decision himself."

"Where's he gone?" asked Neil.

"That doesn't matter. Drop the laser or I *will* shoot."

Neil lowered the gun but didn't let go. The tranchillion that had talked to him looked over to another that was stood by a lever. The power was switched on and Colonel Twochelope started screaming as electricity poured through his body. Neil dropped the laser and, seconds later, the electricity was switched off.

Three of the five tranchillions in the room moved towards him. The one by the lever had moved far enough away for Neil to act. The first tranchillion put his hand on Neil's shoulder and was just about to force him to his knees when Neil sprang into action.

He grabbed the arm and pulled him in close to act as a living shield while he simultaneously disarmed the tranchillion. Neil shot the two nearest to him and then the other soldier before he could pull the lever. Several laser blasts hit Neil's tranchillion shield and he pushed the lifeless body hard towards the last soldier.

He fell with the dead tranchillion on top of him, causing his laser to fall from his grasp. Neil walked over and pointed his laser at the helpless tranchillion's head. Neil recognised the look of terror on his face and lowered the laser.

He left him struggling on the floor underneath the dead weight of the heavier tranchillion and unstrapped Colonel Twochelope from the chair. He laid him on the floor and examined him. He wasn't going anywhere under his own steam, but he couldn't leave him here. Also, he couldn't see a way out.

Neil walked back over to the struggling tranchillion and pulled the dead one off. Then he picked him up and forced him over to the chair. He strapped him in and called for Rebecca.

She appeared in the doorway.

"Capustri. Would you ready yourself at the lever please," said Neil as he pointed towards it. Rebecca walked over to the lever and waited.

Neil stood in front of the helpless tranchillion in the chair. "Now, where is the exit to this room?"

The tranchillion stared straight ahead and refused to answer. Neil nodded and Rebecca pulled the lever. The tranchillion's body started writhing as he screamed until smoke appeared from his clothes. Rebecca switched off the power and Neil asked him again.

"It's in the next room – to the left. It can only be opened from outside unless you have a remote."

"Where's the remote?"

"Colonel Dowdneer has the only one."

"Does that mean we have to wait for him to come back before we can get out?" asked Rebecca.

"Yes, I'm afraid it does," said Neil.

Neil picked up Twochelope and carried him out. Rebecca switched the chair back on and followed him, leaving the tranchillion to fry. She closed the door behind her to muffle the screams and Neil selected a uniform from the pile that Rebecca had removed from the dead soldiers.

"Remind me never to piss you off," said Neil as the screams gave way to the smell of burnt fat.

Rebecca smiled, recognizing her comment from what seemed like years ago. "It must be the Capustri in me."

~

Colonel Dowdneer had taken a minor detour on his way back to the interrogations via his office. He was now sure that the general had begun to suspect him. The time had come for his take-over. It was no longer necessary for him to find out how they knew about him.

He was waiting in his office for Lt Col Maverphoride to show up. There was a knock on his secret door, and he let Marsup in.

"It's time, Marsup. We need to get started right away before we lose the element of surprise."

"What do you want me to do, sir?"

"Send the message to the troops, get everything going, and then meet me at the interrogation rooms."

Maverphoride left the office and Colonel Dowdneer crossed the room to his gun cabinet. He took out his rifle and several spare clips for both it and his pistol. He checked the charge level on the rifle and then left his office.

Five minutes later he entered the corridor that lead to the disused storerooms, eighteen, nineteen and twenty. He'd had the doors to eighteen and twenty sealed so as no-one could get in or out of them. Colonel Dowdneer used the remote and the door to room nineteen slid open. He entered and was halfway to the torture table when he realised that Lt Carphide wasn't strapped to it.

He spun around at a noise behind him and was punched full in the face which knocked him backwards. He kicked out and Neil only just avoided it. Dowdneer tried a quick combo but he was no match for Neil who avoided all three blows and used the heel of his hand to knock Dowdneer into the torture table.

Dowdneer stretched two of his hands backwards to steady himself. Rebecca, who had been crouched behind the torture table, grabbed one arm and pulled hard. Now the colonel was half on the table and again he kicked out at Neil which was deflected to the side. Neil brought his right leg up above his head and down again hitting the colonel full force in the stomach with his heel.

Neil lifted the, now wheezing, colonel's legs up onto the table and both he and Rebecca strapped him down.

"You'll never get away with this! I'll find you damn it!" shouted Dowdneer after he'd regained his breath.

"We've given you the same hour you gave Lieutenant Carphide with one slight difference," he paused for effect as he opened the door with Dowdneer's remote. "The blocks have been removed."

"I hope you die a painful death Dowdneer. God knows you deserve to," said Rebecca.

They left a ranting and helpless Dowdneer to his fate and set off down the corridor with Neil carrying a semi-conscious Colonel Twochelope over his shoulder.

"We have to warn General Zemorphoride," said Neil.

Colonel Twochelope coughed and said something which neither of them understood so Neil put Twochelope down.

"It's good to have you back, colonel," said Neil.

"You need to find Lieutenant Mourneer," repeated Twochelope.

"Right now, we need to get you to safety," said Rebecca.

"I'll be fine, Capustri. Lieutenant Mourneer was going to meet me at the general's office to tell him what he knew. I didn't make it as I was taken by Dowdneer's men. You need to find him and get him to the general before it's too late," he took a few short, sharp breaths. "If I don't make it he's your only evidence against Dowdneer."

"Will do, sir. But first I need to get you away from here. If you're found by Dowdneer's men in your current state you'll be killed for sure," said Neil. He picked up Twochelope again and they left the storeroom corridor.

They were walking along when a voice from behind them said, "What's happened to the colonel?"

Rebecca spun around and brought her rifle to bear on the speaker. He moved back a couple of steps and his hand dropped towards his weapon.

"Don't," said Rebecca.

"Who are you?" asked Neil.

"Private Bowerphille, sir."

"He's all right," said Colonel Twochelope from Neil's shoulder.

Rebecca lowered her rifle.

"Good, then I need you to take over getting Twochelope to medical," said Neil. "He's been tortured with electricity. Trust no-one, private. You may not believe this but Colonel Dowdneer has half of our soldiers under his control and is planning to take command."

"That can't be, sir."

"Trust me. He is. Now get some soldiers, that you know personally, and protect the colonel in the medical bay until he recovers enough to give you his own orders. I repeat – trust no-one."

"Yes, sir."

"We'll try to get a list of soldiers you *can* trust to you soon," said Rebecca.

Neil and Rebecca left him to it and set off in search of Lieutenant Mourneer.

CHAPTER THIRTEEN

December 2171

Resolve / Ganymede

The community lounge on board the star-ship *Resolve* was bustling with people. It appeared that everyone, not on duty, had decided to come down at the same time. Lisa sat at her table, handed John his drink, then ruffled his bleached blonde hair.

John had been watching her advance towards them and smiled, his green eyes twinkling. "Thanks."

"Andrew's on his way," she said before taking a sip of her beer. "I think he's eyeing up the ladies."

Keith looked for Andrew and saw him talking to a brunette with shoulder length hair and a surprisingly dark tan. Andrew bent forwards slightly and said something in her ear and Keith saw her smile.

"Hey, Andy. Get over here with my drink instead of chatting up all the women," called Keith. Andrew looked round and said something else to her. She nodded and laughed then followed him over to their table.

"Give me my drink you sex pest," Keith joked as Andrew put his brother's drink on the table. He looked at the girl and said, "Watch him honey. He's a terrible flirt."

She smiled at Keith.

"Hey, grab a light bulb bro," said Andrew. "This is Roxanne. Is it all right if she joins us?"

Everyone at the table welcomed her, and Andrew relieved the table next to them of one of its chairs. They sat down. "Now, what are we talking about?" he asked.

Andrew, at thirty-one, was four years younger than his brother and looked the most like their father. He had black hair, brown eyes and was clean-shaven with a slim, athletic build.

"We were just talking about the last mission. There was hardly anything to it and we had to miss the concert because of it. I'm not happy," said Lisa pretending to pout.

"There will be other concerts, Lisa," said John.

She glared at him. "I've not been to one for ages and who knows when we'll get another chance."

"Yeah, we could all be dead tomorrow," said John.

That remark earned him a slap from Lisa. "You're terrible, John. But I love you." They kissed and when they parted John had a smile on his face.

"Has anyone heard where we're going next?" asked Andrew.

"I talked to the captain earlier," said Keith. "Apparently, there's been some trouble on Ganymede, so we're headed back there again."

"Did he say what sort of trouble?" asked John.

"No, and I didn't ask, but I'm sure we'll find out tomorrow."

Roxanne spoke up, changing the subject. "You're Neil Bolgon, aren't you?"

Keith fixed his gaze on her and said, "Yes. Yes I am."

Roxanne smiled and pulled the top of her uniform down slightly. "Can you sign my shoulder please?"

"Oh my god. Another one," said John. "You should have been a rock star or a footballer." He passed Keith the pen they kept for just this sort of occasion.

Keith leaned forward and wrote, 'To Roxanne love Neil Bolgon', then signed it underneath, being careful not to use his own name.

"Don't wash for another couple of hours and it should last you years," he said.

Andrew butted in. "Hey, do you mind. I've only just asked you out."

Roxanne looked at Andrew and smiled. "Sorry, I couldn't help myself. Two of my girlfriends have got a 'Neil Bolgon' message written on them and I saw an opportunity."

"Anyway," said Lisa. "Back to the fun. Whose round is it?" They all started laughing and the merriment resumed.

~

Ryan Ross, a 2nd Lieutenant and second-in-command of the *Resolve*, stood to attention as Captain Meade walked onto the bridge.

"Ah nice of you to join us captain. 2nd Lt Ross has been filling me in on the details of your last mission," said the general on the video screen.

[232]

"Sorry, sir. Call of nature. How can I help?" said Captain Meade.

"I have more details on Ganymede, captain. It seems that most of the tranchillions escaped, leaving a few of our soldiers' dead. I want you to bring the deceased back here ASAP, captain. That's your mission," said the general.

"Is that all, sir?"

"I want them all brought back in cryosleep, captain," he paused. "How far out are you?"

"About a day, sir."

"Okay. Just one more thing, captain. Could you get Neil to send me a transmission. I'd like to speak with him."

"Yes, sir."

"Can you make sure he does it from a secure and private access point, captain."

"Sir."

The screen went blank and Captain Meade turned to 2nd Lt Ross. "This is brilliant. We're a combat unit. First, they send us to take down some thieves, who were long-gone by the time we got there, and now we're going to be a travelling morgue."

2nd Lt Ross forced a smile and said nothing.

"Get Bolgon up here."

~

'*Warrant Officer Bolgon to the bridge,*' the tannoy boomed.

Keith got up. "I'd better see what they want. If I don't make it back before you leave, have a good time."

They all waved him goodbye. Andrew was a little merrier, as usual, than the rest but he'd also managed to

[233]

get Roxanne drunk as well. Keith left them to it and started his long journey to the bridge.

On his way, Keith noticed a female officer walking in the opposite direction. She looked mid-twenties with a lovely slim figure and brown curly shoulder-length hair. He considered her brown eyes and almost got lost in them. He smiled as she passed him then he heard her call to him. Keith stopped and faced her.

"You're Neil Bolgon aren't you, sir?"

"Yes, and you are?" he asked, not recognising her.

"Lance Corporal Henderson. Laura, if you prefer," she replied.

"Did you want something, corporal?"

"Yes, sir. I just wanted to say thank you on behalf of one of my pilots that you saved in the battle of Ganymede."

"Any time, corporal. Good job as Green Squadron leader. You deserve to be commended for your part in that battle."

"Thank you, sir. But, sir. How do you know what I did?"

"I read every report afterwards, Ms Henderson. I like to know how the soldiers around me are performing."

"It's Miss Henderson, sir," she paused, "in case you were wondering."

"I've got to go, corporal. Keep up the good work," Keith marched onwards towards the bridge.

My god she was fit, thought Keith. *If it wasn't for this disguise I'm wearing,* he let his thoughts trail off and concentrated on where he was going.

Lance Corporal Henderson shrugged her shoulders and carried on her way. *I can't win them all,* she thought.

Keith arrived at the turbo-lift and stepped inside. He pressed the button for the bridge and waited for the doors to re-open. He was met by 2nd Lt Ross.

"The general wants to talk to you. You can use my office over there. It's secure as the general requested."

Keith walked over to the office and the door closed behind him. He opened a direct link to the general's office back on the moon.

Presently, General Bolgon's face appeared on the screen. "Hello, son. Is the line secure?"

"I only have their word for it, father."

"That'll have to do. Now, how's it going, Keith?"

"It's a relief to be talking to you, sir. At least you know my real name. This is going to be a lot harder than I thought."

"Hang in there, Keith. The reason I called is that Neil has been extremely busy on Ganymede and I'm sending the *Resolve* on a clean-up mission. It looks like he had to kill a few of our own and I'm warning you just in case he was seen."

"He was disguised wasn't he."

"Yes, he was. But just in case the suit failed, or he had to switch it off for any reason. Remember, you look exactly like him. I don't want you recognised. Keep a low profile."

"How do I keep a low profile? Neil's practically a superstar. Everyone here knows him," Keith's thoughts returned, briefly, to the brunette.

"I can't intervene and request you stay on the ship. It would raise more questions. Perhaps feign illness?"

Keith could hear the general's shrug within those words. "I'll think of something. Hopefully I won't be on duty when we arrive there."

[235]

"Have you any more questions?"

"No, sir. I'll report to you later."

The screen went blank and Keith left the office to go for a lie down.

~

Keith entered his quarters, which he shared with Andrew, and found that his brother still hadn't returned from the community lounge. Every berth was the same. They consisted of two small rooms and a toilet. There was just enough space for two people to sit comfortably in the living area. The other room had space for a bunkbed and not much else.

He stripped down to just his chameleon suit, appearing to be naked, before entering the tiny bedroom and sitting on the bottom bunk.

"Wow, Neil. You really do look good naked," said a voice from behind Keith.

He looked round and saw Miss Henderson lying under his covers with just her head and shoulders on view. Keith got up and faced her. "What are you doing here? How did you get in?"

"There are ways around these security doors. Are you coming to bed or am I going to have to chase you?"

"I'm not who you think I am," said Keith.

"Nonsense, Neil. I know exactly who you are."

"I have a girlfriend and she's pregnant. I can't do this," said Keith half-heartedly. Laura sensed the indecision in his voice. She let the cover drop to her waist as she sat up, exposing her breasts.

"I saw that look you gave me earlier. Besides, it looks like you want me, Neil. Or does your cock lie."

Keith looked down and saw that he'd reacted to her before looking back towards her breasts and, finally, her smiling face. *Shit. These suits even react in this* way, he thought. She patted the bed and he couldn't resist any longer. He turned away from her, feigning a last second of indecision, and undid the convenient flap in the chameleon suit that allowed him to use the toilet without taking it off.

Keith released his own penis, which had been straining to get out, and turned back. She didn't notice the difference as he advanced towards her. She flicked the bed clothes off and opened her arms as he got on the bed with her. They kissed as she pulled him in closer and Keith was lost in his own passion. He had not had sex for quite a few years, and he was going to damn well make up for it with Laura.

~

Andrew had been invited back to Roxanne's quarters. He had left John and Lisa in the community lounge so he could spend some quality time with her. Roxanne used her key-card on the door, and it slid open. They both stumbled into her room, giggling. She helped Andrew over to a chair and sat him down.

Roxanne was thankful for the alcohol suppressant tablets she'd taken. She didn't have Neil but with Andrew being his brother maybe she could find a way to manipulate two stories and still trap him as well.

"I'll just get some wine lover," she said as she leant over and kissed him.

"Okay, Roxy. I'll be here."

When she got back to the chair, he'd fallen asleep. She sighed and set both glasses down. Roxanne pulled her micro-cassette recorder from her handbag and said, "December eleventh; have contacted Andrew Bolgon, brother of Neil, and have managed to get him alone. Neil proves too hard to ensnare. Will try to get to him through his brother."

She put the micro-cassette recorder away and watched him sleep. Then she picked up her glass of wine and settled back in her chair to contemplate her next step.

~

John and Lisa left the community lounge half-an-hour after Andrew. They held hands as they walked back to their room. John looked at Lisa as he said, "Lisa, would you like to have a baby?"

She stopped and faced him. "Are you serious, John?"

"Yes, of course I'm serious. Neil and Chloe are having one and I think it'd be lovely to be a daddy."

"But we're at war, John. I could be called into battle at any time."

"Well, if you fell pregnant then maybe you could stay at the base or we could set up a home on Earth."

"I'm not like that, John. I live for the action. You know I do. I'd be bored sitting at a desk."

"I'm not saying it'd be like that. I've not thought it through, Lisa. But it would be nice, don't you think?"

"We'd have to get married first, John. I'd want the baby to have your name."

"You'll do it then, Lisa?"

"We'll see, John. We'll see."

They entered their room and stripped off all their clothes. It had been a long day. They'd been stuck on board the *Resolve* for a while now and it was driving them crazy. They got into bed and within a few minutes were fast asleep.

~

The *Resolve* was orbiting Ganymede. Inside, there was a lot of activity. The duty rosters had just changed, and Keith, Andrew, John and Lisa were all selected to go down to the surface.

Keith and Andrew were suiting up ready to provide fighter cover. Keith noticed that Andrew looked preoccupied.

"Hey, Andy. Is something wrong?" he asked.

Andrew raised his head. "No – not really."

"Come on. Something's wrong. Tell me."

"I do have a problem, but I don't want to burden you with it."

"Spit it out, Andy. Come on."

Andrew hesitated and sat down with only his helmet left to attach. "I'm in trouble," he sighed. "I've got myself into a situation and the only way out *is* to involve you."

Keith sat next to Andrew. "Tell me about it."

"Do you remember Roxanne?"

"Of course. Who could forget that tan she had."

"Well, she's causing me trouble, Neil. She only hooked up with me because she was after something."

Keith waited for him to continue.

"She wants you, Neil. She wants you, alone, in her room or she tells the captain what I get up to with the women on board."

"I keep telling you not to have sex with crew members. It's against regulations," he stopped short remembering what he'd done only a few short hours ago. Keith looked up and saw Andrew staring at him.

[239]

"Tell her I'll meet her after the mission – but in the community lounge. Don't worry, Andrew. Everything will be okay."

Andrew looked at his watch and stood up. "We still have half-an-hour before we leave. I'll go and find her. Be right back."

Keith was glad to be alone for a while. He needed time to think about what he had done. Laura had been great, but she thought she'd slept with Neil. If he took it to its natural conclusion it could only be trouble. His only hope was that Laura had taken it for a 'one-night stand' and wouldn't take it any further. He closed his eyes as he thought about her.

"Penny for your thoughts," said a female voice.

Keith opened his eyes and saw Laura standing in front of him. "Hello, Laura. How are you?"

"Brilliant, Neil. You were amazing. We must do it again sometime."

Keith cringed. He really wanted to, but he knew he couldn't. The only way out of this was to tell her the truth and hope she still wanted him afterwards. But now was not the time.

"You were fantastic, Laura, and I'd love to sleep with you again but first I need to tell you something," he stopped as she sat next to him and she reached for his hand.

"You can tell me anything, Neil."

Keith carried on with his original train of thought. "But I can't tell you until after the mission and I hope you won't hate me, the real me, once you know."

"What could you possibly tell me that would make me hate you, Neil?"

[240]

"It's a distinct possibility, Laura. I hope you'll understand. Look, just come and find me when we're back on board and I'll tell you everything, I promise."

Laura let go of his hand and lifted his chin upwards slightly. They kissed again then she left to get ready for her part of the mission.

A movement in the shadows at the far end of the corridor caught his eye and Keith got up to investigate. By the time he stood where he'd seen the movement there was no sign of anyone, so Keith walked back to his seat to wait for Andrew.

~

John and Lisa boarded the shuttle which would take them to Ganymede. They didn't expect any trouble on this mission. But they were to provide protection for the medical team who were going to replenish supplies at the base. Their job also involved providing cover for the team who were bringing the bodies back for a proper burial on Earth.

"You look upset, Lisa," said John.

"What. Oh no, no it's nothing."

"Is it about what we discussed yesterday?"

"Of course not, John. I… I saw something earlier that has shocked me, that's all."

"Come on, Lisa. Spill it. Nothing shocks you."

"If I tell you I need you to promise me you won't do anything about it. Do you promise?"

"How can I promise if I don't know what I'm promising about."

"All right, John. Just leave it then."

"Okay, Lisa. I promise. Now tell me. The suspense is killing me."

[241]

"I saw Neil talking to a female officer earlier. I don't know who she was because she had her back to me," she stopped talking now that she was getting to the heart of the matter. She really didn't want to tell John about it.

"Come on, Lisa. Tell me."

"They kissed okay! They kissed and then she left him, and I took off."

"Are you sure it was Neil?"

"Of course, I'm sure."

"How could he do this to, Chloe? Do you think he's slept with her?"

"I would imagine so, John. It wasn't a brotherly – sisterly kiss."

"I'm going to talk to him," said John, rising from his seat.

Lisa held his arm and pulled him back down. "You promised, John. Don't say anything – please."

"I suppose it'll keep. But I'm going to confront him about it, Lisa. Make no mistake about that."

They finished suiting up ready for their mission on Ganymede.

~

Andrew walked back into the changing room and found Neil waiting for him. He smiled at Keith and said, "It's done. She'll meet us in the community lounge when we get back."

"Okay, Andy. Let's go. It's nearly time to launch."

They put on their helmets and typed their codes on their wrist-pad's. Both suits hissed as they pressurised. Then they walked into the hanger bay where their fighter, *Star Cruiser One*, was berthed.

They gave each other the thumbs-up sign and climbed aboard the fighter. Once they were in and harnessed, Keith closed the canopy and they were ready for take-off. Keith switched on the comms and said, "Is everyone ready?"

All nine fighters of Red Squadron answered with a 'Yes, sir' and then Keith opened the channel to transmit to everyone.

"Are you ready, Green Squadron?"

"Yes, sir," replied Lance Corporal Henderson – the Green Squadron leader.

"Stick to the plan and everything will be fine," said Keith. He switched on the engines and *Star Cruiser One* lifted off the floor. The rest of Red Squadron followed suit and all ten blasted out into space. Red Squadron settled into a defensive formation around the first shuttle and Green Squadron appeared from their launch bay and did the same with the second shuttle.

"Commence Operation TM. Bring everyone back safely," said Captain Meade over the radio. They all increased their thrust and set off on their flight down to the surface.

~

There were now only four tranchillion prisoners in the prison. They had either been wounded or knocked unconscious during the escape. After a medical examination, they'd been put back in their cells. There were also five humans imprisoned. They had attempted to kill the remaining tranchillions because they'd all lost friends and needed someone to blame.

The two shuttles and twenty escorting fighters touched down next to the prison building and soldiers

[243]

started pouring out of them. 2nd Lt Ross was greeted by the base commander.

"Welcome, Lt Ross. The deceased are this way. If you would like to climb aboard," said the commander.

2nd Lt Ross climbed aboard the astroport and the commander sat next to him. "Are you okay, Lieutenant?"

"Yes. I just don't like coming to these outposts. I prefer to stay on the ship."

"You won't be here long. It's not far."

The pilots were to stay with their fighters. Keith and Andrew got out of their cockpit and sat on the tarmac, their backs against the front landing strut. John's unit had been assigned to go with 2nd Lt Ross and followed behind the astroport. They arrived at the medical building and 2nd Lt Ross followed the commander inside.

There was a sombre atmosphere to the proceedings as 2nd Lt Ross signed the relevant paperwork. There was no laughing or talking going on – it was time to pay their respects to the soldiers that had lost their lives.

"All of the cryosleep chambers have been fitted with anti-grav units. I hope that will make it easier for you, Lieutenant," said the commander.

"It will, Commander."

"Why has the general ordered for them to be put into cryosleep?"

"I have no idea. All I've been told is to bring them back ASAP. Your medical supplies should be in place by now and I'm anxious to get going. Goodbye, Commander," 2nd Lt Ross left the medical building followed by the strange procession of soldiers and cryosleep chambers.

Once all the chambers were loaded, they set off immediately for the waiting shuttles. 2nd Lt Ross didn't want to hang around for too long on Ganymede. He didn't like it here at all.

Keith got up as soon as he saw the astroports returning. "Get up, Andrew."

Andrew scrambled to his feet and stood to attention as 2nd Lt Ross got out of the astroport.

"Get these chambers loaded quickly people," ordered the lieutenant. He walked back aboard his shuttle and waited for the return journey to the *Resolve*.

Keith and Andrew climbed aboard their fighter and went through their pre-flight preparations. The rest of the pilots were busy doing the same. The last of the chambers were loaded aboard the shuttles and 2nd Lt Ross gave the order for them to launch.

~

Keith and Andrew got down from their fighter and headed for the changing room. Keith had just finished tying his laces when Andrew exited his cubicle.

"I've just got to put my boots on then we can go," said Andrew.

"Go where?" asked Keith.

"To the community lounge. You haven't forgotten, have you? You promised."

"Oh yeah. No, I haven't forgotten, Andy. We'll go when you're ready."

Andrew finished tying his boots then they made their way to the community lounge. It was busy again although that probably had something to do with it being the only place for entertainment on the ship.

"We'll have to make this quick," said Keith.

"Why's that?"

"Because we're still on duty."

"Look, over there," Andrew was pointing. "She's over there."

They sat at her table and waited for her to speak. She looked at them and a smile crept onto her face, her eyes twinkled. Neither returned the smile.

"So, you turned up then," said Roxanne.

"What are you after?" asked Keith.

"Why do I detect animosity here?"

"Why do you think?" replied Andrew.

"Look, if all I'm going to get is attitude then we can forget our deal," she started to rise. "I'm off to see the captain."

"Who are you?" asked Keith.

"You know who I am," Roxanne sat back down.

"I know that you said your name was Roxanne, but I want to know what you're doing here," said Keith.

"I'm a soldier, I… I don't understand what you're on about."

"You're no soldier," said Keith pointing at her. He leaned forward. "Now, what are you doing here?"

Roxanne had started sweating and, for the first time in her career, she began to get nervous. She was not used to having her questions turned on her.

"That's it," she stood up. "I'm going to the captain."

"Hey, Neil! I want a word with you!" called John Lyderattle who had just entered the community lounge. "Is this another of your hussy's?"

Keith looked towards his friend who was striding towards them.

"What are you on about, John?" asked Keith.

"You were seen kissing another woman. An officer, no less."

[246]

It was Keith's turn to feel the burn of questions being fired at him. He looked around and saw everyone staring.

"How could you do that to Chloe you tosser," he continued to advance towards Keith.

"Do what? I don't know what you're on about, John."

Roxanne was elated. This was more than she could have hoped for. The great Neil Bolgon cheating on his pregnant girlfriend.

Keith stood and faced John, but he was pushed back into his seat with some force.

"Are you saying that Lisa is a liar, Neil? She's the one who saw you."

Keith got up again as he said, "Please, John. Not here. Let's sort this out in private."

John went to push Keith back into his chair, but he reacted and grabbed John's arm. He twisted it round slightly and, with his other hand, applied pressure to the elbow of John's out-stretched arm, forcing him, face down, onto the table.

John now had his head pressed against the table with his arm held out straight behind, controlled by Keith. He couldn't move and that's when Lisa stepped in. She kicked Keith hard in the ribs which made him let go of John.

"Get off him!" she screamed at Keith as she jumped and spun backwards in mid-air, catching Keith with a vicious back-kick to his stomach. He stumbled backwards against the wall – scattering some of the nearest onlookers. Keith's replicater fell from its socket and clattered onto the floor.

Lisa's follow-up attack never came. This round metal object had just appeared as if from nowhere and, even more amazing to everyone in the room, Neil began to change. The clothes he was wearing began to sag and a mask materialised on his head.

"Oh shit," said Keith.

"Who are you?" asked John who had now stood back up. "And where's Neil?"

Keith tried to make his escape. He bent and picked up the replicater then ran for a gap in the spectators, but John was too quick for him and he was knocked to the floor with a well-placed leg-sweep. He looked up and saw Laura staring at him open-mouthed.

"Secure him," ordered John. He removed the chameleon mask, and everyone saw Keith for the first time. He had greying black hair and a few wrinkles on his face.

"Take him to the captain."

Keith, without the replicater to help, could do nothing and was marched off down the corridor with Andrew, John, Lisa and two other soldiers guiding him towards the bridge.

Roxanne walked in the opposite direction to record what she'd seen. She would find out who the impostor was and uncover what was going on. Then she would have the biggest story of her career and there was nothing her rival, Suzanne Cox, could do about it.

"What is this?" asked John as he turned the replicater over in his hands.

"I can't tell you I'm afraid," replied Keith.

"Maybe you can tell the captain then."

"You don't need to be so rough with me," said Keith as he stumbled forward from a push in the back.

"Are you a spy?"

"I will not answer any questions."

They continued towards the bridge in silence.

~

The turbo-lift arrived at the bridge and the group were taken to Captain Meade's office by 2nd Lt Ross. Keith was placed in a chair in front of the captain's desk while Andrew stood behind and to the side of him. John and Lisa stood guard at the door and Ross left the room, looking for Captain Meade.

A minute passed until the door opened again and Captain Meade, followed by 2nd Lt Ross, entered the office.

"What's going on here and who is this man? I don't recognise him," said the captain.

"I'm with military intelligence," said Keith. "I'm actually on a mission right now which I've just failed. For now, that's all I can reveal. You need to contact General Bolgon and he'll clear this up."

"Okay, what's your name and rank?" asked Captain Meade.

"I'm Staff Sergeant Keith Turnball," he replied.

"Keith Turnball. Keith... I've heard that name before," said the captain.

"I was part of the crew that first explored Anthera, sir."

"Bullshit," came a retort from the back of the room. "That was over a hundred years ago."

Without turning around Keith said, "We left earth in twenty-fifty-two when I was twenty-four. Fifty-eight years later we landed on Anthera and were attacked. We left, having hardly gathered any information about the planet and another fifty-eight years later we arrived back on a world that had completely changed. We were in cryosleep for those one-hundred-and-sixteen years so, although I was born in thirty-one, yes – one-hundred-and-forty years ago, I'm actually only twenty-seven."

John stayed quiet this time and concentrated on guarding the door. Captain Meade opened a link to General Bolgon's office. After a few seconds had passed the general appeared on screen.

"What's wrong, captain?"

"We have a stranger on board and would like you to confirm his story, sir," said the captain. He pressed a button and another, larger, screen mounted on the wall behind him came to life.

"What's happened, Keith? And, more importantly, what have you told them?"

"The replicater fell out, sir. I haven't told them anything specific, sir."

"Okay, Keith," the general turned his attention to the captain. "Captain Meade – clear the room except for Keith. This is for your eyes only, understand."

"Yes, sir," said the captain and he signalled for everyone present to leave. They all filed out and Captain Meade was told about Neil's current mission.

"You mean it was actually Neil who killed all these soldiers we have on board."

"It's quite possible that Neil is responsible for most, if not all, of them captain. I'm awaiting his return to get his report before I pass judgement on the situation."

"Okay, sir. I won't say anything although Neil has a few good friends on board who'll want to know where he is."

"Just tell them he's on a classified mission, captain."

"Okay, sir."

The screen went blank and Captain Meade turned to Keith. "Well, Staff Sergeant Turnball. You'd better change into a uniform that fits and we'll put that suit in my secure room until we get back. You can continue to use officer Bolgon's room – dismissed."

"There's one thing you need to know, sir."

"What's that, Turnball?"

"There's another stowaway on board, sir. Her name's Roxanne and she's in her early twenties with blue eyes, shoulder-length brown hair, about my height and has a dark tan."

"Are you sure, Turnball?"

"She was trying to set up Andrew Bolgon, sir. Although I think she was after Neil. Other than that, I can't say, sir."

"I'll investigate it, Turnball. Is there anything else?"

"No, sir."

"Dismissed."

Keith got up and left the office to get changed.

CHAPTER FOURTEEN

December 2171

Anthera

After four days of fighting, Colonel Dowdneer was undoubtedly winning. His victory seemed inevitable, but Neil was determined not to lose his only real ally amongst the tranchillions.

He was running as fast as he could with Colonel Twochelope draped over his shoulder. The original unit of six soldiers accompanying him were now reduced to three. It had been a hard fight to retrieve the colonel from the medical bay.

A laser blast hit the wall above his head and Neil sank to one knee as he pointed his pistol in the direction the shot had come from. He fired twice then forced himself back to his feet and continued, trying to keep up with the three tranchillions in front of him. One of them stopped and turned as he crouched behind some cover. He took out two more of their pursuers then threw a grenade down the corridor. It hit the wall and disappeared around the corner.

The soldier stood and ran after Neil as the explosion from the grenade ripped apart some more of the ship's walls. Ahead of Neil, one of the soldiers took a shot in the shoulder and dropped his rifle. The soldier next to him took out the threat and was kneeling beside him covering the front. Neil stopped next to the downed soldier and looked at the wound.

"You'll make it soldier. Now on your feet, we need to get out of here," Neil encouraged him to stand. The injured soldier struggled to his feet, holding his shoulder, before reclaiming his rifle with his two left arms. His shoulder was painful, but it was nothing that couldn't be fixed.

"Can you shoot straight with your left?" asked Neil.

"I'll do my best, sir."

Neil lowered Colonel Twochelope from his shoulder and said, "You carry him on your left side and let me worry about the enemy." He lifted the colonel onto the injured soldier's shoulder, who winced slightly as he took the weight, then took his weapon. Neil now held a rifle with his top pair of hands and two pistols in his bottom pair. They moved on with not far to go now.

They came to a point where two corridors crossed. After the first soldier passed the junction Neil saw movement on both sides of him. The ambush was

[253]

sprung, and Neil fired in both directions wasting only three shots.

The soldier carrying the colonel rushed past and the third soldier caught up with Neil. They both ran after the others.

Neil dropped one of his grenades before he turned the last corner in the sprint for the safety of the bunker. One pursuing tranchillion appeared and fired one shot before the grenade exploded, tearing him to shreds.

"Nearly there!" shouted Neil. They could see the open bunker door ahead of them. They were the last of the loyal tranchillions left that had any chance of making it there. After they were through, the general would order the door closed but there was no choice. They were losing too many people and the general had decided to make a stand at the bunker.

The heavily armoured door closed behind them. For the time being they were safe as there was no weapon powerful enough to penetrate it. The injured soldier was led over to the medical equipment and Colonel Twochelope was carried over to a bed in the medical area. Hopefully rest was all he needed.

Neil sought out General Zemorphoride. He stopped in front of him and saluted. The general looked up from the list he was reading.

"You made it back with Colonel Twochelope?"

"Yes, sir. He seems to be fine. Just needs some rest, sir."

"Did we lose any more men, major?"

"Three were killed and one injured, sir."

"At least we got Colonel Twochelope back," he paused then held up the list. "This list. How accurate do you think it is?"

"Very accurate, sir. There were only ten people we weren't sure about and that was only because we ran out of time. Lt Carphide is checking off the list as we speak so we'll soon know how many are left."

"Very good."

After a few seconds, Neil decided to ask the general a question that had been bothering him since they had started gathering at the bunker. "Sir, is there another way out of here?"

"Yes, but it's dangerous. And you'll not be able to get back in the same way," a frown creased his forehead. "Why do you ask, major?"

"Because we'll die here eventually if we don't figure a way out, sir."

"I'm still hoping our people will find us," said the general.

"They will find Colonel Dowdneer – who can make up any story he likes," replied Neil.

General Zemorphoride hadn't contemplated that when he led them all here. A sudden realization that he'd condemned them all to death didn't help matters.

Neil knew what he was thinking and said, "It's not your fault, sir. If you'd not led us here most of us would be dead already."

"Why is he doing this? I don't understand. He was my best friend."

"He wants to take over, but he won't stop there. If it's possible he'll take over every planet he comes across. Your..." he stopped himself. "Our entire race will become feared throughout the galaxy until he picks on someone that is stronger than us," Neil seemed to be getting away with his slip.

"What makes you think that?"

[255]

"I know that's what he's doing," he glanced at Rebecca before continuing. "Lt Carphide is psychic, sir. For the last week, we've been walking among every soldier here and she has been reading their minds."

The general looked at Lieutenant Carphide. "Bring her to me."

Neil walked over to Rebecca. She'd just finished checking her list as he stopped next to her. She smiled.

"I've told Zemorphoride about you being psychic," the smile faded, "and now he wants to see you," said Neil.

"Great."

Rebecca walked over to General Zemorphoride with Neil close behind. She held out the amended list for Zemorphoride to take and said, "The list is complete. Everyone here is loyal to you. You only have to be wary of Lt Mourneer, sir."

"Why is that, lieutenant?"

"He originally joined Dowdneer but defected back to us. There is a small possibility that, when under pressure, he could turn again."

"Is everyone on the list here?"

"After crossing off the dead, eleven more soldiers are absent, sir."

General Zemorphoride took the list and scanned down it.

"I fear they're either dead or being forced to work with the colonel," continued Rebecca.

"Thank you, Lieutenant Carphide. Major Xenorphide has told me about your – ability. Is there any way you can show me how it works?"

"I can't show you how to use it, sir. I was born with it. But I can prove that I am psychic."

"Go on."

Rebecca closed her eyes and concentrated on the general. "Start thinking about anything, sir. Like clothes, colours, food, drink or numbers and I'll repeat what you think."

The general looked at Neil who nodded back to him.

"Yes," said Rebecca to his unasked question. "Red ... thirty-four ... seven ... blue ... pink ... no I'm not ... yes, of course I am. Okay, sir," she opened her eyes again and looked at him.

"That was amazing, lieutenant. I'm going to have you by my side if we get out of this. No-one will be able to lie to me again with you around."

"I think we've confirmed how we knew about everything," said Neil. "Now we must come up with an escape plan, sir. I have some ideas that'll need your approval. But first, I need to see the way out before we can plan anything."

~

"They've escaped into a bunker, sir," said the runner standing before him.

"Get five soldiers to stand guard and if anyone comes out, shoot to kill. Tell the rest of the squad to continue their sweep of the ship," replied Dowdneer.

He was leaning back in the general's chair with his feet on the desk. Everything was going as expected. The one surprise though was Major Xenorphide. The way he'd rescued Colonel Twochelope with only six soldiers to help him was, he had to admit, impressive. But he was now trapped in the bunker with the rest of Zemorphoride's loyal soldiers. All he had to do was wait for the Emperor's troops to find them. Then he could execute part two of his plan.

[257]

The average lifespan of a tranchillion was around three-hundred years and at only two-hundred-and-one he still had plenty of time to see his dreams come to fruition.

"Has anyone found Lt Mourneer yet?" asked Dowdneer.

"He seems to have disappeared, sir," said Lt Col Maverphoride.

"Does there appear to be anyone still opposing us?"

"Not many now, sir. They'll either join us or die."

"Right then, I have a new job for you, Marsup. I want you to find someone who can assess the ships capabilities. I need to know if it can be fixed and what parts are needed, if so. When help arrives, we can hand them a list of what we need and get this thing going again."

"I'll get right on it, sir," said Marsup. He left Colonel Dowdneer's new office to start his search for a suitable candidate for the colonel's new task.

Once I've taken over, my first target will be this system. They've caused me so much trouble. It'll be a pleasure to squash them with the full might of my military, thought Colonel Dowdneer.

The colonel switched on the surveillance footage of the recent interrogation of his three least favourite tranchillions. He watched with pleasure as that interfering idiot, Tchzor Twochelope, wriggled and screamed with pain from the electricity passing through his body. He licked his lips as he saw the fear, once again on Capustri Carphide's face. He started laughing as he watched Xornin Xenorphide, tied to the rack, being held under water before he was rudely called away by General Zemorphoride.

[258]

He continued to watch and eventually saw Xornin's escape. He sat back in his chair. None of this helped. It just made him angry again.

~

"It's an airlock," said Neil.

"Yes," said General Zemorphoride. "But the problem is due to the position in which we crashed. There's a long drop to the ground and no way to get back up once you're out."

They stepped away from the airlock and closed it again. They began walking back down the passage that led to the bunker.

"My plan would still work. We just need to amend it slightly," said Neil.

"Go ahead then, major. Tell us this plan of yours. Whatever you manage to do, we still have only one-hundred-and-eleven soldiers here against three to four-hundred of Dowdneer's troops," said General Zemorphoride.

"I can get thousands more soldiers to help if my plan works. But first, I need a lot of trust and understanding from everyone here," said Neil.

"You already have everyone's trust and most of them respect you as well."

They stepped, one by one, through the narrow doorway back into the bunker. The general sat in his makeshift head-chair and Neil walked into the centre of the room. He closed his eyes and took a deep breath. Then he played his final card. Either this would work or both he and Rebecca would be dead within the next five minutes.

Neil waved Rebecca over. "We're both humans. We are wearing advanced suits that change our appearance. Let me assure you that both Captain Xenorphide and Staff Sergeant Carphide are safe and well back on our moon."

"What are you on about Xornin? This is no time for jokes," said the general.

"This is no joke, sir. When I reveal myself, I won't be able to understand you, so I'll need you to bear with me while I transform back."

There were whispers going around the watching tranchillions while they waited to see where Xornin was going with his fantasy.

Neil reached down and held the replicater while Rebecca did the same. Neil nodded to her and they removed their replicaters at the same time. Slowly they changed into their normal selves to the astonishment of the tranchillions. The shocked silence turned to a loud noise as they all started shouting at once. Some were calling for their death and others for their arrest.

They plugged their replicaters back in and transformed into their tranchillion disguises. One of the tranchillions suddenly charged at Neil but he moved to one side and caught him in a painful hold which twisted one arm up behind his back while Neil used one of his other arms to control the tranchillion by his neck.

"We don't want any violence," said Neil calmly. "We just want to help and try to stop this war between our species."

Another tranchillion rushed out of the crowd and Neil used a front kick on him without releasing his hold on the first one. The tranchillion doubled up as he felt the full force of Neil's kick to his stomach. The crowd of tranchillions were slowly closing the gap, getting ready to rush him and beat him with their numbers.

"Stop!" shouted General Zemorphoride. "Stop at once! That is an order!"

The crowd stopped advancing and even backed off slightly. General Zemorphoride rose and walked the short distance towards Neil. "Let him go, human."

Neil released the tranchillion who walked quietly back to the crowd. He waited to see what the general was going to do.

"This is even more unbelievable than what Colonel Dowdneer has done. How many of my soldiers have you killed, human?"

"Quite a few before I found out the truth about this war. The only ones since then have been in self-defence and they were Colonel Dowdneer's follower's, sir."

"What is your name and rank, human?"

"Neil Bolgon – Warrant Officer Class one, sir."

"You're a very brave soldier, Neil. Revealing your identity when there is no way of escape is truly outstanding."

"Sir," called one of the tranchillions from the crowd.

"Yes soldier, do you have something to add to this discussion?" said the general.

"Sir. I've seen, first-hand, what this soldier can do. He rescued most of our soldiers' single handed from his own people. He even had to kill a few of them. In my opinion, he's on our side and I'd gladly follow him into battle any time. He's the best soldier I've ever seen. It doesn't matter that he's an alien. I'd give my life for him."

"I agree," said another voice from the crowd. This was followed by voice after voice all agreeing to let Neil and Rebecca live and fight alongside them.

[261]

"It seems you have quite a following, Neil Bolgon," said General Zemorphoride. "Everyone is to leave the humans alone for now. Let us hear Neil's plan."

Zemorphoride sat back down and waved Neil and Rebecca over to him. "Sit please."

Neil and Rebecca sat at the makeshift table and began to plan their strategy for defeating Colonel Dowdneer.

"I'll need to take a few soldiers, sir. Mainly flight crew so we can fly the battleport back," said Neil.

"You'll need at least twenty to fly it properly. We should have enough amongst us. Also, I think another fifteen soldiers should go to make sure you get to the battleport," suggested the general.

"I'd prefer as small a squad as possible. It will make it easier to remain undetected by Dowdneer's forces. I take it your flight crew are trained in combat as well," said Neil.

"Of course – just not as intensely as the soldiers."

"Right, if that's the case I'll settle for twenty-five overall."

"There's another problem," said the general. "There are only ten suits here. How do you propose to get them all to the battleport?"

"I'll go with four of your best soldiers. We can get the suits, load them into a rover, and bring them back."

"If you're not seen it should work, but there's still the matter of the distance between the airlock and the ground to consider."

"I'm sure we must have the materials here to manufacture a rope of some sort. Attach a platform big enough to hold the suits and pull them back up that way."

"Let's get started on the rope," said General Zemorphoride.

~

Private Bowerphille knelt over the dead body of his best friend and took a moment to mourn him. He was in the medical bay where, until recently, he'd been guarding Colonel Twochelope. He stood and opened a cupboard drawer. Inside, there was a variety of medical items. He took out a bandage and a roll of tape. Then he opened the drawer next to it and removed a bottle of sterilised water. He dropped his trousers and checked his wound then tied some of the bandage tightly around his leg to stem the bleeding.

Next, he poured some water over his wound and used a piece of cloth to clear the blood away. More sticky, yellow blood started dribbling down his leg while he dampened a fresh piece of cloth. He placed the damp cloth over the wound and wound the bandage around the cloth. He secured the bandage with the tape and pulled his trousers back up. With the bleeding contained he filled a bag with essential medical supplies then picked up his rifle and took what remaining clips he could find from his friend's body.

He'd been knocked unconscious by a grenade and mistook for dead by Dowdneer's soldiers during the battle to save Colonel Twochelope. He'd briefly seen the colonel being hauled over Major Xenorphide's shoulder before he blacked out. He just had to hope the major's team had got him to safety, but he doubted he would ever know. Not now.

Bowerphille peeked out of the medical bay doorway and saw no one around so he hurried as quietly as he could in the direction of the loading bay. His plan was to get as close to the vehicles as possible and wait for a

[263]

chance to get away. Where to, he had no idea, but if he stayed here, he would either die or be forced to do Colonel Dowdneer's bidding.

Bowerphille crept around a corner. He didn't have far to go now for which he was thankful as he felt weak from the loss of blood. There were two soldiers walking towards him. He shot them before they could react then searched their bodies, finding some clips, before carrying on towards his destination.

There were only minimal guards at the loading bay and Bowerphille kept a low profile. He slipped through the doorway, once a guard had passed by, and made his way to one of the side rooms using cover to keep himself concealed. He entered the room and found a dark corner to sit in. He needed to rest again as the injury he'd sustained was sapping his strength the more he used his leg.

~

Colonel Dowdneer hadn't left his new office since he'd taken over. Everything was going well and there were only some small isolated cases of resistance left. He kept some pressure on the bunker door to make sure they didn't get any ideas of escape. The rest of his soldiers were doing a fine job of patrolling the corridors.

A runner knocked on the door.

"Enter," said Dowdneer.

The runner handed over the message and waited. Dowdneer finished reading it and wrote a new one on the notepad.

"Find Lt Col Maverphoride and give him this," said Dowdneer as he handed the notepad back to the runner. He stood and gathered the plans that Lt Mourneer had drawn up. He put them in a secure case which used voice recognition to unlock it.

Dowdneer strode over to the door and left the office. Four security guards fell in behind him. He walked to the nearest lift and selected the lowest level which read 'GARAGE & MAINTENANCE'.

When the lift doors opened, two of the guards stepped out first checking for hostiles. There were none so the colonel exited the lift followed by the other two guards. They resumed formation and carried on until they arrived at the maintenance doors. Dowdneer entered the maintenance room and looked at all the drilling machines that were being made.

"Who's in charge here?" asked Colonel Dowdneer.

A tranchillion looked up from the corner of the room. He was going over the blueprints of the machines with a couple of advisers. "I am, sir."

Dowdneer walked over to him and glanced at the blueprints then said, "How's it going?"

"Fine. We should be on schedule to start drilling tomorrow."

"Are any of them ready?"

"Just one, but the other two will be completed by morning, sir."

"I want the one that's completed to be moved over to the caves as soon as possible. The sooner we get started the better."

"Yes, sir. I'll arrange for the drill to be moved out within the hour."

"Very good, corporal. Carry on," he left for the loading bay.

He saw signs of battle on the way there. The dead had been left where they fell, and he saw some signs of a recent battle. One of the tranchillions groaned and moved slightly. The colonel rolled him onto his back to check his wounds.

"You're dying. Nothing can stop that," said Dowdneer as he released his pistol from its holster. He aimed and fired then rolled the body back onto its front.

"I want whoever is responsible for this found."

"Sir, the comms has just come back online," said one of the security team.

"Get in touch with Maverphoride and find out if he knows about this."

They arrived at the loading bay and entered. Dowdneer saw three rovers being prepared for the transport of the drills.

"Sir, Lt Col Maverphoride has just reported back. He's got a good team together for the damage assessment and reports that the comms system seems to be working."

"Give me that," Dowdneer pointed to the earpiece in the guard's ear. He quickly handed it to the colonel. Instead of fixing it to his head, Dowdneer held it to his ear.

"This is Colonel Dowdneer. The 'maintenance & loading bay' patrol is down, Marsup. Do you know anything about it?"

"No, sir," replied Marsup.

"I want all runners re-assigned to more useful duties now the comms are working again. By the way, Marsup. What was wrong with them?"

"They'd been damaged, but it was extremely easy to fix. I don't know why the general didn't get them back online, sir."

"Probably because he preferred the old way or, maybe, there could be a deeper problem," Dowdneer paused for thought. "Marsup, get the engineer to check the system thoroughly then get back to me when he has a report."

"Okay, sir. Do you want me to investigate the patrol problem?"

"No, Marsup. I'll deal with it myself. Speak to you later," Dowdneer handed back the earpiece and looked round the loading bay.

"Search for any soldiers that may be hiding around here," said Colonel Dowdneer.

His security team started their search.

~

The rope was completed, and Neil's team were suited up and ready to go.

"Good luck, Neil," said General Zemorphoride.

Neil saluted the general and turned to Colonel Twochelope. "Be ready for our return colonel. We may not have much time."

"I'll be staying with the general to help defend the bunker. In case I don't see or hear from you again, good luck and hurry back with those re-enforcements. Oh, once again, thank you for rescuing me twice. I really do owe you, Neil. You're a damn good soldier."

"Thank you, sir. I *will* see you again. Just make sure you don't die while I'm gone," they both smiled and gave each other a brief hug. Neil turned to Rebecca and held out his arms. She moved in closer and they hugged.

"You'll be safe with the general and the colonel, Rebecca," he said quietly into her ear. "I'll see you once we have the suits."

[267]

"Okay, Neil. Hurry back."

They parted and Neil stepped through the narrow doorway to join the rest of his squad. They all put on their helmets and checked each other's suits were airtight then entered the airlock. The rope had already been tied to a secure point, but Neil gave it a hard yank to make sure. It held and he let go.

He walked over to the outer airlock door and waited for the signal from the only tranchillion in the airlock that wouldn't be going. He had the same amount of air supply as they did and was going to stay in the airlock to watch for their return.

Neil pressed the button to release the outer door and the air in the room was vented out before the door slid open, revealing the empty vacuum of space. One of Neil's team had picked up the rope and dropped it over the side. Neil leant out to see if it was long enough but, due to the angle of the ship, the rope disappeared underneath.

"I'll go first to see how far the rope reaches," said Neil. "I'll be back shortly," said Neil. They all acknowledged him, and he grabbed the rope. He lowered himself over the side and was gone.

A minute later he reappeared. "Follow me. Thirty second gaps." He dropped over the side once again and thirty seconds later the next soldier began his descent.

As each member of Neil's team landed safely on the ground they knelt, covering all directions with their rifles. Once the last soldier was on the surface Neil gave the rope a tug and the rope started rising back up to the airlock. Neil signalled for his squad to follow him.

It was a ten-minute trek, across the landscape, to the loading bay. Once they arrived, they spread themselves out and waited for Neil's signal. He moved quietly up the ramp and stopped at the top in a crouch looking for any possible targets. A large machine was being wheeled into the loading bay.

He turned to the two soldiers on his left. "You two secure the suits and wait for the rover to come to you. Go, go."

They left in a combat crouch and disappeared inside the locker room.

Neil turned his attention to the other two. "Stay close. Only fire if fired upon."

They acknowledged then moved deeper into the loading bay. Neil worked his way slowly towards the rovers but couldn't get close enough to take one without being seen. He was wondering how they were going to do this quietly when he noticed movement near the rover that he'd mentally picked as his target.

The tranchillion seemed to be injured and was obviously trying to stay out of sight which meant only one thing to Neil. He'd be on their side. A door opened and in walked the unmistakable figure of Colonel Dowdneer. He was talking to his security guards as he approached the tranchillions pulling the large machine over to the rovers.

All the workers were facing the colonel, not looking in their direction. Neil gave the signal to move forward and they set off keeping behind cover as much as possible. The injured tranchillion saw them coming and realised they weren't Dowdneer's soldiers. He sunk to the floor in relief.

Neil stopped next to him. "I know this one. Get him on board the rover and be ready to go." Neil touched the injured tranchillion. "I thought you were dead."

[269]

"I was unconscious. Did the colonel survive?"

"Yes. He's in the bunker. Save your strength, private."

One soldier slung his rifle over his shoulder using the strap to hold it close to his body. The other soldier opened the back of the rover and got in. He made his way to the front and sat in the driver's seat, waiting to start it up. The other soldier picked up Private Bowerphille and carried him to the rover.

Neil moved down the side of the vehicle and opened the door. "Be ready to move if they see you. Otherwise, wait for my signal." Neil closed the door and, using cover, got as close to the colonel as possible. He was trying to eavesdrop.

"Carry on your search and kill him," said Dowdneer. "The rest of you concentrate on the drill. I want it out of here within ten minutes." The colonel marched out of the loading bay with his security guards.

Neil couldn't risk shooting him, however tempting, because the odds of surviving the retaliation would be slim. Besides, they still needed to keep a low profile or the security in the docking bay could be increased later, making it very difficult to get the battleport.

The drill started moving towards him. Neil retreated to the rover and nodded towards Bowerphille. "How is he?"

"He'll live. But he does need urgent medical attention. He's lost a lot of blood."

"Get back down here and help me push this," said Neil.

The soldier jumped down and they pushed the rover from behind. It was out of sight behind other vehicles and the drilling machine was acting like a mobile wall. They were breathing heavily when they finally got the rover close to the locker room. The soldier climbed back in the rover, covering the area where any likely hostility would come from. Neil ran to the locker room.

"Get the suits inside the rover and fetch an extra one, we have a survivor."

Neil picked up as many suits as he could carry and took them to the rover. He got inside and took over the watch.

"See if there's anything you can do for him," said Neil.

Once the last of the suits were loaded the two soldiers on the ground pushed the rover until it had picked up enough speed to make it to the exit ramp. Then they climbed in, closing the door behind them.

Neil looked at Bowerphille. "Hang in there. We have a medic at the bunker. You'll be all right." He looked up again and said, "Everyone save your air for a while – we'll use the air in here until we need to go back out. And help Bowerphille into a suit."

"They've spotted us, sir," said the driver.

"Okay, start it up. Let's get out of here. Hopefully they'll think Private Bowerphille is making an escape and not come after us."

The engine started and they drove out with only two laser blasts hitting the outer shell of the vehicle before they disappeared down the ramp.

"The comms are working again," said one of the soldiers.

"We can't use it. Colonel Dowdneer could intercept the transmission," said Neil.

"I could talk to them, sir," said Private Bowerphille.

They all looked at him.

"I could pretend that I've escaped in the rover and that I desperately need help. I'm sure Dowdneer won't know who's with you, sir. One of your men could have escaped with me. The general will recognise one of his soldiers. Hopefully he'll realise there's a hidden message, sir."

Neil looked thoughtful. "Okay, that will work. Use Private Bowelope for your name drop."

Private Bowerphille picked up the comms unit and attached it to his head. "Hello – is anyone hearing this? Colonel Twochelope, General Zemorphoride, is anyone hearing this?" He paused and waited for an answer.

There was none so he tried again. "This is Private Bowerphille. I have Private Bowelope with me and we're requesting help. We're in a rover escaping Colonel Dowdneer's men but I'm injured. Can anyone hear this?"

There was static coming from the speakers and he was about to try again when the crackling stopped.

"This is Colonel Dowdneer. Come back private and you'll not be harmed."

"That's a negative, sir. I've seen what you've done already. You killed my friend."

"When I find you, private. I won't kill you; I'll torture you for the rest of your life. You'd better *hope* I don't catch you."

"This is Colonel Twochelope, private. I'm sorry but we can't help you right now. Stay out of Dowdneer's reach and we'll see what we can do. We've got the message. Good luck."

"Switch it off or we'll have to put up with Dowdneer's comments," said Neil.

"Does that sound like they understood our message, sir," said one of the soldiers.

"Yes. That last part was stating what we already knew so to us the meaning was clear – they got the message," said Neil.

Several minutes later the rover pulled up under the airlock and everyone put on their helmets. Once they were air-tight again Neil opened the back door of the rover and the air was sucked out. The four soldiers of Neil's unit exited first and covered every angle then Neil followed.

"You wait there until we find the rope, private," said Neil. He looked up and saw a platform coming. It was swinging slightly, and Neil reached up to steady it once it was within range.

After it had settled on the ground, Private Bowerphille got on the platform. Neil placed a few of the suits on there as well, then tugged the rope and stood back. The rope tightened then the platform lifted off the ground.

"Good luck Private. Hang in there until we get back with reinforcements," said Neil.

"Where are you going, sir?"

"Ask Colonel Twochelope, private. He'll tell you everything."

The platform carried on rising and Neil jumped back into the rover to get the rest of the suits ready for loading.

"That platform was a good idea. We can send most of them up in one go now," said Neil.

"Sir, they've sent out a search party and are heading this way."

Neil jumped out and looked back the way they had come. "They're following our tracks." He dumped the suits on the ground. "Gather round. You," he pointed at one soldier. "Follow the rover and brush the tracks away as we go then get back to the suits and carry on loading. We'll lead them away and come back to you. The signal will be two quick flashes of the headlights."

He turned to the others. "Let's go."

They got back in the rover and reversed towards the oncoming headlights. When they had reversed far enough away from the airlock they stopped, steered to the left, and set off towards the mountains.

The soldier left behind had just finished brushing away their tracks when he saw the lead rover appear over a rise. He ran far enough from the tracks to, hopefully, be out of their headlights reach then dived to the floor and lay still.

The rovers slowed then stopped. As the soldier lifted his head to see if they'd seen him they turned away, following the new tracks. He sighed with relief that it had worked and got up. He ran back to the pile of suits and waited for the platform.

~

"Over to your right. Park it there and we'll set up an ambush," said Neil.

The rover pulled up amidst an extremely rocky patch of ground and they all got out. Neil had a quick look round then said, "You two on high ground." He pointed at the two large rocks that overlooked the whole area.

Neil nodded to the last soldier. "You're with me." They set off to take up positions immediately behind where the rovers were likely to stop. They both settled on the ground, watching and waiting.

Moments later, two rovers skidded to a stop. Their headlights were aimed at the stationary vehicle. The back doors opened on both rovers and two, two-man squads

[274]

jumped out. They circled out in different directions to surround the vehicle. Neil and soldier three crawled slowly towards the back of the rovers.

Neil gave the sign for soldier three to take out any remaining occupants in his targeted rover and Neil readied himself for the other one. Soldiers one and two saw them enter the back of the rovers and used that as the signal to fire.

One of Dowdneer's men peered inside the abandoned rover and looked back towards his partner before his head was knocked back against the vehicle with accurate laser fire from soldier one. The other soldier moved his rifle in the direction the shot had come from as he dived and rolled into a crouch. His suit started leaking air as soldier one shot him in the chest and he was knocked backwards against the rover. The next shot hit his visor and he slumped to the ground.

Soldier two had also taken out both of his targets but made the mistake of getting up. He was knocked backwards off the rock and landed with a thud as one of the drivers shot him. His body started to spasm.

The driver looked round too late and Neil shot him in the head at point blank range. Soldier three had taken too long to get to the front of the rover and was wrestling with the driver. They rolled around the back of the vehicle until they fell out onto the ground. Soldier three came off worse and lost his grip on the driver. He was kicked in the ribs and sent sprawling.

The driver pulled his pistol and aimed it at soldier three. The shot hit the floor only inches from soldier three's head as Neil tackled the driver to the floor. He had managed to hold onto his pistol and pointed it at Neil.

Neil kicked it away and stamped on the visor of the driver's helmet. A crack appeared which grew until it shattered. Neil left him to die on the floor and helped soldier three to his feet.

"Thank you, sir," said soldier three.

"Go and see if he's all right," said Neil pointing to where soldier two had fallen.

When he got there, soldier one was already crouched over soldier two. "His back's broken, I think." They signalled for Neil.

"He's in pain and his suit's leaking," said Neil. "He may be able to make it back, but I think the journey would kill him. It's your call guys."

Soldier one stood and looked down upon the stricken soldier then shot him. His body stopped twitching.

"Take a rover each and we'll get back to the ship. Nice of them to provide us with more transport, wasn't it," said Neil.

They drove all three rovers back to the airlock and, as they approached the group of tranchillions on the ground, they flashed their headlights twice then pulled up next to them. Neil got out and Rebecca walked up to him.

"Did everything go to plan?" she asked.

"Not entirely. We lost a man," replied Neil. "That still leaves us with four highly trained soldiers. We should make it."

Neil moved in front of the small crowd of tranchillions. "We need to stay undetected or it's going to get very hard. The new problem we're facing is that we now have a time limit. When those men fail to report I'm sure Dowdncer will send a much larger force to look for Bowerphille."

[276]

There were rumblings amongst the listening tranchillions.

"If we make it to the docking bay before they come looking for us it might even help," said Neil.

"How's that help?" asked one of the soldiers.

"The more soldiers they send out the less we'll have to deal with."

"You're crazy. There's still going to be hundreds of them inside."

"That's true but they think we're outside and they're also spread out over the entire ship looking for survivors."

"What are we waiting for. Let's go."

They climbed aboard the three rovers and gave the loading bay a wide berth.

~

"I can only send out two more rovers. We need to keep the others back to take the drills out tomorrow," said Colonel Dowdneer.

"I'd still recommend sending them out, sir," said Lt Col Maverphoride.

"It shouldn't have come to this, Marsup. There were only two privates in that rover and one of them was already injured."

"We'll soon know what happened, sir."

"Okay, send two. But I want you to go with them to make sure they perform properly."

"Yes, sir. We'll find out what happened. Do you still want them alive, sir?"

"Of course. Death is far too good for that traitor. I'll teach him some respect."

"I'll get it organised, sir."

Colonel Dowdneer left the loading bay and started the long trek to his office. He needed time to think. Things seemed to be going wrong again. *At least the general is still locked up,* he thought.

Colonel Dowdneer had only been back in the office five minutes when his phone started ringing. He got off the settee in the corner of the room and pressed a button on his desk as he sat down. The phone switched to loudspeaker.

"Colonel, we have found the team. They're all dead, sir. Plus, one other soldier," said Maverphoride.

"One of the privates?"

"I don't think so, sir. I think we were misinformed."

"How do you mean, Marsup?"

"There should be two rovers here, but both have been taken."

"There were at least three of them then. What do you think, Marsup?"

"It was an ambush, sir. And not the work of a couple of inexperienced privates. Those soldiers we sent out were among our best. Something is going on, sir. My guess is that it has something to do with the general."

"Is there another way out of the bunker?"

"I wouldn't have thought so, sir."

"Get back here and go through the ship's plans. Let's see if there is another way out."

"I'm on my way, sir."

~

Neil climbed onto the roof of his rover and reached up to grab the edge of the docking bay entrance. He pulled himself up just far enough so he could see into the bay. They were in luck. He couldn't see anyone in there.

They seemed to be having a lot of luck recently. The only reason they could take this short cut was because of the angle the mothership had settled into when it crashed. He lowered himself down and let go.

"There doesn't seem to be anyone in there. Good call, Sergeant. This saves us a lot of time and effort. I'll go first followed by you two," Neil pointed at two of the more experienced soldiers. "Once the area is secured the rest of you can come up and we'll take the battleport."

Everyone nodded in silent agreement. Neil looked at Rebecca and made the thumbs-up sign. She did the same and he turned back to the docking bay, reaching up once more. Neil again checked for any sign of activity then pulled himself up.

Once he was joined by the other two soldiers, they moved forwards through the force-field and entered the ship. Neil signalled for them to flank left and right while he moved through the centre. He could see the battleport he'd arrived in straight ahead.

Neil stopped at the battleport's ramp and crouched while constantly remaining alert for any hostiles. The other two soldiers signalled the all clear and stationed themselves near the two exits leading deeper into the mothership. Neil ran back to the edge and signalled the rest of the crew.

He helped them up and they made their way into the battleport. They started the launch preparations as soon as they arrived at their stations. Neil helped the last of the flight crew up and waited for the two remaining soldiers to join them.

"Sir, soldiers are approaching from the south corridor," a voice said through his headset.

"Sir, there are soldiers approaching from the north corridor as well," said the soldier guarding that entrance.

"Get back here as fast as you can, we'll cover you," ordered Neil. He signalled to the two soldiers with him to find cover and target a door each. The two soldiers coming from the exits were halfway back when the doors to the south corridor opened and Lt Col Maverphoride strode in.

Neil's covering soldiers opened fire, forcing Maverphoride to duck behind cover. The soldiers approaching from the north corridor were pre-warned when they heard the laser fire. They burst in, firing as they came. Neil scored a headshot on the first one through.

"Hurry up and get inside!" yelled Neil.

Two panels opened on the battleport and laser cannons dropped down – targeting the onrushing soldiers. Neil ducked at the sudden noise of the cannons as they opened fire above his head. Several of Dowdneer's soldiers were cut down. There was no more resistance as the cannons had Dowdneer's soldiers diving for cover. Neil rushed on board and closed the ramp.

The battleport lifted off and started moving forwards. Neil arrived on the bridge and saw an opportunity to help Twochelope and Zemorphoride a little more.

"Shoot the wall next to the force-field as we leave," he said.

The laser cannons fired as the battleport left the docking bay. The wall exploded and sparked causing the force-field to start flickering.

"Get out of here!" yelled Lt Col Maverphoride as he ran for the exit. He and only five others made it through the doors as the force-field gave way, exposing the docking bay to space. Everything not bolted down was immediately and violently sucked out.

One last soldier dived for the doors and was cut in half as the blast shields slammed down. Maverphoride looked at the top-half of the soldier and then bent over as he vomited on the corridor floor.

CHAPTER FIFTEEN

December 2171

The Moon

General Bolgon, accompanied by five people, marched towards the docking bay. The doors slid open as they approached, and the general returned the salute from both guards on duty.

"John, take Suzanne with you to the interview room and wait for us there," said General Bolgon as they entered the docking bay. John Stillson and Suzanne Cox left the group.

The general, Michael Toddwell and two armed guards carried on towards the docked starship *Resolve*. Several of the crew were already on the hanger floor going through the usual checks and Jim could see Keith and his son walking down the ramp.

As Jim drew closer, he also noticed a female soldier, in handcuffs, being led to the interview rooms. He didn't let his attention wander for long and looked back towards the soldiers exiting the ramp.

The general acknowledged the salutes as he stepped in front of Keith, Andrew, John and Lisa.

"Report to interview room one," he said. They all turned to their left and marched towards the interview room in single file. Jim looked back up the ramp and saw Captain Meade at the top. As usual he was the last off his starship. The captain noticed General Bolgon waiting for him at the bottom of the ramp and, accompanied by 2nd Lt Ryan Ross, walked down it. They stopped in front of the general and saluted.

"How did it go, captain?" asked Jim.

"Permission to speak freely, sir?" asked Daniel Meade.

"Once we're in private, captain," replied Jim.

"In that case, sir. The mission was a success."

"Good. Now let's get to the interview room and discuss what happened," he paused. "Who was the female soldier in cuffs, captain?"

They started walking towards the interview rooms. "We're not sure. All we know is that she wasn't supposed to be aboard the *Resolve*, sir."

"A stowaway, captain. How on earth did that happen?"

[283]

"I'm sure we'll find out, sir. But we were reluctant to interrogate her without your permission."

"We'll talk about this in private as well," they stayed silent the rest of the way to the interview rooms.

Suzanne and John stood as the general entered the room. Once everyone was in and settled the general commenced with the interview.

"Okay, captain. You wanted to speak freely. Go ahead."

"You also said in private," replied the captain, looking at Suzanne.

Jim followed Captain Meade's gaze. "Suzanne is our official reporter. There is nothing you cannot say in her presence."

Suzanne smiled at Captain Meade. "I'm being made to be a good little girl. Don't worry about me."

He smiled back then looked towards General Bolgon. "All right then, sir. Why did you send us out against those thieves? It was obvious we wouldn't get there on time. We ended up with a brief visit being asked questions, which we couldn't answer, by the colonists and then, finally, we're sent to Ganymede to become a travelling morgue. Both duties could have been handled by a much smaller starship and at less expense."

General Bolgon frowned but decided not to raise his voice. "I did say you could speak freely, captain so I'll look past the way you just spoke to me." He paused as he looked at everyone present. His gaze stopped on Suzanne.

"You already know about this, Suzanne. So, bear with me. What I'm about to tell you is to go no further than this room," he paused confirming their acceptance. "You also know a few of the details about Neil's mission, captain. That mission is the reason I had to send out the *Resolve*. Your initial assignment was just an excuse to get Neil away from here. I needed Keith, disguised as Neil, to be gone before the tranchillion escape otherwise there could have been complications. I'm sure you'll agree that any physical interaction with Chloe would have been extremely awkward for Keith. I didn't want to put either of them through that."

"So instead of Chloe, Keith fucked one of my officers and got caught," said Captain Meade.

"He did what!"

"Lance Corporal Henderson had sex with Keith, thinking he was Neil and Keith was too weak to say no," said the captain.

"Get Turnball and Henderson in here as soon as possible," said the general to one of the guards.

"Who else knows about this, captain?"

"Sergeant Lyderattle confronted Keith in the community lounge, sir. So, I'd say that most, if not all, of the crew know, sir."

"Oh Jesus Christ. I don't believe it," he pointed to another of his guards. "Bring Chloe Lewis here, and I want to see Sergeant Lyderattle immediately," General Bolgon got up and started pacing the interview room.

"If any details of Neil's mission have been leaked by this, I swear that I'll execute everyone responsible. This could get Neil killed if the tranchillions do have anyone feeding them information."

Everyone in the room stayed silent. No one wanted to incur the general's wrath. The door opened and in walked Keith, John and Lisa. Jim sat down once again and said, "Where's Henderson?"

[285]

"We're still trying to locate her, sir," said one of the guards.

"Well hurry up about it."

General Bolgon looked directly at Keith who seemed to shrivel away under the intense gaze. "What did you do, Staff Sergeant Turnball?"

"I'm sorry, sir. It's entirely my fault. I was weak," replied Keith.

"Did you have sex with Lance Corporal Henderson?"

"Yes, sir. I did," his eyes dropped to the floor.

"Do you realise that your actions could get my son killed," the general's voice was getting louder with every word spoken.

Keith gulped and tried to look at the general, but his shame engulfed him. "I wasn't thinking, sir. She came on to me and I said 'no' at first, but she was too irresistible."

"She thought you were Neil and you still went ahead with it. This could have split Neil and Chloe up. I… I'm furious with you Turnball!" the general had gone a bright crimson colour.

The door opened again and in walked Lance Corporal Henderson. She looked at everyone then saw Keith looking pathetically broken and realised what was going on.

"Sir, I can explain," she started to say before the general interrupted her.

"Both of you should know better than to fraternise with the other soldiers! This!" he raised both hands in the air in exasperation, took a deep breath and regained his composure. "This is what happens. And now I must sort it out," his voice was back to normal.

Jim looked at John. "Sergeant Lyderattle. As Neil's best friend, you should have handled this differently, but

[286]

I do admire your courage. Going up against Neil – you could have been hurt. If you'd handled it differently, we could have swept all this away. Now I'll have to go public to explain this whole mess."

There was a knock at the door and a guard announced Chloe's arrival.

"Ask her to wait outside," said the general. The guard closed the door again and Jim locked his fingers together while resting his elbows on the desk.

"All three of you – front and centre."

They moved into position and the general stared at them. The whole room had gone silent.

"Sergeant Lyderattle, despite your apparent lack of subtlety you will remain a sergeant. Staff Sergeant Turnball, your actions leave me no option but to demote you to sergeant. Your weakness is not an excuse. Lance Corporal Henderson, you knowingly seduced Officer Turnball, who you thought was Neil, into going to bed with you. That could have destroyed the relationship between Chloe, Neil and their unborn child. For those reasons, I'm going to demote you to the rank of private. You'll lose your command of Green Squadron and I hope this will teach you a lesson. Dismissed, all three of you."

Keith, Laura, John and Lisa left the room and walked off down the corridor.

"John, Lisa, what's going on?" asked Chloe who was waiting outside.

John looked at her and said, "You'll find out soon enough." He turned away and walked down the corridor. All of them had decided to go back to their quarters. The interview room door opened, and a guard called for Chloe to enter.

[287]

"What's going on, Mr Bolgon. Is Neil okay?" Chloe looked around the room but there was no sign of him. "He's not dead, is he?"

"No, Chloe. He's not dead," said the general. "But I do have some unpleasant news for you, and I wanted to be the one you heard it from."

~

"You can't keep me here. Why are you keeping me here? I've done nothing wrong," said Roxanne Taylor. "I demand to know why you're keeping me here!"

The guard stayed silent, staring straight ahead, not moving. The door opened and in walked General Bolgon and Suzanne Cox followed by Captain Meade. They all sat in the chairs provided.

"Guard, I think you can take those off her now," said the general.

The guard walked over to Roxanne and removed the handcuffs which had been keeping her hands behind her back. Roxanne rubbed her wrists while watching Suzanne.

"What's she doing here?" asked Roxanne.

General Bolgon looked at Suzanne. "She's with us. Do you two know each other?"

Suzanne nodded then looked at the general. "She's Roxanne Taylor, a fellow reporter at *World News*."

Roxanne gave Suzanne an evil glare. She didn't need to say anything.

"Okay, Roxanne. What were you doing on my starship?"

Roxanne stopped glaring at her rival and looked at the general. "I'm a reporter as blabber mouth over there told you. I was looking for a story."

[288]

"There are reasons we don't let reporters go on our missions. There's danger everywhere we go. You could've been killed. Also, some events need to be kept secret, at least for a little while, for security and to prevent mass panic. A concept most of you reporters seem to ignore," lectured the general.

"As a reporter, I have freedom of speech and a right to print anything I find out," said Roxanne and again she looked at Suzanne. "What's she done to deserve your favour?"

The general ignored her question and said, "What have you found out then, Miss Taylor?"

"I'm not saying anything general. You can read it in the paper."

"She has a micro-cassette recorder which she keeps all her notes on. Everything you need to know will be on there," said Suzanne.

"You bitch!" shouted Roxanne as she slammed her hands on the table and got up suddenly, reaching for Suzanne. The guard sprang into action and knocked Roxanne to the floor. Then he turned her over on to her front and planted his knee into the small of her back. Roxanne screamed out in frustration and pain as the guard caught both of her flailing arms and re-cuffed her hands behind her back.

He picked her up and forced her to sit while she continued to find as many expletives as she could remember.

"That's enough, Miss Taylor," said the general.

She carried on, giving no signs of stopping her rant. Jim nodded to the guard again and Suzanne winced as she witnessed the resulting hard slap across Roxanne's face. The ranting stopped and turned to whimpers as a

[289]

reddening handprint slowly started to appear on her cheek.

"Suzanne. Would you go through her belongings to find the micro-cassette," said the general.

"I could get in trouble if I do that," replied Suzanne.

"You won't," the general assured her. "The only person in trouble here is this young lady. I normally use the correct procedures, but I don't have the time or patience for that right now. My son's life could be in danger and I'm not above having a spoilt, annoying, foul-mouthed little bitch killed if I have to."

Roxanne looked up; a genuine look of fear showed on her face for the first time. "You wouldn't. You don't have the authority. I have a reporter's right to tell the truth. I…"

She was interrupted by the general. "Here, on this moon, I have every right to do anything. It's part of my mandate. If someone needs to disappear, they aren't seen or heard from again. If someone needs to be silenced – they don't talk. Is any of this sinking in yet or should I just have you silenced right now?"

Roxanne opened her mouth to say something then closed it again. She looked defeated and Suzanne felt for her for the first time since their rivalry began.

Suzanne found the micro-cassette recorder and rewound the tape then pressed play. At first there was some non-relevant babble until they came to her re-counting of what happened on the starship.

When they had heard everything that she'd recorded, the general looked at Roxanne again. "I don't suppose I can trust you to keep your mouth shut so, until this whole business is resolved, you'll be held, and this evidence will

[290]

be destroyed. If you cause any hassle for Chloe, Neil or me after this is over, you'll be silenced permanently."

The general waved her away and the guard took her to the detention centre.

"I'm glad I cooperated with you all those weeks ago," said Suzanne.

"I hate having to get heavy handed like that, Suzanne. But I won't have anyone jeopardize Neil or Chloe's lives."

"I understand, sir. Really I do."

"Suzanne, you write up a report about this but, again, I'll have to go over what you write. I really don't have to go into details with you do I."

"No, sir. While I believe the truth must be told, I also see the sense in covering up certain facts. We don't need to destroy people's lives."

The general smiled then drew a deep breath. "Okay everyone, I think that's enough for today. Everyone from the *Resolve* has a week off for R&R. Let your crew know captain."

Everyone filed out of the interview room, leaving John Stillson and the general alone.

"Now, John. Have the bodies been taken where I suggested?" asked the general.

"Yes, sir. Are we going there now?"

"Yes. I want to see their condition. The sooner we get started the greater the chance of success."

They left the interview room and strode off in the direction of 'Research & Development'.

~

Laura Henderson followed Keith to his quarters then called to him as he stopped to open his door. "Keith. Keith it's me, Laura. Can I have a word with you?"

Keith looked at her. "What do you want Laura? Haven't you done enough damage already."

"What! You're not the only one who lost rank today. I'm back to being a private which loses me command of Green Squadron – and it's all because of you, actually."

"What do you mean it's my fault! You seduced me, remember."

"Yes, I did. But I thought you were Neil and then you get found out which brings the whole sorry mess to General Bolgon's attention."

"I'm sorry that you lost your command, but I did try to warn you that I wasn't Neil."

Laura looked round and saw they'd gathered a little crowd. "Can we do this inside, Keith? People are watching."

"Of course, Laura. Come in," Keith opened his door and stood back to allow her into his quarters then he followed her inside and the door slid shut behind them.

"Thank you, Keith. That was all getting a little too public."

"Yeah. The general might execute us if we caused any more scandal just after being reprimanded." He gestured for her to sit which she did. "Can I get you a drink, Laura?"

"Thanks. My throat *is* dry."

"Is coke all right or orangeade – perhaps something a little stronger?"

"Orangeade would be lovely thanks. I've not had any of that in years."

Keith poured their drinks and handed Laura her glass before sitting opposite.

"I just need to know one thing, Laura."

"What's that, Keith?"

[292]

"Did you enjoy having sex with me?"

"Well, yes, of course but…"

Keith interrupted her. "Would you consider doing it again, Laura? I… I think I love you."

Laura nearly spat her drink back in her glass. "Are you serious, Keith? I mean I only slept with you because I thought you were Neil."

"I can look past that. What I need to know is do you fancy *me* at all?"

Laura looked at him. She saw the grey growing in his black hair and saw several middle-aged wrinkles on his face. "How old are you, Keith?"

"One hundred-and-forty, officially. But, due to cryosleep, my actual age is nearer twenty-seven."

"You look as though you're in your forties, Keith." *And that is being kind*, she thought. "Is something happening to your body?"

Keith felt the wrinkles with his fingertips. "Perhaps the ageing slowly catches up with you," he said.

"I'll need some time before I answer that question," said Laura. "You did kind of spring it on me."

"Do me a favour, Laura. Don't tell me yes if it's never going to happen. I think you're beautiful and I couldn't wish for a better woman in my life."

"I'd better be going, Keith. But I will give it serious consideration. See you soon," she left his quarters.

Looks like I frightened another one off, he thought to himself.

~

The lighting was dimmed, and soft music was playing, which was almost drowned out by the sound of hundreds of off duty soldiers and staff all involved in their own

[293]

private conversations. Keith looked around the room at everyone enjoying themselves and remembered the last time he was in a bar. He shuddered at the thought of what had happened.

"It's all forgotten as far as I'm concerned," said John Lyderattle. "I'm sorry for the way I treated you."

"Don't worry about it. We all make mistakes and mine was a biggie," said Keith.

"We're all mates again?" asked Lisa.

Keith held up his glass and they all did the same. "Cheers."

Andrew sat down looking glum. "I don't get it. None of these hot women will have a drink with me."

"Maybe that's for the better, Andrew," said John. "Look what happened last time. You pulled a reporter and dropped us all in the shit."

"Yeah. Sorry about that. Let's have a women free night okay," he glanced round as Lisa murmured something which he didn't catch. "Present company accepted of course," he added quickly.

"Sorry, Andy but you'll most likely have to put up with one more," said John. "I've invited Chloe for a drink."

"I meant for me, John. A women free night for me," said Andrew.

After another round had been bought, they were busy talking about where Neil might be when a female voice asked, "Is this seat taken?"

Laura Henderson was standing there looking, mostly, at Keith. There was a short silence then Andrew said, "Okay... yeah... err, sit down. I'll just get another one for Chloe." He fetched another chair then sat back down.

"I'm sorry about what happened, Keith. If you still want me, I'll be more than happy to see you again."

Keith's bottom jaw dropped open in amazement; he'd been so sure that he had lost her.

"Put your tongue away, Keith you lucky beggar," said John.

That remark earned him a slap from Lisa.

"I didn't mean anything by it, Lisa. You're the only girl for me, you know that."

"Just you remember that. Oh, and, John. You can stop staring at Laura now or we might have another fight on our hands."

"I wasn't… I wasn't… oh, okay then. I was and I'm sorry."

Lisa frowned at him and saw a worried look appear on his face then she cracked up and started laughing.

The whole table joined in the laughter and John called the waitress over for another round of drinks. Keith leaned over towards Laura and whispered in her ear, "Chloe is going to be joining us soon. You know. Neil's girlfriend. She knows what happened. If it starts getting uncomfortable, let me know and we'll leave, okay."

Laura nodded and kissed him. "Thanks for the warning, Keith." They held hands, feeling like a couple of teenagers again, but they didn't care what people thought.

Chloe turned up and sat in the chair provided. She acknowledged everyone then spotted Laura.

"Hello, I don't seem to have met you before," said Chloe.

Laura took the hand that was held out to her and shook it as she said, "Laura – Laura Henderson. Pleased to meet you."

Chloe paused, trying to think where she'd heard that name before, then it clicked. "You... you tried to seduce Neil." She looked at all her friends. "How could you sit and drink with her?"

They all looked away and Chloe turned her gaze back upon Laura with a dangerous fire burning in her eyes.

"I'm sorry about that. Really, I am. But it wasn't Neil I slept with. It was Keith." Laura looked genuinely sorry.

"Do you think that matters? You thought he was Neil at the time. I should kill you... you... you bitch."

Keith stood up. "That's enough of that, Chloe. It was all a big mistake. There's no need for insults."

"There is every need for insults you Twat!" her voice was getting louder as she got more and more angry. Chloe suddenly lashed out at Laura and pounced on her. Laura's chair tipped backwards with Chloe on top. John was up in a flash and pulled Chloe off Laura. As Laura tried to retaliate Keith grabbed her and pulled her away with Lisa's help.

"No one attacks me like that! No one!" shouted Laura, her face turned crimson.

Keith held her chin in both his hands, trying to make eye contact. She looked at him and he said softly, "Laura, she has every right to be angry, and attacking you was wrong, but I think it best if we go quietly and defuse the situation."

"It would be best, Laura," added Lisa.

Laura nodded and tried to calm herself. They left the bar and walked back to Keith's quarters. Lisa watched them go then sat back at their table.

"Is she all right?" asked Lisa.

"Yes, she is. Wow, Chloe. Where did that come from?" asked Andrew.

[296]

"I'm sorry everyone. I'm just worried about Neil. I thought he was with you and it turns out he's off on another assignment and nobody will tell me where."

"We all thought he was with us until we found out. I was even bunking with him. He's my brother for Christ's sake and I still didn't know," said Andrew.

"I'll make it up with Keith tomorrow. And, for everyone else's sake, I'll try to be civil with 'home wrecker' as well."

"That's good, Chloe because taking her on isn't a good idea. She's well trained and I'd hate to see you get hurt," said Lisa.

"Let's all settle down and enjoy a couple more drinks," said John.

They all agreed and the mood at the table calmed with an air of happiness beginning to resurface.

~

Laura sat on Keith's sofa as he made them both a strong coffee. She crossed her legs and her skirt rode up slightly. "Thanks again, Keith for what you said back there."

"It was nothing, Laura. I didn't like the way she was talking to you," he paused as he lifted both cups and brought them into the main room. "It's very unlike her though. She's a good person, normally," he set the cups down and froze for a second when he caught sight of how far up her legs her skirt had ridden.

Laura noticed his reaction and looked down. She smiled and uncrossed her legs, then shifted her weight while smoothing down her skirt.

"Sorry, Keith."

"For what?"

"Making you uncomfortable."

[297]

"No... no I'm not uncomfortable. I just saw your legs and remembered the other night, that's all."

"Would you like to do it again?"

His eyes wandered the room until, finally, he looked into her eyes. "Yes... err no... err, I mean."

"What's wrong, Keith? The other day you were asking me for sex."

"Of course, I'd love to have sex with you. It's just that I really do love you and I don't want anything to go wrong."

Laura leaned forward and held both his hands in her own. She stared intently into his eyes, smiling. "I love you too, Keith. One-night stands are one thing, but I don't go back to someone unless there's a certain something between us."

A look of relief washed over Keith's face and he kissed her passionately. Soon, they started fumbling with each other's clothes. They intended to enjoy themselves.

~

Sirens sounded all over the base and every soldier rushed to their rally points. In the command tower soldiers were hurriedly checking their screens and the radar.

The lift doors opened and in walked General Bolgon. "Status report."

"There's an unidentified starship on our scopes, sir."

"Power up the defences and send a squadron out to meet it. Are you sure there's only one?"

"It's still too far out, sir but it appears to be alone."

Michael Toddwell walked up behind them. "What's going on, sir?"

"We have a situation, Michael. There's an unidentified target closing in. If it turns out to be tranchillion then we have a battle on our hands."

"Sir, don't they usually send out more than one starship," said Michael.

"Yes, but it could be a new tactic, or… well… it's anyone's guess," said the general.

"Sir," interrupted a technician. "They are within communication range."

General Bolgon pressed a button and spoke to the, now obvious, tranchillion starship.

"Identify yourselves or turn around. This is Space Federation airspace. You will be destroyed."

"Don't shoot, sir. This is Neil Bolgon. We're coming in with some friends on board, sir."

"Neil! Oh my god it's you," the general paused as he remembered himself. "Okay, Officer Bolgon. Proceed to docking bay four. There will be a squadron of *Star Cruisers* with you shortly to escort you in. Do you need any medical care?"

"No, sir. Everyone's okay but I do need you there ASAP, sir."

"Will do, Neil. Will do," General Bolgon addressed Mr Toddwell. "Michael, would you stay here please. If any hostiles have followed them, I want you to use all necessary force to eradicate them. You have the command tower."

They saluted and General Bolgon left, with his usual escort of two security personnel, to make his way to meet his son once again.

The tranchillion battleport touched down in the landing bay and, moments later, the exit ramp lowered to the floor. From out of the darkness strode Neil and

[299]

Rebecca dressed in their chameleon suits. Neil had asked the tranchillions to remain aboard until he'd spoken with his father.

The tranchillions waited patiently, and understandably nervously, just inside the battleport. Neil and Rebecca stepped onto the floor and saluted General Bolgon.

"So, son. Where are your friends?"

"Inside father. They are volunteers – not prisoners. We need somewhere to house them."

"How did the mission go, Neil?"

"Quite successfully, sir. The tranchillions are divided. Unfortunately, the rebels are in control of the mothership, so we'll need to take it back by force before we can get to the friendlies."

"It sounds like a major debriefing is needed. But right now, it's rather late in the day. Go back in there and get them to follow you. Take them to section C where they can get some rest. Please make sure that all weapons are left on the battleport, Neil. We don't need any mishaps."

"Dad, we need to come up with some sort of communicator so that both our species can understand each other. Only Rebecca can speak fluent tranchillion. I have to use a *Chameleon Suit* to understand them. Is there anything in the pipeline?"

"I'll get our scientists on it. It shouldn't take too long. We can adapt the replicater technology."

They saluted each other and General Bolgon left the docking bay leaving instructions that the tranchillions were to be left alone. Neil and Rebecca re-joined the tranchillions on board the battleport and Neil pulled his mask back over his head then inserted his replicater so he could communicate with them.

[300]

"Listen everyone. You will be escorted to a place where you can rest but, as I'm sure you can appreciate, no weapons will be allowed to leave here. I'll need you all to leave them behind and follow us in single-file, thank you."

When they had all conceded to the conditions Neil removed his replicater and mask then he and Rebecca led them down the ramp and waited while everyone filed out. Two soldiers entered the battleport to make sure everyone was out then signalled to Neil and they marched off. The two that had checked the battleport stood guard at the entrance and four more soldiers fell into formation around the tranchillions. All of them were careful not to point their weapons in the direction of the aliens.

It was a nervous journey for both parties which went by without a hitch. General Bolgon had cleared a route for them. There was the odd gasp and a lot of whispering going on from the curious soldiers and staff, who were being held back, when the tranchillions were marched past.

They arrived at section C and walked down the corridor until all of them were inside. Neil climbed on a chair so that he could see over the tranchillions and, more importantly, so they could see him.

Neil addressed the human soldiers. "I'm going to briefly change into a tranchillion so I can speak to them. Don't be alarmed."

He pulled on his mask then placed the replicater into the slot in his suit and changed into Major Xenorphide. Then he gave his instructions to the waiting tranchillions.

"Rebecca has got key-cards to every room in this section. They have numbers on them. Each of you take one from her as you pass and that will be your room for the rest of your stay. If anyone has any questions, please ask either me or Rebecca and we'll try our best to answer them."

The tranchillions started taking their key-cards from Rebecca as the doors to section C opened and they filed through one by one to find their rooms.

~

Neil had changed clothes before he left for his quarters. He was tired and wanted the warm comfort of his bed. But word had got around that he was back and when he entered his room, he found it full of his friends. Chloe ran over and wrapped her arms around him as they kissed.

"I've missed you," she said once they'd parted. "I've missed you so much. Don't ever do that to me again."

"Do what?"

"Go off on a mission without telling me. When this lot came back, and you weren't with them, I began to imagine all sorts of things."

Neil looked puzzled.

"Keith messed up," said John. "We've known for a couple of days that you were on a different mission."

"Sorry guys. I haven't been debriefed yet, so I don't know what's going on."

"Can you all let him get in and sit down. I'm sure that he could do with a rest," said Lisa.

Neil sat and they all gathered round him eager to hear what he'd been doing. Chloe wasn't pleased to hear that Rebecca had been with him until he told of how she had almost died twice while on the mission.

"That's all I can tell you guys until tomorrow afternoon. Keep it to yourselves please," said Neil.

"It's good to have you back bro," said Andrew.

"It's good to be back," replied Neil.

They stayed for hours telling each other stories of what had happened to them until, finally, the late hour forced their guests away and Neil was left alone with Chloe.

"The disguises were good then," said Neil. "Even Andy couldn't tell that Keith was disguised as me."

"I'm glad that he was found out. Imagine what would've happened if he'd come back before you," said Chloe.

"Dad would've found them something else and kept them away."

"So now that we're finally alone, what do you say to a little loving, mister?"

Neil lifted her up and she wrapped her legs around his body. He carried her to their bedroom, kissing her and squeezing her bottom. They reached the bedroom and Chloe started undoing his uniform while he laid her on the bed. Neil shrugged off his jacket and shirt and Chloe unzipped his trousers, pulling them down.

"Oooo… pleased to see me," she said.

"Yes babe… it seems like ages since..." Chloe kissed him again to stop him talking.

"Just fuck me."

Neil ripped her clothes off roughly and took a moment to admire her body, then he pulled his pants down and kissed her all over. Both naked – they merged into one, glad to be together again.

~

Neil turned over in his bed and felt for Chloe, but she wasn't there. He rubbed his sleep-weary eyes and got out

[303]

of bed. He opened the bedroom door then remembered the last time and poked his head through.

"Chloe – you there?"

"Yes!" she called back from the kitchen. "Just making breakfast. Sit down, it'll be ready soon."

Neil walked into the lounge and sat at the table before calling, "Love you."

Chloe walked in wearing an apron and carrying a tray with their breakfast on. "A good old-fashioned fry up." She placed the tray on the table in front of, a now ravenous, Neil. "I'll get the drinks." She turned her back to him and Neil admired her soft, firm buttocks and the slender lines of her back. He watched her muscles working gently as she continued walking away.

"You'll go blind," she said without looking back. Then, when she got to the doorway, she turned her head and her blonde hair flicked over her shoulders. She smiled and winked at Neil. He did the same as she disappeared into the kitchen.

Neil started dishing all their favourites onto each plate and when Chloe returned with the drinks her plate was ready for her. She placed Neil's orange juice next to him and they kissed. Neil squeezed her left breast gently as she bent over him. Chloe slapped his hand as she stood up straight. "Naughty. There's plenty of time for that later."

"I'm glad you left the apron in the kitchen dear," he said. They started eating and Chloe decided to ask Neil about Kelly's proposal.

"Babe, you remember Kelly and Rachel, don't you?"

Neil looked up from his food. "Yes."

"I was thinking. Well, we were thinking about having a foursome. What do you think?"

[304]

Neil almost chocked on his food. "Are you serious?"

"Yes I am."

Neil shrugged his shoulders. "If you're fine with it then I'd be more than happy to partake in that. But doesn't one of them have a boyfriend."

"Yes. Rachel has, but he doesn't need to know."

"Like I said, hon. I'd be extremely happy to join all three of you in bed. When did you have in mind?"

"If they can make it – tonight."

They finished their breakfast and Neil got up. He stood in front of Chloe and she rose from her chair. He pulled her towards him, and they kissed. Then she jumped and wrapped her legs around him. Neil carried her back to the bedroom.

"Let's get some practice in," he said as he lowered her onto the bed.

~

Later, after Chloe had gone to work, Neil was sitting in the briefing room. There was a table between him and his father. Rebecca came in and sat next to him. Michael Toddwell sat next to the general and that left two empty seats the other side of him.

"Who are they for?" asked Neil.

"John and Suzanne," replied Jim.

There was tension in the air. "Am I in trouble, dad?" asked Neil.

Rebecca looked up with a frown on her face.

"That depends on the outcome of this briefing, son. Don't look so worried Rebecca," said the general, noticing her frown. He looked back towards Neil. "We're just waiting for them then we'll start."

[305]

Two minutes later, John Stillson and Suzanne Cox walked in offering their apologies.

"Let's get started," said the general after they had settled down.

"Your escape from this base, disguised as a tranchillion, went perfectly. Is that correct?" asked the general.

"Yes, sir. It did. No loss of life."

"Let's move on to Ganymede then. There were quite a few deaths there. What I need to know is, were they avoidable, Officer Bolgon?"

Neil sensed the trouble both he and Rebecca were in. His father was being formal, that meant no favours.

"They were unavoidable, sir. Certain events got slightly out of hand and I was forced to kill several of our own people."

"Start from the beginning, Officer Bolgon," commanded the general.

Rebecca sat up straight and said, "This isn't fair. He saved me twice on Ganymede and once on Anthera – not to mention how many tranchillions he rescued."

The general glared at her and she sat back, looking scared.

"You'll be asked for your opinion, and your statement, when we have finished with Officer Bolgon," said the general.

Rebecca clasped her hands together and started nervously twitching her fingers. Two MPs were watching from behind the security glass waiting for the results of the briefing.

The general again looked at Neil. "Go on."

Neil recounted how he did a recon of the prison building and saw two soldiers go down after requesting a diversion; one injured – one killed. He then entered the building, gathered his information and got back out knocking one guard unconscious in the process. Neil told how he got back outside the fence and to the rendezvous point but found no-one there. He told how he found Rebecca and the tranchillion surrounded by human soldiers and the fact that it was pitch-black.

Neil said how he saw Rebecca and the tranchillion curled up on the floor being kicked by the soldiers. Then the beating stopped and one of the soldiers had grabbed Rebecca's head and pulled it back, saying something to her. Then he kicked her again and pulled out his pistol, pushing her onto her back.

"I had no choice, sir. I needed Rebecca alive and had no time to render them unconscious silently. So, I killed them all and I'll have to live with that, sir," said Neil with not a quiver in his voice.

"Carry on Officer Bolgon," said the general.

Neil continued with his statement. He described how he saw reinforcements arriving and how he led them away without killing any more. He told how he found Rebecca again and how he carried the unconscious tranchillion over his shoulder leading Rebecca via a rope back to the camp but due to her injuries their pace wasn't quick enough to make it back before sunrise.

He told how he left them to get some help and when he returned Rebecca was again surrounded by soldiers. He described how the soldier, who was acting under orders, shot the unconscious tranchillion lying on the floor then turned his rifle towards Rebecca. Again, Neil had no choice but to kill them.

"I shot the one about to kill Rebecca and my reinforcements took care of the rest."

Neil then told what happened the next night. How he knocked out one guard and stunned the other outside the prison building, then how he knocked out four other guards inside. He told how he was walking away when another one asked him to hold the door, so he let him through then stunned the guard and closed the door.

"After that everything started to happen quickly. The unconscious guards were found and the guard that found them called for me to sound the alarm. I entered the control room, distracted the guard and stunned him as well," Neil paused and took a sip of water which reminded Rebecca of hers. She drank some water as Neil carried on with his statement.

He told how he broke into the rifle cabinet then changed into a tranchillion again. How he knocked out another guard who had burst into the control room before opening the cell doors and switching off the power.

"Unfortunately, some more guards were injured or killed when the tranchillions stampeded for the door," said Neil. He paused for another sip of water.

"I had to wait for them all to get out before I could exit the building. I lost about fifteen tranchillions while inside the building either through being trampled on or by being shot. The guards were firing wildly in all directions by then. They couldn't see where the tranchillions were in the darkness and they all ended up getting trampled. When I eventually got outside, I saw a Jeep, with a large laser mounted on it, firing into the crowd of tranchillions – mowing them down as it moved across the tarmac."

General Bolgon sat back letting Neil carry on with his statement while taking the odd note. Suzanne was scribbling away merrily knowing that some of it would have to be omitted.

"I got into position and took out the tyres not wanting to take any more human lives. The driver lost control and the Jeep flipped over. I saw another five incoming Jeeps and we ran for the battleport. When laser fire started hitting the concrete around me, I returned fire as did Rebecca. The Jeep veered off and I took out the tyres again. The soldiers got out the opposite side and we retreated to the battleport keeping them pinned with laser fire. The last few tranchillions were boarding when the other four Jeeps arrived. All five of my team kept the vehicles suppressed until everyone was aboard then we ran on ourselves. As you can see, I had no choice but to kill the ones I did. If there had been any other way, I would have gladly taken it." Neil sat back in his chair and drank some more water.

"Do you need a break before you finish your report, Officer Bolgon?" said the general.

Neil shook his head. "No. Just having a breather, sir."

Next, Neil recounted what happened on Anthera injecting some of his own thoughts and opinions into the facts. Half-an-hour later he was finished.

The general nodded to everyone present. "Quite a story, Officer Bolgon. Quite a story. Now, Rebecca. Your turn. Tell us everything you can remember." He turned to the glass behind him. "As Rebecca is still a civilian, I will not be hard on her. Do not question me about it."

The two MPs behind the security glass looked at each other but stayed silent.

It took an hour for Rebecca to give her statement and when she was finished General Bolgon said, "You may

[309]

go while we go over the notes. I'll let you know later what we decide."

"Thank you, sir," said Neil.

The general, John Stillson and Suzanne left the room. Neil and Rebecca also left.

"Let's get something to eat," said Neil.

"Are you buying?" asked Rebecca.

"Of course. And Rebecca, even if no one else has said it, thank you for all that you've done."

Rebecca nodded and smiled, "Just don't ask me to do it again. I still can't get the image of that tranchillion out of my mind or those spikes dropping towards me."

"Do you need to see someone about that?"

"No, I'll be all right, Neil. Thanks for your concern."

They set off for some dinner.

CHAPTER SIXTEEN

December 2171 – January 2172

Earth

"How have your first twelve days been, David?" asked Madeline after knocking and entering David Turners room.

He looked up from his paperwork. "Lovely, Mrs Tressel. Thanks again for letting me stay. Are you sure it's all right for Gwen too?"

"Please, David. How many times have I got to tell you? Madeline. Please call me Madeline. And, of course she can stay. There's plenty of room here. Although, the farmhouse would be preferable."

"I'm still working on that," he paused to change the subject. "This proposal I've drawn up for the new business is finished. I'd like you to go over it to make sure it's accurate."

Madeline sat beside him. "Let's have a look see." She read the document for several minutes then looked up, smiling.

"Are you sure of the cooperation from the Space Federation, David?"

"Yes. Well I know that General Bolgon will look at the proposal and if he likes it then we only have to show it to the bank."

"We have enough money to cover the start-up costs. We won't need a loan," said Madeline.

"Yes, I know that but if I'm going to be a partner in this venture then I feel the need to put money into it myself. To do that I'll need a loan."

"It doesn't matter, David. We'll put up the money initially and when you have enough saved you can pay us back. What do you think?"

"I'd still like to pay my way."

"Look, David. If I didn't trust you then I wouldn't have offered. You can stay with us until you find a place of your own and then take out a mortgage. That way will be best, believe me."

"All right, Madeline. I accept your offer but first we need to convince the general."

"The only thing I'm not happy about is that David, Guy and Steve will have to join the Space Federation to earn their pardon."

"I'm sorry, Madeline but that is the generals only condition. If it helps any, they'll be aboard my starship and I'll keep an eye on them."

[312]

"Go ahead, David. Take it to him with my blessing. I hope it goes well," Madeline leaned over and gave him a hug which he accepted awkwardly.

He got up. "Are you positive it's all right to bring Gwen back with me?"

"David, that's twice you've asked me in as many minutes. If you ask one more time, I'll change my answer, now stop it."

David left to take the proposal to the general and bring back Gwen for a fortnight's holiday with him.

~

Captain Turner departed the shuttle followed by David Tressel. Turner smiled and began to feel more relaxed in these familiar surroundings. David Tressel, however, was extremely uncomfortable about being here.

Turner saw his apprehension. "Try to relax, David. You're not going to be taken away. You're perfectly safe. I guarantee it."

"It's not easy, David. It feels like I'm walking deeper into enemy territory with every step."

"Come on, we'll get something to eat at the café. And I've got some pills that will help you calm down if you'd like one."

"I might just take you up on that."

They walked to the café and had a meal. David took one of the captain's pills. By the time they had eaten he looked calm again and they set off for the general's office.

When they entered, the secretary looked up and smiled as she saw Captain Turner. She sprang up and ran over to him, her black shoulder-blade length hair flowing out behind her. She thudded into him and he closed his open arms around her, lifting her off the floor as they kissed.

Tressel cleared his throat to remind them he was there, and they parted.

"It's good to see you, David," said Gwen.

"You too, Gwen. I can't wait to get you on your own," replied Captain Turner.

"All my things are packed. When I get off later, we can go. Oh, David. I'm so excited that we're finally going to be together."

"Me too, Gwen. Me too," he said, and they briefly kissed again.

Gwen sat back behind her desk and announced the arrival of Turner and Tressel and was told to let them straight in. They entered General Bolgon's office and sat at his desk as instructed.

"So, you are David Tressel," the general offered his hand across the desk. "Nice to meet you."

David leant forward to shake the offered hand as his face remained blank.

"You don't have to worry Mr Tressel. I'm a nice person unless you cross me," said the general.

"That's what worries me. I have crossed you – several times."

"As long as you and your boys do what I want it's all water under the bridge. I'll give you and them a full pardon."

Captain Turner handed the business plan over to the general which he promptly took.

"Right, let's have a look at this." After several minutes he said, "This all looks very good captain. I see you've put yourself down as partner. Are you leaving me?"

[314]

"Once the war with the tranchillions is over, sir. I would like to retire from active service and do something a little less dangerous. I see this as a perfect opportunity to get a normal life again, sir."

"You've made up your mind haven't you, captain."

"Yes, sir."

"Very well. Once the upcoming mission is completed, I'll grant you early release. It's been a pleasure to have you on my team, captain."

"Thank you, sir. It's been a pleasure to work for you."

"I approve this venture of yours and wish you good luck. I want you all to report here on the third of January to begin your duties. Mr Tressel, you and your people will take an intensive training schedule to get you ready for service once you arrive on the third. I suggest that all three of you try your best to get fit before then."

"We will, sir," replied David.

"You may go now and good luck to both of you."

Turner and Tressel stood and saluted the general before leaving his office. David let out a relived sigh. Turner walked over to Gwen.

"What time do you get off?"

"Five o'clock, but I'll need at least another hour to get my things and have a shower."

"Right I'll book a flight for some time after six. Where do you want to meet?"

"You can come to my quarters if you want."

"David will be with me. He's not got anywhere to stay up here."

"Of course, David. I'll see you both later," she briefly kissed him again and Tressel put his hand up in acknowledgement, not really knowing where to look.

[315]

They left the office and set off to book their flight home.

~

The Land-Rover pulled up outside a converted warehouse. The crates of Etherall and Sodrum were safely locked away towards the back of the building. The front section had been converted into living quarters since the Tressels' forced exile. It was like a home inside, but Madeline was still hoping it wouldn't be for much longer.

David, David and Gwen got out of the Land-Rover and entered the homely end of the warehouse. The Land-Rover pulled off again and disappeared round the back.

"This is lovely. You'd never know from the outside," said Gwen.

"It's only temporary," said Turner quickly, knowing it was his fault they were here. "We'll be moving back to the farm-house as soon as possible."

"It will happen now. I'm just glad we made it back from there," said Tressel nodding towards the heavens. He looked around but couldn't see his mother.

"Make yourselves comfortable. I'll find mum and see which room she has prepared for Gwen," he rushed off, anxious to find out if his mother was okay.

"You're back," said Guy Travis, leaning against the doorframe leading to the warehouse. "I'm sure Mrs Tressel will be very happy to see you," he spotted Gwen. "You must be Gwen. Nice to meet you."

"Thank you," she said with a blank expression.

"Guy... his name's Guy Travis," said David.

"Guy. What an unusual name. Nice to meet you," said Gwen.

[316]

Guy remained in the doorway with a smile on his face.

A short lady, with dyed black hair, bustled through the doorway behind them followed by David Tressel. Gwen thought she looked about fifty and had a friendly face.

"Hello, Gwen," she said as she shook her hand. "Hello, David. I have prepared a room for you next to Mr Turner's. If you want the arrangements changed just let me know."

"My own room is just what I wanted, Mrs Tressel. I'm sure it will be perfect," said Gwen.

"Follow me. Let's get you settled."

Once the guests had left, Guy walked over to David. "How did it go?"

"The general is a powerful man, Guy. I'm glad I went there voluntarily and not as a prisoner. It went well, I think. We should be back in business by the time we get back from up there. The sales from our stockpile should be enough to get us by in the meantime."

"I'm sure glad you made it back. I'd have had a hard time springing you from a Space Federation jail."

"What's been going on while I've been away," said David. They left through the warehouse entrance.

"Is Steve still with us?"

"Yeah. I don't think he's leaving now we're not in so much trouble."

"Hopefully we'll be able to make his position permanent this time. He doesn't need messing around. Who knows, he may even get back with Suzanne when all this is over."

"No. She's still married to her job, isn't she?"

"She seems to be spending most of her time on the moon, but when was the last time you saw a report from her in 'World News'?"

"She printed one last week. It was about the aliens escaping."

"I didn't even know they had captured any aliens. Besides, that's just one story in a month. She's normally much more prolific than that."

"Come to think of it, when I read her report, it didn't seem like her," said Guy. "The story was bland. Like, like a check list. It didn't have her usual, gripping, quality."

They entered the garage part of the warehouse and saw Steve loading a truck with the help of two other workers.

Steve stopped what he was doing when he saw David and they briefly hugged.

"You're back then. How did it go?" asked Steve.

"Fine. We're on track for going legitimate and I'd like to offer you a permanent place with us when it happens. What do you think?"

"I'd love to, David. How long before you know?"

"Probably within the next two weeks, but there's a problem. As part of the deal with General Bolgon, all three of us will have to join up with the Space Federation until this war with the aliens is over."

Steve's face dropped. "I'm no soldier. I'll just get killed."

"None of us are. Well, me and Guy have some experience in combat, but we've never been soldiers."

"What'd happen if I refuse to join?"

"We'll lose the contract, and all be on the run again, unless the general accepts that we couldn't force you to

[318]

come with us. After all you haven't been with us long. I'll see what I can do."

"I need time to think."

"Take as much as you need up until we have to leave which will be January third."

"I'd better get on with my work," mumbled Steve as he turned away from them.

"Do you think he'll come, David?"

"I think so. Yes, I'm sure he will. But if he doesn't, we'll cover for him as best we can."

~

The sleek silver and black starship settled in the court yard of Madeline Tressel's farmhouse. The exit ramp lowered to the floor and out walked David Tressel, Captain Turner, Madeline Tressel, Steve Cox and finally, the pilot, Guy Travis.

Madeline took a deep breath and let out a sigh. "It's great to be back."

Captain Turner spotted the gap where Madeline's front door should have been. "I'll get the Space Federation to pay for a new front door, Mrs Tressel."

She looked at the house. "You'd better young man. Let's see if there's any more damage."

They entered the house and walked through the rooms. So far, the only damage done was the front door and some water marks where the rain had come in through the open doorway. Madeline hadn't had carpets fitted downstairs so a mop and elbow grease would remove the stains.

When they entered the rear sitting room, which was at the front of the house, they saw two people asleep under a blanket. David Tressel walked over and clapped

[319]

his hands loudly above them. They woke up and quickly scrabbled backwards into a corner.

"What are you doing in our house?" asked David.

"We saw it was empty and came in out of the rain. We... we've been here ever since," replied the male squatter.

"How long have you been here?" asked Madeline as she moved forward next to her son.

"I think about a couple of weeks maybe," said the female squatter.

"Well we're back now. This is our house and after you've had a good meal you can be on your way," said Madeline.

"Mother. Just kick them out. They've probably eaten most of our food already," said David.

Madeline turned to her son with a look that told him to shut up. "The last time I checked this was my house, not yours." She looked back towards the couple sitting on her floor. "Besides. Look at them. They obviously have nowhere to go. Just think if it was you in their position."

Madeline held out her hand to the two frightened squatters. "Come on. Don't be afraid. Let's get you something to eat."

"Thank you," said the young man as he encouraged his girlfriend to her feet. They followed Madeline to the kitchen.

"Steve, can you accompany mother and her *guests* to the kitchen and make sure they're all right," said David.

Steve followed them into the kitchen. David shook his head before the rest of them checked upstairs to see if anyone else was hiding up there. The rest of the house was how they'd left it. They opened the windows to rid

[320]

the air of a musty smell that had accumulated then went back downstairs.

"The rest of the house is fine, mother," said David as he stuck his head round the kitchen door. The two guests were eating a meal that Madeline had made for them. "I'll check the outbuildings."

"David. Be careful. There could be wild animals holed up in any of them."

"Okay, mother," he looked at Guy who was grinning. *Honestly – you'd think I was still eleven*, he thought.

Guy didn't say anything. The grin was enough. They walked back outside, and Steve joined them.

"Steve, go with Guy and check the barn. David, you're with me," said Tressel.

They spent half-an-hour checking everything was okay before Guy entered the starship and moved it into the barn, which now looked like a hanger. All the, normally hidden, panels were now on show. The starship settled in the centre.

Guy re-joined Steve at the entrance and pressed a button on his remote. The wall panels slid shut and the starship descended underneath the hanger, disappearing out of sight. Within a minute the hanger looked like a barn again.

"Does everything seem fine?" asked David from behind them.

"Yes, Dave," said Guy.

"Let's get back to mum then."

When they entered the kitchen, Madeline and her two helpers were busy scrubbing the kitchen floor.

"Ah, David. We have two new team members. They've agreed to help us tidy up and will gladly help where they can. I've given them a room to themselves."

"Mother, can we afford to take on any new workers?"

"These two deserve a second chance, David and I'm giving them one. I won't hear anything to the contrary."

David knew he wouldn't be able to dissuade his mother, so he welcomed them to the team.

"Right everyone let's get on with it," said David.

"Hello. Is anyone home!" called a voice from the hallway.

David walked back out and saw Julie Statham standing there.

"Come in, Mrs Statham. Mother's in the kitchen."

"Hello dear," said Julie as she entered and saw Madeline getting to her feet.

Madeline bustled over to Julie with outstretched arms. "Hello, Julie. It's good to see you."

They embraced briefly before Julie looked around the room. "Hello everyone – Steve." She singled him out. "I hope we can still get along."

"Of course, Mrs Statham. It wasn't your fault. How's Suzanne?"

"She's fine. Gone back up there," she raised her eyes upwards. "You know she still loves you, don't you?"

"Does she. Even though I dumped her after you know what."

"She understands and, given time, hopes that you'll understand her reasons for doing what she did or at least forgive her. I think she's going through some changes. She doesn't seem as enthusiastic about her work as she once did."

"What do you want us to do, mother?" interrupted David, eyeing the two new recruits.

"Get these floors cleaned up while I talk to Julie. I'll be back in a couple of minutes."

[322]

"We haven't had anything to eat."

"We don't have much in. Find something to tide you over and we'll go out for lunch," said Madeline.

"I'll get Jeffrey to give you all a free meal at the café if you want."

"Thanks, Julie. We'll take you up on that," said Madeline.

~

The Tressels' business was back on track. After officially re-opening five days previously they'd got most of their old contacts to accept they were now a legitimate company and still able to offer the same price as before.

Julie Statham had accepted a part-time job to help while the boys were away. A temporary pilot had been hired and most of their old work force had gladly returned. The only thing that Madeline was unhappy about was that David, Guy and Steve would be risking their lives fighting for the Space Federation.

In a few hours, they were due to leave to start their conscription and Madeline was fussing over them all.

"They'll return safely, Madeline. I shouldn't say anything, but I feel I owe you," said David Turner. "There's a rumour going about up there that the tranchillions are fighting each other and that we'll become allies with them. The battle should be short with minimal casualties' due to there not being many hostile tranchillions left."

"They're still going up there, David. You can't expect me to be happy about it," said Madeline.

"I really don't think they'll be in much danger, and it will earn them the pardon they need to go legitimate."

[323]

"I know," she sighed. "Just bring them back safe please."

"I'll do my best, Madeline. I'll do my best."

Gwen entered the room. "Is anything wrong?"

"No, Gwen. Mrs Tressel's worried about her boys. Excuse us, Madeline. We don't have long left and I'd like some 'alone time' with Gwen. Try not to worry about them."

Gwen and David left the living room and took a walk outside in the cold January air.

"Did you enjoy your Christmas, Gwen?"

"Yes. I had you and I didn't have to work. It was lovely to spend Christmas on Earth, just lovely."

They continued their walk, leaving behind faint footprints in the wet mud as they went.

~

David Tressel finished off his last-minute business and left the office to find his mother. He found her in the living room and sat next to her on the sofa. "Hi, mum. You all right?"

"Yes dear. You be safe, you hear. I don't want to lose you."

David put his arm around her and kissed her temple. "You won't lose any of us, mum." He wanted to give her his promise, but he couldn't guarantee their safety. "Let's watch something until we go."

Madeline switched the TV on, and their minds were slightly taken off the upcoming events. Guy and Steve were saying goodbye to their families and were due back within the hour.

Forty-five minutes later Steve turned up followed, soon after, by Guy. They loaded their bags into the Land-

[324]

Rover with only one seat folded down in the boot so they could fit all six of them inside.

They all got in and Madeline drove them to the spaceport in Leicester.

CHAPTER SEVENTEEN

December 2171 – January 2172

The Moon

Two days had passed since Neil's briefing. Chloe was with him in their favourite place, the *Artificial Park*. Again, *Regents Park* was programmed in for the week and they both longed for a break so they could visit the real place.

They were walking towards the exit when Chloe stopped Neil by a bench. "Sit down for a minute please."

They both sat and Neil fixed her with a stare. "What's wrong, babe?"

"I want you to marry me before you go away again, Neil," she looked at the ground. When she looked up again there was a tear in her eye. Neil wiped it gently away for her as they kept eye contact. Looking deeply into his eyes she said, "I want her to have your surname, Neil. I want things legitimate. But most of all, I want to be known as Mrs Bolgon before you go to fight these tranchillions."

Neil lifted her chin slightly as she had, once again, lowered her head. He smiled at her and her heart melted, then they kissed a long and gentle kiss, full of love. They parted and Neil said, "Yes, Chloe Samantha Lewis. Yes, I will marry you." He got down on one knee in front of her. "The question is, Chloe. Will you marry me?"

Her heart filled with joy and she jumped into his arms. "Yes, yes, yes," she repeated. Neil put her down and they left the park. They entered a dull, grey, lifeless corridor in complete contrast to where they had just been.

"We'll start organising things just as soon as we find out the verdict of the briefing," said Neil.

When they got back to their quarters the TV screen was flashing the words 'important message'. Neil walked over to it and said, "TV on – receive message."

The screen went blank then John Stillson's face appeared. The image smiled then he said, "Hello, Officer Bolgon. The results of the briefing have been decided and the general requests your presence in his office. Miss Lewis may attend as well."

The screen went blank and Neil said, "Reply. I will be there shortly," he paused to look at Chloe and she nodded. He looked back at the screen. "With Miss Lewis, thank you."

"It looks like we're going to see your father then," said Chloe.

"Yes, we are. Let's get this over with."

[327]

When Neil and Chloe entered the general's office, they saw a room full of familiar faces. General Bolgon was sitting behind his desk with his two advisers either side of him at a respectful distance. Suzanne Cox was at a table to the side ready to take notes and Rebecca was sitting at a table opposite the general with two empty seats next to her. There was no sign of the military police.

"That's encouraging, Chloe," said Neil. "I can't see any MPs."

They sat next to Rebecca after Neil had saluted his father.

"Thank you for coming so promptly, Officer Bolgon." His face changed from serious to smiling as he said, "No need to worry, son. There are no charges."

"Thank you, sir," said Neil.

"No. Thank you for the brilliant execution of our plan. Both of you did an excellent job. The meeting to decide our next course of action will begin in the 'War Room' in just over an hour. I expect you to be there, Neil."

"Of course, sir. Let's get this war ended."

Neil and Chloe left the room and couldn't help smiling at each other.

"Let's go tell John and Lisa you're off the hook," said Chloe.

Rebecca watched them go then walked in the opposite direction with her head down and a tear in her eye.

John, Lisa and Andrew were in John and Lisa's quarters when Neil and Chloe found them.

"We've got good news," said Neil as he and Chloe sat next to Andrew. "They aren't pressing charges."

"Damn right," said John.

[328]

"What happens now?" asked Lisa as she set drinks down in front of them.

"I've got a meeting to attend in about fifty minutes where we'll draw up a plan and then, sometime soon, we'll be going to Anthera," said Neil.

John put his drink down. "How soon?"

"The surviving tranchillions, let's call them the good tranchillions, need our help ASAP so I'm hoping to be on my way back by at least the end of January."

"It doesn't matter how soon we leave," said John. "I mean, tell me if I'm wrong but, our current engines, even on maximum drive, would take months to get us there. They may all be dead by the time we get to them."

"The battleport I came back in can do it in three days. I'll just have to go on ahead with as big a force as it can hold and do my best until the rest of the fleet arrive."

"Couldn't we try to incorporate the tranchillions technology into our engines, you know like, modify them," said Lisa.

"That's a good idea, Lisa. I'll mention that to them."

They finished their drinks and Neil decided it was time for him to go. He kissed Chloe goodbye and was just about to leave when she said, "Oh wait, Neil. We've got something else to tell them."

Neil nodded and waited at the door. Chloe turned back to the others. "We're getting married!" The smile on her face was only outshone by the twinkle in her eyes.

Lisa squealed and jumped up, giving Chloe a big hug. John and Andrew gave Neil a slap on the back and a handshake.

"Can't believe you're finally doing it," said Andrew.

"Yeah we're kind of excited about it. I'm leaving the arrangements to her and possibly Lisa, if she wants to."

"What was that. You want me to help," said Lisa.

"Yes, I'd love you to help with the arrangements, Lisa," said Chloe.

"I've really got to go now," said Neil.

They all waved goodbye to him as he set off to the meeting in the 'War Room'.

He got there with only a few minutes to spare and sat in one of the chairs facing the giant screen. General Bolgon stood to start the proceedings.

"Welcome everyone. The reason for this meeting is to determine what to do about the situation on Anthera. I'll need suggestions once Officer Bolgon has debriefed everyone. Officer Bolgon, would you please step up to the front."

Neil rose from his chair and walked to the front, joining the 'top brass' at the head of the table. The meeting went well and lasted for several hours. Once it was over, Neil was sent to fetch Rebecca from the science laboratory where she was helping to make the translation device. They were to go to the isolation wing to release the two tranchillions still being held there.

They entered the prison complex and were shown the isolation cells. Neil looked in through the small window to see where Captain Xenorphide was. He was sitting on the bed looking at his feet. He looked up slowly as the door opened and Neil, followed by Rebecca and two armed guards, stepped into his cell. Neil nodded to Rebecca and she spoke to the captain.

"Captain Xenorphide. I am Rebecca Chambers, and this is Neil Bolgon – a Warrant Officer in our army."

Captain Xenorphide was staring wide-eyed at Rebecca. "I... I can understand you. How is that possible?"

"I have had your language imprinted into my brain by a race from your part of the galaxy called the *Watchers*."

"I remember you," he pointed towards Neil. "You turned into me and the other one turned into you. How... how did you do that?" Rebecca translated for Neil.

"That doesn't matter," said Neil and, again, Rebecca translated.

"What does matter is that we're no longer enemies and are currently devising a plan to rescue the few tranchillions left that are loyal to General Zemorphoride," said Neil.

"What do you mean?" asked the captain.

"We've been to Anthera to gather information, originally for an attack on your people. But now we have aligned ourselves with your general. During our time there, Colonel Dowdneer has taken over by force and the only tranchillions loyal to the general are with him in a bunker."

"Colonel Dowdneer. A traitor. I don't believe it. He always was a bit," he struggled for the right word, "disagreeable – but even so. He is the general's best friend."

"Was the general's best friend. Now, if he catches Dowdneer, he will execute him," said Neil.

"I'm afraid I'll need more than just your word," said Xenorphide.

"We have orders to let yourself and Capustri go. Twenty-four of your comrades are in section C enjoying our hospitality. They helped me escape so we could bring re-enforcements. They will be your proof."

"Okay, I'll come quietly. But if this is a trick, I swear I'll kill you."

[331]

"This is no trick. Why would we need to? You're already confined. There is one thing we need you to do before you get your proof. We need you to save us some time by convincing Capustri to follow us."

"Of course. That I will do."

"We'll take you to the rest of your people where you can rest easy until tomorrow. Please understand that we have armed guards outside your section for your safety as much as ours. I'm sure you'll understand that having tranchillions here has not gone down well with a few of our soldiers. They have lost a lot of friends and family over the years due to our war."

"Are you hoping for peace between us?" asked Captain Xenorphide as they left his cell to walk the hundred yards to where Capustri Carphide was being held.

"I am hoping for peace as will all of us when they understand the truth about how this war was started."

"And what is that truth, may I ask?"

"Colonel Dowdneer attacked our survey team on Anthera sixty-one years ago then told your people that we'd attacked him. We've been fighting each other thinking that the other side started it."

They broke off their conversation as Captain Xenorphide entered Capustri's cell. Two minutes later they came out.

"We're ready to see our comrades, Neil Bolgon," said the captain.

Neil, Rebecca, the two tranchillions and the two, armed guards set off for section C.

The next day Neil and Rebecca visited section C to find Captain Xenorphide. As they passed through towards the captain's room, various tranchillions recognised them and began cheering. Some even asked how the plans were going and enquired if they could help. Neil told them that, for now, they didn't need any help and that they were here to see Captain Xenorphide.

"Thanks for bringing the captain and staff sergeant back to us," said one tranchillion as they passed.

"You're welcome," replied Rebecca.

"How far off are you from completing that translator, Rebecca?" asked Neil. "All this waiting for you to translate holds up the conversation."

"I really don't know, Neil. I think it's working but they need to programme a lot more tranchillion words in before it'll become reliable."

"We'll have to get you back on that as soon as we're done here," said Neil. "Ah, here it is."

Neil knocked on the door and Captain Xenorphide opened it. "Neil and Rebecca. How may I help you?"

"How are you finding your room?" asked Neil.

"Adequate," answered the captain after Rebecca's translation.

"I'm sorry. It's the best we could find on such short notice and while I trust your soldiers not to cause any trouble, I'm not so sure about ours. For the moment, it's best to keep you segregated."

"I agree, Neil. It will take a long time for both our cultures to trust each other."

"The reason we came here is to ask if you had any engineers here to help with integrating your engine technology into ours."

"I can't willingly allow you to steal our technology. That decision lies with the Emperor and him alone."

"I would gladly ask him, and I'm sure our Confederation would hand over some of our tech in return, but your general and his loyal soldiers are in dire need of help and we just don't have the time," said Neil.

Captain Xenorphide pondered the request for a minute then said, "Okay, Neil. I see your point. To save our people I'll do my best to help. Let's see if we have any engineers out there."

The captain stepped outside his room and called for all twenty-five tranchillions to gather round.

"Are there any engineers among you?"

One tranchillion stepped forward. "I have some experience as an engineer, but I was part of the flight crew for the *Contention*, sir."

"It seems that Corporal," the captain encouraged him to say his name.

"Mayorpe, sir."

"Mayorpe. Corporal Mayorpe is the only one who may be able to help you, Neil."

"Thank you, sir. We'll get you back to your people soon," said Neil.

Neil, Rebecca and Corporal Mayorpe left section C to get started on the engine modifications. The rest of the tranchillions carried on with their exercises.

One of the stationed guards became nervous and raised his weapon when he saw them approaching the laboratory doors.

"Lower your weapon, soldier," said Neil.

The nervous guard didn't respond.

"Lower that weapon soldier. That's an order," said Neil in a more commanding voice.

"But, sir. There's a tranchillion behind you, sir," replied the nervous guard.

"I know soldier. He's with us. We're all friends now. He's come to help the scientists."

The guard lowered his rifle. "Can I see your pass please?" He kept one nervous eye on Mayorpe.

Neil showed his pass and they all entered. They followed the signs to the engineering laboratory and Neil swiped his pass through the card-reader. The light changed from red to green and the big, reinforced glass, double doors slid apart. They entered the laboratory.

A short man with grey hair, who was balding on top, wearing a long white lab-coat hurried over to them. He pushed his glasses further up his nose with the tip of one finger and said, "Ah... This must be the tranchillion who's going to help us." He held out his hand to shake Corporal Mayorpe's.

Rebecca saw Mayorpe's indecision and said, "It's one of our customs to shake hands when meeting another person. Please be gentle with him. You do it like this." Rebecca demonstrated, with Neil, how to shake hands.

Corporal Mayorpe gripped the professor's hand and they completed the custom. "I'm professor Dewis."

Rebecca translated for the corporal who replied, "I'm Corporal Mayorpe."

With the pleasantries out of the way, professor Dewis led them over to the main screen where the schematics for their starship engines were on display. Neil took Rebecca to one side and said, "I've got an idea. I'll get a Chameleon Suit and someone to wear it. If we change that person into a tranchillion they can handle the translation duties leaving you free to complete the translation device."

[335]

"The lab where they're working on it is only a couple of corridors from here," replied Rebecca.

"I'll get right on it, see you soon," Neil left, leaving Rebecca to explain what he was doing.

Several minutes later General Bolgon entered the laboratory. "Report."

Professor Dewis answered. "Well, sir. Hopefully with Corporal Mayorpe's help we can increase the performance of our engines. But it's too early to tell yet, sir." He looked at Mayorpe. "It should be interesting to work with the tranchillion."

"Where's Neil, Rebecca?" General Bolgon stared at her with his penetrating eyes.

"He's gone to get a Chameleon Suit so I can continue with the translation device, sir."

"How do you like your new post, Rebecca?"

"I would prefer to be back in the research centre, sir."

"Once we have no need for your services, I'll see that you get your old job back," he paused, waiting for her to look him in the eyes. "Rebecca. Thank you for what you've done so far. I'll not send you out again, you have my word."

"Thank you, sir."

They both started to concentrate on what the professor and Mayorpe were doing. Another laboratory assistant had fetched two white lab-coats for the tranchillion. They were too small for him, so they didn't do up at the front. Corporal Mayorpe had stretched one round his bottom pair of arms and the other round his top pair.

"We'll have a coat made especially for you," said the general. Rebecca translated for Mayorpe and he smiled showing his sharp, pointed teeth.

[336]

"Thank you, sir. That would be most welcome."

~

It was lunch time and Rebecca had accepted an invitation to join Neil and his friends for a big get-together. They sat at two tables that had been pulled together for their use. Neil had Chloe and Andrew either side of him. On Chloe's right sat Rachel and Kelly, her two best friends. Next to Andrew sat John and Lisa with an empty chair waiting for Rebecca.

She entered the café and saw them. She returned the wave from Chloe and made her way between tables to sit in her chair between Lisa and Rachel.

Neil said, "This is Rebecca Chambers. Rebecca, I believe you've met almost everyone here, so I'll just introduce you to Kelly Hanson and Rachel Walters."

"Hello, Rebecca," said both Kelly and Rachel almost in unison.

Neil signalled to the waiter.

He came over and said, "Are you ready to order?"

"Yes, but could you start with Rachel over there," Neil pointed at her, "and work clockwise around the table. It'll give Rebecca a little more time to choose."

"Thank you, Neil," said Rebecca.

Once the waiter had taken their orders, they started their conversations again.

"So, Andrew. Have you met any more, young ladies since Roxanne?" asked John.

"I've met lots of them, but I've just walked away," said Andrew.

Lisa, who had just taken a mouthful of wine, managed to spit most of it over the table and everyone started laughing.

[337]

"What's so funny?" asked Andrew.

"I never thought I'd hear you say that, Andy," said Lisa, still chuckling and wiping her mouth with a napkin. "You've never had a problem before. What's changed?"

Andrew was about to answer but John had noticed the interest that Kelly seemed to be showing in him. "Well, I think your next girlfriend could be very close, Andy."

Everyone looked at John.

"She's about the same height, slim, very attractive, around six years younger, dark and mysterious with black dreadlocked hair and sitting at this table."

Now they all looked at Kelly and she darted her head from one face to the next then sat back, open-mouthed.

"I... I don't fancy him."

"Really. Then why haven't you taken your eyes off him since we all sat down?" asked John.

"I've been looking at everyone," she now had her arms crossed in front of her chest.

"Look. Now she's denying it. She really wants you, Andy," said John.

"Stop it, John. Leave her alone," said Andrew.

John looked at Andrew and smiled. "You like her too then."

Lisa gave John a brief elbow to the ribs and whispered from the corner of her mouth, "Shut up, John."

"I'm sorry. I didn't mean to embarrass anyone, but I think they'd make a lovely couple."

"John!" said everyone in unison. He closed his mouth and pretended to zip it shut.

"Kelly. I'm sorry for my man's lack of subtlety. I'm sure that if you two do like each other you can sort it out

[338]

later but, for now, Chloe and I have some news for everyone," said Lisa.

The whole table was listening intently to what she had to say, and Chloe nodded her head. "You tell them, Lisa."

"John asked me to marry him not long ago," she turned to him. "The answer is yes, John. I'd love to marry you."

"Oh, brilliant, Lisa. You really mean it?"

"Yes."

They hugged each other and kissed. When they parted, John had a big smile on his face as he announced, "We're also trying for a baby."

Lisa spoke again. "Also, as you know, Neil and Chloe are getting married. And, Chloe and I have decided to have a double wedding. We haven't set a date yet but we'd both like to be married before we depart on the upcoming mission."

"Oh really," said John. "That soon. Do I have any say in this?"

"No," replied Lisa.

"It should be sometime in January," said Chloe.

The conversation turned to weddings with everyone suggesting different ideas. On several occasions, Andrew's and Kelly's eyes met and both looked quickly away. Although Rebecca was happy for Neil and Chloe, she felt a little sad. There'd be no chance for her to have Neil now. Rebecca closed her eyes, forcing the sadness away then continued to enjoy the rest of the afternoon.

But Chloe had seen her reaction to the news. She'd been purposely watching her in fact. And she decided to keep her eyes on Rebecca just in case.

~

Christmas had passed and 2172 was a couple of weeks old. The tranchillions of section C were starting to walk freely, within *Sentry One*, amongst the humans. The translation devices were working perfectly and, with a few exceptions, there'd been no trouble. With the help of Corporal Mayorpe, two star-ships – the *Resolve* and the *Spirit* had been fitted with the adaptations.

The *Resolve* had been sent out with a skeleton crew to test its performance. The travel time between the moon and Ganymede had been reduced to one day. Previously, it had taken three days to travel that distance. All the calculations had been done and the plans altered accordingly. The tranchillion battleport, along with the *Resolve* and the *Spirit* would leave on the twentieth of January. The battleport would arrive at Anthera in three days and the reinforcements would arrive four days later.

With Neil's input and Captain Xenorphide's help the assault had been planned. The initial attack from the battleport would have one tranchillion integrated into each human unit to help with navigation. The ten tranchillions with the least battle experience were to remain on the battleport when the rest proceeded with the operation.

In the strategy room, the final debate was taking place. Captain Xenorphide stood to get everyone's attention. "If what Officer Bolgon has told us is true we need to leave as soon as possible. Even a few days could save lives."

"The captain is spot on," said Neil. "I'll go with the tranchillions in their battleport taking as many human soldiers as possible. We'll get Dowdneer's attention – forcing him to re-focus most of his forces on us. That, hopefully, will lighten the pressure on General Zemorphoride's troops."

"I'd still prefer all three ships to arrive at the same time," said the general.

Captain Xenorphide sat down in exasperation. "Humans. It's a wonder you haven't been wiped out yet."

That response caused most of the humans in the strategy room to start protesting that the tranchillion couldn't be trusted.

"I'm sure the captain is just anxious to get going so he can save his people," said the general.

The room hushed as it always did when the general spoke.

"I'm sorry everyone. I didn't mean to be derogatory towards yourselves," said Captain Xenorphide.

"You're right, Captain Xenorphide. Perhaps I'm being too cautious. I propose that Neil goes tranchillions to weaken the enemy as much as possible before our main forces arrive. I want a show of hands for all those that agree."

Almost everyone in the room raised their hands.

"Right, that's decided. Tomorrow will be a day of rest for the crews of the *Resolve*, the *Spirit* and the tranchillion battleport."

"*Contention* – my battleport is called the *Contention*," interrupted Captain Xenorphide.

General Bolgon stared at the captain. "I apologize, captain." He returned his attention to the room. "The starships will leave on the twentieth and good luck to you all – dismissed."

Neil walked round to Captain Xenorphide and they shook hands. "Lets free your comrades, captain. I'll see you in two days."

"Thank you for fighting so hard. I really do feel that we need to get back quickly."

"We'll drive Dowdneer away or kill him, don't you worry."

"The colonel's days are numbered, Mr Bolgon – of that you can be sure."

~

David Tressel, Guy Travis and Steve Cox dropped their sweat-soaked training gear into the bags provided then hit the showers.

"These training sessions don't get any easier," said Steve.

"They are increasing the intensity every day. As we get better the training gets harder," said David.

"I Don't know about you guys, but I think we're at least twice as fit as we were. Their training methods are amazing," said Guy as he rubbed the soap over his chest.

"Attention!" called Major Chamberlain from behind them. All three turned to face him and stood to attention as they saluted.

"You lot have come a long way in a short time. Ideally, I'd like at least two months to prepare you, but the call came through only minutes ago. You'll be leaving on the starship *Spirit* the day after tomorrow. I suggest no women, no alcohol and no activities that may get you injured."

Major Chamberlain paced in front of them. "You, Private Travis, are a great pilot. Given time you may even challenge Officer Bolgon in a Star Cruiser. Private Cox and Private Tressel – both of you have shown a great aptitude for firearms and leadership respectively. I hope that all three of you stay on to reach your true potential.

I am damn proud of all three of you. I'll leave you to get dressed."

They all saluted and once the major had left, they relaxed and carried on washing themselves.

"That guy is so intense," said Guy.

"He's the one that trained Neil Bolgon," said David.

"I heard that he was already an officer in the SAS before he joined the Space Federation," said Steve.

"Who told you that?" asked Guy.

"Suzanne of course."

"Is anyone in there called Steve Cox," called an unseen voice from the entrance to the shower room.

"Yes, I'm Steve."

"There's a lady out here for you."

"Okay, thanks," replied Steve.

"Sounds like you'd better hurry up, Stevie boy," said David.

Steve left the shower before the other two and pulled on his uniform. His boots were the last item to go on and by then Guy and David were back with him, towelling themselves.

"Go get, Stevie boy," said David as he whipped Steve on the bottom with his wet towel.

"See you guys later."

"See you later, Steve," both men replied in unison.

Steve left the shower room with his washbag slung over his shoulder. He walked into the corridor and there, stood in front of him, was Suzanne.

"How are you, Steve?"

"Okay, Suzanne. What do you want?"

"Can we talk."

"I've got to take these to laundry. You can walk with me if you like."

[343]

Suzanne walked by his side. "Can you forgive me, Steve? I... I know I should have handled things differently with your father and I'm sorry."

"He's still in prison, Suzanne and you put him there."

"Please, Steve. I love you. I'm prepared to do anything. Anything to get you back," she was starting to plead with him. She had never done that before.

"Look, Suze. I've been angry with you for a long time, but I do still love you," he stopped walking and turned to face her. He saw tears in her eyes and realised that she was being genuine.

"I'm about to go to Anthera and fight against the tranchillions, Suze. This is not the time or place to be making life changing decisions."

"But I needed to let you know before it was too late. I'll quit World News and work for a local if you want..." she stopped as he gently quieted her.

"Shh, Suze. Meet me tomorrow in my quarters and we'll discuss it then."

"Okay and, Steve. Thank..." he kissed her in mid-sentence then left her in the corridor as he strode off to the laundry room.

~

Back in the shower-room, Captain Turner had turned up to congratulate the boys on how well they'd done.

"I never expected you three to do so well. Where's Steve?" asked Captain Turner.

"A woman turned up for him. He must have left with her," said David.

"Do you know who she was?"

"No, we didn't see her. Sorry, sir," said Guy.

[344]

"Hey, you're even remembering to use 'sir' when addressing an officer."

"We try our best, sir," said David.

"Well, I'll let you get on. I've got to oversee the preparations of the *Spirit*, make sure you both have a good rest tomorrow. You deserve it."

Captain Turner left them to get dressed. Once they were dressed, they went in search of Steve.

~

"Come on come on, there's only an hour to go," said Kelly while trying to get Chloe to sit still for her. "Once I've finished your hair you can find your shoes. In fact – Rachel... Rachel."

Rachel appeared from the room next door. "Yes, Kelly."

"Can you find Chloe's shoes please? She seems to have misplaced them."

"Okay, but I need a couple more minutes with Lisa."

Kelly nodded. "I'm going to be half-an-hour here anyway. But that doesn't leave much time to find the shoes and get to the registry office."

Rachel left and picked up the long flap of white silk again. "Sorry girls but they've asked me to find Chloe's shoes. She's lost them."

Now that she could see what she was doing again, Rebecca carried on with the buttons she was doing up. They started in the small of Lisa's back and rose all the way up to the base of her neck.

"I know where they are, Rachel," said Rebecca. "She was supposed to pick them up from Trisha on the way here. I'll bet you anything they're still there."

"That's in *totally* the wrong direction," said Lisa.

[345]

"I'll go as soon as I've finished here," said Rachel. "I'll just about make it back before she has to leave."

"I need two more minutes. These buttons are a bitch to do up, Lisa."

"Sorry but I just had to have this dress as soon as I saw it."

"It was bloody expensive. I don't know why Neil's father decided to buy both your wedding dresses. Neither of you are his daughters," said Rachel.

"Well Chloe will be his daughter-in-law soon and her..." Lisa stopped herself just in time. The knowledge she had nearly given them was private. Chloe would tell people if she wanted. "Her parents can't buy her a dress. I'm a friend of the family and rather cute. Maybe he thought it wouldn't seem proper to buy one without the other."

"Why did you stop what you were saying?" asked Rebecca.

"There's something about her past that I'll not reveal."

"Oh, come on. What is it?" said Rebecca.

"Leave it. I mean it."

"Okay, Lisa," Rebecca pressed her lips together with the effort of pushing the last button through its hole. "There, finished," she said triumphantly. Rachel lowered the silk flap and fastened it at the bottom either side of Lisa's hips.

"You look lovely, Lisa," said Rachel.

"I do don't I," replied Lisa with the biggest grin on her face.

"Soon you'll be known as Lisa Lyderattle. It has a certain ring to it doesn't it," said Rebecca.

[346]

"One with a big fuckin diamond in it," said Lisa. They all started laughing.

"I've got to go now. You'll manage the rest, Rebecca?" said Rachel.

"Yes of course. Go, or she'll be going barefoot," replied Rebecca.

Rachel walked to the next room and said from the doorway, "I'm off to get your shoes. If I'm not back by the time you leave, put a note on the outside door. It'll save me having to search the rooms. See you all soon."

"Thanks, Rachel. I don't know what's wrong with me lately," said Chloe.

"You're pregnant. The baby's sucking the intelligence from you with every passing minute," said Kelly.

Rachel left the room shaking her head and ran off to Trisha's quarters.

~

In another room, only a few hundred meters away, both Neil and John were ready to go. John had on a black suit with red silk shirt underneath and was relaxing in an armchair.

"I bet those girls are still deciding what make-up to wear and which colour handbag goes best with their outfits," said John.

"If they make it on time it doesn't matter," said Neil.

Keith and Laura were sitting in the corner – their jobs done.

"You both look lovely," said Laura. "Not at all like soldiers."

"That reminds me, Laura," said Neil. "I'm going to ask dad to reinstate your rank and command of Green Squadron. We're going to need the best on Anthera."

[347]

"Thanks, Neil. Do you think he will reinstate me?"

"I can only try. I do have some influence but, at the end of the day, it's his decision."

Neil finished polishing his shoes and put them on. "What do you guys think?"

Neil had a black suit on the same as John, but he'd chosen a white shirt instead.

"I'll go along with Laura," said Keith, not hearing Neil's question.

"It won't be long before you two are getting hitched. You're already doing everything she says," said John.

"Hey!" exclaimed Laura. "I don't tell him what to do."

"Yes, you do. You're used to doing it. It comes with being in command. You used to tell nine other men what to do," retorted John.

"That's different, you annoying little..." she tapered off as she couldn't find the right word.

"Hey! Less of the little. I'll have you know that Lisa's a very lucky girl. The size of my..."

John was cut short by Keith. "John there's a lady present."

John looked at Laura. "She ain't no lady. Just like Lisa. Being a soldier means you kill people and that knocks all the ladylike tendency's out of you."

"That's a load of bollocks," said Laura.

"See – see," said John waving a finger in Laura's direction. "Even when she tries to defend herself, she swears. That's not at all ladylike."

Laura shrugged in defeat and shook her head.

"You know all this is harmless banter," said John. "We *are* still friends?"

"Of course, John. Of course," she started smiling again. "Besides, if I had taken it personally, you'd be flat on your back by now."

"You had better tone it down at the ceremony," said Neil.

"Oh, I promised Lisa I'll be on my best behaviour."

"He's right though, Keith. He's doing as he's told and getting married today, hopefully, without any fuss," said Neil.

Laura and Keith looked at one another and Keith shook his head at Laura's silent question. They smiled and kissed.

~

With just two minutes left before they were due to leave, Rachel got back with Chloe's shoes. After she'd caught her breath, and Chloe had her shoes on, Rachel said, "Trish sends her regards and hopes that you like them."

"I'll thank her later," said Chloe.

"Right, let's go," Kelly stood. "Time waits for no man – or woman," she added.

When they got to the registry office Chloe had a sneak peek inside the reception room. It was packed and at the back sat four tranchillions. Captain Xenorphide, Capustri Carphide and two of Neil's new best friends, Marsup Mayorpe and Putil Ptierwelope. Putil was one of the tranchillions who helped in the rescue on Ganymede.

"Don't they look frightening," said Rachel, indicating the tranchillions. She had also taken a sneak peek.

"I'm sure we look frightening to anything smaller than us," said Chloe.

"I don't trust them. I mean until recently we *were* fighting them."

[349]

"If Neil says we can trust them, that's good enough for me."

At the far end of the reception room both Neil and John were waiting for their brides. Keith and Andrew were stood next to them in their roles as best men. Andrew, who was Neil's best man, leaned over and whispered into Neil's ear, "Good luck, bro."

Neil took Andrew's hand and smiled. Then he pulled him in close and patted his back. "Thanks," he whispered.

Just then the music started, and everyone turned to the double-doors at the back of the room. Neil spotted Suzanne off to one side as his gaze swept over the entire congregation. She was busy writing notes.

The double-doors opened and in walked General Bolgon, dressed in full military uniform, with Chloe on his left arm and Lisa on his right. Following behind, holding the veil's, were Kelly and Rachel with Rebecca and Laura carrying the rings on little cushions made for the occasion.

The ceremony went extremely well and at the reception party afterwards everyone got drunk – including Neil who normally chose not to. Most of them were going to regret their excesses the next day.

~

The departure date had finally arrived and, after saying goodbye to their loved ones, three-thousand soldiers and crew boarded the *Contention* and the starships *Spirit* and *Resolve*. All the crew were going about their usual checks. No faults were found and the ready signal from all three star-ships lit up on the main desk in the control room.

General Bolgon opened a link to all three ships and gave his final speech. All three-thousand personnel were lifted by his battle-cry as they cheered. Now he could do no more. It was up to the brave men and women leaving in those starships to end this war.

The *Contention's* engines started, and the exhaust ports began to glow. It lifted off the hanger floor and hovered as the hanger doors started opening. The exhaust ports glowed brighter and the tranchillion battleport moved forwards into the exit corridor and out into space.

It was quickly followed by both two-thousand-meter-long human starships. They moved into formation, with the *Contention* taking the lead. All three accelerated forwards at full thrust. The *Contention* engaged its short-range Hyper-drive and disappeared.

In three days, it would be orbiting Anthera. Four days after that the *Resolve* and the *Spirit* would catch them up. The battle at Anthera would soon begin.

CHAPTER EIGHTEEN

January 2172

Anthera

"They should have been back by now," said Colonel Twochelope, pacing the room.

"Have a little more faith in their abilities, Tchzor. The very nature of a stealth operation means that it could take a little longer than anticipated," replied General Zemorphoride.

"I think we should send someone else, sir."

"There has been no 'comm' chatter. If they'd been spotted or captured, we would have heard about it on the radio. Now, calm down and start acting like a colonel."

Colonel Twochelope sat and controlled his breathing; calming himself. Once he had control again, he opened his eyes and said, "Shouldn't Neil's people be here by now. Surely they've had long enough."

"Patience, Tchzor. Any day now they'll be back. I can feel it."

They heard running feet coming from the only corridor leading off the main room. The tranchillion slowed to a walking pace as he approached them. "They're back, sir."

"Okay, go and help," said General Zemorphoride. "See, colonel. The stealth mission *was* a success and the humans *will* help us."

They heard running again but this time the tranchillion burst into the room. "They've found us. I think the team's dead, sir."

Colonel Twochelope jumped up and gestured for two soldiers to join him as he ran towards the airlock. He looked through the glass and could see the rope still dangling over the side. The sentry was sitting with his back to the wall, one hand on his shoulder. The hand dropped as he lost strength and Colonel Twochelope saw the wound. The suit had re-sealed itself, but he could see that the sentry was in trouble.

"Can we close the outer door from here?" he asked the visibly shaken soldier.

"Yes, sir. But you need the code."

"Get the code as quick as you can. Go, run!" ordered Colonel Twochelope. *If they get enough soldiers inside that airlock we could be in trouble*, he thought.

A head appeared and one of Colonel Dowdneer's soldiers scrambled into the airlock. He knelt and pointed his rifle towards the colonel.

[353]

"Quick with those codes, there's one aboard already!" he shouted towards the main room. When he looked back the soldier had slung his rifle over his shoulder and was placing charges on the inner airlock door.

Oh no, they'll suck us all out, he thought.

The soldier returned and entered the code. The lights inside the airlock started flashing and the outer door began to close. Dowdneer's man inside the airlock was talking to someone on his radio. Suddenly he ran towards the closing outer airlock door.

Colonel Twochelope realised what was going to happen and started running towards the main room. "Come on, run – run for your lives!"

They all ran as fast as they could and dived through the doorway.

"Close it quickly! And lock it!" yelled the colonel in a panicked voice.

Just as the door closed, and the general typed in the code to lock it, there was an explosion and they could hear a whistling sound coming from the other side of the door.

It started creaking and dents appeared in the centre as the air was ripped out of the corridor. Then all fell silent. The outer airlock was sealed and the rope – severed. The soldier still on the rope fell from near the top. Although the fall was not as fast as it would have been on a planet with earth's gravity, it was still enough for him to be killed on impact.

"They tried to kill us all with a charge, we could've been sucked out into space," said Colonel Twochelope.

"What are we going to do now, sir?" asked one of the soldiers.

[354]

"We'll have to ration our food and hope the humans come and save us," replied General Zemorphoride. "It all rests on them now."

The entire room stayed silent, most of them believing they were doomed.

~

Dowdneer stood over his communication screen. "Is it done, Marsup?"

"It's done," replied Lt Col Maverphoride, "but we didn't get the result we wanted, sir."

"What happened, Marsup?"

"The explosion had the desired effect. A lot of debris and one body was sucked out, but they somehow over-rode the airlock door and closed it. We have no way of knowing if they are alive or dead, sir."

"They'll be alive, Marsup. I can't be that lucky. Let's hope that plan B works."

"I'll get back inside, sir and see how it's going."

"Okay, Marsup. I'll see you soon."

Colonel Dowdneer slammed his fist on the table and made everything on it jump. *At least following those soldiers helped us find out how they were getting out. That's something I suppose*, he thought.

He was about to sit back when the intercom buzzed. Dowdneer pressed a button. "Yes!" he snapped.

"Sir, something just appeared on the radar."

"Have you got a visual yet?"

"No, sir. It's still too far out."

"Get onto Lt Col Maverphoride and tell him to hurry up in case it's hostile."

"Sir."

Several minutes passed until the buzzer sounded again and Dowdneer answered it. "Yes."

"Sir, it's the *Contention*. The one that escaped a while ago, sir."

"What defences do we have?"

"Just the fighters' and one battleport. We don't have sufficient power to use the lasers, sir."

"Why?"

"There must be a fault in the communication circuit, sir. I think it's draining the power."

"Launch the fighters but save the battleport."

We might need to escape in it later, he thought.

Within two minutes all remaining fighters were launched to begin an attack on their own battleport. Moments later, the *Contention* launched its own fighters.

Let the battle commence, thought Colonel Dowdneer.

"Sir, there's something wrong. Somehow, they've managed to get reinforcements. No... no it can't be."

"What is it. Spit it out soldier," commanded Colonel Dowdneer.

"Alien fighters', sir. Some of them are alien fighters."

Colonel Dowdneer sat back in his chair, closed his eyes and sighed. "How many?"

"A lot, sir."

"Carry on. Kill as many of them as you can," Colonel Dowdneer opened his direct line to Lt Col Maverphoride. "Marsup."

"Yes, sir. What's going on? There seems to be fighting above us."

"Make sure you stay out of sight. You won't stand a chance if those fighters zero in on you. We may have to use the back-up plan after all. We can't defend ourselves if all our fighters are destroyed."

[356]

"What about the lasers?"

"I know why the general didn't re-open the communications system. It's damaged somehow and seems to be draining the power."

"I'll ready the rovers when I get back, sir."

"Shit... shit, shit, shit!" Colonel Dowdneer picked up a large ornament from the desk and threw it against the far wall where it smashed into thousands of tiny fragments. "Arrggghhh!" he screamed out in frustration.

"How... how did they get the aliens involved," said Colonel Dowdneer. "Perhaps they were captured again. This doesn't make sense."

There was no one else in the room.

~

The Star Cruiser looked out of control as it barrel-rolled continuously towards Anthera's surface. Neil kept his eye on the rear-view screen and waited for the pursuing tranchillion fighter to get closer then he said, "Now."

Andrew pressed a button that released a container full of smoke out of the rear of the Star Cruiser. Neil stopped the barrel-rolls and pulled up sharply, taking Andrew by surprise and to the brink of unconsciousness, before banking to his left. The tranchillion emerged from the smoke and hit the ground at full speed. The resulting explosion would have been blinding and deafening to anyone on the surface.

"Whoo-hoo!" yelled Andrew. "That was brilliant."

"There's no time for celebrations. We've got two more coming in," said Neil.

After twisting and turning and several evasive manoeuvres Neil managed to lure one of the fighters into his sights. He fired then continued his evasive manoeuvres as the fighter exploded and hit the ground.

"Hang-on, sir. I'm coming in," said Capustri Carphide from her tranchillion fighter. The pursuing fighter suddenly lost power and dropped towards the surface after Capustri took out its engines. The distinctive fluorescent yellow markings sprayed all over her fighter shone as she flashed past Neil's Star Cruiser.

"Thanks, Capustri. I owe you one," said Neil.

"Any time, Neil."

The battle continued furiously for five minutes until the tranchillion fighters were all destroyed. Neil scanned round to make sure there were no hostile fighters left.

"You may approach, Captain. All hostiles have been eliminated," said Neil.

The *Contention* descended and landed near to where the Star Cruisers had already settled. Neil walked over to the battleport followed by Andrew. The rest of the pilots stayed close to their fighters.

The rear exit ramp opened and out drove sixty ground assault vehicles. Each one had a single unit of ten soldiers inside which would split into two equal squads when they got to their designated way-points. Every assault vehicle, except one, set off as soon as they hit the ground.

"Within ten minutes the mother ship should be surrounded," said Neil to Andrew. "When I'm on board the AV, you'll have control of Star Cruiser One. Your co-pilot is on the AV. Just make sure you come back, okay."

Andrew gave Neil a quick hug. "You stay safe, Neil. What you're doing is a lot more dangerous."

The AV pulled up beside them and, after waving goodbye to Neil, Andrew led his co-pilot towards Star

[358]

Cruiser One. Neil climbed aboard the AV and was welcomed by John and Lisa. Both were wearing combat suits.

"Let's get this done," said John.

Neil smiled at John then turned to the comms man. "Can I have the microphone?"

The comms man handed it over and Neil adjusted the frequency until he found the channel that General Zemorphoride was on.

"General Zemorphoride. Do you read? This is Neil Bolgon. Do you read?"

There was a moment of static before the signal cleared and the general's voice came through. "This is General Zemorphoride. Is that Neil's voice I hear?"

"Sod it. He can't understand me without those new translators," said Neil. He called Putil over and the tranchillion changed seats with the comms man.

"Can you talk to him and find out what's going on?"

"Of course," Putil took the microphone and repeated Neil's earlier question.

"Who am I talking to?" asked Zemorphoride.

"Private Ptierwelope, sir."

"Where is Neil Bolgon?"

"Right here, sir. I'm acting as translator."

"Tell him that the escape hatch has been damaged and cannot be opened so we'll have to go out through the main door."

Putil repeated the instructions to Neil.

"Ask him what the situation is like in there."

Putil waited for the reply then said, "The supplies are getting low and rationing has been enforced. It was never designed for that amount of people."

"How long have they got?"

"About four days," repeated Putil.

"All right. Tell him we'll be there as soon as possible."

Neil searched his memory for details of their plan and came up with a few amendments.

"Unit twelve, prepare for entry but wait until I get there. Unit one, move to unit twelve's position. Be ready as back-up." Neil gave the microphone back to the comms man and touched the driver on his shoulder. "Move out to unit twelve's position," he ordered.

~

General Zemorphoride addressed his people. "Listen everyone. The human, Neil Bolgon, has returned. He knows what our situation is and will rescue us shortly. Everyone will keep to the rationing in case it takes him a few days to get to us. That's all."

The situation didn't look much better than before he'd heard from Neil but at least he had come back. Colonel Twochelope approached the general.

"What did he say, sir?"

"He said that he'd be here as soon as possible."

"How many soldiers has he brought with him?"

"He didn't say."

The general sat back behind his desk, sighed, then looked at Colonel Twochelope. "That human – Neil Bolgon – is quite the soldier, Tchzor. It would be so much easier for them to destroy us all and go home."

"If that happens it won't be Neil's decision, but I honestly can't see them going down that route, sir."

"Why's that, Tchzor?"

It was Colonel Twochelope's turn to sigh as he pulled a chair closer and sat down. "I've got something to tell you, sir. It's how I knew about Neil being here and how I knew about Colonel Dowdneer."

"You knew before he revealed himself?"

"Yes, sir. I found out the day he had his quarters bugged."

"Why didn't you tell me, Tchzor?"

"I couldn't at that time, sir. The only evidence I had that his intentions were to help and not destroy us were voices in my head."

The general frowned and leant forwards. "What do you mean, voices?"

"There's another civilization from our part of the galaxy called the *Watchers*. I don't know if that's what they're really called or whether it's just a simplified version that we can pronounce, but that's the name they gave me. They are telepathic and can talk to us in our minds. They told me that Neil would be coming, and they also told his female companion about me."

"They have never talked to me, Tchzor."

"They can only talk to certain individuals who are psychic. You're not, sir."

"Well I guess all we can do is wait for Neil and hope that he can get to us."

"He will get to us, sir. He will get to us," said Twochelope then added a thought which he kept to himself, *I just hope it's before we die.*

~

They had arrived at the loading bay. It was the only way in now that the docking bay was sealed off and the escape hatch damaged. The normal way in and out for the troops would not be viable as the mothership was resting on its hull, the landing gear smashed and irrelevant.

[361]

They were in a stand-off now as Colonel Dowdneer had realised that the only way in or out was via the loading bay. He'd stationed the greater part of his troops in defence of it.

The forcefield was all that stood between Dowdneer's troops and Neil's two units. It kept the air inside the mothership, and anything solid would go through but lasers were another matter. As they were essentially an intense beam of radiation in the infra-red spectrum they couldn't pass through.

Both forces could see each other and neither wanted to be the first to step through and into the line of fire. Neil was busy trying to work out a plan-of-attack when John and Lisa joined him.

"They're dug in well, Neil. How are we going to get in?" asked John.

"I've no idea. The only option is a direct assault to take them by force but to do that we need the *Resolve* and the *Spirit* here to overwhelm them with numbers."

"Isn't there another way in?" asked Lisa.

"There were two other ways. The back way via the escape hatch which was the original plan until Dowdneer found and destroyed it. The other way in was err... destroyed by me as we escaped the first time."

"Well at least that keeps them from sending out any more fighters or battleports," said Lisa.

"They sent out some fighters to intercept us when we arrived. Where did they come from?" asked John.

"Good question, John. Let's ask Captain Xenorphide," said Neil as they walked towards the assault vehicle. Neil picked up a headset and attached it to his ear.

"This is Neil Bolgon. I need to speak with Captain Xenorphide."

"Yes, Neil. What's the situation?" replied the captain.

"Dowdneer has amassed what must be the greater part of his troops to the loading bay. We're not getting in here any time soon."

"Great. Have you any alternative entry points figured out yet?"

"No, sir. At least not yet. That's why I'm calling. Is there another entrance for your fighters to exit? The one's that intercepted us had to have come from somewhere."

"Hold on while I check."

Neil looked away from the screen, on the radio's main unit, to check on the situation in front of him. Nothing was happening. It seemed to Neil that Colonel Dowdneer was content to sit it out. Time was on his side. The general and his soldiers had little time to spare and the colonel knew it.

Neil looked back at his screen as the blankness was replaced by an image of Captain Xenorphide.

"There are multiple exits from this side of the ship, but all are too high to be reached from the ground."

"Can the battleport fit in the exits?"

"No, they are launch tubes for the fighters."

"How good is your crew at holding a steady position in flight?"

"Do you mean hovering, Neil?"

"Yes. I have an idea on how to get in. If anything went wrong at least we'd have got supplies to the general. But we'd need rescuing as well," he shrugged. "That's all I can come up with."

"How long can they last, Neil?"

"Judging from what they said – by the time the fleet arrives they won't have had any food or water for two days. And fighting through Dowdneer's men, even with an overwhelming force, would take at least two more days."

"What's your plan then, Neil?"

"I lead a small unit in through the launch tubes to reach the bunker followed by three or more units to hold the corridors between the bunker and the docking bay. If there isn't any resistance, we get them out. If there is, the back-up units retreat, and my unit stays in the bunker to await rescue."

"Sounds good to me. I'll be expecting you back soon."

"Okay, sir. We're on our way."

Neil left the radio to the operator again and called back his unit. They got back on board the AV and waited for Neil. He left instructions with units twelve and one to use grenades to help them through the force-field and do the best they can to cause a distraction.

Neil got in the AV and they moved off to the other side of the mothership.

~

"All the tests are complete, sir. Basically, the ship's dying," said Lt Col Maverphoride. "There is a possibility that the back-up generators can be fixed which, given time, will restore the batteries. However, to do that the power-drain must be nullified."

"You mean switching the comms off again don't you," said Colonel Dowdneer.

"I'm afraid so, sir. It's the only way. Once the power fails completely the life support will fail as will the force-fields protecting us from space. The shield doors may not even function to cut off the vacuum. If that happens the whole interior would be gutted and sucked out into space."

"It doesn't look like we have much choice then. Keep the comms open while you're fixing the generators just in case you need to report back. We'll go from there."

"Okay, sir. Are there any orders on the loading bay situation?"

"No. They're staying outside, and we'll stay where we are. By now the general will be running out of supplies since we've cut off his little expeditions," Dowdneer started chuckling. "As long as we keep them out, the general and his troops will cease to be a problem."

Marsup left the room and started his search for the engineers he needed. Colonel Dowdneer stayed where he was and continued to think about different ways to win. As far as he could tell he had every situation covered.

~

The AV ascended the ramp and stopped inside the loading bay of the *Contention*. Everyone got out and, once the ramp had closed, took off their helmets.

Captain Xenorphide strode into the loading bay and everyone saluted him.

"Situation report," commanded the captain.

"Once the suits are fully restored, we'll immediately prepare to enter the *Dragen* through the fighter launch tubes, sir," said Neil.

"Are you sure you can do this?" asked the captain.

"Yes, sir."

"Okay, everyone going on the mission get some rest and good luck."

An hour later the teams were suited up and ready to go.

"Is unit three ready?" asked Neil.

"Ready, sir."

"Right, let's get on with it. You all know what you're doing."

Every soldier present nodded and they moved over to the access tunnel that would connect them to the mothership.

The battleport lifted off and flew towards the *Dragen's* launch tubes. It hovered in line with an exit hole and the access tunnel extended towards the mothership. While they waited for the green light Neil gave his final rallying speech.

"The aim is to get them out but once we engage the enemy Colonel Dowdneer will send reinforcements. I'd say that we'll have about five minutes from first contact before they arrive. There could be anywhere from ten soldiers up to around four or five hundred. If it looks like we can't hold our escape route, we enter the bunker or retreat to the *Contention* and wait for the *Resolve* and the *Spirit*. The supplies we've brought will be more than enough to last the few days we'll need them. Let's aim for extraction but remember, if anything goes wrong, stay with your designated tranchillion and good luck."

They started filing through the tunnel after putting on their helmets with Neil, Putil, John, Lisa and a young, but excellent, soldier named Private James White going through first. Neil's team reached the launch tube.

"Do you know anything about these tubes, Putil?" asked Neil.

"Just that they launch the fighters from them. The pilots get into the fighters in the docking bay then a

[366]

magnetic clamp attaches to them and they're carried to the launch tubes. There's a maintenance hatch built into the side which is where we'll access the ship."

"That's good enough for me," said Neil.

After passing through a force field within the launch tube they emerged into the fighter's space and moved over to the maintenance hatch. Neil looked round at his team.

"We'll just have to open it and hope that there's no-one on the other side," he said.

"If you open it carefully then there's a good chance that no-one will notice you anyway," said Putil. "We use a mobile ladder to reach the hatch from the other side."

"How far is the drop?" asked John.

After a brief pause, he replied, "Oh I'd say about thirteen feet roughly. I've never measured it."

"We should all be able to take a drop like that," said John.

Neil opened the hatch slightly and peeked through. There was no-one in the immediate vicinity, so he opened it further and stuck his head out then he withdrew back into the launch tube.

"Looks clear and the mobile ladder is only about twenty feet away. Putil and I will go first and bring the ladder back if the coast is clear," said Neil.

They all nodded. Neil re-opened the hatch and lowered himself down until his arms were at full stretch then he let go and dropped the remaining seven feet to the floor. As his feet hit the cold metal surface of the docking bay, he bent his knees and rolled into a crouch, bringing his rifle up in front, scanning for any movement.

There was none and a moment later Putil landed next to him just using knee spring to cushion his fall. Together they moved to the edge of the launch tube and looked out into the deserted docking bay. The shield doors were down blocking any potential entry that way, but Neil supposed they could be opened to allow a major assault access to the mothership.

This was the opposite side of the ship to where Colonel Dowdneer's main force was lying in wait. If they managed to keep their presence unknown, they might be able to use this docking bay.

"It's empty, Putil. Let's get the ladder over to the hatch."

"Yes, sir," replied Putil. They walked over to the ladder – while remaining aware of any possible hostiles. They grabbed each side of the ladder and pushed it into position. Within another minute all of Neil's team was on the floor and ready to move.

Neil touched his helmet near his ear. "Sergeant Phillips. The docking bay is clear. We're moving to secure the exit. Do you copy?"

"Yes, sir. We're in the tube and ready to access the hatch."

"There's a ladder set up for you. Last team through needs to move it away."

"Copy that, sir. We're coming through."

Neil signalled for his team to move and they ran across the hanger floor to the main exit covering all angles with their rifles.

"You go first, Putil and we'll follow. Try to stay silent. If a target needs taking down, do it hand-to-hand unless compromised. Is everyone clear?" said Neil.

They all nodded and Putil opened the door, looking both ways down the corridor, then he moved off with the rest of the team close behind. They kept going until they came to a left turn where they halted.

"Hold here until team two catches up," ordered Neil.

Shortly team two arrived and Neil addressed their team leader. "Hold this position and keep Capustri on patrol. Capustri, do your patrol as suggested but don't leave their sight."

"Yes, sir," said Capustri as she started her patrol of the surrounding corridors. The rest of her team set themselves up on the corners to watch for any tranchillion patrols that may stumble across them.

"Let's go," said Neil to his squad. They all set off following Putil again until the next major turn off where they waited for team three to catch up. They continued to advance like this until their objective loomed in front of them.

"How many guards?" asked John.

"I can't tell from here but there must be at least four of them," said Neil.

"There is another way round. We could attack them in a pincer movement," said Putil.

"Okay, John, Lisa. You go with Putil and when you're in position we'll take them out. Set your rifles to stun in case you have to use them."

Putil set off with John and Lisa. They were approaching one of the corridors that led to the bunker when Putil signalled for them to wait. They took up positions covering both directions and waited for Putil's return.

A few seconds later he was back carrying an unconscious tranchillion. He signalled for John to open a door across the other side of the corridor. John and Lisa entered the room with their rifles leading the way.

[369]

The room was empty with no other exits so Putil laid the tranchillion on the floor and hurried over to a wall cabinet to his left. He opened the cabinet and removed a handful of cross-shaped objects.

"What are those?" asked John.

"Wrist-binders. We keep them in cabinets all over the ship just in case," said Putil.

"In case of what?" asked Lisa.

"We are very strong and if one of us needed controlling for whatever reason these are the easiest way," he held one up to show them. "We can't break one of these open and if the prisoner starts to get unruly, we simply use this," he took a small, finger sized, remote out of the cabinet and pressed the button on it. All the binders gave off a short electrical charge.

"Guaranteed to put its captive down but you have to aim it at the binders."

Putil turned the unconscious soldier onto his front and touched one end of the cross to his wrist. The end wrapped around the wrist and moulded in place. Putil restrained all four of the tranchillion's wrists.

"We'll leave him here. In ten minutes, they'll change guards. Let's get moving," said Putil.

John radioed his latest Intel to Neil then followed Putil and Lisa. They took their position and John let Neil know they'd arrived.

Simultaneously Putil, John and Lisa attacked from their side while Neil and James took out the guards' opposite. They were totally surprised by the attack and not a single shot was fired.

Neil switched the frequency on his radio to the position he had last contacted General Zemorphoride on then he handed it to Putil.

[370]

"Come in, General Zemorphoride. This is Putil Ptierwelope. Come in," he repeated until he received an answer.

"Putil. You're back. Where are you?" asked Colonel Twochelope.

"I'm outside the bunker door with Neil Bolgon, sir. We have taken care of the guards and would like to enter."

"Confirm your identity."

Putil looked at Neil. "He wants me to confirm my identity." He shrugged his shoulders.

"Who are you talking to?"

"Colonel Twochelope."

Neil told Putil about how they met him. "Remind him of that and he'll let us in." *Sorry Rebecca*, he thought.

"Colonel. When you and Neil entered Rebecca's room you found her in human form and topless. That's how you found out about them, sir."

The bunker door opened and in walked Neil's team carrying all four unconscious tranchillions fully bound. They laid them in a corner and Neil approached General Zemorphoride.

Neil's team handed out translation devices so everyone in the room could understand each other.

"They're coming," called Private James White from the door.

"James, John, Lisa – take them out then cover the first corner." Neil then said to the general, "Let's go."

General Zemorphoride stood. "Everyone, grab a weapon if you've got one then follow Neil."

They heard shots outside and Neil stopped at the bunker door. He peered out and saw an injured tranchillion crawl around a corner further up the corridor.

"Sit rep," called Neil.

John spoke up. "Three hostiles dead. One injured, sir."

"We can assume that the word's out. Expect extreme resistance within ten minutes. Let the survivors past then follow on. James."

"Yes, sir."

"You're to lead the survivors back to the docking bay. Don't stop for anything," he turned to Putil. "Take White's position. Everyone ready... move out."

Neil left the doorway and advanced towards the corner the injured tranchillion had escaped around.

~

The tranchillion leaned back against the wall, coughing and holding his leg. He reached to his mouth and wiped the sticky yellow liquid away with the back of his hand. He'd been hit in the chest and leg. He knew he didn't have long as he touched the transmit button on his earpiece.

"Come in, Colonel," he started coughing again. "Please come in, sir."

"What's up?" came Dowdneer's reply.

"There's aliens inside," more coughing and his blood splattered the floor between his legs. "The bunker – they're escaping."

Neil appeared at the corner and fired twice – ending the conversation. He heard Dowdneer's voice on the downed soldier's commlink but resisted the urge to reply. Neil ran back to the others.

~

[372]

The engineer attached the last circuit in place and screwed the cover shut. "That's it, sir. Shall I?"

Lt Col Maverphoride nodded. "Let's see if it works."

The engineer flicked back the safety flap and pressed the start button. The back-up generator started humming and the power level dial started lighting up indicating that it was working. Marsup smiled then opened a direct line to Colonel Dowdneer.

"The back-up generator's working again, sir," reported Marsup.

"Good. Now give me five minutes to check on all operations then switch off the comms and come back here," said Dowdneer.

"Understood, sir. I'll be with you soon."

Marsup waited for the allotted time then changed channels and contacted his engineer waiting at the comms station. "Switch it off then go back to your normal duties."

The comm system went dead and the generator's indicator changed as the hum gradually got louder. The dial now indicated full capacity.

"Good, it seems to have worked. You may now go back to preparing the vehicles," said Marsup.

The engineer left and Marsup made his way back to Colonel Dowdneer with two soldiers in tow.

~

Neil's unit was last through the docking bay door. He was pleased to see that General Zemorphoride had already organised his defences. There were only two entrances into the docking bay and the general had them both covered. Neil walked over to him.

[373]

"Do you want to hold this bay or retreat to the *Contention*, sir?"

"We'll stay. Dowdneer has no way in without getting slaughtered. When are your troops due?"

"About three and a half days, sir."

"In that case, I think we'd better get the shield doors open to allow the rest of your troops in. It's going to be a hard three days."

"No doubt," replied Neil.

General Zemorphoride looked down at his translator. "How does this work?"

"I don't know, sir. I leave that kind of thing to the scientists."

"It's very clever. Maybe your race will have something to trade for our hyper-drive technology after all."

~

Colonel Dowdneer was satisfied that everything was going well. The aliens were waiting outside with no way in. The general was inside the bunker with no way out and with the comms about to be switched off the power levels should start to rise.

The comms system on Dowdneer's desk started crackling then a weak voice came through the speaker. "Come in, Colonel." Dowdneer heard some coughing. "Please come in, sir."

Dowdneer pressed a button. "What's up?"

"There's aliens inside," the next bout of coughing left him in no doubt that this soldier was in trouble. "The bunker – they're escaping," Dowdneer heard the unmistakable sound of a laser then the link ended.

"Soldier come in. Come in damn it!"

[374]

Dowdneer realised he was dead and pressed the button again. "Marsup, are you there?"

The comms system went dead.

"Aarrrgggh! Not again!" he shouted.

The door opened and one of Dowdneer's guards entered with his laser drawn.

"Get me a runner, quick," said Dowdneer.

How did the aliens get inside? It's not possible, he thought. A runner entered the office.

"Ah, go to the loading bay and send half of the soldiers defending it to the bunker. Tell them to use extreme caution as there are aliens on board."

The runner left his office. Dowdneer got up and started pacing.

Lt Col Maverphoride found Dowdneer still agitated when he entered ten minutes later. "What's wrong, sir?"

"Wrong. Wrong. What could possibly be wrong, Marsup. Oh, maybe a little thing like aliens running around in my ship perhaps. How the hell did they get on board!"

Another runner entered the office. "Sir. The starboard docking bay doors have been opened."

"That's their entry point, Marsup. It's not far from the bunker." Dowdneer then said to the runner, "Get to the soldiers I sent to the bunker and tell them to secure the starboard docking bay."

Colonel Dowdneer picked up his rifle, checked the charge level, then said, "Marsup – go to the loading bay and select eighteen soldiers, an engineer and a medic. Bring them to the battleport. We're switching to plan B. Leave instructions for the soldiers defending the loading bay to start attacking the aliens ten minutes after you leave. Is that clear?"

"Yes, sir." Marsup left Dowdneer's office and the colonel un-holstered his side-arm, checking the charge level on that as well. He opened his desk drawer and picked up all the spare clips he could find then inserted them onto his belt.

"Let's go," he instructed his guards as he left his office.

~

The door leading to the corridor opened slightly and stopped for a few seconds. Then it opened further and a tranchillion soldier stepped through, scanning the area in front of him. He looked at the, now open, shield doors then stepped further into the docking bay. Another tranchillion stepped in behind him. The other door into the docking bay opened and two more tranchillions entered.

Laser fire suddenly took all four out. Both doors opened again and this time the assault team came in firing. A barrage of laser fire answered them, cutting down several soldiers before they retreated to the safety of the corridor.

"It's a bottleneck, sir. If we go through, we'll die," said one of the survivors.

"Then we'll have to set up a trap of our own and wait for them to come to us," replied their commander. "Send a runner to tell the colonel."

~

The flight crew were ready and Dowdneer paced in front of the battleport waiting for Maverphoride to arrive. An engineer and a medic had already arrived and Dowdneer was getting impatient. The hanger door opened and in strode Lt Col Maverphoride with the requested eighteen soldiers following on behind.

"What took you so long, Marsup?"

"What. I was quick."

"Never mind. Get in everyone."

With Colonel Dowdneer the last to board, he entered the cockpit, "Take off and land at these coordinates, but stay low and fly quietly. Have the aliens outside moved to the loading bay?"

"Yes, sir."

"The coast is clear. Take off."

The battleport lifted off from the hanger floor and slowly moved out into space. It settled down on the surface and five *rovers* emerged from the back. They waited outside.

Colonel Dowdneer gave his final instructions to the pilot then got into the lead *rover*. The battleport lifted off and started searching for targets.

"Let's go driver. Stay close to the cliff face until we must cut across the flat lands. We definitely don't want to be seen in these."

The group of five *rovers* moved off unseen in the darkness and laser fire started to light up an area around the other side of the mothership. Dowdneer smiled. *Die you alien scum, one day I'll be back, one day you'll pay.*

~

Fighters flooded out of the *Contention* as Andrew, now leading Red Squadron, took off from the surface. The lone battleport had killed hundreds already.

"All right everybody, we need to divert that battleport away from the ground troops," ordered Andrew. He flew straight towards it firing continuously before banking away at the last second. Their lasers were proving ineffective against the battleport's shields.

"Keep at it, it's working. Now let's try and lead it away from our troops," said Andrew.

The battleport had turned towards the *Contention*, which was manoeuvring into a position of attack, and focused all its firepower on it. The *Contention's* shields flickered, weakening. The battleport fired again and the last few shots penetrated the *Contention's* shields. It shook violently as the impacts damaged the hull and fires broke out in the damaged areas. The *Contention* dropped away from the fight and landed on the surface of Anthera.

"It's too powerful. How can we defeat it?" said one of the pilots.

"Just keep up the pressure and don't give in," said Andrew.

~

"Are we just going to sit here?" said one of Dowdneer's soldiers.

"Until we hear from the colonel, we'll confine them to the docking bay," said Sergeant Omirphoride, their commander.

"We've been in a stalemate for an hour already. When will we hear from him?"

Sergeant Omirphoride looked at the disgruntled soldier next to him. "I've already sent a runner to the colonel. Now sit tight." His warning glare forced the soldier into silence.

Twelve minutes later the runner came back, out of breath. "Sir... I can't find him."

"What do you mean you can't find him?"

"I've been all over the ship, sir. There's not a trace anywhere."

"He's left us to die hasn't he," said the disgruntled soldier.

Sergeant Omirphoride drew his side-arm and pointed it at him. "Shut. Up. Soldier. Or I'll shut you up myself."

"No... no I won't," he looked round at all the surrounding soldiers. "Can't you see what he's done. Dowdneer forced us to overthrow the general then, when things got a little too hot to handle, he flees and leaves us to die."

"Last warning soldier," said the sergeant.

"Come on everyone. We're supposed to be a peaceful race. Look what Dowdneer's turned us into…" the sound of a laser firing abruptly silenced the disgruntled soldier.

All the surrounding soldiers suddenly pointed their weapons at Sergeant Omirphoride. "Drop your weapon, sir."

The look of surprise on the sergeant's face would have been comical in any other situation, but all the faces looking at him were deadly serious. Only one other soldier had taken the sergeants side and was quickly changing targets with his laser. "What do we do, Sergeant?"

"All of you put your weapons down, and Colonel Dowdneer won't hear about this mutiny," said Sergeant Omirphoride.

"I repeat, put your weapons down. I'm relieving you of your command."

Sergeant Omirphoride realised that he couldn't regain control and slowly placed his laser on the floor.

[379]

"And your rifle, sir," the soldier watched him lay his rifle down. He looked at the only other hostile soldier. "And you."

The other soldier did as he was told.

"Now lay face down."

One of the soldiers ran over with two wrist binders and they secured both prisoners.

"What do we do now?" asked one soldier.

"We surrender to them," he nodded towards the docking bay door.

"They'll kill us as soon as we walk through."

The soldier looked down at the two prisoners. "They can go first. The general's in there. Hopefully he'll accept our surrender."

"And if he doesn't?"

"Either way we'll die eventually. At least surrendering gives us a chance of survival."

"I'm with you."

They all agreed, secretly thankful to stop the fighting. Both prisoners were forced to their feet and positioned at the entrances to the docking bay. The surrendering tranchillions held their pistols at the side of the prisoners' necks then pushed them through the doorways.

"Don't shoot! We surrender! These two are now prisoners! We surrender!" They held position – waiting for a reaction.

General Zemorphoride stood up from behind his cover. "We'll accept your surrender if you leave your weapons outside. Come in with your hands in the air then lie down in the centre of the room."

The laser disappeared from the prisoner's neck.

"Do as you're told everyone," said the leading soldier. He walked through the door pushing Sergeant

Omirphoride in front of him then, in the centre of the docking bay, he forced the sergeant to the floor and lay down next to him. The rest followed his example and the general's soldiers were sent to check the corridors.

They came back through. "Everything's fine, General."

"Collect their weapons." The general then addressed the surrendering soldiers. "You'll forgive me if I don't fully trust you all. I want you over in that corner," he pointed to his right, "where we can keep an eye on you."

Colonel Twochelope walked over to them. "Why have you surrendered to us?"

The leading soldier spoke up. "Because Colonel Dowdneer hasn't been seen or heard from for over an hour. We think he's abandoned us."

Colonel Twochelope looked at the general. "Now can I lead an assault against the remaining traitors?"

"Not yet. First, we need to stop the battleport. It's taken far too many lives already."

"Any ideas how we're going to do that?" asked the colonel.

"Tell them what's happened here and that Dowdneer deserted them. That might convince them," said Neil.

"They won't surrender. In case you hadn't noticed they're winning out there," said Colonel Twochelope. "We have nothing that can damage them."

"No. Neil's right," said General Zemorphoride. "We might not be able to damage the battleport, but morale is a different matter. Get in touch with the *Contention*. Tell them to get us a direct link to the hostile battleport."

A few minutes later, General Zemorphoride was talking to Captain Xenorphide. "Are we ready, Captain?"

"Yes, sir. You have control of the radio."

"*Resistance*. This is General Zemorphoride. Come in," he waited for a reply.

"I repeat. *Resistance*, this is your general speaking. Reply at once."

"This is the *Resistance*. Are you begging to surrender?"

"No. I'm ordering you to surrender. Colonel Dowdneer has fled. Most of his troops in this ship are dead or have surrendered. I'm giving you the same chance."

"We'll never surrender, general – never."

"I urge you to reconsider. The fighters will be recalled, and you'll be allowed to land safely. The humans have two star-ships arriving soon. They *will* blast you out of the sky if you insist upon this pointless battle any longer."

"I think it's a trick to make us give up our advantage. I'll..." the transmission was suddenly cut.

"What's going on up there?" called the general. He looked around as he said, "Can anyone see where they are from here?"

"No, sir. They're out of sight."

"Sir, this is *Resistance*," a new voice sounded on the speakers. "We have subdued the captain and request a safe flight down."

"Thank you. Who is this?"

"Lance Corporal Rimorlope, sir."

"Land it safely then come out without weapons. Any hostilities shown will be responded to with full force. Do you understand, Corporal?" said the general.

"Yes, sir."

"Right, that's sorted. Now, Neil and Tchzor, take some men with you and either hold the rest of them in the loading bay or get them to surrender. The rest of you split into five-man units and take out any of Dowdneer's patrols that you find. We'll be able to hold this bay with ten men now. Get going."

~

Two days had passed, and the loading bay was still impenetrable. The one-hundred-and-thirty tranchillions still in there refused to surrender and assaulting their position was impossible without losing a lot more lives. All Dowdneer's patrols had been stopped and the forces outside the mothership were all concentrated on the loading bay.

Two large, human starships descended towards Anthera and hung menacingly over the *Dragen*. They manoeuvred into position on both sides of the mothership.

"This is Captain Meade. Do you require any assistance down there?"

"This is Captain Xenorphide. It's nice of you to join us. We have control of the situation. Although a hundred-and-thirty of Dowdneer's soldiers still control the loading bay. We've been awaiting your arrival before attempting an assault."

"I'm sending help now, captain."

Inside the *Dragen*, the news that the two human starships had arrived a day early had filtered to Neil's squad.

"Be prepared everyone. They could become desperate at any time," said Neil.

"Something's happening," called out Colonel Twochelope.

Neil looked through the window next to the door and saw the tranchillions inside moving about with a purpose. "Like I said, be ready in case they come this way."

Inside the loading bay the tranchillions were huddled together. They had put on their helmets. They spread out into several straight lines.

"For Dowdneer!" they screamed with their weapons held high as they started forwards towards the forces waiting outside. By the time they'd reached the force-field separating them from space they were running 'full speed' at the humans.

The ferocity of their attack took everyone by surprise. Line upon line of tranchillions flew out of the loading bay and descended upon the human soldiers. Several AV's were accosted to escape. Most of the tranchillions were simply ploughing through the human soldiers as if they weren't there. The soldiers started flying in all directions, like pins in a bowling alley, as the tranchillions knocked them out of their way.

After the initial shock of the tranchillions running at them had worn off, the soldiers further out were picking them off with their lasers. But, with added fury driving the tranchillions forward, it took several shots to put one down.

The escaping AV's were targeted by Star Cruisers patrolling above. Not one of them escaped.

Neil's squad poured into the loading bay but, at his command, they waited behind the force-field. There were several stray laser bolts hitting the force-field. It made sense to stay behind its shimmering protection. The battle was over within minutes.

"What made them do that?" asked Neil.

[384]

Colonel Twochelope answered, "They had two choices. Attack or surrender. They must have been extremely loyal to Dowdneer's cause."

Neil shook his head and stepped through the force-field to see if he could help the wounded.

~

From a great distance away, Dowdneer watched as two huge human starships descended towards the *Dragen*. Through his binoculars, he observed the last of his forces burst from the loading bay and attack the humans. For a moment, he thought they were going to prevail then he watched, with a grim look on his face, as they were mercilessly cut down by laser fire.

He turned away from the scene and addressed Lt Col Maverphoride. "Let's go. To the cave. No one will be joining us."

Colonel Dowdneer climbed back into the rover and they set off towards the mountains.

CHAPTER NINETEEN

February 2172

The Moon

"No, John. We need more time to prepare," said General Bolgon.

"But Dowdneer has escaped the ship. He could be anywhere on the planet," said John Stillson.

"And that kind of operation will require a dedicated team to carry out a full search of the entire planet. The new *Arrant-Scour* class ships will be perfect for the job."

"Sir, those ships may be about four weeks from completion but, to do the kind of search you're suggesting, we'd need thousands of them," said Michael Toddwell.

"No, we wouldn't. Several hundred maybe, not thousands," said the general. He waved his hand in the air. "Anyway, enough talk of future ventures. In the here and now my main concern is defending that mothership. Dowdneer could try to take it back. That's why I'm keeping the *Spirit* out there as a deterrent. The *Augur* will relieve the *Spirit* after the allotted time."

A buzz sounded on the general's desk. He reached down and held the intercom button, "Yes, Gwen."

"Captain Meade is here to see you, sir."

"Send him in."

Captain Meade entered the office and stood to attention in front of the general's desk. "You wanted to see me, sir."

"Yes, Captain. Please sit."

Daniel did as he was told.

"I've gone over all the reports on the Anthera mission and we've decided that your entire crew deserve some R&R. A standard two weeks should be sufficient for most of them. Any of your crew who were injured will be allowed a further two weeks or until they have fully recovered."

"Thank you, sir."

"Congratulate your crew on a job well done. Dismissed."

Captain Daniel Meade got up, saluted, and left the office.

The general pressed his intercom button again. "Gwen, can you get Suzanne Cox for me please?"

"Yes, sir."

[387]

"Now, John. I think that you have enough to be going on with. Report any changes in any of your current assignments," said the general.

Mr Stillson got up to leave. "Will do, sir. See you later, Michael." He raised his right hand with two fingers outstretched and placed them against his temple then flicked his wrist in a farewell gesture to Michael.

"Now that I have you on your own, do you have any suggestions, worries, thoughts on the report from Anthera?" asked the general.

"No, sir. The plan we've come up with is, in my opinion, the best course of action. Although, we do need to start searching for Dowdneer as soon as possible."

"I think so too, which is why I want you to drop everything and concentrate on getting the *Gargantuan* and the *Arrant-Scour* fighters ready for deployment within the next two to three months."

"Yes, sir."

"I would also like to continue the studies of Anthera. So, I want you to get together a team to build a small settlement under our protective atmosdomes. A research team can work from there. Again, all necessary equipment and personnel needed can travel on the *Gargantuan*. It's certainly big enough. If all goes well, I think we can safely say that it'll have been fully tested. Also, I want that new tranchillion engine tech incorporated into the engines."

"Yes, sir."

"Once Suzanne has gone, we'll visit R&D."

"I hear that the soldiers are coming along nicely, sir."

"No problems attaching the arms and legs?"

"None, sir. The bodies are responding well."

[388]

After five minutes of friendly chat between them, Gwen buzzed through to announce Suzanne's arrival. Suzanne smiled at them both then sat down.

"Suzanne, thank you for coming. We have gone over your report and I'm happy to say that it has been approved. You may submit it as soon as you wish," said General Bolgon.

"If you don't mind, I think I've fulfilled my deal with you and I'd like to make this my last report for you – sir," she added, still not used to military talk.

"I don't see why not, Suzanne. Are you packing in reporting altogether?"

"I'm not sure. I've come to realise over the last couple of months that my personal life could do with a little TLC."

"Right," the general held out his hand and Suzanne shook it. "It's been a pleasure doing business with you," he picked up the report that she'd written and handed it to her. "I'm sorry to see you go," he smiled. "Goodbye and good luck."

"Goodbye, sir."

"You can call me Jim, Suzanne. You don't need to keep calling me sir."

"Okay. Thank you, Jim," said Suzanne with a smile. She left the office for the last time and felt like a huge weight had been lifted off her shoulders. Now all she had to do was wait for Steve to get back and start mending some bridges.

~

Neil watched Chloe move around the lounge. It seemed like an eternity since he'd left on his last mission.

"Come over here," he called out to her.

She walked over and sat on his lap, facing him.

"I'm so glad you came back alive. I..." her words stopped as he kissed her. After a few seconds, they parted.

"I love you, Mrs Bolgon," he said as he smiled.

Chloe returned the smile. "I love you too, Mr Bolgon."

"Do you like being known as Mrs Bolgon, babe?"

"I couldn't imagine having any other name."

The doorbell chimed and Chloe left Neil's lap to look at the screen next to the door. She smiled as the door slid open. John and Lisa stood there.

"Hello, Mr and Mrs Lyderattle, come in please," she said with a slight theatrical bow.

"What's wrong with you?" asked John.

"I'm just very happy to be Mrs Bolgon."

"And I'm very happy to be Mrs Lyderattle," butted in Lisa.

Chloe closed the door behind them, and they all sat down.

"Quite a battle, don't you think," said John.

"It had its moments," replied Neil.

"What about the way those tranchillions rushed our soldiers," said Lisa.

"I still can't believe they did that. I'm just glad they chose to rush the others," said Neil.

"Yeah, in the tightly confined space of the corridors they'd have had the advantage," said John.

"Why?" asked Chloe.

"Once they were among us, we wouldn't have been able to use our weapons in case we shot each other," said Neil.

"Anyway. Where's the beer?" asked John.

Chloe grunted slightly as she started to get up, but Lisa put a hand on her shoulder, "You stay there, Chloe. I'll get them." Lisa noticed her belly. "My, what a bump you've got there; can you feel it kick yet?"

"Not yet. That's at least another three months off."

"The reason we came around," interrupted John in his usual way, "was to tell you that we've been given two weeks leave and we've decided to go to Spain to work on our tans."

"That's nice, John. We'll go to London because I promised to show Chloe the real 'Regents Park' but I suppose we'll go somewhere else as well."

Lisa came back with John's beer and opened one for herself as she sat down.

"Oh, there goes the door again," said Chloe, allowing Neil to answer it for her.

"It's Rebecca," he opened the door.

"Hello, Neil. Is this a bad time? I can come back later," said Rebecca when she saw John and Lisa.

"No of course not, come in come in," said Neil.

Rebecca walked over to Chloe. "How are you?"

"Fine thanks. Just feeling fat. How are you?"

"The general's got me my old job back so I'm extremely happy."

"Glad to hear it, Rebecca. Thanks for coming around," said Chloe.

"If we get a few more we could start a conga," said John.

Neil looked round at everyone and felt lucky to have such good friends. He caught Chloe's eye and smiled at her. She snuggled into his chest as he put his arm around her.

"Ah, look at them," said John which caused Lisa to snuggle into him and he was forced to put his arm around her.

Neil laughed. "You're getting the hang of it, John. It really doesn't hurt you know."

"My god. Neil made a joke," retorted John.

Rebecca sat back in her chair, watching them, and again she felt sad – just for a moment – but Neil saw it and remembered what had almost happened back on Anthera. That kiss hadn't been just because they were stuck on Anthera. She genuinely loved him.

"Is anything wrong, babe?" asked Chloe breaking his line of thought.

"No, why you ask?"

"You looked miles away for a second, that's all."

Neil couldn't help looking at, Rebecca. Chloe moved his chin back towards her and looked in his eyes. "Are you sure?"

"Yes, I'm sure."

~

The body twitched – even under heavy sedation – as the robotic arm was attached to the, still human, shoulder. All that was left of Private Price was his torso and head. All his limbs had been surgically removed, ready for the robotic limbs to be attached.

The door to the laboratory opened, allowing General Bolgon and Michael Toddwell to enter. Besides them, John Stillson was the only other person allowed in or out of this laboratory. The general had granted this project 'Top Secret' classification. Anyone who managed to violate security were to be executed immediately.

"What are you doing, Professor?" asked General Bolgon when he saw the arm. "I want to be able to attach different arms and legs as the technology advances."

"But, sir. This is how we do it," replied the professor.

"No. I want a permanent socket welded to the shoulder that can have different arms attached to it."

"We only make one type of arm, sir."

"For now. But in the future, we may be able to attach, say, a rocket launcher to the socket or... or... a jet pack, via both shoulder sockets. Use your imagination, Professor."

"Okay. I'll redesign the limb attachments. Is there anything else, sir?"

"Yes. Robotic limbs are no good if the body can be damaged easily. I want an impenetrable body shell attached to protect the torso," the general looked thoughtful for a moment. "And the head must also be covered. Apart from the risk of these soldiers being recognised, it would be unfortunate if one bullet or laser to the head could put them out of action."

"Okay, sir."

"How are the brains coping with the reprogramming?" asked Michael Toddwell.

"Well, so far we have encountered very little resistance to the intrusion, but these things take time. We have to be a little more delicate with our approach to the human brain."

"Keep up the good work, Professor," said General Bolgon. "Let's go, Michael. I want you to start the arrangements for the other projects we discussed earlier."

They left the professor silently cursing what was essentially a restart of his project.

[393]

How do they ever expect me to get this finished if they keep changing the parameters? he thought.

TO BE CONTINUED...

EPILOGUE

The sun blazed in the blue sky as the treetops gently swayed in the breeze. Everything about this planet was tranquil. Even the few sky-cars, that were flying about their business, would not pollute this planet anymore. At the first sign of pollution becoming a problem, the emperor had ordered change. These new vehicles used solar power and their batteries could last the whole night even if used constantly.

Emperor Zemer Putilnorphille stood on the balcony of his bedroom in the royal palace enjoying the view of his kingdom. He enjoyed the responsibility of being emperor for his entire race and even at two-hundred-and-seventy years old he felt as driven and healthy as he did when he first took over from his father seventy years previously.

He pulled his long flowing robes around him and left the balcony. Moments later, he heard a knocking at his door.

"Come in," he commanded.

The door opened and his *head guard* walked in, kneeling before him with his head bowed.

"Rise my friend. What is so important that you would interrupt my private time?"

"Sorry, Emperor but I have an urgent message from control."

"Okay, hand it over, Wimpor," he held out his hand and Wimpor Wmporphille handed the information disk to him.

Emperor Putilnorphille took it and sat at his desk. He inserted the disk into his info block and waited. The face of his Chief Communications officer appeared – looking very excited.

"Emperor, we have received a faint, but unmistakable, signal from the lost mothership, *Dragen*. It sends a message that they've had engine problems and have crashed on the outermost planet of a system called *Sol*. We would like your permission to send a rescue party," the message ended.

The emperor faced his head guard. "Tell them to send out two motherships. One for the survivors and the other to repair or destroy it if unsalvageable."

At last, he thought. *We have found the 'Dragen'. This is a good day. I miss having my brother at my side.*

Emperor Zemer Putilnorphille remembered his former surname fondly. The name he'd had to renounce, as his father had before him, when he took the royal name of Putilnorphille. He smiled. It would be nice to speak with Zermiten again.

His forehead creased and he closed his eyes, *I hope he's still alive. He must be,* he thought.

ABOUT THE AUTHOR

Simon was married to his beautiful wife, Samantha, until she passed away shortly before the original publication of this book. He has three children – Daniel, Chloe and Ryan.
He lives in Leicestershire and has done ever since his birth.

Simon has written stories since early childhood but has never tried to publish anything until around 8 years ago. He tried various agents and publishers until deciding to self-publish this novel.
Simon's favourite authors are AGATHA CHRISTIE, STEPHEN KING, JACKIE COLLINS, DANIELLE STEEL AND PETER F. HAMILTON to name just a few.

Simon also enjoys Formula One, Football, Snooker and watching X-Factor and Strictly Come Dancing. He is also in an air-rifle league and takes his eldest son along with him. Daniel often gets a better score than his dad which pleases him very much.

Simon spent several years as a carpet fitter/retailer after leaving school. He stopped work to care for his wife, who had a long-term illness, and children – two of which are registered disabled. This allowed him enough spare time to write his novels and dream of success as a novelist.

Now read the unedited first
two chapters of the sequel
(Probing Anthera).

GALAXY AT WAR

BOOK TWO

PROBING ANTHERA

CHAPTER ONE

August 2172

Earth / Moon

48 days to go

...Earth...

Tears streamed down her cheeks as she screwed up her face. "It hurts."

Neil squeezed her hand a little more, trying to offer some comfort. "I know babe. Deep breaths." He tried to emphasise what he said by taking deep breaths himself. Chloe squeezed his hand tighter.

"Long deep breaths," emphasised the midwife looking at Neil before re-focusing her attention on Chloe. "Push now. That's it. Push, push, push."

Chloe pushed, roaring out her pain at the same time. As she relaxed, the midwife said, "Okay now, rest and wait for the next contraction. Keep your breathing long and deep. You're doing fine."

"How much longer is this going to take?" asked Chloe through gritted teeth. "It's been six hours already."

"Now you're in established labour – no more than an

hour. But there is no telling with these things," replied the midwife.

"I'll go for the next few minutes then," said Chloe.

The midwife smiled and was about to say something else when Chloe's body stiffened once again.

"Here comes another one," said Chloe.

Neil had moved to kiss Chloe's forehead while they were talking but he now resumed his position. Chloe's hand tightened as she anticipated the next contraction.

"Long deep breaths, Chloe," said the midwife as the contractions started again. "Push."

Chloe did as she was told, and the head appeared.

"Stop pushing – stop pushing," said the midwife. She turned the baby.

"Now, when you feel the next contraction push gently, Chloe. Ready?"

Chloe nodded. She just wanted this over and done with and, as she started another contraction, she pushed again. The baby slid out and started crying. An overwhelming relief washed over her, and the pain was gone.

"It's a girl," said the midwife as she held her up for them to see. Then she placed the baby on Chloe's chest.

"Look at her, Neil. She's beautiful," Chloe's tears were now of joy rather than pain.

"Does it still hurt?" asked Neil.

"No. Not anymore," she smiled.

"Do you want to cut the cord, sir?" asked the midwife.

Neil looked around and saw the scissors offered him. "Err... no... no thank you."

The midwife placed a clamp on the cord then snipped it. "What are you going to name her?"

"Tanya," said Chloe quickly. "Tanya Samantha

Bolgon."

Neil smiled once again, and he reached out a finger to stroke his daughter's cheek. "She's perfect, babe. Absolutely perfect." He bent over and kissed Tanya's head.

"Shall we weigh her now?" asked the midwife from the other side of the bed.

"Oh yes... yes," said Chloe. She smiled as she released her precious baby.

Neil leaned over her again and gave her a hug. "How are you feeling?"

"Drained," she sighed. "And tired. You go and let everyone know and I'll meet you all back on the ward."

"Okay, Chloe. See you later," he kissed her on the forehead. "You did well, babe. Really well," Neil left the room and went in search of his family and friends who were waiting for news.

Tanya was brought back to her, wrapped in a blanket.

"She's a healthy 7Ib 4oz's," said the midwife as she handed Tanya back to her. Chloe held her daughter for a few minutes, gazing down at her and Neil's creation. Tanya opened her eyes and stared at her mother for the first time. Chloe held one of her tiny hands and smiled fondly. Tears of joy rolled down her cheeks, brought on as the emotion of the last six hours got the better of her.

"You're perfect, Tanya. I love you so much."

~

Neil looked at his watch when he couldn't see Andrew and the others. *Quarter past one*, he thought. *I'll try the restaurant.*

After another couple of minutes spent navigating the many maze-like corridors, Neil entered the hospital restaurant and quickly looked left and right. He moved further in before spotting them and walked briskly to their table.

"Hi, Neil. Has she had it?" asked John Lyderattle, Neil's best friend, when he saw the joy etched all over Neil's face.

"Yes, John. It's a girl," Neil was positively beaming as he spoke.

"Congratulations," said Lisa Lyderattle.

"Yeah... congratulations, bruv," Andrew stood and gave his brother a hug.

"Have you named her yet?" asked John after sitting back down to finish his food.

"Yes. Tanya, Samantha."

"That's lovely, Neil," said Lisa with a wink, knowing that Tanya was the only name Chloe had wanted.

"Are you hungry, bruv?" Andrew offered Neil some of his dinner.

"No. I'm too excited to eat. Maybe later."

With his mouth full of food, John said, "If you hang on a minute we'll be finished, and we can all go to the ward together."

"John. You shouldn't talk with your mouth full. It's rude," scolded Lisa.

"Sorry," came the muffled reply as he continued to eat.

"Chloe should be coming out of the delivery room soon," said Neil, suddenly at a loss for what to say.

"Are you sure you don't want this? I've had enough."

"Actually, thanks, Andy. I am hungry, and if it's going to waste."

Andrew smiled and pushed his plate across the table. "You're welcome, bruv."

~

"Mrs Chloe Bolgon please," said Jim Bolgon.

"And you are?"

"General Bolgon. Chloe's father-in-law."

"Ah, yes. Room three, which is just down there on the right," said the nurse as she pointed. "But she's not back yet, sir."

"Has she had the baby?"

"I'm not at liberty to say."

"Of course not. Do you need me to wait outside?"

"No no, you'll be fine. But first I need you to sign in."

Jim took the pen offered and made his mark. He was still in his uniform, as the call he had received over six hours previously had taken him by surprise. He had left the running of *Sentry One* to his two capable assistants and he knew Gwen could handle his office for a while.

The nurse read the details he had just given. "Mrs Bolgon won't be long."

"Thank you, nurse Swanson," replied the general as he read her name badge. He gave back the pen and walked towards room three. Jim opened the door and stepped inside, closing it behind him. He stood at the window looking out on all the people busily going about their business.

He was still at the window when Chloe was wheeled in holding her daughter in her arms. He turned around and smiled as he saw Chloe and Tanya.

"Hello, Jim."

"Hello, Chloe. How's the baby?"

"She's fine, Jim, and gorgeous and perfect," she looked down at Tanya. "This is your granddad, Tanya."

After helping Chloe onto her bed, the porter and the nurse both left the room. Jim moved over to her.

"Would you like to hold her?"

"Of course," he reached out and gently cradled

Tanya's head as he rocked her side to side. He looked up, the lines around his eyes showing more than ever as he smiled at Chloe.

"She's beautiful. She has Neil's eyes."

The door opened and in walked Neil, John, Andrew and Lisa.

"Well done, son," said Jim as Neil joined him to look at his daughter again. Jim handed Tanya to Neil and sat beside Chloe. He mouthed the words 'well done' to her as well. Neil moved to the end of the bed where there was a little more room and was surrounded by his friends.

Chloe looked at all the people she loved most in the world at the foot of her bed and held out her hand to Jim. He took her hand and kissed it. As far as she was concerned everything was all right in the world.

"Thank you for being a father to me, it means so much."

"You are the daughter I never had, Chloe and I'm proud you would think of me as your father," he smiled and squeezed her hand.

~

...Moon...

John Stillson, the forty-eight-year-old assistant of General Jim Bolgon, entered the twenty-five-thousand-meter long hanger in which the *Gargantuan* was being built. After he passed through numerous security checks, he entered the main hanger and marvelled at the sight of the, almost finished, ten-thousand-meter long carrier.

There was still quite a lot to do and it looked like it was going to slip from its scheduled completion date of the sixteenth, which was only six days away. He stood and watched some painters working their magic on the third letter of the carrier's name.

It is beautiful, he thought. *Absolutely beautiful.* After his brief contemplation of the *Gargantuan,* he carried on along the iron walkway. He was there to inspect the latest addition to the blueprints.

As he entered the carrier the chief designer hurried towards him. "Hello, Mr Stillson. Could you have a look at these please."

John looked at the notes written on the clipboard. "What does this mean, Collins?"

"Well, sir. There is something wrong with that system, but we don't know if it's a hardware or software problem."

"What is the system supposed to do?"

"It's a fail-safe to cool the engines if the main system goes down."

"And why can't you fix it?"

"It's part of the tranchillion redesign of our engine and no-one here knows how it's supposed to work."

"Okay. I'll see if I can get Corporal Mayorpe and his team to finish it off. Until then, get on with everything else and put it out of your mind. We could even, perhaps, leave it until we get to Anthera and they could look at it then," John closed his eyes, frowning slightly, as he waved a hand in a dismissive gesture. "Now let's get to the navigation deck so I can look at what I came here for."

John followed the chief designer and made a mental note to speak to General Bolgon about the matter as soon as he got back.

~

"Hello, Captain Meade," said General Bolgon's secretary, Gwen Smith. "The general isn't here yet, but Mr Stillson and Mr Toddwell are waiting for you inside. You may go in."

"Thank you, Gwen."

The door to General Bolgon's office opened and Captain Meade stepped through. "Hello, John – Michael. Where's the general?"

"General Bolgon has a proposition for you. He will be here shortly."

The captain sat to wait for the general to arrive. He looked towards John Stillson. "So, how's the *Gargantuan* coming along?"

"A few teething problems but it will be ready for the twenty-fourth," replied John.

"Is there anything you would like to know about it?" asked Michael.

"Well, I've heard that it dwarfs our current carriers; is that true?"

"Yes, it does. It's ten-thousand meters long and twice the height of the current ones."

"Will it actually be able to move?"

"As long as it stays in space," interrupted John. "And it's still fast due to the tranchillion technology on board."

"It still needs more additions but the tranchillion general still refuses to give us the data we need. They won't give us their hyperspace technology either," said Michael, feeling a little annoyed at their refusal to cooperate.

"That's perfectly understandable, Michael," said John. "I'm sure once we have negotiated with their emperor, and taken some of our technology in trade, they will give us hyperspace travel."

The door to the office opened and in walked General Bolgon. "You started without me I see."

"No, sir. We were just talking," said John.

General Bolgon sat and placed his hands on his desk. "Right, John. How's the *Gargantuan* coming along?"

"Just fine, sir. But we could do with Corporal Mayorpe and his team to sort out a couple of teething problems."

"Can these problems wait until they get to Anthera?"

"I think so, sir. It's to do with the back-up to the cooling system for the engines, so unless the main system breaks down there won't be a problem."

"Is everything loaded and ready for launch day?"

"Not yet. It's mainly the *Arrant-Scour* ships we're waiting for," said John.

"We need another four days for the production lines to finish off the amount you specified," said Michael.

"Is everything else on board?"

"Yes, sir. The *Star Cruisers*, three-quarters of the *Arrant-Scours* and all the necessary equipment to build the Atmosdomes. Basically, we're just waiting for the last quarter of the recon fighters and a lot of minor things like seats, inner panels, some wiring and the rest of the painting."

"That's very good, Michael. We need to get back to Anthera as soon as possible or Dowdneer could attempt to take back the mother-ship."

"I don't think he'll try. Our presence there will surely be a big enough deterrent," said John.

"The *Vigour* is a pretty big deterrent I'm sure, but the sooner the *Gargantuan* arrives, and we are regularly patrolling the planet, the better I'll feel," said General Bolgon. He turned his attention to Captain Meade. "Which brings me to the reason you're sat here, Captain," he smiled.

Captain Meade, also smiling, said, "Yes, sir."

"I want you to captain the *Gargantuan*. I think you're the best candidate."

Captain Meade's smile faded then he shook his head.

"Sorry, sir. But no. I want to stay with the *Resolve*, sir."

The general frowned. "Why Captain? I consider this appointment to be very important. There is a distinct possibility that this carrier could be the head... no, the flagship of our fleet for years to come."

"Sorry, sir, but I'm happy where I am. The crew know me and I them, plus I feel an attachment to the *Resolve*, sir."

There was a look of disappointment on General Bolgon's face as he shook his head. "Very well, if you're sure, Captain."

"I'm sure, sir. Absolutely sure."

"Okay. Michael, start reviewing profiles for an alternative," the general looked back towards Captain Meade and stood, inviting him to do the same.

"I'll let you know when to be ready for departure as you will be accompanying the *Gargantuan* to Anthera," the general shook Captain Meade's hand. "Dismissed."

Captain Meade saluted the general then left the office.

"Well, I didn't see that coming," said Michael. "I really thought he'd jump at the chance to captain the *Gargantuan*."

"Have you got any ideas, John – Michael?"

"Well the natural selection for me would be Captain Stevenson of the *Impetus*," said John. "Henry Warner has already been promoted to captain of the *Spirit* after Turner left so he's out. I don't think Ryan Ross is ready yet either. Besides he's not the right rank."

"No, keep Ryan with Captain Meade for now. We'll watch him and promote him to lieutenant next year if he deserves it," said General Bolgon.

"I second Captain Stevenson," said Michael. "Lieutenant Yamashita will naturally step up to captain the *Impetus*."

"We go for Captain Stevenson then," said Jim. "I'll leave you to sort out the details, Michael. Then arrange a ceremony to make the rank changes official."

"I'll get right on it, sir," said Michael.

"Off you both go. I need some time to think."

Michael and John left the office and caught ex-Captain David Turner kissing Gwen. Michael cleared his throat and said, "David, we'll have less of that please." He smiled and shook David's hand.

"Nice to see you, Michael. And you, John. Err, is the general available?"

"He's just requested to be left alone for a few minutes but I'm sure he'll see you. Bye, Gwen – bye, David," said Michael before leaving the room followed by John.

"Well I guess I had better buzz him then," said Gwen.

David sat on the edge of her desk and waited, gazing at her hair tumbling over her shoulder as she sat.

"Sir. David Turner to see you," she said after pressing the intercom button.

"Okay, Gwen. Send him in."

David got off the desk and kissed her once more. "Until later, lover."

Colour filled Gwen's cheeks. "Love you."

David entered the office and saw General Bolgon sitting behind his desk with a bottle of whisky in his hand.

"Would you like a shot?"

"No thank you, sir. I'm working."

"What can I do for you, David?"

"Well, the business is doing good, sir."

"Call me Jim," interrupted the general.

"Jim – err okay. The business is going well and I would like to ask you if we could possibly buy extra Etherall."

"I don't see why not. How much were you thinking of?"

"About two tons."

"Can you sell that amount?"

"We've been working it out and, taking all our customers into account, we believe we could easily sell that amount."

"Okay, Gwen has the contracts. Is there anything else, David?"

"Yes, sir... I mean, Jim. We would also like to start selling Sodrum if that's all right."

"You'll need to get the appropriate licence but I can make five tons available to you initially. More if you do well."

"That would be brilliant, Jim. I'll make the arrangements then get back to you on that."

General Bolgon had just downed his third whisky in a row in front of him as he said, "Okay, David. I'll speak to you again."

"Err, sir. Far be it from me to interfere with your business but, don't you think you should cut back on the drink a little."

"You're right, David. You shouldn't interfere. Now if you're finished, I'll see you later."

David left the office and stopped by Gwen's desk. "Do you think the general's drinking too much?"

"I do but I'm not in a position to tell him. Both Michael and John have tried."

"He still misses his wife, doesn't he?"

"Oh yes. Not that he will admit it."

"Is there anything we can do?"

"I don't know, David. I just don't know."

CHAPTER TWO

August 2172

Earth

41 days to go

"I'm sorry to lose you, Suzanne. Are you sure you won't reconsider?" said the editor of World News British Division, Harvey Miller.

"No. Sorry, Harvey. I definitely want to concentrate on my private life and I'm never at home while working here," replied Suzanne.

"Come here," he held out his arms. Suzanne walked around the desk to hug Harvey.

Once they had parted, Suzanne said, "You've always been more than a boss to me. You have been a really good friend and I thank you for it."

"You can come back anytime you want to, Suzanne.

There will always be a job for you here."

"Thanks," Suzanne picked up her small box of personal items which she had already cleared off her desk. She walked over to the office door and Harvey hurried to open it for her.

"Bye, Harvey. I will see you soon."

"Bye, Suzanne and good luck."

Suzanne left his office for the last time and said her goodbyes to all the staff as she walked to the lift. She shifted the weight of the box onto one arm as she waved goodbye to her colleagues. The doors opened behind her and she stepped backwards into the lift holding in the overwhelming desire to cry before the doors closed in front of her.

She tried to compose herself in the few moments she had alone. The bell pinged and the doors slid open to reveal Roxanne Taylor waiting to enter. Suzanne pushed past her rival, trying to leave without making a scene.

"Finally off then, Suzie," gloated Roxanne.

Suzanne faced her. "What's it look like, Roxy." She retorted in an equally taunting way, all thoughts of leaving quietly, vanishing.

"Good riddance to bad rubbish if you ask me."

"I thought you'd be happy. I mean, you might *actually* manage to get a front-page story now."

"You bitch. My work's always been good enough for the front page."

"Maybe Harvey will use your dribble a little more now."

"Hey that's not, I mean, my work's not," she let out a frustrated breath and took a step towards Suzanne.

"You're going to miss the lift."

Roxanne turned and hurried to press the button, but the lift had already left. Roxanne knew that she would have to wait for five to ten minutes before its return. She turned around to resume her ranting, but Suzanne had already left.

"Aarrggh!" yelled an extremely frustrated Roxanne. "What are you looking at!" she snapped at the receptionist who was slowly shaking her head.

She turned back to the lift and stabbed the button, seething inside that Suzanne had, once again, got the better of her.

~

Steve finished counting the crates of Etherall and picked up his clipboard to record his stock check. He looked up and adjusted his hard hat as he heard his name being called.

"Hi, David. Hang on," he put down the clipboard after making a note of where he was then walked over to his employer.

"Steve, Suzanne's here for you. You can take an early lunch if you want," said David Tressel.

"Thanks, David. I've marked where I am. Did she say what she wanted?"

"No. But I'm glad you two seem to be getting along again. You both deserve it."

"Yeah, let's hope it all works out," he winked. "See you later."

"See you later, now get going."

Steve ran off in the direction of the farmhouse, eager to see Suzanne. He slowed down as he neared the door and opened it. He entered the kitchen, which was where Suzanne could nearly always be found when she visited the Tressels.

Suzanne looked up from her conversation with Madeline Tressel and Steve admired the way her brown, curly hair bounced as she moved her head. Her skin glowed bronze due to the recent hot summer weather.

"Hi, Steve. I've come to take you out for dinner."

Madeline half-turned to look at him. "Ah... good. Now, you two have a good time and I'll see you later."

"Thanks, Mrs Tressel," said Steve.

"I'll make a special visit after hours sometime soon, Mrs Tressel," said Suzanne. "I'm glad to hear that business is booming. You deserve some good fortune."

As Steve and Suzanne left the kitchen, David and Guy entered. They all acknowledged each other. Guy and David sat at the table, opposite Madeline.

"Guy wants to leave us, mother," said David.

"Are you sure, Guy?" said Madeline.

Guy nodded.

"What are you going to do. All you've ever known is flying. Have you got another job lined up already?"

"Yes, Mrs Tressel. I've decided to join the Space Federation permanently. I'm aiming for a *Star Cruiser* position."

"Is it dangerous?"

"Every job has its risks, but I love flying and my recent taster with the Space Federation has made me realise that I need more than being a delivery boy – no offence. I have the potential to be the best fighter pilot in the Space Federation."

"That role has already been filled. By Neil Bolgon no less," said David.

"Oh him. He's getting older and another reason I'm going. I can learn from him while he's still at his best."

"Makes sense I suppose," said Madeline.

"Good look with your new direction," said David.

"When do you leave?" asked Madeline.

"Tomorrow, when Mr Turner goes there to pick up

some Etherall."

"We'll miss you, Guy," said David.

"I'll miss you both as well," Guy got up from the table. "I'd better get my work finished. See you later."

~

"When do you go back?" asked Steve.

"Go back? What do you mean, go back?" replied Suzanne, risking a quick glance towards him before concentrating on the road.

"To Leicester. To *World News*," he held both hands up in front of him and bent a single finger on each hand to emphasise the last two words.

"I don't go back, Steve. I quit *World News* and have taken a job here, in Hinckley," Suzanne glanced at him again and smiled at the look of pure shock on his face.

"Y... You've quit *World News*. W... why did you do that?"

"Because it took up too much of my time. My new job should mean I'm available to be with you a lot more, that's why."

"You gave up your dream job to be with me more; are you ill?" Steve reached across to touch her forehead with a smile on his face.

Suzanne knocked his hand away. "Don't, I'm concentrating."

Steve sat back, deep in thought, then said, "What's your new job, Suzanne? Are you still with a paper?"

"Yes. I've joined the team at our local, the *Hinckley Times*."

"Well, at least you should be home at night then."

"Ah here we are," said Suzanne.

"Let me guess; we're going to Jeffreys for dinner."

"Of course, Steve. I've still got to tell my parents

what I've done."

They got out of the car and walked, holding hands, down the pedestrianised street pausing at the odd shop window on their way to Jeffreys.

Before they entered the café, Steve pulled on Suzanne's hand and she turned to face him.

"Suzanne, I love you so very much. Thank you for quitting *World News*. I promise that I'll try my best not to let you down," he bent his head towards hers and they kissed.

A passing shopper looked at them. "Get a room."

They both looked up but couldn't determine who'd made the comment from amongst the crowd. They smiled at each other again then entered Jeffreys, holding hands. They sat at a table and waited. A lady appeared from the back, with dyed black hair, carrying an order pad. When she saw them, her face lit up and she gave them both a hug.

"Suzanne – Steve, how lovely to see you both. What can I get you?"

"A jacket potato with side salad please, mum," said Suzanne.

"And I'll have the mega-burger with chips please, Mrs Statham," said Steve.

"Oh please, Steve. We've known each other a little too long for that. Call me Julie."

"Okay, Julie."

"That's better. Now, I'll get these going."

"Have you got five minutes, mum? I've got something to tell you."

"Of course, dear. Just let me serve these other two customers then I'll be with you."

"Can we have two cokes as well, Julie?"

She took the orders into the kitchen then returned to

the café floor to take some more. After another trip to the kitchen, Julie sat at their table. "Jeffreys going to call me when he needs me. So, what's on your mind?"

"Mum... I've quit *World News* and joined the *Hinckley Times*," Suzanne looked expectantly at her mother, hoping for approval.

There was a blank look on Julie's face as she took in the information and Suzanne's joyful smile faded.

"What's wrong, mum?"

Julie's vacant stare disappeared. "What... oh, I don't believe it, Suzie. I would have never thought. Am I dreaming?"

Steve started laughing at Mrs Statham's shocked expression and Suzanne shot him a look which was meant to shut him up. Steve calmed himself. "It's true, Julie. She's given up her old life for me. I'm just as amazed as you."

"What's so amazing about me quitting my job?" Suzanne couldn't believe how he could find it funny then Julie started laughing as well and Suzanne's gaze switched back to her.

"It's brilliant news, Suzie," said a grinning Mrs Statham. "Brilliant news."

Suzanne finally caught on with what they had found funny and joined in the laughter. Mr Statham appeared in the kitchen doorway. "Julie. Food's ready." He gave a look of puzzlement in their direction then disappeared back into the kitchen.

"I've got to get on, see you in a few minutes."

Suzanne watched her mother walking away then turned to Steve. He was looking intently at her.

"Is something wrong?"

Steve took a deep breath. "Suzie. We've been back together now for four months and I couldn't be happier than when I'm with you. You are everything to me and after what you've just done it makes me realise, more than ever, that you feel the same way." He stood up then got down on one knee. "I seem to remember doing this once before. Let's make it work this time. Suzanne Cox... will you marry me again?"

Suzanne looked around at all the diners who had stopped eating to see what her answer would be. She also noticed her mother and father in the kitchen doorway then she locked eyes with Steve and her face beamed.

"Yes, Steve. Yes, I will marry you."

Cheers and clapping erupted from everyone present as they kissed.

~

Julie Statham had organised a large gathering for dinner that night to celebrate Steve and Suzanne's engagement. Even though it was short notice most of the invited had turned up.

"Your mother knows how to throw a dinner party, Suzanne," said Guy.

"I'm amazed that she organised all this in a few short hours," replied Suzanne.

"I'm amazed that almost everyone was able to make it," said Steve.

The lounge door opened, and Mrs Statham entered. "Would everyone like to move to the dining room please."

They all filed through and took their places at the table. Julie had enlisted the help of the cafés cook. She wanted both Jeffrey and her to be able to enjoy the night along with everyone else.

Five side-tables had been placed end-to-end on which the buffet was set out. Everyone began to select their own favourite foods from the vast amount of choice the cook had prepared. The background noise was just like in a busy restaurant and the air was electric with joy and happiness.

Suzanne felt a new warmth in her relationship with Steve. She was sure that their marriage would last this time. She was determined never to put work before their relationship ever again.

After they had both finished their mains, Julie thought that the time had come for a little discussion with her friend, Madeline. She approached her and tapped her on the shoulder.

Madeline turned around. "Yes."

"I was thinking that you've been working hard all your life and that you should take an early retirement. Imagine all the things we could do if you were free to go out any time you wanted."

"Oh, I don't know, Julie. I like my work and I've not been long turned fifty-six," her brow furrowed. "Why are you asking me this?"

"Neither of us is getting any younger and we don't need to make any more money. You see, here's the thing…" she paused, struggling for a way to say what she was thinking. "I would like to see the world and we," she nodded in Jeffreys direction and he nodded back, "have already decided to tour as many countries as we can possibly manage. We would like you to come with us. What do you think?"

"I'm not sure, Julie. It's a big step to leave everything and David needs me."

David had heard the proposal and he leaned over to catch his mother's attention. "Mum, I think Julie's idea is great. All your life you've given up your hopes and dreams to look after your family. I think it's your turn to do what you want." David shrugged and continued. "I'll be fine, and so will the business. But I *would* like a postcard from every place you visit."

Madeline held her son's hand. "Thank you, David. But I'll need time to think this over and," she turned to face Julie, "thanks for including me in your plans. I'm really honoured that you thought of me. I'll give it a lot of consideration and get back to you."

"Okay, Madeline. I hope you say yes though. It wouldn't be the same without you."

The rest of the night went smoothly, and they all continued to party until well into the next morning.

~

It was mid-day the next day and almost everyone who had attended the party the night before had not yet risen. At the Tressels farmhouse Madeline, David and Guy were waiting for a space shuttle to land outside.

"He should be here soon," said David.

"Are you still sure about joining the Space Federation. Surely there's still enough time to back out if you wanted," said Madeline.

Guy shook his head. "I've already signed up and besides, this is what I want to do. It has been an adventure working for the both of you but, since we went legitimate, a lot of the risk and excitement has gone."

"I understand, Guy. We are just worried that you might get killed," said David.

"If I do – I do. You both know how I want my funeral. But I'm not going to get killed so it's not an issue."

They heard a shuttle landing outside and, as the engines wound down, Madeline gave Guy a hug. "You be safe," she said with her eyes watering.

"I will, Madeline. Thanks for all you have done over the years. I'll visit every chance I get; I promise."

As they all stood, David took Guy's hand and shook it then gave him a reassuring pat on the back. He was struggling for words and trying to hold in his emotions as he looked at Guy.

Guy bailed him out. "I know man, I know."

David sighed. "Your skills as a pilot have saved not only me, but everyone working for us from time to time. I'm honoured to have you as a friend. If you ever need anything, just call," David let go of Guy's hand and smiled.

"Sure, David. I'll miss you both," Guy picked up his travel bag and they followed him to the door. "Just keep my room spare for when I return. Love you both."

He opened the door and saw David Turner waiting by the ramp of the shuttle. He walked over to him.

"Emotional?" observed David.

"Oh, you bet, let's go."

"I'm surprised there aren't more people here."

"Big party last night. I suppose most of them are too pissed to be up yet."

"Any special occasion?"

"Steve and Suzanne are getting remarried."

"Tell them congratulations!" shouted David to the waiting Tressels.

They gave the thumbs-up sign in acknowledgement.

Guy disappeared inside the shuttle after giving a final wave and then the ramp closed behind them. Moments later, the engines whirred to life and Guy left the Tressels to begin his new career.

Available From:

SMART CARTRIDGE
1 CHURCH WALK
HINCKLEY
LEICESTERSHIRE
LE10 1DW

THANK YOU FOR READING THIS BOOK.

THE NEXT IN THE SERIES IS COMING

SOON.

Printed in Great Britain
by Amazon

64547293R00251